Hearts of Stone

Hearts of Stone

Audrey Pembroke

ROBERT HALE · LONDON

ISBN 0 7090 7773 4

Robert Hale Limited
Clerkenwell House
Clerkenwell Green
London EC1R 0HT

2 4 6 8 10 9 7 5 3 1

Typeset in 10/13 Sabon
Derek Doyle & Associates, Shaw Heath.
Printed in Great Britain by
St Edmundsbury Press, Bury St Edmunds, Suffolk.
Bound by Woolnough Bookbinding Limited.

Prologue

March 1815

'COME on, my lovely . . .'

William Freer paced back and forth across the limestone cave, one of several along this part of the Dorset cliffs.

Every so often he came to the entrance, where a broad ledge dropped to the open sea, to listen. Hearing nothing but the slap of waves on the rocks below, he turned back into the gloomy vault. Amelia had more than a mile to come, and mostly uphill.

A single candle flickering on a rock shelf silhouetted the supporting pillars of stone, or 'legs' as the quarrymen called them, and faintly illuminated the yawning mouths of galleries. Constant drips of moisture echoed eerily as they plopped into pools on the tacky clay floor.

The other quarrymen had long since gone, and William hated himself for hiding like a coward until his beloved brought the promised certificate of exemption from service.

Thanks to Boney's recent escape from Elba the press-gangs were in full swing, and only yesterday Amelia had told him she was carrying his child. He must stand by her, for her father's reaction when he found out would be to disown her rather than allow her to marry a common quarryman.

Henry Warren, respected JP had risen from quarry boy to stone and coal-merchant, and was proud of his freeholder's vote. Now he coveted the title his daughter would gain by marrying the Honourable, though impoverished, Mr Maltravers.

The wait seemed interminable, and William longed to be in the barge moored under the cliff. A spark of light out at sea would tell him the black-painted smugglers' barque was there, and unless he sent an answering signal immediately, the captain wouldn't wait.

At last came the sounds he was listening for. A slithering accompanied by the rattle of loose gravel. Someone was sliding down the steep cliff path, then came short, hurried footsteps.

A low sweet voice called his name.

'William, William, are you there?'

He was at the entrance, hugging her, embracing her hungrily until she laid her head on his shoulder and wept.

Worry creased his brow.

'Couldn't you get it?'

'Yes, oh yes. Father didn't notice the certificate among the other papers he had to sign, but William . . .' She sobbed, shaking her head as she gave him the document. 'I tried again, but Father would have none of it, and he's expecting Simon Maltravers to ask for my hand tonight. There's nothing to do but elope.'

'Your father doesn't know about—?'

'Oh, no. I couldn't tell him. It would make things worse, especially for you. At least this way we shall be together . . . Look, I have the jewels *Maman* left me. They'll fetch enough to get you started as a mason in London . . .'

William picked up his plaited-straw nammet bag containing his best tools, then looked at her.

'You'm quite sure?'

She nodded, and they stepped outside. He'd just taken her hand to help her down the steep rock steps when a loud voice hailed them from the cliff top. The half-moonlight was too generous.

'You there – Halt! I impress you in the name of King George into His Majesty's militia!'

Amelia almost fainted from shock as twenty armed men, blazing torches held aloft, ran down the steep path. How did the press-gang know they were here?

Her question was answered when she saw the tall swaggering figure of Simon Maltravers.

She'd been missed when Maltravers arrived for dinner, and her father guessed where she was. Her own father had betrayed them.

Beneath his hawk's beak of a nose, Simon's lip curled.

'I'm sorry to interrupt your lovers' tryst,' he drawled, 'but the officer has authority to take you. Quietly, or otherwise.'

William gave Amelia's hand a reassuring squeeze.

'Pardon me, Sergeant,' he said to the leader of the press-gang, 'this document exempts me from service.'

The sergeant took it, read it in the torchlight, then shrugged as he handed it to Maltravers.

' 'Tis in order, sir. Signed by Henry Warren, JP.'

Maltravers perused the document as though he'd never seen one before.

'Ah, it even bears your description,' he said flippantly. 'Five feet, eight inches tall, ruddy complexion, dark hair and grey eyes . . . aged twenty-one, and rentpayer of this cliff quarr . . .'

He looked William up and down, while his voice became heavy with sarcasm.

'Also a fisherman, whom the cities of London and Westminster cannot do without for their supply of cheap fish . . .'

His sneer became a malicious grin as he looked at the girl trembling beside the quarryman.

'So, my little might-have-been fiancée would rather elope with a worthless nobody. Well, for all your father cares, it will be quite in order if I destroy any paper he has signed by mistake—'

'Oh, no! You can't . . . please, *please don't*!'

It was done, even as she tried to snatch it from him.

Maltravers tut-tutted as he brushed away the shreds, then barked at the sergeant:

'Take him!'

Transfixed with dread, Amelia stood weeping as they dragged her lover away.

'I think you should reconsider your situation, m'dear,' drawled Maltravers, still beside her. His eyes were black slits as he gazed down at her. 'Why not let me take you home? I might still be persuaded to marry you . . . if your father makes it worth my while . . .'

Amelia recoiled in disgust.

'I'll be damned before I marry you,' she flung at him. 'Go away, and leave me alone!'

'Be damned, then.' He made a mocking bow and left her, confident her father's determination would ultimately prevail.

But resentment lent Amelia strength. She wasn't entirely alone, and she still had *Maman*'s jewels. She would run away to her Aunt Mary in Dorchester.

Placing a hand reverently over her abdomen, she vowed to be waiting with her baby when William returned.

For return he would . . . she, and God willing.

CHAPTER ONE

September 1832

'I can see the bay up yer!'

Perched like a sparrow on the broad muscular back of the lead draught-horse, Tommy Freer grinned down at his big brother who was dwarfed walking alongside.

'Oh ah,' Will grunted in reply. There was no need on the downward slope for the bull-hide whip he carried. The three hefty shires had pulled many loads of stone down from the quarries to the shore, trailing a cloud of dust, or squelching through mud, according to the weather.

Behind them, to the south, undulating slopes bounded by the English Channel were broken by slag-heaps and muddy hollows, evidence of the numerous stone-mines, called quarrs. Above and beyond the stone workings Lackford Hall commanded a view of the whole area.

Rich pastures swept up the other side of the valley to the north, meeting the lower slopes of the hills that stretched away to the west as far as Tommy could see from Hercules' back. The ridge excluded the outside world, except for ships that sailed around the head.

As they neared the town, fanning eastwards around Swanwick Bay, the small boy shivered in the cool September air. Showers the previous night had given way to the first light frost of autumn, hardening the ruts in the road, and soon more heavy wagons would follow.

The parish church stood in the valley beside a small river, all that remained of the great lake that existed before time began, and in its demise left the layers of stone that had given men their livings for centuries. Tommy had learned that much at school.

A woman clothed in black came to the doorway of the rectory classroom across the road from the parish church. As she swung the bell in her hand, sleepy-eyed children appeared from grey stone cottages and trotted down the hill.

At the junction where the road branched off to the church, Will pulled on the brake, calling 'Whoa!' The wagon rumbled to a halt, and he reached up to Tommy.

'Down y'get, young un, and behave yerself – or else. D'ye hear?'

Tommy nodded, eyes widely innocent.

'Yes, Will. Thanks fer the ride.'

At seven years old he didn't understand Will's surliness when transporting a load of stone. For him, riding on Hercules' back was a delight – until Widow Hyer began ringing her bell. Its strident clanging could be heard for half a mile.

He pulled his ruched-up jacket straight and ran to join the other children.

'Where's Charlie?' asked Mary Dyke. A pretty girl of twelve, she was a class monitor. 'Widow Hyer really needs her today, with old Barton's inspection.'

'I dunno.' Tommy shrugged, looking back up the hill. There was no sign of his sister, who was nearly as old as Will. 'If she don't hurry I'll have to cover for her.'

He wished school was over, so he could run to the quarr and find his dad.

Clutching her shawl closer around her skinny shoulders with her free hand, Martha Hyer pursed her lips. She was proud of her healthy pupils. They came from a stalwart generation that had withstood the wars with Napoleon, and overcome the cholera, smallpox and influenza.

The only difference in their social levels was, some were poorer than others.

Thankfully they'd obeyed her summons; even Tommy Freer was early, but she couldn't see that sister of his.

Well, there was no time to waste.

'Sarah Taylor – you'd better be head monitor today!' Martha nodded at chubby Sarah who stepped forward simpering with importance.

At a sharp blast from her whistle, the rosy-cheeked children ceased chattering and filed inside.

Martha looked at Tommy Freer. She'd suffered a pang, seeing his big brother drop him off on his way to the weighbridge. Will could have made something of himself, but was barely nine years of age when he'd gone to work a man's hours in the family quarr.

She sighed and clapped her bony hands, signalling the children to don their smocks.

Still in line, each pupil tied the strings of the garment on the child in front before settling on the hard benches.

Martha marked the register. Absenteeism due to lack of the weekly fourpence was not unusual; reason enough to give a week's holiday at quarter-time when rents were due. Not much absence was due to sickness, except it seemed, for one person.

'Charlotte Freer!' Martha's black, boot-button eyes flicked the room, her thin lips pinched in annoyance. 'Tommy, where is your sister – not recovered yet?'

Tommy stood up. 'I dunno, miss. Our Charlie should be yer by now.'

He crossed his fingers behind his back, trembling for the sin he committed. It was only half a lie. His sister was fibbing when she got sent home early yesterday, saying she was unwell.

She'd gone to work for Fred Cooper the cowman, and was helping with the milk round this morning. It was true that he didn't know where she was; she should have been here by now.

He'd promised not to tell on her, so Tommy stared with all the round-eyed innocence he could muster.

'Did you give her my message?' snapped Martha Hyer. 'I wanted everyone here on time today – especially your sister,' she added acidly. After all, as a pupil-teacher the girl was paid ten shillings a year.

'I – er forgot,' Tommy lied, blushing. He tightened his crossed fingers, and mumbled an apology. He might have got away with it if not for the impending visit of the Reverend Barton.

Widow Hyer tut-tutted. She recognized exaggerated innocence.

'Perhaps I was wrong to trust her ... she's more wayward than I thought. Doesn't she care what the rector will think?'

'Course she do, ma'am,' cried Tommy. ' 'Tain't her fault I fergot!'

'That much is true,' snapped his teacher. 'Well, let's see if we can improve your memory. Sarah, the "Poor Memory" marker, if you please.'

Sarah Taylor scurried to the box of cards denoting various vices and virtues.

Gloatingly, she held up her selection by its strings, and popped it over Tommy's head. He blushed with shame, and scowled as the rest of the class tittered.

His sense of outrage was mollified when Widow Hyer called out:

'Stop laughing, Billy Hart! Come here, and let me look behind your ears. Dirty boy. Mary Dyke, bring a basin of water, and soap and flannel, please . . .'

The morning wore on and still Charlie had not come when the parson arrived.

'Class stand,' commanded Widow Hyer as the worthy gentleman stepped over the threshold, removing his black stovepipe hat.

They all stood stiffly to attention until Reverend Barton motioned them to sit.

'Except you, boy,' he said, pointing at Tommy. 'What's this?' He fingered the card dangling round Tommy's neck. 'Poor memory? I find that hard to believe in such a bright young lad. Tommy Freer, isn't it?'

He rocked back and forth on his heels, thumbs tucked behind his coat lapels, one eyebrow cocked questioningly at the boy.

'Y-yes sir,' replied Tommy with a hangdog look. 'S-sorry, sir.'

'Sorry for what? Explain yourself, boy.'

Tommy studied his feet, embarrassed by the fibs he must tell.

'I should've told me sister you was visitin' today, sir,' he mumbled. 'She was off sick yes'day, an' would've made sure to be yer today, b-but I fergot.'

The parson turned swiftly to Widow Hyer.

'His sister is sick? Nothing serious, I hope?'

'Oh no, Reverend,' Widow Hyer hastily assured him. 'We're very fortunate to live by the sea, where the air is clean.' Her gaze proudly scanned the class. 'They may be poor, but none is starving, and what they lack I endeavour to make up for with teaching, and – er – discipline.'

She nodded towards Tommy, who, red as a boiled lobster, stood shuffling his feet.

'Hm, yes. I can see the boy's memory improving already,' said the parson, and Martha caught the twinkle in his eye.

'Tell you what, lad, if you can remember your seven times table I shall pronounce you cured, what?'

Tommy looked up, startled. He swallowed, and took a deep breath. Staring in anxious concentration, he recited, parrot-fashion:

'Seven ones are seven, seven twos are fourteen . . .'

Martha Hyer almost smiled when she told Sarah Taylor to put the card back in its box, and motioned Tommy to sit down.

12

Tommy was overcome with relief, but he was worried about his sister. She'd promised, 'cross my heart and hope to die' not to let him down, and whatever else she did, it wasn't like her to break a promise.

The parson tested the pupils' reading, then hurled questions at them. Satisfied at last, he congratulated the widow.

'Excellent, Mrs Hyer. Your efforts bear fruit – ahem – always glad to write a good report . . .' The school was his brainchild. 'Now, a word with you, if I may?'

Instructing Sarah Taylor and Mary Dyke to supervise, Martha followed the parson to the door.

'The sick child,' he asked earnestly, 'you're certain it's not the cholera, or influenza?'

'Absolutely not.' Martha shook her head firmly. 'You remember Charlotte Freer, the one I recommended for the post of pupil-teacher? I believe she does a job of work outside school: I think her absence is most likely connected with that.'

She refrained from saying she was disappointed the girl had let her down today. 'The Freers haven't had it easy . . .'

'Hm, I know,' put in Reverend Barton. 'Life's a struggle for the quarry folk.' ·

'Yes,' said Martha, fussing with her shawl. 'But Charlotte has a more – er – colourful background than most . . .' She paused, uncertain, but now was as good a time as any . . . 'Her mother had a lady's education . . . and as well as looks and poise, Charlotte has a working knowledge of French—'

'You mean she has quality,' interrupted the parson again. 'Handed down from that French grandmother of hers.'

Martha nodded, annoyed by his interruptions, but warming to her theme.

'It's a pity, the grandfather's estrangement from the family. He could have done so much for them. Charlotte would make a fine governess.'

The parson was bound to have connections.

'It's such a waste, don't you think, for any child not to reach his or her potential?' she concluded, fixing him hopefully with her beady eyes.

'Quite so, Ma'am. How old did you say the girl is? Just turned sixteen? Well, rest assured, I'll keep her in mind . . . Good day.'

He bowed his head respectfully, donned his tall hat, and left.

13

'Whoa, Ned!' Raven-dark hair flying, cheeks pink from cold and haste, Charlie halted the milk-float in the dairy yard of Lackford Hall farm. She leapt down, and yelled: 'Come and give us a hand, Dick!'

'I'm in trouble today,' she groaned, as together she and the groom backed Big Ned so that he reversed the cart into its stable space. 'Fred was up all night with a sick cow, and I had to do the round alone. Now I'm late for—'

Dick interrupted her.

'Ned needs a rub down.' He flicked back his dark mop of tousled hair.

At eighteen he was two years older, thickset, and of medium height. With his handsome devil-may-care expression, and work-shirt open at the throat, he caused many a sigh from local maids. But Charlie had no time for his manly charms.

'Will you see to'n – please, Dick?' Lifting her pointy chin, she gazed at him, her grey eyes commanding rather than pleading.

It got his back up, she was stuck-up and needed bringing down a peg or two.

'You'll have to give I somethin' in return,' he said, a contemptuous twist on his lips as he blocked her way.

'What?'

'Give us a look at yer tits,'

Charlie's mouth fell open with amused indignation. Then she shrugged.

'It'll have to be quick, then.'

With a sigh of resignation, she unbuttoned her bodice, and pulling it open revealed small, round, white breasts. Their rosy nipples hardened visibly in the chill autumn air.

Dick gaped, his mouth slack, and Charlie laughed at his Adam's apple wobbling.

She wasn't coy about her body; in the Freers' cramped cottage privacy was scarce. All the same, if Ma or her dad found out . . .

She began rebuttoning her bodice.

'Right, now let me pass—'

'Just a minute.' Dick put out a hand, meaning to slip his fingers inside for a feel, but she slapped it away.

'You've had your look, now let me pass or I'll tell my dad what you made me do.'

Dick withdrew his hand as if she'd bitten it.

'All right, but I'll expect somethin' more, next time you ask a favour.'

She didn't answer. About to dash across the yard, the sound of a man's booted steps halted her.

'Oh, sugar – it's old Lackford!' Charlie's hand flew to her mouth, her eyes wide with alarm. 'I don't want him to see me; my dad's two months behind with the rent!'

'Get up in the loft, quick!' cried Dick. 'I'll tell you when he's gone.'

Charlie didn't miss the gleam in his eyes, but she had no choice. She scrambled up the ladder, and crouched in the hay, holding her breath as the squire walked into the stable and stood right beneath her hiding-place.

He sat on a lower rung of the ladder, waiting for Dick to finish rubbing down Big Ned.

Charlie was dismayed, it wouldn't be worth going to school this late, and tomorrow she'd be hauled out before the whole class.

More fibs, she thought, stifling a sigh. Then curiosity overcame her panic as she peered through a gap in the floorboards. It was the first time she'd seen Sir Alan Lackford this close; she always kept out of his way when she saw him coming.

Rumour said he'd driven his wife to suicide, and sometimes he was referred to as 'that ogre'. Even if his wife was mad, they said, to do such a thing he must have made her that way. Apparently he'd gone a bit queer when, as a serving junior officer he'd seen his father blown to bits by a cannonball at Waterloo. His mother died soon after, of a broken heart.

Charlie, intrigued by such tales, was surprised to see that Squire was several years younger than her father. He was tall and lean, and he had big blue eyes.

'Tell you what . . .' he was saying, and as he looked at Dick standing respectfully before him, she saw that his fair hair receded from a high brow, and curled around the back and sides. His hands were slender, not rough and workworn like common folks', and reminded her of Ma's description of Charlotte Annereaux. It was her French grandmother's small fortune that had helped make Henry Warren the important man he was.

Charlie grimaced. Horrid old man, he'd always disliked her dad, so they'd had little to do with him, and never addressed him as 'Grandfa . . .'

Whoops, Sir Alan had stood up; was he going?

15

She drew back and held her breath, but he kept talking.

There *was* something strange about him. Although soft-spoken, he gave the impression of quiet persistence, of a man used to having his own way.

Charlie wondered if folk spoke of him contemptuously because he was rich, and they were so poor. He had no need to shout and holler to be obeyed, people respected money and jumped to attention when he wanted something.

He had the power to employ or not, and to provide a roof or not; which amounted almost to having the power of life and death over a person.

'It's always the way,' her dad once said. 'Folks like us slave to scratch a livin', while the gentry grow wealthy on our backs.'

He'd begun his inland quarr on Lackford land before she was born, having survived Waterloo and returned to marry Ma. As well as rent, he had to pay sixpence on each ton of worked stone, not to mention the parish poor rates, and the salt tax.

All the quarrymen grumbled, the stone should be for their own profit to support their families. Even now Will was down at the weighbridge, where yet another penny per ton was added to their costs.

Oh yes, they toiled for a pittance; if it wasn't for the smuggling which most dabbled in they would starve. Dear God, if the preventive men caught them red-handed, they'd have to arrest more than half the community.

Charlie jumped as Sir Alan's voice grew louder, and broke in on her thoughts.

'I shall want the two bays tomorrow when I go to Bridport, there's a matter to sort out in my rope-making factory.'

Squire's father, the late Sir Hugh, had done well over the years of trouble with Boney, when several warships were built at Bridport. He'd bought land in the Swanwick area when he'd married, and now it was all Sir Alan's except for the strip containing the disused cliff quarr belonging to his mother's brother, the Honourable Simon Maltravers.

'I'll inspect the horses, now,' Sir Alan was saying. 'How's that colt today?'

He moved away with Dick in tow, and Charlie looked for an escape. If Dick thought he was getting any more favours from her, he could think again.

Warily she pushed the hatch open. On this side of the stable she'd be hidden from sight, but it was too high to jump.

She searched until she found a length of old rope. She tied one frayed end around a beam and dangled the other through the opening. There would be a five-foot drop, but she could manage. She must be gone before Dick came back.

Charlie tugged on the rope to make sure it would bear her weight, then clambered through the hatch. She winced as the rope burnt her hands, but slithered down until she found herself dangling with her arms above her head.

'Sugar!' she gasped, loosing her grip to land on all fours. She jumped up, hoisted her skirt to her knees and fled.

Once satisfied she was far enough from Lackford property she slowed to a walk. There was no point hurrying home early and alarming her mother; better gather some feed for Bess, the donkey, until it was time for the afternoon milking.

Ever since she'd realized her birth was a disappointment to her dad she'd striven to please him. He'd suffered another, more bitter blow when a second son was stillborn between her and Tommy. Ma was ill for a long time, and though his attitude softened towards herself, he never showed the same pride and affection as he did for Tommy.

Not that she begrudged her little brother, everyone was fond of him. But she sympathized with Will, taken for granted into employ in the family trade, and unpaid while an apprentice. Yet somehow the money was scraped together to send her, then Tommy to Widow Hyer's school.

A special understanding developed between her and Will, but lately he'd become aggressive, and quarrelsome. He accepted all their parents could offer, but never did more than he had to in return.

As Charlie searched the hedgerows for milk-thistle, Bess's favourite, she thought regretfully of her dad. At barely forty he was already suffering from the ailment common to quarrymen, stone-dust in the lungs.

His cough became more persistent, and he'd persuaded Widow Hyer to keep her at school to help with the younger pupils in return for improving her prospects.

Charlie knew that Will had been born out of wedlock, and what the despised Maltravers had put her parents through all those years ago. Her Dad's regiment was detained to invest Paris after Boney's final defeat, and when he came home the following spring, his ship's captain married him and Ma at Weymouth. But back in Swanwick, having been away from his quarr for more than a year and a day, Dad lost his right to mine

17

the stone. They had no money, and Henry Warren had long since disowned his daughter.

'Your dad knew the downs vein was good on Squire Lackford's land,' Amelia had told her. 'With his help we were able to begin again – literally from scratch!'

William Freer was in debt from the start, borrowing from the Company of Marblers and Stone-cutters to pay the 'fine' to sink a shaft.

Her ma had almost shed tears at the memory.

'He had to work all the hours God gave to build the retainer wall, and dig his shaft in six weeks.'

They had to borrow to buy food until the quarr yielded an output, then, as fast as one debt was paid, another was outstanding.

The only help they received from old Warren was if it profited him, like hiring his wagons and horses. He would buy their surplus stone when there was a slack time, but at pathetically low prices.

Charlie frowned over the humiliation her parents endured. Working his own quarr was the one way her dad could provide Will with honourable employment, but he'd had so little time for her brother, outside of teaching him the trade. Then her birth complicated things, with another mouth to feed. Now, because Dad had Will's help, he did find time for Tommy.

He'd be taught the trade too, but only as something to fall back on. A better life was intended for the young un.

Sometimes it seemed their dad blamed Will for the harsh life he'd been forced to lead, when surely it was his own fault for making their mother pregnant outside wedlock.

Charlie thought fleetingly of Dick, and grinned wryly. No man was ever going to take advantage of *her*. She liked school and being a pupil teacher too much, although how long she'd keep that privilege if Widow Hyer found out about today . . .

Charlie shook the thought away. They weren't an unhappy family, it was just that she longed for her dad to be proud of her.

She smiled again, a small secretive smile. Every night, behind the modesty curtain Ma hung around her bed, she counted the pennies she had stored under her mattress.

One day she would be free of tedious struggles, and poverty.

CHAPTER TWO

'Yer's the chain, lad, good as new.' Amid fumes of smelted metal, Sam Roper the blacksmith helped Will to haul the heavy iron links into the empty wagon.

Will grunted his thanks, then glanced over his shoulder towards the weighbridge office. His brows drew together in a frown.

'Summat wrong, Will?' Sam rubbed his hands in the rag he took from the pocket of his leather apron, and gave Will a gap-toothed smile. 'You look like you lost a guinea, and found a tanner.'

'You ain't far wrong.' Will's face relaxed as he turned to the blacksmith. 'Old Skinner tried to put one over, chargin' too much. He reckoned the load was over three ton, so I made him weigh it again afore I paid'n. 'Twas only another ha'penny.'

By the time he'd off-loaded the slabs and stacked them at the bankers, the morning was nearly gone.

'Dad'll be in a mood; he was expectin' me back wi' the chain afore this.'

Sam pursed his lips. Horace Skinner was known for his 'mistakes', but the youth's arrogance irked him.

'How's yer dad these days, be his cough any better?'

'Naow,' Will shook his head. 'He's sloggin' away at a new seam. He'll have more stone ready fer haulin' when I get back. At least Bess'll be rested.'

Sam was concerned about William Freer, they'd known each other a long time.

'Yer dad works too hard—'

'You try tellin' him, Sam,' said Will, feeling exasperated. Anyone would think his dad's cough was *his* fault. 'Trouble is, when he gets tired he cuts corners; he ain't bin round checkin' the legs lately. I try to tell'n,

19

but he acts like I don't know nothin', yet I finished me apprenticeship two year ago.'

Sam grunted sympathetically.

'Well, this repair'll cost you ninepence. I s'pose when you've paid fer the wagon an' horses you won't have enough for the club. Give me summat on account if you want, and make it up next week. Unless . . . I could do wi' another horse-trough.'

Will hesitated, lifting his cap to scratch his thatch of brown hair as he considered Sam's offer. Paying into the sick-benefit society they could afford a doctor if needed, also, if his contribution lapsed he'd miss out on his free pint of beer as receipt.

He decided to accept.

'Aah, me dad'll be much obliged, Sam,' he said, declining any responsibility for the debt. 'I'll see you have one or t'other by the end o' next week.'

He paid twopence on account, and drove on to the Dun Cow. Not that being in debt was any disgrace, his dad often paid for candles with a catch of fish, or traded a stone slab for a loaf of bread.

All the same, a man who was owed was the one you looked up to.

When he'd finished at the pub Will drove up the track to his grandfather's stables. It wouldn't do to keep Merchant Warren waiting.

Despite the old man's contempt for his family, Will admired Warren's standing in the community. He came from the same humble background, yet had made his way in society. Saving up to buy his own horse and cart was the first step towards becoming the wealthy coal- and stonemerchant he was today.

As a youngster, when his dad came home exhausted and irritable Will had often been on the receiving end, making him think he was to blame. Then, when he was big enough to sweep up the chippings from dressed stones, he had to work in the quarr. At age ten he learnt to 'walk' the slabs, and examine them for flaws, then how to decide what each was best fitted for.

Now he was a qualified stoneworker Will no longer blamed himself for all that went wrong. The more wishful his thinking, the more he hardened his heart, especially as his wages helped Tommy's schooling.

'Never mind, son,' his dad would say, 'the quarr'll be yours one day.'

So he was biding his time. As he had no learning for anything else he meant to be the best mason in the district.

He'd seen the swanky young men come home on visits from the cities where they'd gone to make their fortunes. Well, he too would exchange his fustian trousers and hobnail boots for a pair of stripes and polished shoes, and a silk shirt with a white scarf round his neck. He might even pay the shilling fine to marry a girl from outside.

One day he'd be a well-to-do merchant like his grandfather.

Will's respect for Merchant Warren, however, did not extend to the man with him in the stable yard. The Honourable Simon Maltravers stood head and shoulders above the corpulent merchant. Dad's old enemy had few friends among ordinary folk: he leaned too hard on them to buy leases.

It seemed to Will that kowtowing to his betters was the price a self-made man must pay for rising above his humble beginnings.

He returned his grandfather's perfunctory nod, ignored Maltravers, and began unharnessing the horses. He enjoyed handling the lovely gurt animals, and stroked their velvety noses, but Hercules, whom he put back between the shafts, was his favourite.

While he pretended indifference to the lowered voices of the older men, he was surprised to see Maltravers pocketing money which the merchant gave him, rather than the other way round.

'For last night's use o' the cliff quarr,' said Henry Warren. 'Look outside your back door after dark.'

Maltravers cast a wary glance at Will.

'Amelia's boy?'

'Aah, that's her little bastard – all grownup – and with the makings of a fine mason. He'd have good prospects if . . .' Henry Warren clamped his lips.

Maltravers raised an eyebrow.

'If you unbent, and forgave your daughter?'

'Aah, perhaps,' muttered the merchant. 'There's something to be said fer seeing yer own flesh an' blood carry on . . .' Noting Maltravers wince, for the man's wife was barren, Henry hastily added: 'How's your good wife these days?'

Maltravers grunted.

'Ailing, and complaining as usual about coming down in the world. Since corn prices fell she's had to manage with only our cook, and one maid.'

Henry Warren scuffed a boot.

'Sorry I asked,' he mumbled. He wasn't the only one upset when his plan for Amelia's marriage failed, and though Maltravers' interest was financial, a title in the family had seemed a worthwhile deal.

When Sir Alan came of age Maltravers had relinquished his steward-ship of the Lackford estates and eventually married the daughter of a wealthy Poole banker. Jane wasn't to know his capital came from salvaging wrecks – and smuggling.

Now Maltravers seemed glad of the chance to moan.

'She never lets me forget the bad investment I made, expanding my wheat production with her dowry. But she forgets how much I spent repairing that crumbling ruin under the hill.'

Henry Warren regarded him knowingly, for Maltravers had bought Underhill Manor to impress his father-in-law, with money he'd rather have gambled. Now he sensed that Maltravers envied his nephew, a squire and titled landowner – with heirs.

He himself was no landowner, but he was a man of property, includ-ing his own merchant ship *Esmerelda*. He enjoyed the power and influence he wielded, and he just might consider leaving Will well provided for . . .

'Hmph,' he said gruffly; he'd forgotten what it was to feel affection. He forced himself to concentrate on what Maltravers was saying; the man always needed money.

'I daren't put my tenants' rents up again, it would cost too much, evicting those who can't pay,' complained Maltravers. He shrugged impatiently, and eyed Will. 'Yon lad's sure of himself, he has a way with horses. He'd be a good man to employ.'

It was a question as much as a statement, and Maltravers' lip curled at the merchant's immediate frown. 'At least you're on speaking terms with him.'

'Business only,' growled Warren. 'He's the only one of the family I can bring myself to deal with.'

'And he doesn't know you once wanted him adopted?'

The malice in Maltravers' voice told Henry Warren that he was still bitter about the past. Amelia had produced two healthy sons.

'Aah, only so his ma might marry you, but . . .' The merchant heaved a sigh, 'The little fool threw away her chance, an' now she's struggling.'

Maltravers sounded casual.

'Ah well, that's life, but I'm surprised you en't employed the lad on the gang.'

Warren hissed through his teeth.

'You could be right. He's got small regard for his parents, yet he's still the obedient son.'

He thought of the contraband he brought in hidden under *Esmerelda*'s false bottom, and the bales of wool, taken out with the stone, bound for his contacts on the Continent. Maltravers, whose cliff quarr was a temporary hiding-place, helped to thwart the preventive men by feeding them false information.

Most tenant farmers would rent out a horse or two at night, and there were always volunteers willing to carry the barrels and bales, but no one dared cross him or Maltravers.

Will came over, leading Hercules hitched to the wagon.

'I need Hercules to get the chain home,' he said bluntly.

He hoped the merchant wouldn't charge extra.

To his relief Henry Warren gave him a curt nod.

'Don't take too long!'

Will's thanks gleamed in his eyes as he nodded at the old man. He swung himself up into the driving seat and cracked the reins, causing Hercules to move at a hefty trot.

Henry Warren shook his head.

'Hm, I wonder if he could be trusted on the smuggling run? I need to know he can keep his mouth shut.'

Maltravers stared after Will, thinking how devastated Amelia and William Freer would be if their son, already fond of drink, was completely ruined – thereby ruining the family.

For now, he was content to use Henry Warren and anyone else who suited his purposes.

If Will had known the older men's thoughts he would have eagerly joined their gang, for even now he was thinking he could earn a few bob as a tub man. Only last night in the White Horse, the talk touched on a recent smuggling run, and he'd overheard how Dick obliged with a couple of horses while Squire was away.

Around the time he was born, after Boney's defeat, the demand for cliff stone for harbours and fortifications declined. Everyone knew the abandoned caves were used to land and hide smuggled goods, but the ringleaders remained unknown. Whoever they were, folk admired the clever way they timed the landings and avoided the preventive men.

His thoughts thus occupied, Will relaxed his hold on the reins. His way was uphill, and Hercules plodded on willingly enough.

Passing a rough track that led down the wares to the cliffs, Will remembered there were also rich pickings when a ship foundered. Folk had to be quick, before the landowner asserted his rights of salvage. That was another of his parents' failings, they were too honest.

Will began to whistle. He'd had the whole morning away from underground toil, and with a pint downed, and pleasant ideas for making easy money, his mood lightened.

Then his thoughts returned to his dad, and he grimaced. With a queer little pang of regret he visualized his dad getting up in the dark of early morning, and taking a candle to gaze on the sleeping faces of Ma, Charlie and Tommy before leaving for the quarr.

With the onset of the dark winter mornings and evenings, neither he nor his dad would see daylight for months.

William Freer senior rested on his haunches to consider his next move. He could have done with Will's help, but they had to take advantage of the fair weather. The easier the transporting, the less it cost.

He allowed his thoughts to flit back along the dark tunnel, and out into the sunshine. Down across the fields, in their cottage, Amelia would be preparing supper. Dear girl, always so welcoming, and loyal. She never rebuked him for their mean way of life, and they were as happy as any in their circumstances. They were better off than farm labourers, and there were plenty of fish in the sea.

Thinking of Amelia helped to dispel the depression he suffered whenever he felt he'd failed his children, especially Will, his first-born. There was hope for the other two. With a bit of learning Charlotte should be able to become a companion, or even a governess.

He sighed, then smiled briefly as he thought of Tommy. The kid would soon be here.

Suddenly his candle spluttered.

'Blast!' He hadn't noticed it burning low; he'd have to go back to the tunnel entrance where he kept his candles and tinder-box.

Scrambling along, he coughed, and swore again for not remembering to bring a spare candle earlier.

Returning with a newly lighted one, he noticed once more the wooden prop supporting a rock in the ceiling he and Will hadn't had time to let down. He'd make it their first job tomorrow.

Back at the spot where he was working with his paddle, a long steel bar fashioned like a chisel at one end, he inched out the last bit of clay

24

holding back the slab, then used the bar to lever out the stone. It came away suddenly, and fell neatly on to the strong elm trolley he'd placed ready to catch it. He secured it with ropes, and harnessed himself to the trolley in preparation for the backward run.

He took a deep breath, and felt the rope bite into his hips as he took the strain, but once he got the load moving it eased with the momentum.

Just a hundred yards to the bottom of the slide, and he could rest.

He was thinking of Tommy's happy face again, when he was overcome by a sudden spasm of painful coughing. Still stumbling backwards, he bumped into the wooden prop and knocked it awry.

The last thing he heard before he was felled by a crushing weight was a noise like a cannon shot.

At last school was over. Tommy's spirits soared, the weekend ahead was a reward for enduring the week gone by. He poked out his tongue at Widow Hyer's back in return for the frosty look she gave him as he walked past her.

'Hey, Tommy, where's Charlie to? Gone to look fer yer mem'ry?'

Tommy ignored Billy Hart's taunts and rushed up the hill to the quarries. By the time he came within sounds of metal ringing on stone, and the grunts of toiling men, his legs ached, and he gasped for breath.

He slowed to a walk as the rough track got steeper, balancing on ridges with arms outstretched, or placing one foot in front of the other in the deep ruts. It was a risky pastime and when he heard the prolonged blast of a cow-horn, he leapt aside. A laden wagon, too heavy to brake, hurtled downhill, forcing its struggling team of horses forward, while the carter ran alongside.

Tommy gained the top of the hill, and ran until he came in sight of the Freer quarr. It seemed very quiet compared with the others.

He called out, but apart from a welcoming 'Hee-haw' from Bess there was no answer. The donkey was tethered to the capstan, but Will wasn't back yet, and his dad must be underground. Bess was quivering and restless, picking up her feet and stamping as she did when there was an adder around.

Tommy picked up a stick and searched, but could see no snake. After soothing the animal with soft words nuzzled into her cheek, and caressing her with hot grubby hands, he went into one of the stone work huts.

His dad's coat still hung on its wooden peg. Tommy's eyes went to the shelf above, where there was a battered metal box his dad had brought back from the war many years ago. Now it had a special use. Tommy reached up for it and carried it outside to the edge of the mine.

At the top of the paved slide Tommy gave the box a hearty kick, and grinned as it bounced and rattled its way to the bottom. The signal he was here would bring his dad out any minute, to climb the rough-hewn steps like a mountain goat. He would carry Tommy down on his shoulders and show him the work he'd done today, then they would walk home together.

Five minutes passed, and Tommy began to think his dad had gone without him, but not leaving Bess like that, surely?

He called out, childishly indignant at first, then fearfully. His dad had never gone without him before, and the donkey was restless again. Something was wrong.

What should he do? It was too dangerous to climb down by himself, besides he'd promised not to, on pain of a belting if he tried.

When Charlie arrived with her arms full of green stuff, Tommy was hopping about at the top of the slide shrieking in panic:

'Dad, Dad! Why don't you come?'

Charlie's instincts took over. If her dad had had to leave early he'd have left a message with someone at another quarr to look out for the boy.

She dropped her bundle where she stood.

'Tommy – run and tell the men at Chapman's quarr they're needed here. Then go and find Will, and don't come back without him!'

Relieved to be told what to do, Tommy obeyed with tears gushing down his face.

'Oh dear God, no,' Charlie muttered, 'not a founder. Please don't let it be a founder!'

Hoisting her skirt with one hand, she steadied herself with the other and clambered backwards down the steep rock steps. Her heart thumped with fear, and knowing.

Forty feet down she peered into the mouth of the mine, her teeth biting into her pinched lips.

There was no glow from a distant candle, no sound.

She ventured into the blackness, and slid her hands along the tunnel wall until her fingers found the ledge and the hollowed-out stone where the tinder-box and candles were kept.

Turning to the faint daylight from the tunnel mouth, she fumbled with flint and steel until a spark set the tinder smouldering. What took seconds to kindle a brimstone-tipped sliver of wood and light a candle seemed like hours.

Pocketing a spare candle she smothered the tinder, and moved on, muttering a plea.

Through eighteen years her dad had tunnelled ever deeper underground to fetch out good stone suitable for paving, and roof slates. It was stuffy and she soon grew hot and sticky with the perspiration of fear. She wanted to call his name but dare not, in case of disturbing loose rocks. There was no scurrying of rats or mice, not even beetles or spiders in this barren world of stone and unbreathing clay. Only her shuffling footsteps broke the silence.

She hadn't gone more than a hundred yards before she reached a corner where a new lane branched off. As she lifted the candle to try and see down it, the light flickered. A draught was coming from somewhere.

'Dad?' she whispered loudly into the endless dark, and waited, listening, so as not to imagine sounds that weren't there.

Then she heard the rattle of small stones sliding on grit. Such a little sound, but it confirmed her worst fears. She gasped with a sob: 'A founder!'

Holding the candle aloft Charlie took cautious steps forward, then stopped. There was no sign of her dad, only a piece of wooden prop sticking out of a pile of rocks and rubble.

Terrified of another fall at any moment, she scooped up a handful of damp clay, made a rough ball against the rock face and stuck the candle into it. Then she clawed at loose dirt, and fallen rocks, grunting with the effort of pushing aside those too heavy to lift.

Panic lent her strength, and she worked feverishly, pausing only to wipe the sweat from her brow. She thought she heard a faint groan, and redoubled her efforts. God, she'd never felt so hot . . . .

She took more care to lift rather than drag the stones, and was rewarded with the sight of a hand, then an arm. Now she could see his face, ashen, eyes closed. The rocks had tumbled in such a way as to prop each other up, leaving a small gap over his head. The rest of his body lay hidden, crushed beneath the mound.

'Dad, oh Dad,' she whispered brokenly. 'It's me, Charlie.'

His eyes fluttered open.

'Oh, thank God I found you . . .'

Tears streaked her dirty cheeks, and she sobbed as he tried to speak.

'Hang on, Dad. Help's coming . . . *please* hang on . . .'

27

'Charlotte? My pretty girl, Charlotte . . . as good as yer ma . . . stupid bloody vool, I be.'

'Dad, don't. You're no fool, you're a grand – Da-ad?'

His head lolled to one side, his eyes upon her, yet not seeing her.

When Will arrived with the men from Chapman's quarr they found her kneeling beside the half-buried body, sobbing her heart out.

CHAPTER THREE

'CHARLOTTE. My pretty girl, Charlotte.'
Almost her dad's last words, Charlie repeated them over and over. Her father *was* proud of her. If only he'd shown her more affection, maybe his passing would be easier to bear.

And Ma was devastated.

Charlie tried to comfort her.

'His last thoughts were of you, Ma' It was true, he must have been thinking about Ma when he said '. . . as good as yer ma, and so pretty.'

She'd always tried to be equal to any boy, thinking to please him, and never thought about her appearance. Now his words became enshrined in her memory – his parting gift to her.

In return she vowed never to allow anyone to call her by her proper name. She was *his* Charlotte alone.

While she, Ma and Tommy comforted one another, Will hovered in the background, seemingly indifferent. Now and then he muttered angrily: 'I told'n so . . .'

Ma said it was his own pain coming out.

Their ma wasn't as weak as Will might have thought. The first thing she did, when she recovered her wits, was apply to the company for permission to keep the quarr open. Though Will was competent, he was not of age, and having him work for her was one way of protecting Charlie and Tommy from his bitterness.

The shilling that bought a widow the freedom to manage her husband's quarr also gave her the right to employ an apprentice, to which idea Will strongly objected.

'It won't cost you anything,' Amelia pointed out.

'No, but he'd have to be accommodated, and it would be another mouth to feed.'

Charlie felt sorry for Tommy, poor lamb. He seemed to feel his dad's loss more than anyone.

He gazed at their ma with enormous dewy eyes when she tried to comfort him.

'Dad's happy now. He's gone to heaven where he doesn't have to work, and be tired all the time—'

Tommy stamped his foot. 'But he's gone away from me,' he stormed. 'Well, I won't go to school!'

Frustrated with grief Amelia snapped at him:

'Would you rather go and work in the dark quarr – without Dad?'

Tommy was afraid of the dark where bad things happened, so he went to school.

'It's what Dad wanted,' Charlie argued, when Will demanded that their little brother should be his apprentice.

They reached a compromise when Tommy, who had transferred his affections to Bess, said:

'I can be donkey-boy after school and at weekends, so I can help.'

'Glad somebody round yer can see sense,' Will growled. 'If you want to keep him at school, you'll have to pay fer it – and you'll have to dam well help in the quarr!'

She did. Instead of going back to school herself, she helped Will in whatever way she physically could. She helped load and push the trolley underground, and above ground she stacked the slabs she could 'walk', and fetched and carried tools to the blacksmith. Amelia allowed her to wear her dad's old trousers for the work.

Over the following weeks Will changed so much she sometimes feared he would strike her, or even Ma. Although he'd been moody and selfish before, she'd understood him. Now their closeness waned, yet he worked hard and took pride in not cutting corners. They were no deeper in debt than anyone else.

'Will behaves as if he hates us,' Charlie complained to her mother. Things were hard before, but life had its lighter moments. 'There's no fun any more.'

'I can understand him,' said Amelia, 'he had ambitions. Now he's the breadwinner he has to work all the hours God sends.'

Charlie didn't have the heart to reply that her dreams, too, were shattered. What little money she'd saved helped pay for the funeral, and now she spent her spare time earning money for Tommy's schooling. Instead she said:

'Will even works nights sometimes, surely there's no need . . .'
Amelia shrugged.

'We must do all we can to help, only it wouldn't be so bad if there was a little kindness left in him.'

They toiled on through the winter to build up their supply of stone for when the sea and weather were favourable for transporting once more.

Will took refuge from his lot at the pub most evenings, and Amelia railed at him.

'I'm not working my fingers to the bone so you can waste money on booze!'

Will stood up and barged the table with his fist, his face a scowling mask.

'Bide quiet! What I do in me own time is my business.' A slab of stone for a pint of beer, and the landlord profited by selling them on to the stone-merchants.

One Saturday, Charlie was underground with Will to help with the hauling while Tommy led the donkey. With each circuit around the capstan a ton of stone was raised another six feet.

Meanwhile she and Will were preparing the next stone. They were near the mouth of the tunnel when Tommy screamed, and they saw the previous load halt half-way up the slide.

Charlie was first up the rough steps to see what was wrong.

Bess had collapsed from exhaustion, and Tommy was lying across her body, sobbing.

After a swift examination, Charlie shook her head.

'She's beyond any help we can give her . . .'

Will ignored Tommy's frantic sobs, and swore.

'The rent's due, and I ain't fallin' any further behind. Charlie, you and Ma will have to push the spack 'til we save up fer another donkey.'

They had to give in. 'If not,' Will threatened, 'I'll open up the three foot vein, and send Tommy in while I do the haulin'!'

The only solace Tommy found for his doubly broken heart was in school. By learning his lessons well, he gained praise and affection from crusty Martha Hyer.

The Freers were never out of debt. Candles were a regular outgoing, like chisels and punches which had constantly to be honed at the blacksmith's.

31

'You look tired, maid,' Sam Roper told Charlie one day. 'Like yer ma last time I seen her in town.'

There wasn't much Sam didn't know, but he was a likeable fellow.

Thankfully Charlie lowered the heavy plaited-straw basket.

' 'Tis good to get away for a bit,' she admitted. It was a clear spring morning, and she looked towards the hills, away from the dismal quarrs.

'Will says he wants all the chisels seeing to, and he needs some wedges for the "legs".'

'I got some you can have cheap. Why don't 'ee sit theeself down and rest, maid, while I temper this lot?' The burly blacksmith pointed to an upturned barrel.

'Thanks, Sam. But I mustn't be long. Will said not to wait if you're busy.'

'Hmph,' grunted Sam, pumping bellows until the coals glowed red-hot. It wasn't like Charlie to be so meek, so that's how things were with the Freers, poor buggers.

Using a pair of tongs, Sam thrust a blunted punch into the fire.

'Will ain't taken a partner?'

'Naow,' sighed Charlie. 'He won't even agree to take an apprentice. When he's up to date with the rent, he says. Well, pigs might fly. He hates owing the gentry.'

'Don't matter 'bout me, then?' quipped the blacksmith, hammering the red-hot end of the tool on his anvil. There was a fierce hiss when he dipped it into the water-trough, and a spurt of steam.

He glanced at Charlie from the corner of his eye as he examined the new point, and she gave him a fleeting smile to cover her embarrassment.

'Of course it does, Sam, but you know what I mean. Owing our own kind ain't so, so . . .'

'Hoomiliatin'?'

'Aah, that's right.' Relieved because he understood and wasn't offended, Charlie grinned broadly.

Sam scrutinized the chisels.

'Some o'these 'ave seen better days'n all . . .'

He stopped, and laid the tools down to stare past her.

Charlie turned to see Sir Alan Lackford leading his big roan hunter into the smithy's yard.

'Oh no, not him,' she groaned in dismay.

'Don't fret, maid,' said Sam, wiping his hands in his neckerchief. 'I've known Squire since he was a little'n. He ain't so bad. Pestered me as a boy, wantin' to watch me work, an' still does, now an' agin . . . Mornin', Squire. What can I do fer you?'

Charlie stood up, feeling awkward and untidy. To curtsy wearing trousers seemed ludicrous, but she tucked a loose strand of hair into place and bobbed tentatively.

Apart from a curt nod his lordship ignored her.

'My horse cast a shoe,' he told Sam, 'and as I'm some distance from home I hoped you could oblige.' His tone was pleasantly polite, but it was still an order. He darted a glance at Charlie over his shoulder. 'You don't mind?'

She gave a slight shake of her head. It was the done thing for the gentry to take precedence, but how unfair it was, she thought, that his sort were always tall, as if God meant you to look up to them. She once said as much to her ma.

'It's because they live above ground, in fresh air and sunshine – and with plenty to eat,' Amelia said. 'Not like quarrymen, and coal-miners who barely see the sun from one day's end to the other.'

'I'll get back to yer tools presently, maid,' Sam told her as the two men turned to the horse.

Charlie grimaced at their backs and thought about Sir Alan's reputation. Was he as bad as he was made out to be?

Suddenly she felt a prick of alarm. The last time she'd seen him this close was when she'd hidden in the loft above his stables. The day of her dad's death, six months ago. Squire's unexpected presence here might be another bad omen!

Her eyes grew big with unaccountable fear.

'I have to go, Sam,' she called. 'I'll come back later!' The squire turned his head at the sound of her voice, but she was already running.

Will might be fed up with waiting. If his ill humour got worse, neither she nor Ma would be able to stop him making Tommy work in the quarr. Too many small boys were killed in accidents due to inexperience, or lack of strength.

'What ails her?' Sir Alan asked the blacksmith, his brows raised in surprise.

Sam stared after Charlie.

'I can guess,' he said sadly, and shook his head. 'I never seen anyone so changed. Name's Charlie Freer. Her dad was killed by a founder last autumn; now she and her family are tryin' to keep the quarr goin'.'

33

Sir Alan nodded. 'Freer; ah yes, tenants of mine. Damned bad business.' He looked puzzled. 'Charlie? Strange name for a girl. Short for Charlotte, I presume?'

'Oh, aah sir. Named after her gran'ma on her mother's side. French, *she* was. Come over durin' the Terror – one o' the survivors Henry Warren rescued when 'er ship got wrecked. That's how they met.'

'Merchant Warren?'

Sam Roper nodded. 'The same. Best move 'e ever made. She were so glad to be out o' France she married'n. She had some jewels, an' that's how he got started. One man's meat, as they say . . .'

'Ahem, quite so.'

'Aye sir. They only had the one girl survive; he was more int'rested in his business, an' took it fer granted his missus was happy, content with their one child. But she was pinin'. The story goes that her parents were in prison when she escaped, and got sent to Madame Guillotine.'

The blacksmith sighed. 'In th'end she died of the cholera. A couple o'years later the daughter Amelia runned off wi' young Freer . . .' Sam shrugged. 'She had a good home, and a governess, but she were lonely . . .'

He broke off, and bent to nail on the horse's shoe, fearing he'd touched a tender spot. Squire was lonely ever since his wife . . . and his young uns only tiny tots.

He finished the job in silence, then straightened up.

'Anyways, Miss Freer's like to be rude to anyone using her proper name since her Dad died,' he added. 'Her little brother always called her Charlie, and the name stuck.'

Sir Alan tut-tutted.

'How old is she – twenty?'

'Nearly eighteen, sir. Looks older 'cause she's had to grow up quick – too much hard work an' responsibility, if you ask me.'

'She looked so frightened – of me, d'you think? Rent owing?'

'Aah, no sir. 'Tis her brother she's afeared of. Her and her ma are strugglin' to give the young un proper schoolin', but Master Freer would rather the boy pulled his weight in the quarr. Charlie's afeared of upsettin' him.'

Sam regarded the squire with a bemused expression, and rubbed his stubbly chin. As long as tenants weren't behind with the rent, what did the gentry care for their troubles? At least this one, for all his eccentricity, was more human than Maltravers, his rogue of an uncle.

His thoughts were unexpectedly confirmed.

'Well, when Miss Freer returns, will you tell her I'm sorry for the inconvenience and give her this as compensation. And one for you.' Sir Alan paid the blacksmith, adding two extra half-crowns.

Sam suppressed a whistle, and touched his brow instead.

'That's most kind, if I might say so, sir, an' I thank you kindly on 'er behalf.'

He jingled the coins in his hand, and saved his gap-toothed grin until the squire rode away.

'Aah, he be eccentric, an' thass a fact.'

To Charlie's relief there was no cause for alarm at the quarr. Will was his usual moody self.

'You'm back early, 'tis a wonder you ain't skivin' off while you had the chance.'

'You said not to wait if Sam was busy,' Charlie retorted. 'He was busy, so I came on.'

Fool, she chided herself, now she would have to knuckle down again.

But Will was busy fashioning a scullery sink for the grocer's wife.

'I don't need you yet,' he said grudgingly. 'Get on over to the dairy and see if Fred's got yer pay fer last week.'

Charlie was only too pleased to oblige, and hurried away before he changed his mind.

'I'll call for the tools after,' she yelled over her shoulder.

She felt more cheerful when she returned to the smithy with her wages from Fred.

Sam grinned. 'I got somethin'll make you smile,' he said, and gave her the half-crown from Sir Alan.

'He left this – for me? What's come over him? Dick's always saying how tight-fisted he is. The kitchen-maid told him Squire won't even let them have the scraps off the plates.'

Sam puffed out his barrel of a chest.

'Trouble with havin' servants,' he said knowingly, 'if you go easy on 'em they take too much fer granted. But he can afford to be gen'rous to them as does him a favour outside his employ. Takes after his father – manners maketh man, I s'pose. Anyways, it might be just as well not to tell everybody, aye?'

Charlie agreed. She liked Sam, and trusted him to know best.

*

Amelia stared when Charlie came home at supper time with a batch of sticky buns, and a sugar-loaf. She looked like the cat that got the cream.

'Here y'are, Ma, for the jam you always say you'll make when you can afford the sugar.'

'What the hell . . .' began Will.

'We don't owe anybody anything,' said Charlie. 'Let's just say my ship came home.' It was a term smugglers used, and she winked at Tommy who was already half-way through a bun.

Amelia saw the imperious way her daughter looked at Will. She grew more like her grandmother every day. Sadly, since William died, her eyes held the same haunted look as she'd seen in *Maman*'s, pining for those lost to her.

Will had her father's looks, and pompous manner. Both men wanted to possess rather than belong, but Will lacked his grandfather's patience.

'Where'd you get the money,' he persisted now. 'You didn't use yer pay from Fred?'

'No,' said Charlie airily. 'I helped somebody, and he was grateful, that's all.'

'He! He – who?' Will shouted. 'If somebody gave you money you should pass it on to me, not squander it!'

Charlie stared at him defiantly and sat down at the table.

'What about you? You'd waste it on booze!'

With an ugly expression, Will leaned across the table, and put his face close to hers.

'You never lifted yer skirts fer some gent, I hope—'

He drew back as a resounding slap landed on his cheek.

'How dare you, you *bastard*!'

Will nearly knocked the table over in his haste to slap Charlie back. He would have boxed her ears as well if Amelia hadn't pushed between them. Usually even-tempered, she felt utterly frustrated. What with their poverty, and trying to keep the quarr going, she had no one to turn to, and this quarrelling was unbearable.

'That's enough!' she shrilled. 'If your father could see you like this he'd tan both your bare backsides – big as you are!' In her distress she was at a loss for words to express herself. Next moment she began to chide them in French. *'Mon Dieu, ces enfants! Ils sont tous imbeciles, n'est-ce pas?'*

Charlie and Will stared at her. Until now, apart from teaching

Charlie, Ma only ever used her *Maman*'s language in fun.

In that moment Amelia felt she was nothing but a drudge, and yearned for the comfortable life she'd once led. Then, seeing her youngsters' shocked faces, the moment passed and she regained her senses.

Choking on a great sob, she gave them each a push.

'Sit down!' she cried in English, and covered her face in her hands as she sank into her chair.

Glaring at Will, Charlie got up and put an arm around Amelia's shoulders.

'I'm sorry, Ma. We're not sick in the head, just a bit stupid. I never meant to hurt you.'

'I believed you'd both grown up,' sobbed Amelia. 'I never thought to see the day when children of mine would hate each other.'

Will looked down at his clenched fists.

'Well, she started it,' he muttered. It was the nearest he would come to apologizing.

'If you must know,' Charlie told him, 'Squire came to the forge and Sam had to stop doin' your chisels to shoe his horse. He asked Sam to give me half-a-crown for my trouble of having to go back. Anyway, I paid our bill out of it.'

This mollified Will, but roused his curiosity.

'Why should Squire give you money fer nothin'? He sacked a maid last week fer helpin' herself to logs from his wood-pile.'

Charlie shrugged. 'Don't ask me. He's supposed to be eccentric.'

Will scowled. 'That half-crown would've paid the rent that's owin'.'

Amelia dried her tears, relieved the situation was back to what passed for normal these days.

'Don't begrudge us a bit of pleasure, my son.'

'I don't,' said Will, 'but you'd better make the most of it. Lady Day's next week an' I'm still a month behind with the rent. There's a deal o' haulin' to do.'

The following week saw Charlie and her Ma treading the spack beneath a light but steady drizzle, broken only by an occasional heavy shower.

Because of rent-day, Tommy had a week off school, so they made him shelter in Will's quarr hut and practise his letters.

On the Friday, Will sent Tommy to Lackford Hall with a message to say he would pay the rent by the end of next week, making the wet weather his excuse.

The two women toiled in ankle-deep mud, and by mid-afternoon Amelia told Will she must rest. The hauling was almost finished.

'Thee'd best go on home, then,' said Will. 'Tommy can help.'

Charlie immediately objected.

'The little feller might catch a chill—'

'I started when I was his age,' Will insisted, 'so I don't see why he shouldn't do a bit.'

Tommy heard their raised voices, and came quickly to Charlie's side. 'It's all right, sis.'

They managed, but Charlie was tired, and wet through. By the time the trolley reached the top of the slide it was all she could do to unchain the load and lever the slabs off the trolley. Panting, she leaned on the long arm of the spack to recover her breath.

'Only one more load, sis,' said Tommy. He sent the empty trolley rattling back down the slide. They both listened for Will's shout to begin hauling again.

It came too soon: 'Righto!'

Tommy began giggling; while pushing with all his puny strength his feet stuck in the mud.

Neither sibling heard the approach of a horse, picking its way along the muddy track towards the boundary wall.

' 'Tain't funny!' Charlie snapped at Tommy. 'For God's sake let's get – this'n – done – afore he finds more . . .' Her words came jerkily with the physical effort. Suddenly she lost her footing in the slippery mud, and fell.

Directly her weight came off the spack it sprang back out of her hands, tearing itself from Tommy's grip as well. He staggered, too surprised to realize the danger.

Lying prone in the mud, Charlie reached out helplessly towards him. 'Get down, Tommy. For God's sake, duck!'

It happened so quickly. Tommy stood uncomprehending while the spack, released from tension, gained speed as it spun backwards. The long wooden pole was the same height from the ground as Tommy's head.

Charlie screamed, and shut her eyes.

She didn't see who jumped over her, and caused a scuffle that ended with Tommy shouting: 'Hey!'

But she heard a man's grunt, and the crunch of the spack halted in mid-flight. Then silence while she lay still, teeth clenched, too scared to open her eyes.

Then came the slurp of sucking mud as someone walked backwards, and stepped over her once more. It must be Will, come up for something just in time.

Faint with relief she opened her eyes to see Tommy picking himself up from the sticky morass where he'd been shoved out of danger.

'Oh, thank Go . . .'

She looked wonderingly over her shoulder, expecting a scowling Will to yell abuse. Instead she saw Sir Alan Lackford. With mud to the top of his riding-boots he brought the spack to rest, the capstan now unwound.

Open-mouthed, and speechless, Charlie stared at him; he was shaking from the exertion. His roan mare stood patiently by, head bowed against the wall, her hindquarters to the rain.

'Phew!' The squire dragged a hand across his brow, leaving a muddy smear that she would have found funny at any other time. 'Are you all right, Miss Freer?'

Weakly, she accepted the slim hand he extended to help her up.

'Sir,' she gasped, 'you saved Tommy's life!'

'It was a near thing.' He nodded at Tommy who silently handed him his hat which had fallen into the muck. 'Perhaps it was just as well I came.'

Still in shock, Charlie blinked, wondering what he meant. She saw he was drenched, too, and tried to express her gratitude.

'Won't you come into the hut, out o' the rain, sir?'

'Yes, yes,' he said. 'A good idea, and you'd better sit down.' He manoeuvred her on to a half-worked stone, then he and Tommy followed suit.

As Charlie looked at him, trying to find words to thank him, she was startled by the intensity of his gaze. His blue eyes were clear and direct as he lifted one eyebrow.

'Don't you think conditions are too dangerous for hauling?' he asked. 'For anyone, let alone a young woman and a boy?' Hands on knees, he sat back with his arms straight, still looking at her, his brow creased with genuine concern.

Aware that she must look like a drowned rat, Charlie made a futile attempt to pat her hair into some kind of order. Dropping her eyes from his penetrating stare, she mumbled:

' 'Tis how we're placed at present, sir.'

39

She began to explain how hard Will was working to catch up with rent. Before she could finish her brother appeared, his face twisted with rage.

'What the hell's goin' on up yer? Who let that load come shootin' down the slide like that? You should've known I'd be comin' up after the last'n. Be you tryin' to kill me?'

He froze as he saw Sir Alan, who stood up.

Charlie made to stand too, but the squire laid a hand on her shoulder and she yielded to its pressure.

'Your little brother nearly *was* killed, Master Freer, when your sister slipped, and lost her grip on the spack. I just happened to arrive in time to prevent the accident being fatal.'

'You let go the spack?' Will spat the words furiously at Charlie. 'You should've known better!'

'I *slipped*. Will—'

'She couldn't help it,' Sir Alan interrupted. 'Conditions are too dangerous for hauling, and quarrying is no work for a woman. Haven't you a work-pony, or an apprentice, even?'

Will had to swallow his rage.

'I don't know why you'm here, sir, but I'm glad you happened along.'

'I came about the rent, as you never came to the Hall yourself. My bailiff received your note, but I decided to find out for myself how you were placed.'

'Well, sir,' said Will bluntly, 'I reckon you got yer answer.'

'Hm, yes. Tell you what, Master Freer, I've no desire to see your debt settled over your siblings' dead bodies. They've undergone a considerable shock, you should take them home.'

Sir Alan inclined his head towards Charlie, who pulled herself up.

'Allow me to say thank you, sir,' she said awkwardly, 'for what you did.'

'I'm glad I was able to help,' he replied brusquely. He strode across to his horse and mounted, calling to Will over his shoulder: 'Come to the Hall after supper; we'll discuss the matter more satisfactorily.'

Charlie was fast asleep when Will came home that night. She awoke late next morning, wondering why no one had awakened her. To her surprise Will was with Ma in the kitchen.

'Why aren't you at work?' she asked him.

They both turned to stare at her.

'What's the matter, are we to be evicted?' Surely not, after Squire's kindness yesterday, but they looked so strange.

'Charlie,' her ma greeted her, ladling porridge into a bowl. 'You need not work in the quarr any more.'

'Why, is Will getting an apprentice?' Charlie's eyes widened in alarm. 'I'll not have Tommy—'

'Sit down, eat your porridge, and listen,' said Amelia firmly.

Charlie obeyed, darting a wondering look at Will who avoided her eyes.

'Squire needs a maid at the Hall, and offered you the position,' said Amelia.

Charlie gulped, and laid down her spoon.

'You mean go and work in that gurt house, every day? No more milking?'

'Nor working in the quarr,' Amelia repeated quietly.

Charlie glared at Will.

'What did you tell his Lordship?'

Will sat astride his chair, rested his arms on its back and glanced uneasily at his mother.

'I told'n just how things stood,' he said. 'I cain't manage wi'out yer help, an' we cain't afford a donkey. I told'n me ma's not too strong, an' how we want to keep Tommy at school.

'Then Squire said: "Suppose you had a strong pony to do the haulin' and an apprentice?" He knows a good lad at the orphanage, eleven years old, and strong.'

Will's tawny eyes darkened in mute appeal as he looked at Charlie at last.

'So how . . . ?'

'Squire suggested you could live in, then the lad could 'ave yer bed, and yer share o' food. That way 'twouldn't cost anythin' extra—'

'Oh-aah,' gasped Charlie resentfully. ' 'Tis all right for someone who's rich, with plenty of beds and food to tell others what to do.' She played angrily with her spoon in her porridge. 'Imagine being able to tell someone to leave home, what to do with their life!'

'Think, Charlie,' said Amelia. 'Think about us, of the benefits to the family. Will would have more time, he could build us a lean-to, and I could start my own straw-plait industry. It will be better for you, too.'

Charlie endeavoured to calm down. The idea of not living at home any more was unthinkable, but if Will had an apprentice, it would make life easier for Ma, and Tommy could carry on with his schooling.

Another thought hit her. She would earn wages. They wouldn't be much, but with free board and lodging she could save for her future.

There was just one snag. She looked sharply at Will.

'And how are we supposed to afford a work-pony?'

Will dropped his gaze again.

'I told'n I got no money fer a donkey, let alone a pony what needs more lookin' after, then he said: "Listen lad. Yours is a respectable, 'ard-workin' fam'ly. You deserve to get on". 'Twas his idea—'

'What? *What* was his idea?'

'He said . . . as my sister is a good worker, an' contributes to the fam'ly upkeep anyway—'

Charlie interrupted, frowning.

'You and him were discussing me, without consulting me?'

'He's consulting you now,' said Amelia forcefully.

Charlie looked at her ma's worn face, the tired eyes, and felt ashamed. Perhaps the shock of Tommy's brush with death was making her nervy and irritable. Nevertheless, apprehension welled up inside her as she allowed Will to finish.

'Squire said,' Will risked a glance her way, 'that he was willin' to give I – as your wages a year in advance – a good strong pony. He's got one in his stable that his daughter's outgrown—'

Will got no further. Unable to believe her ears, Charlie stood up, leaning on the table with both hands for support, for she felt weak with shock, and anger.

'You think to settle my future – *with nothing in it for me* – just like that? Well, I won't go!'

'*Charlotte!*'

Charlie gaped at her ma in abject dismay. Her own mother, taking sides against her!

'Charlie,' said Amelia, in the same tone she'd used when Tommy didn't want to go to school. 'You can't want us to go on struggling, straining our insides? It's right you should go.' She drew a deep breath. 'Your father would want you to, if only to better yourself.'

Charlie felt as if she were in the midst of a founder.

Encouraged by their Ma's insistence, Will said:

'Squire an' me shook hands on it.'

Until now Charlie felt she had nothing to lose, and had willingly done the right thing by Tommy, to honour her Dad's wishes.

Sacrificing her freedom to become a bond-slave was different. For a whole year she'd be at everyone's beck and call in that gurt house, obliged to perform any task she was given.

She sank back speechless, her brain reeling.

She'd been traded for a pony!

CHAPTER FOUR

Charlie spent the weekend in a daze as she washed and ironed her few good garments.

'Good fortune has come to this family at last,' her ma declared.

Charlie's eyes blazed at Will.

'Oh aah, it has for some!'

'I'll make it up to you somehow,' Ma promised.

Will was almost his old self, teasing her in a brotherly effort to soothe her trampled feelings.

'You never know, it could be a step up the ladder. You might even marry Dick – he's got good prospects . . .'

Charlie flared at him. She'd not thought of marriage to anyone, least of all a horse-groom with an eye for the ladies.

'I'll make the most of my time in that gurt house, and when the year is up, I'll find a real position, properly paid! One day, Will Freer, you'll come to me, cap in hand!'

Tommy didn't want her to go.

'Nothin's the same any more,' he remarked sadly. First his Dad died tragically, then poor Bess, just as cruelly sudden. Now Charlie was leaving home. 'Can't I come with you?' he asked. 'I could clean old Lackford's boots.'

His doleful look broke her resolve.

'No, you can't – and he's not that old, anyway,' she snapped, then hated herself. She hugged him. 'I'm sorry Tommy, I'm not angry with *you.*'

She forced a smile, though her eyes smarted with unshed tears. 'School for you, young un. That's what this is all about – to make a gentleman of you, so one day you'll go to Parliament and fight for poor men's rights.

'Anyway, someone's got to look after Ma, and I'll be home on my days off.'

Tommy pouted. 'Huh. once a month?'

'I'm only a couple o' miles away, perhaps we can meet after school sometimes. Listen, when Will's apprentice comes, it'll be like having another brother, and you've got a fine pony to fuss over.'

She wondered about herself. Squire would work her fingers to the bone, and no one would fuss over her.

Lackford Hall, a gabled three-storey stone mansion, stood on a breezy knoll, its imposing appearance softened by knots of trees within its walled grounds.

Charlie had seen it many times when she drove the milk-float up the carriage road, before taking the left fork to the stables at the rear. Sometimes she fancied herself sweeping up the avenue of poplars in a real carriage to the front of the house, and being handed down as 'Lady of the house' by a liveried servant. Lifting her rustling skirts of silk brocade, she would – very gracefully – climb the steps into the arched porch and enter the wide front door, tilting her nose at the footman who took her cloak.

But there fancy ended. She had never thought she would see inside, even as a servant.

Early this Monday morning, three weeks before Easter, as she trudged up the slope with her bundle of belongings under one arm, the big house seemed as threatening as it was imposing.

She couldn't help thinking of the rumours concerning Sir Alan, and his wife's mysterious death. Four years ago she'd taken her own life. Why? Was she mad, or desperately unhappy? What reason could there be, folk asked, other than it was due to him, the 'ogre'?

He hadn't seemed like an ogre to her, Charlie thought, as she walked round behind the house, yet he'd bargained away her freedom.

She came to the stables, and hesitated. She had no idea where to go or who to report to.

Hearing a familiar whistling she guessed Dick was mucking out, and stepped into the stable doorway.

Dick looked up, and with an extra loud 'Phee,' stopped work to lean on the rake.

'Welcome to "Happy Hall",' he said. 'I heard we was to have a new maid-of-all-work; well, if this ain't my lucky day.'

Charlie scowled. 'What's good luck to some, is bad luck to others,' she retorted. 'I only came to ask who I have to see. All I was told was I had to come on Monday.'

'Deary me, upset at leavin' home, are we?' The young groom shook back his mop of dark curls. 'Yer Uncle Dick'll look after ye – if yer nice to 'im. And think o' the money. 'Twill come in handy fer a dowry.'

What money, thought Charlie bitterly, too proud to tell him she was a bond-slave.

'I've got no time to stand here talking to you,' she said. 'What's the housekeeper's name?'

'His Lordship ain't got no housekeeper. Cook and the maid do everything. He's got a steward who does the finances – oh an' a bailiff, but 'e don't live in.'

Dick sounded scornful of Sir Alan. 'The master has three older sisters, so he knows how to run a house. Sometimes he goes into the kitchen tryin' to teach Cook things. Oh, very manly our master is!'

Charlie was in no mood for Dick's banter, and though not normally squeamish, the stink of manure and rotting straw was making her feel sick.

'Tell me the woman's name!' she demanded crossly.

'Mrs Biggins, also known as Mrs B.'

'Thanks. I'll go and find her.'

'He's got some *lovely* kids . . .' Dick called after her. 'Wait 'til you meet 'em!'

She ran to escape the sound of his laughter, hoping the house staff weren't as coarse.

Gripping her bundle, she rang the back doorbell long and insistently. A large ginger tom came and rubbed around her ankles, purring as if they were lifelong friends.

There was no immediate response, so she bent to stroke the cat. At the sound of approaching footsteps, and someone muttering, she stood up stiff and straight.

The door was opened by a large, plump woman wearing a white mob-cap and apron. Her sleeves were rolled up and she had flour up to her elbows.

'Well?' she demanded formidably. Her frown said the intrusion was interrupting her important work.

Charlie adopted the strategy her Dad taught her. Attack was the best form of defence.

Lifting her chin she said, 'You must be Mrs Biggins. I am Miss Freer, the new house-help, hired personally by the squire, Sir Alan Lackford—'

'I know who the squire is – and who I be,' began the woman, her hands planted on her ample hips. Standing on the step gave her an advantage, and she looked down at Charlie. 'You'll be takin' yer orders from me, so you'd best come in an' get started – an' leave all yer airs an' graces outside.'

She held the door open, allowing Charlie to squeeze past her, then slammed it shut. Leading the way along flagstones, past the scullery and into the kitchen, she added with a sneer: 'Come from a quarryin' family, don't yer?'

'I do, and I'm proud of it,' Charlie retorted, pricked into haughtiness. 'I've had several years at school, and I can read and write – among other things.'

Mrs Biggins turned to her, an unpleasant leer making her mouth lopsided.

'Well, you ain't gonna need them things yer, so you might as well ferget 'em.'

Charlie fought to control her rising temper, if only for her family's sake. She was saved from saying something she might regret by the appearance of a noisily fraught, untidy female kicking her way backwards through the kitchen door, her arms full of crumpled bed linen.

'Maisie,' said Cook, 'this yer be Miss Freer, if you please. Come to help by the invitation of Sir Alan hisself.'

Her mockery was lost on the housemaid.

Charlie, who had expected some friction, was unprepared for Maisie's venomous reaction.

'Huh, so you'm the new one we bin hearin' about. I seen you from a bedroom winder, talkin' to Dick all friendly-like. We got an understandin', me an' him, so you leave him alone!'

'I've known Dick since he was nine years old, when he came out of the orphanage,' Charlie flashed back. 'I wasn't aware he was spoken for.' Not that she cared, but she wasn't letting Maisie, or anyone else, bully her.

Maisie dumped the laundry on the floor.

Without bothering about the strands of fair hair that had fallen over her face, she stood with clenched fists on hips.

'You stay away from him or you'll be sorry.'

'That'll do, Maisie. Take Miss Freer to the attic and show her where to put her things. And don't let Master Dick hear you two squabblin' over him. He's vain 'nuff as 'tis.'

'Yes, Mrs B.' Glowering, Maisie led the way up the back stairs. Two flights led up to the third and top storey. A long, low-ceilinged room under the eaves served as a dormitory. There were six beds, in rows of three against two walls. Only two were made up.

'Put yer things in there,' said Maisie, indicating a large cupboard at the far end of the room. From a chest under one of the dormer windows she took a pair of patched sheets, and some blankets. 'And you can make yer own bed.' She put the pile on one of the bare mattresses, adding: 'Not now, later, after you finish work.'

'I'll just change my clothes,' said Charlie firmly. She'd worn her one Sunday dress, thinking she might have to see the squire.

'Well, don't be long about it,' sniffed Maisie. 'It won't do to annoy Mrs Biggins. Come straight down to the kitchen.' She flounced out of the room, leaving Charlie with a distinct yearning for the freedom she'd forfeited.

She looked out of a window. There was a wonderful view of valley, hills and the bay, but she couldn't twist around to see a whole panorama like she could from a hilltop. She felt even more like a prisoner.

The bed nearest the door had more space around it, and a screen for privacy folded against the wall. Charlie guessed it was Mrs Biggins's. There was a small table and stool beside the bed, and a large chest of drawers. On its top Cook's prize possession looked to be the little wooden-framed swing-mirror in the midst of her ornaments.

Charlie changed into a patched and faded but clean woollen skirt, a blouse and her apron. After putting her things away, she peeked into the tiny mirror and tidied her hair. Seeing her own sorrowful expression she told herself sharply to stop moping. Tommy was keeping up his schooling, thanks to her, and Ma no longer had to tread the spack.

'You should be proud of yourself,' she told her reflection, and bared her teeth in a mock smile. She almost lingered to make her bed for sheer defiance, then decided not to. The others had already taken a dislike to her, so she'd best find her feet before standing up to them.

She was set to work fetching logs and coal from two enormous wooden bins outside the back door, for the kitchen and copper fires. After helping Maisie with the laundry there was a short break at midday for soup, a hunk of bread and a mug of tea. This much was like home.

Afterwards, Maisie showed her the pantry where the best crockery and candles were kept, and the wine decanted. There was a big stone sink for washing up, and a large pine table.

Maisie left her there, polishing silver candlesticks while she took in the master's afternoon tea-tray. Fudge, the ginger tom, whose curiosity over Charlie seemed satisfied, followed the serving-girl.

Charlie's resentment of her new circumstances eased as she admired the exquisite silver. She'd never seen such fine things before, let alone handled them.

The pantry door opened, and a portly little man with a folder under his arm stood looking down his nose at her.

'The new servant, Freer?'

Charlie nodded and stood up, to be on his level more than out of politeness. She expected him to tell her his name, but he only said:

'Leave that, and come with me.'

Stubbornly, Charlie continued rubbing a candlestick with her cloth.

'Mrs Biggins ordered me to do this job, and not stop until I finish,' she objected. 'On whose authority am I to defy her?'

'Ho, I was warned you were a hoighty-toighty miss. All you need to know is, I take my orders from the master, and he wishes to see you.'

Charlie's boldness dissolved. Nervously she began wiping her hands in her apron.

'Wash them properly, and hurry,' he snapped.

Although no taller than she, his legs were long in proportion to his body and she had trouble in keeping up. She followed him along a flag-stone passage to a carpeted hallway. It was a large square shape, and had pale-green walls adorned with portraits. An enormous crystal chandelier marked the centre of the moulded-plaster ceiling.

The little man paused outside a pedimented oak door.

'The master will receive you in the library,' he said, and pushed open the door. 'Miss Freer, the new servant, sir.'

'Ah, thank you, Ponsonby. Come in, Miss Freer. Oh, Ponsonby – take that dashed cat out, will you?'

Charlie found herself in a lofty room with three walls lined with shelves of books from floor to ceiling. On the fourth side, daylight streamed in through three full-length bay windows; Sir Alan sat in front of the middle one, behind a solid mahogany desk.

Although prepared to resent him, for she always thought of herself as 'one of us', and of him as 'one of them', it was only the first time she

49

was to wonder at Sir Alan's politeness while her fellow servants were so rude.

He beckoned her forward.

Aware that she looked a mess, she pushed back her hair, and smoothed her skirt. Expecting him to rebuke her for her manners and shabby clothes, she began apologetically:

'I was polishing silver, sir, in the pantry,' then stopped. She should wait for him to speak first.

For a long moment Sir Alan sat with his elbows on the desk, hands clasped beneath his chin. He regarded her absently, as if wondering why she'd come.

'Ye-es,' he said at last. He leaned on the desk, and stood up. 'Looking after this room will be one of your duties.' He made a careless gesture with his arm. 'I'll go into details later. First, I want to show you around.'

Charlie swallowed a gasp. The squire – showing a servant around?

'S-sir?' was the only comment she could manage, not even knowing whether one was expected.

His height and closeness as he stepped around his desk made her feel small, and ragged. But as he ushered her to the door, he appeared not to notice her patched and faded skirt, or the apron smeared with stains from silver-polishing.

'I prefer to show new employees around myself, and explain their duties,' he said, striding through the hall. 'That way there can be no misunderstanding. You all have specific tasks, so if you have any questions, come to me. Now the dining-room, in here, is the most important room in the house.'

Charlie followed him into a long room where twelve upholstered Queen Anne dining-chairs were placed around a massive oval table. Sir Alan pulled open the drawers of two matching side-chests to show her where the fine table-linen and place-mats were kept.

Another crystal chandelier hung from the moulded-plaster ceiling, and around the walls were more life-sized portraits. Gilt-framed mirrors reflected light from the pelmeted french windows opposite.

Charlie drew in her breath. The Freer cottage would fit twice into this handsome room.

At one end was a huge open fireplace with an Italian marble surround, and at the other a rosewood commode with a cupboard containing dainty china, and drawers for the best cutlery.

'You will set the table for dinner, clear the dishes afterwards,' said Sir

Alan, 'then lay it ready for breakfast.'

As Charlie gaped around the room, he coughed politely to regain her attention.

'The table must be rubbed up every day, and beeswax applied once a month. The chairs also, and you're to polish the floorboards around the carpet edge once a week.'

Glancing down at the floor as he spoke, Charlie noticed he was wearing carpet-slippers. They were more fashionable than the knitted ones Ma made back home.

Sir Alan led her into the adjoining drawing-room, which was furnished with a grand piano in a corner, and an escritoire under one window. Two couches, one each side of another big fireplace, were arrayed with satin cushions; tapestry footstools stood on the floor in front of them.

Charlie barely took in the ornaments and statuettes placed on tiny tables.

'Apart from dusting, your first duty each morning is to go through the front of the house, opening curtains and shutters,' said Sir Alan. He crossed the hall to a wide flight of polished stone steps.

Charlie recognized the local marble, formed by its clusters of tiny shells. Seeing them was like meeting an old friend in this terrifyingly grand house which, for all its splendour, seemed to lack something, like a person unconscious.

She saw he was waiting, watching her as she ran up the steps after him, and felt ashamed of her appearance.

As if reading her thoughts he murmured: 'Hm, those clothes will never do.'

Sudden resentment smothered her shame.

'They're good enough for fetching coal, and other kitchen chores—'

Before she could add 'sir', he raised his voice, ever so slightly.

'But not good enough for the front of the house. I'll see you're provided with a proper housemaid's dress.'

He ignored her grudgingly murmured thanks, and showed her the bedrooms.

'This was my wife's.' He sounded casual. 'It's only used when we have extra guests.'

The room was plain, with only essential furniture. A bare-branched chestnut tree rustled in the breeze outside the wide window, drawing Charlie's attention to the view. She gained the impression of a large wood stretching out below, but Sir Alan was moving on.

They continued along the first-floor landing, and Charlie tried to hide her delight at the marble busts and gracefully posed nude statues, each in its own niche. Sir Alan was mounting the second flight of stairs, carpeted this time.

Charlie slid a hand up the oak banister rail, drooling over the intricate carving. Wait until she described all this back home!

The children's rooms, another guest room, and a playroom were situated on the third floor. These were smaller – but still bigger than any room at home.

Sir Alan indicated one with pretty feminine draperies.

'My daughter's room, and my son has the old nursery.' He allowed her to look in.

She saw the rocking-horse in a corner near the window, and noticed the top of the chestnut tree outside. This room was directly above their mother's.

'My children are away at school, but they come home for holidays between terms . . .'

Sir Alan sounded very matter-of-fact.

Remembering the way Dick had described his children as '*lovely*' Charlie said:

'I look forward to meeting them, sir,' and hoped her voice didn't betray her apprehension.

'You will meet them in the course of your duties,' he replied shortly, 'but strictly speaking they're not part of your assignments. Don't let them interrupt your work.'

'Oh, no sir, of course not.' Praise the Lord! 'Might I ask how old they are?'

'Isobel is twelve, and Hugh is nine. They will be home for Easter, so we must begin by spring-cleaning their rooms tomorrow.'

Charlie soon learned that whenever the master said there was a task 'we' must do, he meant it was a job for her. It occurred to her that he expected rather a lot. All this, on top of her kitchen chores?

She looked up to see an amused light in his eyes, but her expression must have seemed downcast.

'Why so grave, Miss Freer? Don't you think you will like it here? It's better than quarrying, surely?'

'Oh yes sir. But Mrs Biggins told me to see to the fires first thing every day, and help in the kitchen and laundry in the mornings, and she says there's plenty to fill the afternoons. Oh sir, how am I to fit it all in?'

Charlie could see no end to the hours of hard work.

'Miss Freer, you are working for me, not Mrs Biggins.'

'But Mrs Biggins said I must take my orders from her.' Charlie panicked as another thought hit her, and she lashed out in frustration. 'And what am I to do? Keep changing my dress to suit whichever part of the house I'm in?'

She flinched as he replied calmly, and very quietly:

'Don't be impertinent, Miss Freer. Mrs Biggins knew I was absent this morning, and no doubt thought it best to give you useful tasks until I returned.'

She did that all right, thought Charlie. Cook and Maisie had been horrid. In her resentment his low tone seemed more menacing than Will's brutal anger. She coped with her brother, for at home she had the right to answer back. Sometimes she'd deliberately provoked him. But here she was bought and paid for, an object like the master's other possessions, and she was unsure enough not to know when she was giving provocation.

'As I was saying,' he went on, seemingly unaware of her humiliation, 'your day will begin and end with shutters, and curtains, and the lights, of course. You will be expected to perform extra chores in the kitchen and laundry only if there are guests, so you'll find that pantry duties will fit in comfortably.

'You may take an hour out at luncheon – after mine is served, and you will have two hours off in the early evening before my supper at eight. Afterwards, when you have cleared and reset the table for breakfast the rest of the night is yours. You may attend church on Sunday mornings, and have one Saturday off each month. Is that fair?'

She had to look at him then. 'Indeed it is, sir,' she answered, and was surprised that his eyes held hers.

'If you should need more time off because of problems at home, you have only to say, and I will release you.' She bit back a smile of contempt as he added: 'You would, of course, be expected to make it up, but you could do so an hour at a time.'

She was glad to escape back to the pantry. It was getting dark as she finished polishing the last silver candlestick, and Maisie came in carrying a blue serge dress.

'Here,' she said bluntly, 'you'm to put this on. Then you better hurry up and do yer evenin' duties in the posh part o' the house, *your lady-*

ship!' Her green eyes glittered. 'An' don't think you can start givin' orders just because you'm working in the best rooms!'

The scullery-maid was clearly jealous that a new girl should be put over her.

Charlie tried to make friends.

'Thanks, Maisie. Please don't look at me like that, I have to do what I'm told, same as you.'

'Well he should've promoted me,' grumbled Maisie. 'It ain't fair.'

'I'll ask him to let us change places if you want,' offered Charlie, losing patience.

Swift as lightning, Maisie's expression changed.

'No,' she gasped, 'don't 'ee do that. If he thinks I ain't satisfied he'll tell I to find work somewhere else!'

Charlie was genuinely surprised.

'Would he really do that?'

'Oh aah,' Maisie said, then resumed her normal cunning look. 'There's one thing though, you'll see more of his kids than me an' Mrs B, an' I ain't sorry 'bout that!'

Gracious, thought Charlie, has the big ogre bred nothing but little ogres? She wouldn't say so; there was no sense in giving Maisie ammunition to use against her.

For the next fortnight she smarted beneath their contempt, performing menial tasks if the master had given her 'nothing better to do'. But she took heart from her brief meetings with Tommy during her spare time in the early evenings.

She didn't tell the others where she went. Let them think what they pleased, she had too much pride to justify her actions to them.

To help her self-control whenever Cook or Maisie scorned her, Charlie muttered French phrases under her breath. It gave her an amused satisfaction, so that she became indifferent to their insolence.

Most of her duties took her away from the domestic area; she made odd visits to the kitchen or laundry to carefully wash a piece of fine lace-work, or to iron family garments. When the master sent her to see how a particular culinary dish was progressing, she had to use all her tact. She tried to make his orders sound like requests, and remained outwardly impervious to personal remarks.

With the realization that Squire treated her courteously, she became aware of a dignity she'd never experienced before. Not that she recognized it as dignity. 'I'm like a housekeeper, but without the title,' she told

Dick when he came to the back door to receive his wages.

' 'Tis to keep yer wages down,' said Dick airily. 'If Squire was to give you the post official-like, he'd have to pay you more.'

Charlie smiled ruefully, and kept quiet about her true position.

Sir Alan gave each member of staff their wages personally, visiting the kitchen while Charlie was in another part of the house.

She would have appreciated his tactfulness if only he didn't ask the other women: 'Have you seen Miss Freer?' They made snide jokes about him seeing her alone, and it was in the dormitory at night that her new-found calm was hardest to maintain.

'Better watch yerself, *Miss*, after what he did to his wife,' said Maisie maliciously one night, as they prepared for bed.

'What do you mean?' asked Charlie sharply. 'Honestly, your stupid remarks have gone far enough!'

Maisie was afraid of Charlie when she lost her temper.

'Well,' she began soberly, 'he did drive her to her death, didn't he. Nobody knows what went on in private, do they.'

'No, they don't,' snapped Charlie. 'So what right have you to say such things?' Still, curiosity overcame her hostility. 'How did she die?'

'Too much laudanum.' Mrs Biggins nodded. 'She'd bin havin' lots o' headaches; I reckon it got her down, meself, Master's bein' away so much. She suffered real melancholy those last weeks. Missin' London fer sure.' She sniffed contemptuously. 'Squire never should've dragged her away. A different life altogether she led, afore she met 'im. I seen her bored to tears at times.'

Despite her aversion to malicious gossip, Charlie began to feel accepted.

'How did they meet?' she asked.

'Durin' the celebrations over Waterloo, and bein' rid o' Boney at last. Miss Helen Jamieson she was then. She were older than 'im; I reckon she fell fer 'im when he stood afore the King to receive his father's medal fer givin' his life fer 'is country. Women love a man in uniform.'

Mrs Biggins looked at Charlie in earnest. 'She was only just "out" that year, and was enjoyin' all the balls and parties like rich young ladies do.'

'She thought she was marryin' a hero,' sneered Maisie, 'because his dad was one.'

'They got on well while they was travellin' round the county,' Cook went on, ignoring Maisie's interruption. 'He showed her Bridport, an' how his grandfather had built up the rope-makin' business, an' all that, but even Dorchester was a bit tame fer her. So then she wanted to spend "the season" in London – an' he let her, to keep her happy, even when he couldn't be with her. Then havin' the babes put paid to her rovin'.'

Cook sighed witheringly. 'Oh she tried, but travellin' made little Isobel sick, an' *he* objected to her goin' away an' leaving the child with somebody else. Then, after Master Hugh, she started gettin' headaches, an' when they was old 'nuff, she asked'n to send the kids to school rather than employ a tutor. They was at loggerheads over that; he wanted to keep 'em home, but she got her way in the end.'

Cook lowered her voice to a conspiratorial whisper. 'Them headaches o' hers never got better, and sometimes she'd shut herself away fer two or three days. Then, after *it* happened, Squire was stricken – wouldn't let nobody near him fer ages.

'Nope,' she continued, 'he blamed hisself. 'Twouldn't have surprised me if he'd bin next to go. His Uncle Maltravers was afeared fer 'im; kept comin' an' goin' all the time.'

Somehow Charlie couldn't see Maltravers being concerned about his nephew. Then Maisie changed the subject.

'Hetty heard 'em quarrellin' a few days afore.'

'Who's Hetty?' asked Charlie, surprised.

'The maid you replaced,' said Maisie. 'Hetty Cauldon – old Biddy's granddaughter.'

'That old witch,' gasped Charlie. Biddy Cauldon was a fearful old hag with the 'evil eye' who kept to herself in her cottage on the fringe of the primrose wood.

Charlie had seen saw her once, in the village. The old woman wore a black patch over one eye and, while children ran away, adults felt safe from her powers.

'I didn't know Biddy had a granddaughter.'

Charlie felt sorry for the girl she'd never met; no wonder she'd turned out badly.

'Not many people did,' said Mrs Biggins. 'Afore the master employed her, Hetty was brought up in the workhouse because th' old woman couldn't keep her.'

'Where's Hetty now?' wondered Charlie.

'Livin' with her gran,' said Maisie.

Charlie frowned. 'And Biddy is able to keep her now?'

'Well, she'm bigger an' stronger now,' said Cook, 'and more useful. Old Biddy do work her hard, diggin' their vegetable patch to earn her keep. She's got a cow, and chickens too. Folks be frightened of her "evil eye" an' pay well fer her services, whatever they be, in case she do take off her patch and curse 'em.'

As she shuddered with repugnance, Charlie noticed that Maisie had clammed up. She wondered why.

'I suppose Hetty wanted those logs she stole for her Gran,' she murmured. 'It does seem mean to dismiss her for something so petty.'

Maisie spoke then.

'I reckon she knew too much. She had most to do with her ladyship, bein' her chambermaid—'

'Lady Lackford died four years ago,' protested Charlie. 'If Hetty knew something, why wait all that time to dismiss her?'

'Hetty got the push fer stealin' logs,' put in Mrs Biggins, sharply. She pulled the screen around her bed. 'If the master gives his servants an inch, they'll take a yard.'

Charlie remembered Sam Roper saying something similar, but now Mrs B was tired of talking.

'That's 'nuff, Maisie,' she snapped. 'No point lettin' yer imagination run away 'cause you got a bad case of sour grapes.' She blew out her candle. 'Now shut up, an' go to sleep, or I'll see the pair o' you spend tomorrer down the cellar. Dick's away early, so he won't be fillin' the fuel bins.'

'Huh!' said Maisie, pulling the covers over her head. Evidently Mrs B meant it.

Charlie lay still, with her eyes closed, but sleep was a long time coming. Maisie still felt spiteful because she hadn't moved up from scullery-maid. Now she's got it in for *him*, too.

I can take care of myself, thought Charlie, but the master . . .

Despite her indifference to him, she sensed he was vulnerable, and for some reason, that bothered her.

CHAPTER FIVE

As Easter approached the weather became unusually cold. A bitter wind from the Russian steppes brought a threat of snow, and seeing to the fires in the best rooms was an essential part of Charlie's routine.

One day she paused in the library to look through the nearest window. There was no sign of Squire, and knowing his concern for the new lambs she assumed he'd gone to check them.

The sky was iron-grey, and the bone-chilling wind still blew. Before the air lost its rawness, snow must fall. She shivered, and turned to dust the shelves.

There were some French books she'd been curious to examine, so now she took her chance. She mouthed the words until they sounded familiar and she understood them.

Recognizing the word Aesop, she was delighted to find the French version of his fables, and fingered the pages as she painstakingly translated the captions under the line-drawn illustrations.

Sir Alan came in so quietly she was unaware of his presence until he coughed politely.

'Oh,' she gasped, and closed the book. It unnerved her, the way he would so suddenly and so silently appear.

'I'm sorry if I startled you,' he said, stepping to her side. He took the book from her and looked at it.

Was he being sarcastic? She knew the gentry disapproved of the lower classes being educated, for fear they would get above themselves.

'Can you read French, Miss Freer – or do you just like the pictures?'

She'd expected a rebuke for touching his books without permission, and took his amused tone for mockery.

'A little, sir,' she replied, bridling. 'My French grandmother taught my mother, and I've learned from her, but I haven't seen much of the language written down.' Instinct warned her to be cautious. 'We had

Aesop's Fables at school,' she added shyly. 'In English, of course.'

'How interesting,' he said, sounding vague.

He's not interested, thought Charlie, he's just trying to remember why he came in here. She nodded towards the window, and deliberately dropped the 'sir' as she addressed him.

'Looks like snow. It seems more like Christmas than Easter.'

'Ah yes,' he said, more urgently. 'I want you to leave the library and light the fires in the children's rooms. I want them well-aired, beds too.'

'Yes sir.' She turned to leave the room, but he called her back.

'Here, you may borrow the book if you wish, and any others you'd like to study.'

He'd taken her by surprise.

'Th-thank you sir. I . . .' stammered Charlie. She tried to express her appreciation: 'I'm hoping to become a governess one day.'

He looked at her strangely

'That's good,' he said gravely. 'I happen to believe in furthering the education of . . .' He broke off, and gave her the book.

'Of the poor?' she finished for him, then realized too late that he'd interrupted himself out of respect for her feelings.

For once his normal infuriating calm became ruffled.

'Miss Freer,' he snapped, 'does it never occur to you that you are an inverted snob? We are all placed in this world by accident of birth.'

She had to look at him then, and saw his blue eyes grow pale.

'Sir, I – I don't know what you mean,' she faltered, feeling foolish, yet indignant.

'I can no more help my background than you can yours,' he went on, icily. 'Your kind seem to think that mine lack feelings. I'll tell you what, there are insensitive people in every walk of life. Think about it!'

He turned on his heel, and left her holding the book of *Aesop's Fables* in trembling hands.

Sir Alan Lackford felt annoyed for allowing a mere chit of a girl to ruffle him. Miss Freer was used to hard work and responsibility, and capable of intelligent conversation. Yet, dammit, she'd almost made him forget he was a gentleman. It was just as well he had to pay the bailiff a visit, he could do with some cold fresh air.

He crossed the yard to the stables, stabbed afresh by grim memories of the mental agonies he'd suffered when his wife died. For the manner of her death had been the final rejection.

59

Helen's indifference became noticeable after Hugh was born. The birth was difficult, and prolonged, so he understood her attitude – up to a point. But she distanced herself, even from the children, and became increasingly withdrawn. God knows he'd been patient, but she thwarted all his advances, no matter how tender. She seemed not to care for his needs.

Her death was a great shock, nevertheless, and his emotions were in turmoil for months afterwards. Not to mention the shame. Publicized in the news-sheets, her suicide was a topic for gossip, and put his reputation in question. He'd felt guilt, fearing he was to blame, as well as remorse and self-doubt.

He came from a family of women, yet he had never understood his wife.

At least his children were away at school, where they would learn to stand on their own feet. Also, they were removed from gossip, and servants' whispers.

And he'd discovered the strangest thing. He was pitied by the lower classes, when he preferred their contempt.

Dick led out the roan mare. 'Here y'are, sir. All saddled and ready to go.'

Sir Alan nodded.

'Thank you, Dick. Oh, use the two bays tomorrow to pick up the children, put plenty of warm rugs in the carriage, and make sure the footwarmers are in place, will you?'

'Aye, sir.' Dick touched his cap politely.

Sir Alan caressed the mare absently, then swung himself into the saddle and nudged her into a walk, his mind still busy.

Miss Charlotte Freer was different – for she it was who had brought on his present mood. He detected no self-pity in her. Sadness, yes, but there was also boldness, a recklessness the other servants lacked. She was shy, and knew her place, yet beneath her quiet manner there was defiance – and indeed he had witnessed her pride erupting!

He addressed his servants as befitted their particular station: Ponsonby, his steward; Mrs Biggins, his cook; Dick the groom; and Maisie, a sort of maid-of-all-work, whom he had acquired from his Uncle Maltravers. Just as he couldn't imagine himself addressing Maisie as Miss – er . . . whatever – so he could not bring himself to address Miss Freer by any other name. Out of respect for her feelings, as Sam Roper advised, he would not address her as Charlotte, but he was damned if he would call her by that ridiculous boy's name she preferred.

Now he knew she was reasonably well educated, with potential. The mere act of calling her Miss Freer brought the girl a measure of respect.

He touched the mare's flanks, and as she broke into a canter, the thought hit him.

He held Miss Freer in higher regard than was due to her station.

Perhaps it was because she'd borne her loss so bravely, and was about his own age when he lost his father. And she'd given up her freedom for her family's sake.

Yes, she had breeding, that one.

Mrs Freer, the girl's mother, was well brought up but there'd been a clash of personalities. Her father, Merchant Warren, married above himself only to disinherit his daughter for obeying her natural instincts.

Will and Charlotte Freer were the end results, the girl having inherited the larger share of grace and potential. With learning she could fit in with any company.

Hm, he thought: she wants to be a governess. Well, why not? When her year was up he could help her find a post.

He was in sight of his bailiff's cottage before he remembered the accounts book. He'd taken it home to study, and carried it upstairs last night when he developed a headache. It was still in his bedroom.

He wheeled his horse to return and fetch it.

'Damn you, Charlotte Freer,' he muttered, urging the mare to a gallop.

In Hugh's room, Charlie threw an armful of logs into the basket by the fireplace. Then she knelt to shove fiercely scrunched-up bits of paper into the grate and added the kindling. She was annoyed for feeling this way about upsetting *him*. He was the master, and she deserved a rebuke for speaking out of turn.

But fancy calling her a snob. The others would smirk if they knew. Well, she was unlikely to be dismissed before he'd got his money's worth out of her.

She was subdued when she entered the kitchen to ask Cook for the warming-pans, and wasn't sorry the woman misunderstood her manner.

'So, them brats of his are comin' home tomorrer. He's already ordered next week's menus. Get out my way, Fudge, you darn cat!' Mrs Biggins kicked out irritably at the ginger tom rubbing around her ankles. 'Maisie, get busy on them bellows. Miss Freer needs some red-hot coals.'

Maisie obeyed with a scowl.

'Gawd, wi' weather like this they'll run amok indoors.' She gave Charlie a scornful look. 'You'll 'ave yer work cut out then.'

'It's going to snow,' said Charlie. 'They'll have more fun outside.'

'Well, don't say you ain't bin warned,' muttered Maisie, shovelling coals into a warming-pan. She closed the lid. 'Yer take this'n, while I get t'other ready.'

'Thanks Maisie,' said Charlie with a tight-lipped smile. 'I'll remember.'

She took the long-handled copper pan, and hurried upstairs. Thank goodness Sir Alan was out, she'd rather not bump into him again.

She moved the warming-pan around between the sheets in Isobel's bed until it cooled, then returned to the kitchen for the second one for Hugh's bed.

'Have you seen that cat?' asked Cook. 'I chased him out fer sniffin' in the cupboards. Master won't like it if he's upstairs in the posh part o' the house.' Her inference was that Charlie would get the blame.

'Thank you for telling me,' said Charlie. 'I'll keep my eyes open.'

She left the two women up to their elbows in feathers as they plucked fowls ready for the first of the big meals to come.

When she'd finished in Hugh's room she found Fudge curled up on Isobel's bed, and shoved him off. As she stretched across to smooth the crumpled counterpane, she caught sight of herself in the full-length mirror on the other side. She'd never seen herself full-length before coming here, now she straightened slowly.

She went to the window and peeped out. Hart the gardener looked tiny, tending his glasshouse in the distance, while Dick slopped water from the pail he was carrying into the stables. Ponsonby never came up here, Cook and Maisie were busy in the kitchen, and Squire was out.

While her back was turned, the offended Fudge washed his fur where she'd touched him, and went to the door. It wasn't quite shut. The cat hooked a paw around its edge, and pulled it ajar. Then he sauntered out, tail erect in search of another comfortable spot.

Charlie returned to the mirror, and studied her reflection. She was startled by the grave face that stared back at her.

'I am Miss Freer,' she mocked herself, tilting her pointy chin. 'Housekeeper – or as good as – to Sir Alan Lackford, Squire.'

She took off her apron, discarded it on the floor, and shook out her hair with a delicious feeling of luxury. Next she undid the top buttons of her bodice, and tucked the corners under, to emulate the more daring fashions of fine ladies.

The contrast between her white breast and ruddy complexion made her smile, then she recalled Ma saying how like her French grandma she was. She wished she'd known Charlotte Annereaux.

She stepped back, scooped up her tresses to pile above her head, and swivelled round to see the overall effect. She was pleasing to look at, but who, apart from her ma, was there to care?

Dick, perhaps?

Charlie recalled that day in the stable when she'd opened her bodice to oblige the groom. She was younger then, and saucy, without a care in the world, before . . .

Oh God, that was the very day her dad died.

Two big tears of shame spilled down her cheeks and she loosed her hair.

She rebuttoned her bodice, then, as she bent to retrieve her apron another movement reflected in the mirror caught her eye.

Behind her the door was slowly being pulled shut.

She gasped, she hadn't realized it was ajar. Who could have been watching her?

Fearful now, she quickly did her hair and hurried downstairs. Cook and Maisie were still busy. If they'd caught her preening herself they'd have leapt on her, shrieking disapproval.

Was it possible that Ponsonby wanted something upstairs after all? Certainly not in Isobel's room. Or was it Dick? She wouldn't put it past him, knowing the master was out, but he'd want something for keeping quiet.

Sir Alan moved very quietly in carpet-slippers. She dismissed the idea; he'd gone off on his horse.

While she finished her day's work in silence, Cook and Maisie eyed each other, misunderstanding. Madam was dreading the arrival of the two brats!

Charlie went to bed early, but her restless mind turned to what Squire said about there being insensitive people in every class of society. She thought about Henry Warren.

Nobody would guess he was her grandfather, the way he treated Ma.

Will was insensitive, too, with more reason. She wondered how he was getting on, and if Sandy the new lad had settled in. She hoped that he and Tommy were friends. She saw them all at church on Sundays, and had learned that Tommy now helped Fred with the milk-round.

Her little brother had pouted.

'He won't let me drive the float yet.' While his face lingered in her mind she drifted into sleep, unaware her pillow was damp from tears.

Snow fell overnight, and next morning the darkly heavy clouds promised more.

Charlie was fetching logs from the bin outside the back door when Dick found her. He looked immaculate in the Lackford livery, but had lost none of his cockiness.

'Master says to ask you to light the fires in his brats' rooms early, and make sure there's plenty o' logs an' coal. I'm to meet 'em off the post-horn coach at Frometown. Brr!' He rubbed his hands gloved together. 'I only hope it don't get held up in any snowdrifts.'

Charlie's apprehension grew. The master usually gave her her orders. She hadn't seen him since yesterday when he'd stormed out of the library.

'Isn't Squire going with you to meet them?' she asked, tentatively.

'Naow. He's more concerned to see his sheep and cattle sheltered and fed. If this yer weather keeps up there'll be real problems.' Dick stepped closer. 'Shame you can't come along o' me. I'd enjoy your company.'

Before she could stop him he'd thrust his arm around her waist and jerked her to him.

'Give us a kiss, Charlie—'

'Let me go, you fool,' she hissed. 'You'll get us both into trouble.'

'Master's out, an' nobody else be outside.' He kissed her forcibly, and groaned. 'Charlie, why don't you sneak out to me one night?'

She might have welcomed the feel of his strong arms around her, for she felt starved of affection, but with an effort she struggled free, and shoved him away.

'There'll be hell to pay if Maisie sees us,' she panted. 'She says you and she have an understanding.'

'That's what she thinks,' said Dick. 'I'd just as soon have you.'

'You mean you'd like me as well. Go on with you!' Charlie lifted a hand, threatening to slap his face if he came near again.

Dick's face twisted in a scornful sneer.

'Well, I never knowed you afeared o' anyone afore – or be you too proud these days? Gettin' too big fer yer boots?'

He stalked off, mouthing insults about stuck-up females.

By mid-afternoon Charlie was satisfied all was in order for the children's arrival, and had a fire going in the sitting-room where Sir Alan would take afternoon tea with them. As yet there was no sign of him; he'd come in for luncheon, then disappeared once more.

It snowed again before Dick returned with his charges, calling to Charlie and the others, who stood to attention in the doorway, that he'd only just managed the climb up Hell Hill. The steep hill between Corvesgate and Swanwick was notorious for its tortuous bends.

Isobel was well grown for a twelve-year-old, and was clearly smitten with the groom's dark good looks. As Dick went to hand her down from the carriage she removed her muff, and with mischief in her eyes, reached out her arms to him.

'Carry me,' she ordered.

Dick obeyed cheerfully. He swept her into his arms so suddenly she shrieked, and laughed in his face as he carried her up the steps and across the threshold before putting her down.

Charlie saw Mrs Biggins's lips tighten, while Maisie watched balefully.

'Will that be all, mistress?' Dick asked cheekily.

'That will do for now, thank you,' she replied haughtily, 'until it stops snowing, then you shall take me riding.'

'Righto, miss.' Dick raised his coachman's top hat, and stared boldly at her before he averted his eyes as a good servant ought. 'I'll fetch your little brother.'

The pouting boy was already climbing the steps, and brushing snowflakes from his coat.

'I'm not like my silly sister,' he said. 'I can manage perfectly well, thank you.'

'Aah, young master, that you b'ain't.' Catching Charlie's eye, Dick smirked and winked. He leapt nimbly into his seat and proceeded to drive the carriage round to the stables.

Isobel, meanwhile, looked Charlie rudely up and down and ignored Maisie completely.

'Where's Papa?' she demanded of Mrs B.

'You'd better ask Miss Freer, mistress,' said Cook, indicating Charlie. 'She's the new housemaid, your papa gives her the instructions these days.'

'Oh?' Isobel lifted her eyebrows insolently, and tilted her dainty nose. 'How long have you been with us?'

Despite the girl's rudeness, Charlie was amused, for it seemed as though Isobel was acting – and hadn't she learned to do the same? What with Maisie and Mrs B, and trying to please the squire, she often felt she was playing a part instead of being herself.

She bobbed a curtsy.

'Only a few weeks, Miss Lackford.'

'Is that all?' cried Isobel. 'Why hasn't Papa come to meet us, instead of leaving us to be greeted at the door by servants?'

'Because of the weather, miss,' said Charlie, and noted Cook and Maisie gloating at her discomfort. 'Your father must see to the care of his livestock—'

'You mean his old sheep are more important than us?'

'Some new-born lambs are already lost,' Charlie replied, detecting an impassioned plea beneath the girl's complaint. 'He'll be here soon; let me take your coats.'

Isobel and Hugh shook themselves out of their hats and coats, making Charlie stoop to pick them up from the floor.

She saw that both children had their father's blue eyes, but while Hugh shared his fair hair with a kink at the ends, Isobel had a glorious mane of red-gold tresses that curled naturally.

The girl tossed her head arrogantly.

'Well, what are you two gawping at?' Her rude question wiped the smirks from Maisie and Mrs Biggins's faces. 'You may go back to your work. You've done your duty by us.'

No one had introduced Charlie to Hugh. With her arms laden, she straightened up, determined not to let these precocious children get the better of her. As Hugh continued to glare, she was reminded of Tommy in a bad mood, and bit her lip to stifle a giggle.

'Hello, Frank,' she said, and marched into the cloakroom.

'My name's not Frank,' he cried indignantly, and ran after her. 'It's Hugh!'

'Oh? I beg your pardon, Master Hugh.' Charlie gave him a broad grin, and curtsied. Isobel looked furious, and opened her mouth to scold, but stopped and looked the other way.

Charlie was amazed by the change in the young girl's features as Isobel's rage turned to delight. Her eyes grew large and luminous, and her lips stretched into a warm smile of welcome.

'Papa! Oh, Papa, here you are!' She rushed to greet Sir Alan, and rebuked him happily. 'We missed you not meeting us!' As Hugh threw himself on his father, Sir Alan looked over their heads at Charlie. His brow furrowed slightly.

Had he heard, and disapproved of the way she spoke to Hugh? She hadn't been exactly polite. Well, he was obviously pleased to see his children.

Charlie closed the cloakroom door, and went to stir up the fire in the sitting-room before she fetched the afternoon tea-tray.

Mrs Biggins had put out a freshly baked fruit-cake, designed to appeal to growing youngsters' appetites, and Charlie sighed. What a difference two boisterous children could make to this soulless house. If only they were more pleasant.

Recalling the change that came over Isobel at seeing her father, she thought how young they had been when their mother died. Isobel was eight, and Hugh only five, when they'd been packed off to boarding-school. How abandoned they must have felt. No wonder they liked their father to meet them.

Now Charlie's duties included taking early morning tea to the children, and stirring up their fires. Isobel, having regarded her frostily, and disdained to reply to her greeting, would then leave her room untidy.

Hugh was less brittle; his curious gaze, as he watched Charlie's movements, betrayed a yearning. If he wasn't afraid of Isobel, she thought, he might consent to a little mothering. As it was, he would sneak into the kitchen when he smelled baking, and Mrs Biggins would just happen to have some broken pieces left over from a batch of cakes or biscuits.

Charlie began to get behind with her chores. Hugh, too, left his room in a mess, but his untidiness was due to boy's carelessness, with no malice intended. From the first day she managed to get a smile out of him.

She deliberately hesitated.

'Good morning, Master . . . er . . . Hugh.'

He rose to the bait. 'I'm glad you remembered my name.'

'I like your name,' she said, 'so I'm not likely to forget it. I have a good memory, you know.' She said anything she thought might draw him out.

'Is Papa going to be here, today?' he asked wistfully.

'I don't know, yet. It's stopped snowing; you could go out and build a snowman.'

'Will you help?'

Charlie remembered Sir Alan's instruction not to let them interfere with her work.

'Tell you what, Master Hugh, if you and Isobel tidy your rooms, I could be finished much sooner. I can't play before I've done my work.'

She wished she could say: *your father will go out with you.*

Hugh scrambled round obligingly, but Isobel had overheard.

'We could order you to come outside,' she said belligerently as Charlie passed her.

'I would be in trouble if I didn't do my work,' Charlie retorted over her shoulder, 'and you would be cold because you'd have no fires.'

Fortunately the gong sounded for breakfast.

Later, she was pleased when Sir Alan took his children to look for stranded sheep, with Jim the shepherd. Hugh was excited, because he loved Jim's border collie, and the shepherd was training up a younger dog. Isobel remained unmoved; she preferred horses.

When they returned at lunchtime Charlie had the main rooms warm and welcoming. She went to the entrance hall to take their wet things.

She saw that Isobel's back and shoulders were damp as a result of a snowball fight with Hugh.

'I think you should change your dress, Miss Isobel,' she prompted, thinking of the influenza. 'You don't want to catch a chill, or worse—'

Isobel rounded on her. 'Don't you order me about,' she exclaimed, tilting her nose.

'Do as Miss Freer suggests, and don't be so rude,' said Sir Alan coolly. 'And while you're changing, you'd better think about apologizing.'

'Me, apologize to a servant?' Isobel protested.

'You'll get no luncheon otherwise,' he replied, icily matter-of-fact. 'Don't bother coming down unless you're prepared to do so.'

The aroma of freshly baked rolls and oxtail soup wafted back, as Cook and Maisie carried trays of steaming food to the dining-room.

Isobel's eyes followed hungrily.

'Oh,' she cried, running upstairs, and Charlie saw there was more hurt in her expression than anger.

She carried their wet things into the warm kitchen and hung them on the hoist over the range to dry. Meaning to fetch Sir Alan's things, she turned quickly and collided with him. He was right behind her, bringing them himself.

'Oops, beg pardon, sir!'

'My fault,' he murmured, and handed her his greatcoat. While she was hanging it up he said:

'I'd like to apologize for my daughter's rudeness, Miss Freer. I hoped she would learn better manners at school.'

Something made Charlie want to defend the girl.

'I think she was disappointed to come home and find only servants to welcome her.'

She knew she risked speaking out of turn, and did not dare look him in the eye as she added: 'She misses her mother, I think.'

He made no reply, so she chanced a glance at his face. He was staring at her. Only a twitch of his jaw betrayed any feeling, of what she couldn't guess.

Once again she felt inadequate in his presence. However, she stammered on: 'I hope – that is, perhaps Miss Isobel will be happier when I am gone home tomorrow. It's my Saturday off.'

'Ah, yes.' He gave a flicker of a smile, and nodded. 'I hope you find all is well.'

'Thank you, sir.'

The gong sounded.

'If you'll excuse me,' she said, 'I'll run up and fetch Miss Isobel's damp dress.' His daughter might find it easier to say sorry in private, for Charlie had no wish to shame the girl, or cause her to miss luncheon.

In her haste to escape, she missed the gleam of appreciation in the squire's eyes. She knocked on Isobel's door.

'I've come for your dress, Miss Isobel,' she called.

After a moment's hesitation Isobel pulled open the door, and thrust her damp dress into Charlie's arms.

'I'm sorry I was rude, Miss Freer,' she said, impeccably polite.

'Very nicely said, miss.' Charlie gave her an encouraging smile. 'I trust you will enjoy your luncheon.'

She stood aside to let Isobel pass, then followed her downstairs.

CHAPTER SIX

Soon the roads were snow-bound. Hell Hill became a solid sheet of ice, and supply wagons to and from Frometown couldn't get through to Swanwick.

Easter festivities were suspended, and those unable to go about their daily business helped on the farms, for livestock had to be hand fed with rations of hay. The situation eased slightly when the wind dropped and men went fishing.

As if the unseasonal conditions weren't bad enough, after Charlie trudged two long miles through the snow on Saturday morning she saw her mother usher her grandfather inside as she neared her home. He was carrying a basket.

Charlie pushed the door slowly open, and hesitated on the threshold as if she were the intruder.

Henry Warren had removed his black stovepipe hat, and was lifting the cover from his basket to reveal loaves of bread.

Amelia's astonished expression turned to gratitude, while Will's scowl betrayed humiliation.

'What's this fer?' he growled.

'I know your work's at a stand-still,' said his grandfather, gruffly. 'The weather's affectin' you same as everybody else—'

'There's plenty o'mackerel in the sea,' said Will. 'We don't need charity.'

'Will!' cried Amelia, embarrassed.

Henry Warren bowed his grizzled head as if to show he understood, but raised bushy brows and returned Will's glare.

'Who says it's charity?'

The sound of the door shutting made them all look round.

'Charlie – here you are!' Amelia hurried across the room to hug her daughter. 'Look what your grandfather's brought us!'

'What does he want?' muttered Charlie.

'I'm not sure,' replied her mother, taking her coat. 'The snow's making life hard, and I reckon even he doesn't want to see us starve.'

'He'd never give anything away for nothing,' said Charlie.

'Hallo sis!' called Tommy from his corner by the fire. He was playing cards with Will's apprentice boy, Sandy.

Charlie had expected a hug from her little brother, but guessed he didn't want to appear a cissy in front of the apprentice boy.

She returned his cheery grin, while Sandy jumped up to shake hands. He was obviously named for the colour of his hair, and his face was a mass of freckles. Charlie was flattered by the boy's manners.

She gave Tommy the parcel she'd been carrying.

'Look after this,' she said, darting a warning with her eyes in the old man's direction. She didn't want Merchant Warren to know what she'd brought from the hall.

There would never be any love lost between them, and Warren clearly wasn't pleased to see her. His smile vanished into his thick beard as he looked sideways at her. Still, it must have taken guts for the old man to face them after all these years. Warren gave Charlie a perfunctory nod, and continued his conversation with Will.

'Don't never look a gift horse in the mouth, m'boy. You help me, and I'll see you'm all right.' He eyed Will deliberately. 'Everybody's cold, and hungry, and my ship's stuck over in Holywell Bay. She's carryin' a full cargo of coal. I need men I can trust, and good wi' horses. I've seen the way you handle Hercules.'

Charlie saw Will's eyes gleam at the praise. The old man knew how to get his way.

'Cap'n Ford an' his crew had to walk home o'er the hill last night,' the merchant went on. 'They'm going back today, but he won't risk sailing her around the head. We got to drag the cargo overland.'

He turned to Amelia who stood, hands on hips, watching them.

'I know we ain't seen eye to eye, but I want to let bygones be bygones. I'm asking Will to join my work-gang. There'll be a free sack o' coal for you, and a pint o' beer for him when the job's done.'

Amelia looked at Charlie, who shrugged.

'Sounds all right, I suppose,' she said, seeing the light kindle in her mother's eyes. Making friends, after all these years? A pity it couldn't have come sooner, before Dad . . . 'I only hope you won't be disappointed, Ma.'

71

Henry Warren turned back to Will.

'If all goes well, lad, I may find more to your advantage. Are you on, then?'

'Might as well, there's nothin' doin' in the quarr.'

' 'Tis going to be a bad year, weatherwise,' the merchant muttered. 'I reckon there'll be some good pickings from a few wrecks. You won't be sorry you obliged me.' He nodded at Amelia, and donned his hat while Will opened the door. 'Foller me down to the stables soon as you'm ready.'

'Fancy us being able to do something for him,' said Amelia when he'd gone. She began stoking the fire from her meagre supply of furze. 'I enjoyed seeing him crawl, I must admit.'

'I didn't enjoy seeing him at all,' Charlie stated flatly. 'I'd be careful if I was you, Will.'

'You ain't me,' snorted Will, dragging on his woollen hat, 'so don't give us yer airs and graces you bin pickin' up at Lackford Hall.'

Hunching into his lambskin jacket he stomped out.

Charlie glared after him, stung by his remarks. She hadn't asked to be a bond-servant.

She signalled Tommy to unwrap the parcel.

'Spuds!' he cried, seeing the potatoes Charlie had baked in hot ashes overnight.

Sandy looked delighted, too.

While Amelia fried the mackerel Will had caught last night, Charlie put the spuds to warm, then sat back with a contented sigh. Here in Ma's tiny kitchen was the homeliness she missed at the hall.

After the meal Amelia showed Charlie her straw-plait work, an art she'd learnt from her aunt in Dorchester, years ago while awaiting Will's birth.

'Thanks to you, Charlie, I've made plans. Once I've got a little business going, and Will's finished building the lean-to, there'll be room for you when your year is up at Lackford Hall.'

'Oh, Ma . . .' Charlie couldn't express herself. Her own plans to become a governess were hardly formed, there was no point in raising Ma's hopes, nor in disappointing her.

But Amelia had picked up a bundle of plaited strips to sew together while they all sat round the fire.

'Now, tell us all your news.'

Soon she and the boys were asking, 'What's it like at the hall? What's the squire like?'

A pass cut through the ridge a mile from where it ended in white chalk cliffs, forming a circuitous route into the tiny hamlet of Holywell.

Will sat behind Hercules, leading the convoy of horse-drawn sledges up the long slope past the old water-mill which marked the last dwelling on the Swanwick side. The return journey would be mostly downhill, but the combined operation would take the rest of the day.

As he watched the rythmic swaying of Hercules' hindquarters, the nodding black-maned head, Will admired the strength and patience of the great beast. He felt less antagonistic towards his grandfather now, and with a pony, and an apprentice to help, the quarr was at last showing promise.

Although it faced east Holywell Bay curved in behind the ridge, so was protected from the worst of the gales that blew across from the steppes; rowing out to *Esmerelda* wouldn't be too difficult.

With the crew, Will estimated that at least a hundred men were there. Some he recognized: they frequented the pubs or went fishing, and his lip curled at the sight of Horace Skinner. He was more surprised to see Maltravers huddled on deck with Henry Warren. They were talking to Captain Ford and his mate, and seemed to be watching the approach of a customs-house cutter.

Maltravers and the merchant climbed down into a dinghy at *Esmerelda's* side, and Captain Ford directed a man to row them out to meet the customs men.

Will guessed it was about the anchorage fee, and as tax officials were so unpopular, it was less trouble to meet them head on.

He was put straight to work and saw no more. At least it was warm in the hold, where he helped shovel coal into sacks which were then hauled up and passed from man to man into the waiting barges.

Will soon worked up a sweat, and stopped only to tie his neckerchief round his face to prevent choking in the filthy cloud of black dust.

After what seemed more like days than hours, he and his colleagues were sent to the galley for ship's biscuits and hot tea before the journey home.

One of the last to leave the ship, Will shared the same loaded dinghy as the mate. Empty sacks were laid over the cargo, and he had to lean back for the mate to get past and position himself between the oars in the bow. Surprised that his bottom met with hard smoothness instead of lumpy coal, Will curiously lifted a sack and saw barrels stacked beneath.

He gave a low whistle. So that's what the old man meant when he said he wanted men he could trust. Well, the old rogue had come to the right man!

He looked up to see the mate watching him through a haze of cigar smoke.

The man's eyes narrowed dangerously as with one hand he pulled the cosh from his belt.

'You just help wi'the carryin' son, and you'll do all right. But if yer tongue wags . . .' He lifted his cosh and made a cut-throat gesture.

Will was no coward, and deliberately held the mate's gaze as he took his place at the second pair of oars.

'Aah, don't 'ee fret,' he said. 'Me Granddad Warren an' me have come to an understandin'.'

The mate grunted and relaxed. They rowed ashore in silence, but Will's mind was busy.

No wonder the old man and Maltravers had gone to meet the customs men. They'd been eager to avoid a search. He remembered seeing the two men together at Henry Warren's stables the day his dad died. Now he understood; each was useful to the other, and both were up to their necks in the 'trade'.

The blizzards ceased and the sky lightened, but there was still no thaw by Easter weekend.

It was a fun time for Isobel and Hugh. They kept warm by sledging, and ambushing each other with snowballs. When they deliberately aimed at Charlie, if she came out for logs or coal, she gave as good as she got.

While Isobel remained distant, Hugh warmed to her, and the three of them could be seen running and ducking, with shrieks of laughter.

If Sir Alan appeared, Charlie made an excuse to the children about her chores, hoping he might take over where she left off. Have some fun. But he unbent only enough to take them around the estate to see how his tenants fared.

The first to call at the hall was Fred the cowman. Milk was in short supply because the cattle couldn't graze, and winter stores of hay were almost finished. Moreover, hens ceased to lay, and flour supplies dwindled.

Sir Alan was continually preoccupied, and his children transferred their interest to the stream of ragged individuals who came to his back door.

'The poor are always with us,' Hugh quoted pompously, one morning.

'You sound like great-uncle Simon,' said Isobel witheringly. 'I don't know why Papa allows Cook to bother with them.'

Charlie heard these remarks, and spoke sharply:

'It's surprising what hunger can do, Miss Isobel. Better to beg than steal.' When Isobel stuck her nose in the air, she added: 'These are the people whose fathers went to fight Boney, some of them beside your own grandfather.'

'Tell us about him!' cried Hugh.

'You must ask your father. I know very little about Sir Hugh Lackford, except that he died a hero, and was greatly respected by everyone. But I do know he wouldn't refuse to help people at times like this.'

She meant to make them think, but Isobel stubbornly refused to melt.

'I've had enough out here,' she said cuttingly, and tossed her gold-red curls. 'I'm going inside to read. Coming, Hugh?'

It was a command rather than a question, and Hugh sheepishly followed his sister.

However, Charlie noticed that Isobel listened in when she read to Hugh at bedtimes. It was something, apparently, that their mother had little time for.

Anxious about the plight of her own family, Charlie was more perturbed by the arrival of the Honourable Mr Maltravers and his wife, Jane, to Easter Sunday luncheon.

She instinctively disliked the man who so resented her parents, yet was well disposed towards her crafty grandfather. Also, she still felt bitter that Warren had chosen to carry on the feud until he needed Will's help, and would never like either man.

She sensed an atmosphere between Maltravers and his wife, and her feelings against him deepened. Jane Maltravers was small and gaunt, her pale, pinched face wore the look of a woman unfulfilled. There was no display of affection, as there had been with her parents; rather, a kind of distancing between them. However, she must be polite to them.

Charlie had to help in the kitchen as well as keep up her own duties, and she and Maisie waited at table. Both young women wore smart, dark-blue serge dresses and Charlie thought how nice Maisie looked when neatly dressed, with her blond hair tidy.

The main topic of conversation in the dining-room was the inclement weather.

'Things couldn't be worse,' Sir Alan said. 'We have famine conditions building up. I want to organize a road-clearing operation so that supply wagons from Frometown can get through.'

Simon Maltravers nodded agreement.

'What do you have in mind?'

'We should enlist all able-bodied men, as diggers,' said Sir Alan, 'and organize them into three gangs. Start the first two at opposite ends of the worst stretch of highway, working towards each other, and put the third gang in the middle to work outwards in both directions.' Maltravers gave a dubious frown.

'What about the cost?'

Charlie glanced sideways at Maisie as they cleared away empty dishes. The Honourable Mr Maltravers was unlikely to volunteer any finance for the operation.

Sir Alan's enthusiasm remained undimmed.

'They'll work for nothing,' he exclaimed. 'It's for their own benefit, after all. It will give them something positive to do towards helping themselves.'

'That'll warm 'em,' quipped Maltravers, with his superior smile. 'Very clever, nephew. Give 'em hope, and a challenge fighting the elements, and they'll do the rest. I couldn't have thought of a better idea myself!'

I'd like to see him push a shovel, thought Charlie. How two-faced he was; he pretended to be so friendly, yet caused a deal of gossip behind his nephew's back. Maltravers' attitude had long since earned the locals' contempt. He'd been an unpopular landlord as Sir Alan's guardian years ago. Now, greedy for money, he was always trying to push leases on to his quarrymen tenants.

Squire might be eccentric, but he had his tenants' welfare at heart. It seemed clear to her that Maltravers despised his nephew's concern for ordinary folk. Yet Sir Alan couldn't see it. In fact, she'd never actually heard him criticize anyone.

Like old Warren, Maltravers would never go out of his way for anyone unless there was something in it for him.

Charlie saw Jane Maltravers stifle a yawn, and Isobel begin to fidget. The girl looked bored, a sure sign of trouble brewing. At that moment Charlie could think of no reason why she should look up to any of them.

The last thing she expected as she began serving the sweet course was to be addressed by Maltravers.

'Ah, the new maid. Amelia Warren's daughter, aren't you? You have your grandfather's looks, my dear.'

'Amelia *Freer*,' Charlie corrected Maltravers frostily, annoyed by his comparison.

Jane Maltravers lifted her sharp nose, presumably in disdain, Charlie thought, because her husband conversed at table with a servant. How quickly she changed the subject.

'And how is school, Isobel?'

Unfortunately she unwittingly gave the girl her chance to liven things up.

'Did you know I'm learning French at school, Madame Maltravers?'

The wife of the Honourable Mr Maltravers arched her thin brows, and Isobel missed her father's cautioning 'ahem', his usual way of interrupting.

Unconcerned whether Mrs Maltravers knew French or not, Isobel swept blithely on.

'*Oui*, madame.' She waved a careless hand in Charlie's direction, '*Elle s'apelle Charlie! C'est drôle, n'est-ce pas?*' She giggled, adding '*Mon père l'avait trouvé dans une carrière sale!*'

'Yes,' put in Hugh, who understood, but was unaware that he was adding to the insult aimed at Charlie. 'They find all sorts these days in dirty old quarries, old bones, and fossils . . .'

He was drowned out by Isobel's shrill laughter, but Jane Maltravers looked bewildered.

Charlie felt like slapping Isobel's face, but she had the presence of mind to see that Jane Maltravers wasn't sure whether to laugh or not.

Sir Alan looked extremely embarrassed. The muscle in his jaw twitched ominously. If Isobel was punished again, she would be more disagreeable than ever.

The girl needed to be put down, and Charlie could not resist the urge. She forced a little laugh, and patted Isobel on the shoulder.

'*Tiens, Mademoiselle Isobelle*,' she said, with a perfect French accent, '*Madame Maltravers ne parle pas le Français. Est-ce-que vous avez besoin d'un interprète, peut-être?*'

She knew there was no way Isobel would wish her to translate what she'd said. Hugh had already said enough.

Isobel's mouth dropped open in astonishment, and her face went crimson. Muttering an excuse about needing to go upstairs, she rose from the table and fled from the room.

'Begging your pardon, ma'am,' said Charlie to Jane Maltravers, not daring to look at her employer. 'Miss Isobel was telling you that my father was a quarryman; he too fought for England against Bonaparte. He . . . died, last autumn, ma'am, and Sir – Squire – has kindly helped my family by employing me.'

Charlie could barely control her trembling, and for once she was glad Maisie was near.

'Can you carry on, please Maisie, while I fetch the custard?'

She glanced apologetically at Sir Alan, who was staring at her appraisingly. He couldn't be so surprised, could he?

'I see that studying the French book I lent you is paying off, Miss Freer,' he said.

He smiled, and suddenly he looked younger and more handsome.

Charlie blushed, bobbed a curtsy, and hurried to the kitchen.

She took her time to pour hot custard into a serving jug, to allow her fluttering stomach to settle, and barely noticed Mrs Biggins's nagging.

'Did you hear what I said, miss?' Cook stood hands on hips, head to one side.

'Oh, sorry. What?'

'Just give 'em a little drop each. There's no milk to make more.'

Charlie nodded absently, and headed back to the dining-room. She came down to earth when Isobel met her at the foot of the stairs.

'You never told me you spoke French!'

She spoke accusingly, but Charlie saw fear in her eyes.

'You never asked, Miss Isobel,' she murmured, her anger gone. She smiled, and risked a wink. 'Everything's all right. I explained to Mrs Maltravers what you were trying to tell her. There's no harm done.'

For the first time Isobel gave Charlie a genuinely friendly smile, as the fear in her eyes changed to relief.

'Oh Charlie, you are a brick!'

The Lackfords and their guests took coffee in the drawing-room, while Charlie, up to her elbows in hot soapy water washing dishes, felt happy for the first time since she came to the hall.

She hummed a tune as she carried the dinner plates back to the dining-room.

As she bent to put them away, someone came into the room. For some reason her heart skipped a beat, and she turned her head, expecting to see Sir Alan.

It was Simon Maltravers, apparently come to retrieve Jane's long mittens from the back of the chair where she'd left them.

Charlie was startled, and stared up at him. At fifty his hair was still black, and he might have been described as good-looking if only he was better-natured. His eyes were menacing beneath the thick brows, and with his supercilious mouth and hawk's beak of a nose, he looked like a great black bird of prey.

He spoke to her, his tone heavy with sarcasm.

'It would seem quarry folk are more intellectual than one would give them credit for.'

So, he had come to belittle her. Charlie closed the cupboard door and stood up slowly. She felt uncomfortable, afraid, even.

She also hated having to be polite, and lowered her eyes to hide her fear.

'I've had some schooling, sir; you know my background.'

'Yes, I know it.' He sounded spitefully emphatic. 'If your mother had had any sense she could have been well off, and you wouldn't be a servant. You'd have been the daughter of a gentleman – my daughter.' He paused before adding pointedly: 'You might even have made a good match with someone, like my nephew.'

Charlie flushed with something more than fear, or anger. She had been aware of a strange sensation lately, whenever the master came upon her unexpectedly. Yet, surely there was nothing in her manner that this man could misinterpret?

What was Maltravers up to, she wondered, annnoyed that he was deliberately dragging Sir Alan into this unwelcome conversation. The man was a menace; if he was laying the basis for more rumours . . .

She tried to change the subject, but her confused emotions caused her to speak recklessly.

'Thank you for your concern, *sir*,' she flashed at him, 'but the last thing I'd wish is to be your daughter. My father meant the world to me.'

His dark eyes narrowed.

'So,' he muttered through clenched teeth, 'the young whelp is just like her bitch of a mother. I'll make you pay for that remark . . .'

Charlie panicked, and pushed past him. All she wanted was to escape, but in his usual catlike fashion, Sir Alan had appeared and was barring the doorway. She had no idea how much he'd heard, and ached to warn him that his uncle was intent on making mischief.

Maltravers didn't know either, and swiftly changed his attitude.

'Your servant was telling me, Alan, that she's happy to be your servant.'

His smug tone seemed lost on his nephew, for the squire remained unblinking.

'I'm beginning to think her talents are wasted, Uncle,' he said, evenly.

'Huh,' grunted Maltravers, clearly intent on belittling her. 'Because of a French book?' He rounded on Charlie. 'What else have you read?'

Charlie didn't know why, but Sir Alan's presence renewed her confidence, and anger sharpened her wits. She made herself look at Maltravers, and chose her words deliberately.

'If you mean I'm not well read, sir, you are quite right. But I would like to be.' She lifted her chin, and clasped her hands tightly before her in an effort to stop them shaking.

'I hope you'll pardon my saying so, but it seems to me that some people confuse the intellect with intelligence. It's true, my folk are not intellectual, yet once upon a time all our ancestors were cave-dwellers. Including yours.'

Maltravers directed a face-saving grin at his nephew, as if he was willing to overlook the girl's insolence.

'And,' Charlie went on, unable to stop, 'if they weren't intelligent none of us would be here now, but you could hardly say they were intellectual.'

She stopped abruptly. Had she gone too far?

But Sir Alan laughed aloud, and appeared not to notice her trembling.

Simon Maltravers paid her a spurious compliment as he addressed his nephew.

'Well, damme. Clever little thing you have there, m'boy! However, I must go, my wife is waiting. Goodbye, nephew.'

He turned on his heel, and stalked from the room.

Sir Alan took a spotless white handkerchief from his pocket, and blew his nose.

'You surprise me, Miss Freer.'

Despite her wobbly knees, she smiled as she averted her eyes.

'I surprise myself sometimes, sir.'

He chuckled again.

'It seems you do come from educated stock.'

Charlie replied as evenly as she could.

'Widow Hyer is a good teacher. Her father was a distinguished scholar, at Oxford, I think.'

'Well said, m'dear.' The term of endearment came so naturally, that for a moment she thought he was going to touch her. Then his expression changed and he spoke gravely.

'You don't like my uncle, I think?'

His words caught her off guard. He must have heard everything.

'I – I . . . he frightens me.'

'Really? Are you also afraid of me?'

Charlie swallowed. His tone demanded she look at him and give an honest answer.

'I respect you, sir,' she replied.

Passing the dining-room to go upstairs to the playroom, Isobel and Hugh stared at each other. It was ages since they'd heard their father laugh like that.

'Papa likes her!' said Isobel, her eyes wide with surprise.

'I'm glad,' said Hugh. 'He's much nicer now she's here.'

CHAPTER SEVEN

SIR Alan and Maltravers commandeered all available workhorses. They gave Will and Dick the task of leading them across the valley to Corvesgate where they would seek supplies from Frometown on the far side of the ridge. There they would load hired carts, and with four strong horses to pull each one, they would return across the heath and avoid Hell Hill.

Meanwhile, the two landowners rounded up all the able-bodied men, and spaced them along a three-mile stretch of road. Working in shifts, they continually dug, scraped and shovelled, throwing up walls of snow on either side of the highway.

Charlie was obliged to accompany the children who wanted to watch. They were joined by Tommy and some quarry boys, who soon made friends with Hugh. Isobel was in a tolerant mood, and demonstrated her new-found respect for Charlie by behaving herself.

While Maltravers supervised the far end of the operation, Sir Alan directed from the middle to the Swanwick end, lending a hand as necessary.

As Charlie stood by, she considered the last twenty-four hours, and felt quite baffled. She actually liked Sir Alan for himself; what was more surprising, he seemed to like her. So often, in the way he spoke, it was as if he were addressing a friend more than a servant. But then, he was polite to everyone, and perhaps was pleased his children accepted her. The atmosphere had certainly improved since their homecoming.

What concerned her was the fear she'd felt since yesterday for Sir Alan's reputation. The master seemed blind to his uncle's malice, and even if she plucked up courage to warn him, how could she criticize Maltravers to the master's face?

She was also afraid for her family, as Maltravers' demeanour had unsettled her nerves. It sounded as though he still bore malice against

Ma. Could it be envy? Ma had borne sons, and though he'd married well, Maltravers had none to carry on his name.

Why else would he still bear a grudge? If he started the rumours he'd hinted at, Sir Alan would have to dismiss her, which wouldn't help her, or the Freers' reputation.

She'd grown fond of Isobel and Hugh, and feared for them too. What damage a man like Maltravers could inflict!

That her grandfather had taken a shine to Will was small comfort – speak of the devil, there was Henry Warren now, distributing tots of rum along the line of diggers.

Charlie thought disparagingly that it wasn't like him to be so generous. The rum was probably smuggled anyway. Then she suffered a prick of guilt. He was human, after all, and clearing the highway was in everybody's interest.

All the same, she still suspected that the merchant's unusual generosity was a front for some reason, and now he had Will in his grasp.

The gangs worked non-stop throughout the day, and into the night by the light of the waning moon. By Tuesday lunchtime the wagons rolled in amid noisy applause, and back slapping. In fact, Will and Dick were made more fuss of than the men who'd toiled for more than thirty hours.

A few days later the thaw set in, and by the time his children returned to school a week late, Sir Alan found he was free to accompany them all the way.

'I have business to attend to in Dorchester and London,' he told Charlie as she helped him pack. 'I shall be away for some time.'

Charlie felt surprisingly disappointed. Isobel was much less frosty now, and the prospect of being left only with Cook, Maisie and Dick was dispiriting.

Well, at least the master would be out of reach of Maltravers' malice.

Early in the evening before the departure, Isobel asked Charlie to help her wash her hair. It was long, and thick, and Charlie felt a warm glow in performing this motherly duty. Isobel knelt in her shift with her head over the bathtub, meekly obeying Charlie's directions to hold her head down, and keep her eyes shut.

'Look out – here comes the last rinse!' Charlie upended the large jug of warm clean water, running her fingers through the glossy auburn strands to get out all the soap.

'Ooh, that's lovely,' gasped Isobel. 'Do it again, please!'

'I will if you like,' said Charlie, chuckling, 'but it'll have to be cold water.'

Isobel squealed, 'No-o thanks!' Just then a tap came at the door, and Sir Alan poked his head round.

'Miss Freer, come to the library when you've finished, will you?' He stared at Isobel who, spluttering and laughing, called for the towel.

'Why yes sir,' said Charlie, looking over her shoulder at him. What could he want? She hoped he didn't think she was being too familiar with his daughter. Oh dear, she'd been so pleased to be friends with Isobel, she hadn't realized how fine a margin there was between being a good servant and stepping out of line.

After she'd given Isobel's hair a good rub, and brushed it, Charlie hurried anxiously to the library. She felt tired, yet her brain was working overtime.

Before the Maltravers' visit, when she and Isobel became friends, she'd been heedless of giving Sir Alan reason for sacking her. She'd sometimes spoken out of turn, confident that he'd want his money's worth until her year was up.

Now that she'd decided to like him after all, she feared he might tell her to leave before he came back. There wouldn't be so much to do, with Easter over and the family gone.

Now she really wanted to stay, if only to gain a higher post when she did leave. But that was months ahead.

She knocked on the library door, and heard him call:

'Come.'

He was in his easy-chair by the fire, stroking Fudge. It was the first time she'd seen him with the cat on his lap, and she felt calmer.

He rose politely, still holding the cat, and indicated the stool opposite him.

A good sign.

'Ahem. Miss Freer, you probably realize that I am concerned about my children's manners . . .' He held up a hand as she opened her mouth to demur. 'I am aware that the loss of their mother has something to do with it, and – ahem – I can see your presence has a beneficial effect on them. Therefore, I think you should be in a position deserving of more respect. That is why Ponsonby and I have discussed which room you should have as your own.'

Charlie was so surprised she stared at him, open-mouthed and uncomprehending. Only minutes before she'd been half-expecting dismissal. Now she was to have her own room – and privacy, something she'd never had.

Her relief turned quickly to dismay.

'Oh, but sir, what about Mrs Biggins, and Maisie? Won't they be . . . er put out?' She looked down at her hands, clasped nervously in her lap. 'I'm still a newcomer to them.'

Sir Alan sighed in exasperation.

'I know all about servants' petty differences, and I am quite capable of evaluating the worth of each.'

At his change of tone, Fudge jumped down from his lap, and rubbed around Charlie's legs. Sir Alan's eyes followed the cat's movements, then he added:

'I won't enlarge on that, but I will say I'm glad that they regard you as one somewhat apart—'

'Sir?' Charlie gaped at him.

Sir Alan gave a shake of his head, as if impatient that she needed further explanation.

'What I mean is, it will come as less of a surprise to them, my making you housekeeper.' He ignored Charlie's gasp. 'I'm satisfied you are capable of managing household affairs; more to the point, it will be more seemly for the children when they come to you for guidance. They need a firm female hand.'

Charlie gave a small smile and shook her head, not at all sure that she welcomed the promotion. Yet Squire seemed confident of her abilities.

'In short,' he added, they need 'someone whom they respect. They are too used to getting their own way, and much too fond of ordering my servants about.'

'So I've noticed,' she murmured.

'Well, shall you accept the new post?' He got up and stood over her as if impatient for her answer. 'It will, of course, warrant a small increase in wages, so you'll receive a shilling a week henceforth. Ponsonby will deal with the wages in my absence.'

A shilling a week to call her own! She could begin saving for her future . . .

'Th-thank you sir,' she blurted, blinking up at him, uncertain whether to stand and curtsy. 'I would like it, very much.'

'Good.' He stepped back, crooking a finger before his mouth to give a polite 'Ahem.'

Charlie stood up, thinking the interview was ended. But Squire hadn't finished yet. He regarded her seriously.

'It will mean your staying on until Isobel goes to finishing-school. By which time I can help you find a post as a governess elsewhere, would you like that?'

'Oh—' Charlie opened her mouth, and shut it again before she could say: *why, yes sir. Thank you sir.* After her year he might pay her more.

Sir Alan was still speaking.

'We decided to give you Hugh's room. Now the children are growing up they need more space. Hugh will go into Isobel's room, and she will have one of the guest rooms.

'I'd like you to supervise their decoration. I'm sure you have an idea of Isobel's preferences, and you may order any alterations you think necessary to suit Hugh. You'll have a free hand with your own room, but you will, of course, be expected to see to that yourself.'

'Of course, sir.' She looked down to hide a smile. He apparently thought she was regarding her dress, for his next words surprised her again.

'I shall bring back some material so you can make a dress suitable to your new position. In the meantime, come, I've something to show you.' So saying, he strode out of the library.

She was too stunned to follow immediately, then ran to catch up.

Taking a lantern from the porch, Sir Alan went outside, and led her across the yard to the entrance to the cellars. It was nearer than going through the house to the scullery entrance.

'Come.' He unbolted the door and went in. As he descended a flight of stone steps which curved down into what seemed like a vast, dark cavern, he held the lantern high.

'Take care, Miss Freer.'

She followed cautiously into the musty darkness. He waited for her to reach the bottom, then put out his free hand.

'You'd better hold my hand, the ground is rather uneven.'

She obeyed meekly, and blushed as his warm strong fingers closed around hers. He guided her along a sort of cobbled sidewalk lined with stone gutters, and once she stumbled where the cobbles dipped.

'Yes,' he said, tightening his grip to steady her, 'watch out for the drains. My grandfather built the house over the site of an ancient brewery; it belonged to a monastery centuries ago, before the Dissolution. Now . . .'

Charlie vaguely remembered Widow Hyer saying something about a dissolution, during a history lesson on Henry VIII; but without giving her time to catch her breath the squire was explaining about the different areas beneath the house.

'It wouldn't make any difference if I showed you in the daytime,' he said, 'because even then there's little enough light with the trap-doors open.' He swung the lantern to indicate the coal-chute below one trap-door, 'and as you can see, logs are stored under the other one. I hope you're not afraid of the dark?' This time he paused for her answer.

'Er, no sir. It's a bit like the quarries, they're dark all the time.'

'Ah yes, of course. I'd forgotten.'

He sounded annoyed by the reminder. Why, she couldn't imagine, and when another thought hit her, she suppressed an urge to giggle.

She'd worried about Simon Maltravers starting new rumours. What would he say if he knew they were holding hands in the cellars, and at night?

Sir Alan had no inkling, and perhaps he wouldn't care anyway, she thought. It's what came of being rich and having to kowtow to no man.

But he was speaking again, as he shone the lantern around.

'We're under the domestic area here – those steps lead to the scullery entrance, and behind that wall is the wine cellar, where I normally only come.'

Charlie thought he sounded rather gruff. 'Yes, sir,' she answered, for lack of anything better to say.

He led her, still by the hand, to the end of the wine-cellar wall.

'This is the front of the house, and here's what I want to show you.'

They were in a big underground room fitted with shelves. He released her hand and hung the lantern on a hook.

'See these old trunks? They contain my late wife's things; we must sort them out. Look through them and take anything you think will be serviceable. We must get rid of the rest – before Whitsun, what?'

Charlie hesitated. She remembered Cook saying: 'Master went queer when she died. Didn't want to see anything belonging to her, and couldn't bring himself to touch the stuff. Had 'em stored in the cellar to rot. Gawd, what a waste!'

Charlie fished for some appropriate words. Plain 'thank you' didn't seem enough.

Standing with his back towards her, he seemed perturbed at her silence, and passed a hand across his brow.

'No doubt you've heard I kept all my wife's belongings,' he muttered over his shoulder, 'hoarding them like a squirrel.'

He meant servants' gossip, and she felt a twinge of pity – which he wouldn't want. She must say something.

'I – I did notice, sir, when you showed me her room, how impersonal it seemed, that you had removed all reminders. I – I'm very sorry, sir, I know how it feels to lose someone . . .' She stopped as he turned to her. His face looked ashen in the lamplight.

'You and I both know how it feels to lose a beloved father – we were of an age, were we not?'

'Oh – so we were, sir.' It hadn't occurred to her before that they had both lost their fathers when aged between sixteen and seventeen.

As Sir Alan went on, he sounded frustrated more than sorrowing.

'Well, you do *not* know how it feels to lose one's spouse in the manner of my wife's death. To discover that all you've done for the one you loved meant nothing to them. You do *not* know what it meant to the children for their mother to desert them in that fashion.'

Charlie wanted to interrupt, to say she did understand, but he rushed on in his agitation.

'You have no idea, Miss Freer, how rejected and inadequate such an action makes one feel; no understanding of one's grievous sense of failure.'

He paused, and as he put a trembling hand over his eyes she feared he would take leave of his senses. What an effort it was costing him to deal at last with his wife's belongings. And how humiliating to be seen thus by a servant: surely a measure of his distress.

She didn't know what to say, or if he expected her to speak. Had it not meant stepping out of line, she would have given him a motherly hug. As it was, she prayed for the right words.

'No sir,' she ventured, 'I don't know. But – what about her feelings? She must have been terribly unhappy for some reason. Perhaps she was -er – unwell?'

'Perhaps she was unwell,' he sighed, endeavouring to recover himself. 'No one knew why she did it; even the doctor found nothing wrong when she had bad headaches and kept to her room for days on end.' He turned abruptly, back to the shelves. 'Anyway, the worst is over, and we have resumed our lives. I couldn't bring myself to part with these things then, but I want to be rid of them now, and would like them put to good use.'

What could she say? That he shouldn't blame himself? She knew nothing about his marriage.

'I appreciate your kindness sir, and would you mind – if I find something I think my mother might use?'

'No, no. By all means,' he almost snapped. He retrieved the lantern. 'Use your own discretion.' He began to retrace their steps. He didn't take her hand this time, but at the bottom of the steps he stood back, and passed her the lantern. 'Here, you go first and I'll follow. Get you used to the steps.'

'I'll do my best, sir,' she said, as she moved past him, 'to have everything sorted out when you return from London.'

'Yes.' He coughed. 'I'd be much obliged.'

By the time they reached the library he had regained his composure. He opened a drawer, and took out a bunch of keys.

'You'll need these. One of your duties will be to report to Ponsonby when the supply of coal is low, Hart will keep the logs topped up. Indeed, check with Ponsonby if in doubt about anything. Oh, and if you find the others difficult, they'll take orders from him.'

Charlie nodded gratefully. Cook and Maisie were bound to feel resentful, and Squire was sparing her as much aggravation as possible.

Now he seemed to have nothing more to say. In his present state of mind he most likely wished to be alone. She took a step towards the door.

'Miss Freer . . .'

'Sir?' She half-turned to face him, and saw him frown, as if he was deciding what to say.

'One more thing. When you sort through those things, keep your eye open for a silver jewel-casket, will you? It's a family heirloom handed down through the Lackford wives. When we cleared out her room, there was no sign of it. It's the only thing I would wish to keep.'

'Yes, of course, sir. Goodnight.'

When we cleared out her room, she thought, as she climbed the stairs to the attic. If in this case 'we' meant the other servants, anything was possible. Even theft, for such a valuable heirloom sounded tempting. Hetty, perhaps – or even Maisie?

She tossed restlessly all night. Each time she had a waking dream she found it hard to get back to sleep with Cook's snoring. How wonderful to have her own room!

The family breakfasted early next morning, and while she was clearing the dishes, Isobel and Hugh came to say goodbye.

'I shall miss you both,' she said, and Hugh hugged her.

'You'll still be here for summer holidays, won't you?' There was a note of anxiety in Isobel's voice, which both flattered and moved Charlie.

'I'm looking forward to them already,' she assured her.

Isobel shook her hand.

'Goodbye, Miss Freer . . . Charlie.'

'Goodbye, Isobel. Have a safe journey.' Charlie looked up to see Sir Alan waiting for them.

'I'll write to you,' Hugh called over his shoulder. 'When you write back, put in some French sentences, and next holidays you can help me with my essays.'

Charlie laughed, '*Au revoir, Maître Hugh.*'

'*Au revoir!*' they cried together.

Had their father not been there, she would have blown them a kiss.

He watched them run outside, then came across to her. She wished he'd merely nodded from the doorway, for she hated this goodbye more than she'd ever foreseen when she first met his children. Her eyes were swimming.

'I'll miss them, sir,' she said apologetically.

'Never mind,' he said, 'you have enough to keep you busy, I think?' There was no trace of last night's upset, in fact there was a gleam in his eyes. 'It's Isobel's birthday in July,' he added. 'She's having a new dressing-table and full-length mirror. I thought you might like her old one for your room.'

Charlie gulped. Why must he watch her like an eagle studying its prey? Was it her imagination that he'd spoken so meaningfully?

Had *he* seen her that day, when she had preened herself before Isobel's mirror, and someone had pulled the door shut? She had a dreadful sinking feeling that he had, how, she would never know. Judging by the gleam in those blue eyes, he'd found it amusing.

She pretended not to notice, but couldn't prevent the flush that burned her cheeks. It took all her self-control to reply, and she could no longer look at him.

'Thank you, sir. It will be useful when I make my new dress.'

'Good,' he said.

She forced herself to look up again for politeness' sake, and saw his mouth lift at the corners. Then he nodded, and was gone.

Charlie ran to one of the dining-room windows, and watched the carriage drive down the avenue of budding poplars until it was out of sight. Her heart felt strangely heavy, and there was an ache in her throat.

Suddenly, unexpectedly, she wanted her ma.

CHAPTER EIGHT

EVERYONE had more spare time with Sir Alan away, and on the first evening Charlie went home to tell Amelia her news.

'So much for my higher position,' she remarked drily. 'I'll be in the dirty old cellar half the time.' Soberly she told her mother how upset the squire had been.

'I felt so sorry for him, and embarrassed. I suppose he didn't care, as 'twas only me and none of the others.' Charlie looked at Amelia, her brow creased with concern. 'Oh, Ma, that must have been an awful time for him.'

Amelia watched her daughter carefully.

'So, you'll be staying on when your year is up.' Softly she added: 'Is there anything else you need to tell me?'

Charlie couldn't describe her feelings that morning, they were so new.

'Only that he's bringing me some stuff to make a new dress,' she answered, 'and he's giving me Isobel's old mirror.' Here she blushed, and added hastily: 'It will come in handy. Oh, and I've got his permission to pass things on to you. I can do what I like as long as it's all gone before he comes back. I can't get over him allowing me to see him like that,' she added in a whisper, and stared at the half-amused expression on her ma's face.

'You should be flattered,' said Amelia wisely. 'It means he felt able to trust you, but it's a privilege you must keep to yourself.'

'Oh, I didn't think of it like that,' said Charlie.

She felt a bond forming between herself and the master, though it was probably only because of relief on his part that she got on well with his children. Yet he'd pointed out how they'd both lost a father at a similar age. And now each had witnessed the other in a weak moment, if she could call flaunting herself before the mirror a weak moment. Deep down she knew these things were more important than anything else she'd learned. She felt strange, almost as though new, and she wished she could open her heart to her Ma.

Amelia recognized calf love when she saw it. Normally it wouldn't bother her, but to think that Charlie was falling in love with a man so far above her station – it could only lead to heartbreak. She smiled wistfully.

'Well, maid, now you know what growing up feels like.'

Yet Amelia knew she had at least two good reasons for being grateful to Sir Alan. He'd saved Tommy's life and, by employing Charlie, had bettered all their lives. 'So,' she murmured, hugging her daughter as Charlie took her leave, 'life at the hall suits you.'

She sounded more confident than she felt, and was relieved when Charlie replied:

'Only until I leave to become a governess, Ma.'

Rummaging through the disused furniture in the cellar, Charlie found a wash-stand with a bowl that was still serviceable, and a chair. They would do for her room.

Then she began to sort through Lady Lackford's belongings, keeping any garments she could alter, or which Ma could use.

She supervised the decoration and arrangement of the children's rooms, and helped Maisie spring-clean the whole house ready for Whitsuntide, the biggest holiday of the year.

Curtains and counterpains were laundered, carpets beaten, cupboards and drawers cleaned and tidied.

Charlie discussed things with Ponsonby, who was fair, if aloof. He knew his master's requirements, and when he approved her ideas he ordered materials and hired workmen.

Maisie sulkily obeyed the new housekeeper's instructions, but accepted the items of clothing Charlie offered her from Lady Lackford's chests, even admitting a grudging admiration.

'You won't catch me goin' down there,' she said with a shudder. 'I wouldn't care how much I was paid!'

Charlie wasn't afraid of the dark, but she did fear being shut in since her dad was buried alive. She used the scullery entrance mainly, but always made sure the yard door was hooked back. In her apron pockets she carried spare candles and friction matches.

Local esteem for Sir Alan had risen since his road-clearing success, while Dick's involvement in the rescue had made him more smug than ever.

'There's no need for fires now,' he said, when she asked him why the fuel bins were almost empty. 'Anyway, I'm goin' to the blacksmith's to get the kids' palfreys shod.'

He made her see that all she'd achieved was more responsibility, and that she stood to take the blame for any inefficiency.

Dick leered at her. 'If you want it done now, you'd best do it yourself – unless you promise me somethin' for bein' a good boy.' He sidled closer, and Charlie itched to slap his face.

'*Allez au diable*!' she hissed through clenched teeth, and felt a sliver of satisfaction as he reddened under the insult he didn't understand. 'Don't bother about conditions,' she scorned, 'I'll see to the chore myself!'

'Please yerself,' snapped Dick, 'but one o'these days you'll get on yer high horse once too often.' He stalked off, leaving her shaking with rage and remorse at her own incompetence.

It was useless to complain to Mrs Biggins, and if anything was said to Maisie it would cause more trouble. As for Ponsonby, a housekeeper was supposed to be in control of the household.

She felt a failure already.

Upstairs, she changed into an old patched skirt and apron, and covered her hair with a scarf to protect it from dust and cobwebs. The task shouldn't take long, she need only set the fires in case of a chilly evening when the master returned. A couple of sacks would do. She would have to wash and change afterwards, so she went into the kitchen to put some water on to heat while she worked. With a smug smile on her lips, Cook watched Charlie fill the kettle.

'You'll have to make do wi' cold water. I ain't bothered to keep the fire in 'cause I'm off to me sister's in Frometown fer a few days – it's all right, I got Master's permission afore he went. You an' Maisie'll have to look out to yerselves.'

Charlie tried to look as though she couldn't care less.

'I hope you enjoy your visit, Mrs B. Perhaps you'll benefit from the rest.'

Mrs Biggins opened her mouth to retaliate, then evidently changed her mind.

'I'll be off. I got to catch the carrier.'

The small victory took the edge off Charlie's sense of failure, and she felt the sooner the task was done, the better. She took a lantern and crossed the yard to the cellar entrance, it was nearest the coal shute.

Down in the coal-store she hung the lantern on a hook, then let off steam, shovelling until she'd filled two sacks. She 'walked' them to the bottom of the steps, and by the time she'd bumped and heaved each bulging sack to the top, she was exhausted.

It was almost dusk. Mrs Biggins was long gone, and Charlie was not looking forward to washing in cold water. She went back for the lantern, then locked the cellar door and leaned against it to regain her breath.

She was startled by a girlish giggle, followed by murmuring voices. The sounds came from Dick's quarters above the stables. Charlie made a wry face. The groom was back, and not surprisingly he and Maisie were taking advantage of Cook's and the master's absence. She wiped a grimy hand across her moist brow, and began to drag the first heavy sack across the yard to the back door. As she returned for the second, she heard Maisie's voice rise indignantly.

'I never ought to let you 'ave yer way, Dick Farmer, after you bin takin' advantage o' young mistress. Why, she's such a baby an' don't know any better.'

Charlie stopped in her tracks, and strained her ears. They were discussing Miss Isobel!

'Don't you believe it,' she heard Dick protest. 'She'd take advantage of a poor stable-boy if she had half the chance; she'll be quite a woman one o' these days.'

'Aah, she'll be ripe for the pickin',' retorted Maisie. 'Takes after her ma, I shouldn't wonder!'

Charlie swallowed a cry of dismay. When Isobel went riding it was part of the groom's job to escort her. Was the girl in danger from his advances? A strong, handsome fellow like Dick could soon seduce a woolly-minded adolescent schoolgirl.

Maisie clearly didn't like it either, for Charlie heard her shout 'Bastard!' before Dick muffled her cry. Next moment Maisie let out a long sigh, and Charlie bent to her task. She didn't want to hear any more. What a lout Dick was, tormenting Maisie until she was putty in his hands!

Charlie grunted with the effort as she heaved up and emptied each sack into the coal-bin, then went inside to wash and change.

Up in the stable loft, Maisie lay on her back and moaned softly as Dick's fingers caressed her with practised skill. Her eyes were closed, but she opened them when he rested a hand between her thighs.

'Young miss is only learnin' me to *read*,' he said huskily, his ardour aroused.

Next moment he needed both hands to grip her wrists and stop her clawing him. He chuckled, and sprawled on top of her.

'Why,' Maisie spat at him, 'because she fancies you – you bas-? Uh, ohh . . . Dick, you torment.' She went limp as he kissed her, and allowed him to knee her legs apart.

He entered her slowly, paused for a long moment then withdrew, causing her to sigh with disappointment. She arched her back, desperate for contact with that part of him that at this moment mattered more than anything else in the world.

Dick freed her arms, and thrust back inside her, while she pulled him greedily into her for the final pulsating ecstasy.

At last, spent and gasping, Dick rolled over and lay by Maisie's side. He'd never enjoyed a woman more.

When their panting eased, he leaned over her on one elbow.

'Listen, maid, you cain't blame a feller fer lappin' up attention from a pretty young miss like Lackford's daughter. A poor man gets little enough in this life.'

'Especially when he's bin a orphan,' Maisie murmured. She snuggled against him, torn between her ignorance of his early years, and what she knew about him now.

'You ain't really jealous o' young miss, then?' he asked gently.

'Not so much o' Miss Isobel, no.' There was a sob in her throat as she cast one leg possessively over him. 'But I seen the way you look at Charlie Freer. You keep away from her!' Maisie felt confused by hurt and hostility, for despite her passion she despaired of him.

'Oh, maid, like I said, she's too stuck up fer me.' Right now Dick was full of tenderness. 'Nobody can replace you, Maisie. You must know that.'

'I do,' she answered slyly. 'I do, I can tell by the way you come crawlin' back every time one of your females on heat sees you for what you are.'

'Why d'you put up wi' me, then?'

'Because *I* feel this way too, and – and I know you'll always need me in the end, you . . .'

She broke off to push him back, and climbed on top of him.

*

Charlie tried to forget her worries, and immersed herself in organizing her own room. With the workmen's help she furnished it with the things from the cellar, and they carried her bed down from the servants' dormitory; she'd also been allowed to keep Hugh's closet. At length she gazed around, pleased with the result.

She saw her reflection in the mirror, and remembered the gleam in the master's eyes when he'd seemed to allude to that earlier occasion. She felt a peculiar flurry of excitement. Then she felt annoyed with herself. These alien feelings were disturbing, and the master wasn't really giving her anything, just moving his belongings around. This room was hers only while she worked for him.

It occurred to her that she belonged to him: he'd paid for her in advance. The thought caused yet another strange sensation to stir, deep within herself. She turned, half-expecting to see him framed in the doorway. But of course he wasn't.

At first it had irritated her the way he crept up on her, as if to catch her stealing. Now she'd become used to his ways, and had begun to anticipate seeing him.

She felt sad when he and the children went away, she told herself, because she'd grown fond of *them*. Yet several times lately she'd looked up from her work, and been vaguely disappointed he wasn't there.

She missed him!

What was wrong with her? One minute she thought of Dick and Maisie, and resolved not to allow any man to have his way with her, and the next, she was pining over the master. She wondered whether that gentle, eccentric man could . . . he had fathered two children . . . Charlie pulled a rug from the floor, and hurried outside to beat it vigorously. As soon as she felt more sensible, she worried about Isobel again.

Should she warn Sir Alan of the situation when he returned? Say, for instance, that she knew how it felt to be denied a father's affection? Unless he paid Isobel more attention the girl would seek it elsewhere. Like in the arms of the groom.

How she could speak of it Charlie had no idea. There was nothing to be done at present, so she allayed her fears by exploring the house.

There were times when she felt exultant, having the place almost to herself. She wandered through the rooms to look at books, and paintings, and examined embroideries to her heart's content. Ponsonby never bothered her, he seemed satisfied that the alterations proceeded smoothly.

97

One day Charlie looked through the window in Lady Lackford's room. The view was partly blocked by the budding chestnut-tree outside. It was a lovely tree, and grew so close she could have slipped through the window and climbed down it.

She smiled wryly; how easily she might once have done so.

She studied the walled garden below, with its shrubs and flowers. There were some dainty-leafed maple-trees, and soon-to-bloom rhododendrons enveloped the path that led to the gate. Woods stretched away into the valley beyond.

She visualized Sir Alan and Lady Helen in happier days, walking hand in hand through the oaks and beeches, and sighed. Those days were long gone.

Suddenly she remembered Maisie's words, about Isobel taking after her mother.

What could she have meant?

Charlie returned to the kitchen. While Mrs Biggins was away she and Maisie took turns to prepare the evening meals for themselves and Dick. The maid and groom gave her no trouble, apart from sneering at her 'rise' in wages, and status. Probably to hide their own misdemeanours, she thought, and was tempted to reply that she actually earned less than them. Instead she said:

'Oh, come on, you've both had it easy lately. I can always ask Ponsonby to give you more work if you like.'

They left her alone then, and Charlie considered hinting to them that they ought to marry. It was so quiet at night, on the floor above her room, she suspected Maisie was sleeping with Dick in the stable loft. She felt challenged by their sullen stares, but refrained from interfering.

A week later Mrs Biggins returned refreshed, and let everyone know it.

'Miss Freer, the coal-bin's nearly empty, and there's no logs at all. Where's that Dick? Maisie, leave them spuds, and go an' find'n.' She rounded on Charlie. 'Fine housekeeper you be. Seems I got to do your job on top of me own. The larder's still got to be turned out, and I want plenty of hot water for scrubbin'. The master'll be put out if all the spring-cleaning ain't done afore he gets back fer Whitsun.'

'There's hot water in the boiler,' retorted Charlie. 'I saw to the kitchen fire myself. If everything's not quite ready it's because we didn't know exactly when you'd be back.'

Despite Cook's bossiness, Charlie was glad to have her support in pulling the groom into line. Mrs B's return also put an end to his and Maisie's reckless amours. Charlie had little respect for Maisie, but felt sorry for the girl. If Dick put her in the family way she could lose her job and be put on the parish.

Charlie returned her attention to mundane tasks. She made inventories of household linen and crockery, and helped Cook to finish the orders before the Whit Tuesday holiday. Candles must be replenished, and the larder stocked with flour, sugar, and spices.

Outside, while checking the kitchen-garden with Hart, she was gratified to see Dick working hard to load the fuel bins.

When she was satisfied they'd listed sufficient supplies she took the orders to Ponsonby. The little man surveyed her neat handwriting imperiously.

'Hm, seems all right – flour, sugar, wheatmeal – salt? Yes, you've got salt . . .' He paused to add some scribbles of his own, 'Wax polish for Master's boots . . . Right, tomorrow you shall go to Frometown market with Dick; he'll show you where the master makes his purchases.'

Next morning Charlie wore her best housemaid's dress, and while the groom hitched the two bays to the wagon, she asked Ponsonby about money.

'I shall ride over myself and pay the bills at the end of the month,' he informed her.

Dick winked at her, and grinned.

'He's afeared we'll take the money, and elope.'

'Don't start!' Charlie frowned at his ill-timed humour, for Maisie stood by the back door, watching them.

Charlie refused to sit up front with him, and climbed into the back of the wagon where there was a pile of empty sacks. Maisie sniggered then, and threw Dick a kiss which he returned.

The journey was a bumpy ten miles, and Charlie was glad when they reached the market town. She refused Dick's proffered hand, and jumped down by herself.

Her coolness towards the groom paid off. He showed her around politely, and kept his distance. When they were done she helped him load the wagon.

'No room in the back now,' he observed. 'Will you ride with me, madam – or walk home?'

Ignoring his insolence, she climbed up beside him.

'You know, Dick, you're good at your work when you will. Don't you

99

want to impress Squire, and get on?'

'What's the point?' he asked, and stared ahead. The road followed the old Roman way across the heath, and the ruined castle at Corvesgate could be seen on the horizon. 'He'd give I more responsibility, but not much extra money.'

'I know,' said Charlie. She'd learnt that lesson. 'But he'd make up for it with privileges, like a tithe cottage, should you needed married quarters. Then you'd have your own plot to grow vegetables, and get eggs and milk for nearly nothing.'

Dick looked at her askance, and cocked an eyebrow.

'Be you comin' down off that high horse, and askin' to marry me?'

Charlie laughed then.

'No, I'm not. But Maisie would like to, you know very well she would.'

Dick shrugged. 'I reckon so, but I don't want she ownin' me. I seen men in the pubs, their wives make their life a misery with their naggin'.' He grinned. 'I like to keep my women where I want 'em.'

Charlie saw she was getting nowhere, and changed tack.

'I've known you since Sir Alan took you from the orphanage,' she said. 'You may think you're a nobody, but you could make Maisie so happy. If only you'd treat her with respect – keep only unto her – and have children of your own.'

She was thinking of the status marriage would give him. It was what her grandfather had been after when he tried to marry her ma off to Maltravers. At least Dick and Maisie wanted each other. But Dick disagreed.

'You sound like a preacher,' he growled. 'I don't want no kids, they might end up bein' orphans like me.'

Charlie sighed, and resisted the urge to ask: *What if you put Maisie in the family way?* She would put her foot in it then. It seemed that Dick sought love, yet was unable to give it.

Now he lost patience.

'And who be you to tell I what to do?'

They were through Corvesgate, and had begun the ascent of Hell Hill, the last lap before the level home stretch. Despite his aggression, Charlie took advantage of the slow pace to reason with him.

'If you must know, I'm tired of being the butt of Maisie's jealousy. She's got her sights set on you, and is healthy and hard-working and ready for marriage. She'd make you a dam good wife!'

Dick continued to stare moodily ahead. Exasperated, Charlie added: 'Why can't you grow up, and take responsibility for your own life? It's not fair to just use Maisie, and build up her hopes—'

Dick exploded.

'Stop lecturin' me, damn you, Charlie Freer!' He cracked the whip angrily over the backs of the already straining horses. 'Why don't you mind yer own bloody business?'

Charlie lost her temper.

'Listen,' she shouted, 'I only want to help because I think you and Maisie would be good for each other. Well, you're right, it's none of my business. But that now I'm housekeeper, Miss Isobel *is*!'

She had his attention now, and as he turned to glare at her, she finished her tirade.

'You were much too familiar with her last time she was home, and if you don't keep your distance in future, I'll report you to the master!'

Dick turned on her savagely, and for a moment she thought he would use his whip on her.

'Bitch! So that's it – sucking up to the master. Marry Maisie, or else—'

'Don't be so rude,' she snapped. 'I mean what I say. Leave Isobel alone!'

Dick sat back resentfully, his face black as a storm cloud. He enjoyed flirting, but he'd never meant the master's daughter any harm, and he'd had enough of this! They'd come at last to the end of the long pull up Hell Hill, and he whipped up the horses. The wagon jolted at speed, but Charlie hadn't quite finished.

'Don't you care if you hurt Maisie?' she yelled in his ear. 'The master values you – you could build a good life together. Think about it!'

Dick drove so furiously, she lapsed into silence all the way back to Lackford Hall.

CHAPTER NINE

Dick was offended by Charlie's interference, but he thought about what she had said. He had to admit he was afraid of responsibility, and was treating Maisie unfairly. There was something else Charlie had said, about him being good at his work, and that the master *valued* him.

Dick tried to imagine being his own master. It was easy for someone like Sir Alan, but what hope did a poor man have? To be as well off as Henry Warren would be enough, but he'd have to work like the devil.

Well, more responsibility would be a step in the right direction.

Marriage.

His thoughts returned to Maisie, and their love-making. He smiled as he remembered her jealousy over Isobel and Charlie, then another thought hit him. Maisie had no one else, he was more important to her than anyone in the world.

It was a sobering thought.

Suppose, just suppose he did ask her to marry him. They'd be given a tithe cottage like Hart and his wife and kids, and they would gain social standing, respect.

Maybe, one of these days, but he needed time. Meanwhile, he would treat Maisie with more respect.

The welcome improvement in the weather brought on spring growth almost overnight. Birds sang loud and long in a frenzy of nest-building, and as the coast and countryside recovered, men's work resumed.

By mid-May Henry Warren's *Esmerelda* was only one of a fleet of ships in Swanwick Bay. Anchored in as far as they dared, each ship waited to be loaded or unloaded.

Coal, timber, and food supplies were brought ashore, while slabs of stone for pavements, and blocks for construction and renovating city buildings were loaded in their stead.

At the Freer quarr Will taught Sandy to punch grooves on paving stones. He left the boy to practise while he went down to the shore to labour at the bankers.

With the other men, he humped one stone at a time on his back to the waiting high-wheeled carts. Horses drew the loads into the shallows where each slab was transferred into a flat-bottomed lighter, then ferried out to a merchant ship to be manhandled a third time.

Will toiled carefully. Any stone damaged would have to come back, and precious pennies would be lost. The pay was poor, but it meant cash in hand at the end of the day, for the sailors were anxious to make sail while the wind and tides were right.

Will was between loads when he saw his grandfather arrive, and speak to Captain Ford.

'How's it going?' he heard Henry Warren ask.

The captain nodded. 'We'll make it.'

The merchant watched his grandson bowed beneath a hundredweight of stone. The lad had skill, and was strong, and willing. All he needed from life was a chance.

'Hmph,' he muttered into his beard. Old age was making him sentimental.

Will walked back up the beach, rolling his shoulders before the next slab, and caught his grandfather's eye.

'I'm surprised you and t'others don't build a pier,' he grumbled. ' 'Twould ease the loadin' and make it quicker. This way be awful slow.'

'A good suggestion, m'boy, but when times is hard the old-fashioned ways ain't so bad.' Henry Warren tapped the side of his nose, his eyes wary. 'We don' want to make it too easy fer the excise men to inspect, do we.'

'Uh, no, 'course not,' Will mumbled, embarrassed to be so naïve in front of the captain. He grunted and turned doggedly back to his work.

Just then Simon Maltravers rode along the beach, and signalled to the two older men.

'Aye aye,' said Captain Ford, 'he's back from London.' Maltravers dismounted, and jerked his head in Will's direction. 'I admire his persistence.' There was contempt in his tone.

'The lad's all right, he's got grit,' defended Henry Warren. 'So what's doin' in the City?'

'I hope you're right.' Maltravers lowered his voice. 'You'll need all your best able-bodied men in future. The government's re-forming the

Dorset Yeomanry to deal with smugglers.'

Captain Ford gave a low whistle, while the merchant raised an eyebrow.

'We'm only small fry here,' Warren reasoned. ' 'Tis all this talk o' reform that bothers me. If they reduce the tax on malt it'll ruin our liquor trade. You reckon the bill will go through?'

'Eventually,' said Maltravers gloomily. 'Before this year's out, anyway. Since Easter, the House has sat for hours debating raw cotton and soap, among other things. Now Lord Althorpe's pointed out that if they reduce import duties there'll have to be an income tax.'

'Hmph, we don't want that, either,' grunted Henry Warren.

'There's a lot of hot air blowing around the House,' Maltravers went on. 'What with the state of the Church in Ireland, the Bank of England, and Wilberforce on slavery being the main issues, I'd say we've a few months to make a big haul before the bill goes through.'

Leading his horse, Maltravers walked up the beach with Henry Warren to the Ship Inn, while Captain Ford finished supervising the loading.

'Aah, I've had a good run fer me money,' said the merchant, 'and there's always salvage. Like I said, signs are 'tis going to be a rough year for shipping.'

All the same, he regretted what he saw as the beginning of the end. He'd made good money during the war with Boney, but since the Royal Navy had taken over the customs cutters, the trade was dwindling.

'Then I trust *Esmerelda* won't be among the forthcoming wrecks,' sneered Maltravers. 'One thing's for sure, we'll need some good horses to shift the goods with the yeomanry taking over. Why don't you send that grandson of yours to see young Farmer up at the hall while Squire's away? No harm in being prepared.'

He didn't add that if ever he was caught he would implicate his nephew, and the Freers.

Will wasn't altogether surprised when at dinner-time over a tankard of ale, his grandfather said:

'I'm payin' you off now. I want you to drive a load o' coal up to Lackford Hall and give the groom a message.'

Will knew better than to ask questions, and an hour with Hercules was better than loading slabs of stone.

Maisie banged a saucepan down on the draining-board, slopped water everywhere as she scoured the sink, then wrung out the dish cloth so viciously that Mrs Biggins lost patience.

'I dunno what's come over you, Maisie. Calm down, or I'll speak to our new housekeeper. No doubt madam'll have a word in Master's ear when he comes back.'

Mentioning Charlie got the expected reaction.

'Don't you dare, Mrs B. That hussy's done enough already!'

Cook overlooked the girl's vehemence.

'Why, what's happened now?'

'Aah, never mind.' Maisie didn't want to tell Cook that Dick had gone off her since he'd driven Charlie to market.

'All right, miss, don't tell me,' said Cook. She scowled, and hung her apron behind the door. When Maisie was in a huff she was stubborn and careless.

'Summat to do with your love life I s'pose. Dick Farmer's got you danglin' like a puppet. You take care, 'tis me day off an' I don't want to find nothin' broke when I get back!'

So saying, she rolled down her sleeves, donned her hat and coat, and flung out, leaving Maisie seething in the scullery.

Something had happened between Dick and Charlie, Maisie could tell. For two weeks now he seemed to have cooled to the point of avoiding her. She'd never known him to be so busy, and that Charlie always pretended to be so nice.

Putting two and two together, Maisie was highly suspicious, and twice as resentful. She must watch her tongue because *Miss* Freer had gone up in the world, and Dick hadn't taken the hint when she reminded him it was Cook's day off. And with old Lackford away . . .

It was the last straw.

Smouldering beneath an outward sulky calm, she helped Charlie hang fresh curtains, and make up the beds in the newly prepared rooms. She could see the upstart was pleased with herself, no doubt expecting praise when the master returned.

Charlie noticed Maisie's doleful face and felt disappointed. Dick evidently hadn't taken to the idea of marriage.

'Thanks for your help, Maisie. Now I can get finished in the cellar, thank goodness.'

She had been as good as her word to Sir Alan, and had cleared the underground room. Anything she or the other staff couldn't use she'd sent to the poorhouse, and some pieces of furniture were gladly accepted for the schoolroom by Widow Hyer.

'You're welcome,' said Maisie shortly. She hurried downstairs while Charlie went to change into the old clothes she wore in the cellars.

Going down there, was she? Mrs B was away, and the master . . .

Something snapped in Maisie's mind. It was time haughty Miss Freer was taught a lesson.

Wearing her oldest patched skirt and apron, Charlie came into the scullery to fetch a broom and a dustpan and brush.

'What will you do now?' she asked the maid.

Maisie shrugged. She didn't know, and she didn't care. There was one thing uppermost in her mind.

'Tell you what,' said Charlie, inadvertently adopting Sir Alan's phrase, 'see that sack near the back door? I found it squashed up in a corner down there, and haven't opened it yet. Why don't you look through it and see if there's anything you want?'

She opened the cellar door, then remembered something. So far there'd been no sign of the silver casket Sir Alan had mentioned. She waited while Maisie emptied the sack.

There was a pair of satin-heeled slippers, silk stockings, a woollen shawl, a black-velvet dress, and various undergarments, but no casket.

Charlie saw the look of horror on Maisie's face, as the maid recoiled.

'What's wrong?'

'That's the dress *she* was wearin' the day she died. It's 'orrible – fancy offerin' me that!'

Charlie gasped.

'Oh Maisie, I'm sorry, I didn't know!' These things must have been the first to be bundled up and stowed away and, being squashed into the corner, were last to be found. Sir Alan wouldn't want to be consulted about them.

'Maisie,' she protested again, seeing the girl's unrelenting scowl, 'as if I meant . . .'

But Maisie wasn't listening. Her revulsion was the spark that gave her pent-up rage full rein. She picked up the dress and shoved it at Charlie so hard the housekeeper reeled back through the open cellar door.

'I hate you, Charlie Freer, pretending to be Lady Bountiful – and now you've stolen Dick away from me!' She pushed Charlie again. 'Go on, get down in yer cellar. See what else you can find!'

Charlie used the broom in her hand to save herself from falling down the steps, at the same time realizing what Maisie was doing. She lunged for the door, but had to duck the brush and dustpan that Maisie hurled at her. They clattered past her down the stone steps.

In that second the kitchen-maid slammed the door shut and rammed home the bolt.

In the pitch darkness Charlie banged with her fists on the door.

'Maisie, you've got to believe me, it's not what you think. I don't want Dick, and he doesn't want me. Please, Maisie, open the door!'

She stopped to listen, and heard Maisie's footsteps recede. A sickening wave of panic swept over her, and turned her legs to jelly so that she crumpled to the square of cold stone landing. She didn't dare move in case she fell down the steps.

What a fool I am, she thought, trying to overcome her panic with self-reproach. She'd been using the scullery entrance as she'd been up and down so often with boxes and trunks, and this time she'd forgotten to open the door from the yard. It was locked on the outside, so she was trapped until Mrs Biggins returned, and that wouldn't be for hours.

Charlie clasped her hands, and prayed for Cook to return early, and come into the kitchen before going upstairs to bed. How was she to endure? She'd starve before Maisie relented.

How she wished Sir Alan was home. It would all come right if he was there.

She scolded herself for the thought, and tried to calm down. All right, so she was stuck here in the dark, but someone was bound to come along sooner or later, and she would bang to get their attention. She might even sleep the time away, if it weren't so cold and uncomfortable.

She still faced the door, so she put out a hand to feel it and keep a sense of direction. As she steadied herself with the other, it came into contact with the velvet dress.

For a moment she shared Maisie's revulsion and was about to fling it aside, then she stopped. There was something caught up in it that felt like crumpled paper.

Her curiosity made her think more clearly. It was, after all, a beautiful dress. Could the paper be a suicide note, overlooked when the dress was so hastily disposed of?

She felt the dress all over. There was the neckline, and a sleeve . . . She felt for a side seam, and slid her fingers down it until she found a pocket. Of course, the paper was in the pocket.

As she pulled it out and pushed it into an apron pocket, she suddenly smiled.

In her panic she'd forgotten the spare candles and Lucifers she always carried with her in the cellar.

The relief she felt cleared her brain, and she regained her nerve. Now she did push the dress to one side, then with one hand on the door, she swivelled gingerly around and leaned her back against it.

Breathing more easily now, she rubbed her clammy hands on her shirt, then struck the end of a match against the stone floor and lit a candle.

She dripped a tiny puddle of melted wax on the floor and stuck the candle in it. Now she could see down the steps. If she lit the second candle and found her way to the log-store, she could climb the log-pile, and push open the trap-door. If not, she would have light for one hour.

Better not think of that.

Hope renewed her strength. Taking the broom, she left the first candle on the steps in case she had to come back to the scullery entrance.

There was a lantern hanging on the log-store wall. She lit it, and blew out her spare candle to keep for later. Hart had replenished the log-pile, but was it high enough for her purpose? As she looked up at the trap-door, a glimmer of daylight filtering through the cracks spurred her on.

The logs shifted under her weight, and she climbed warily on all fours, for fear of pulling the whole lot down. It would be like her dad all over again, buried beneath a founder. But the thought of spending hours shut up in the musty darkness filled her with dread, so she kept going. Somehow she managed to drag the broom up with her.

At the top of the wood-pile she straightened tentatively to test her balance.

Praying the logs would stay steady she held the broom up to the trap-door. It reached, but she couldn't get any leverage. The tantalizing gleam of daylight through the cracks made her weep with frustration.

Nearly finished, the lantern candle sputtered. She must get down again while she could still see what she was doing.

She was half-way down when she heard booted footsteps above her. Someone was crossing the yard.

She tried to shout, but was breathless from her dangerous climb, and her taut nerves made her voice hoarse. Now she heard the sound of cart-wheels, and iron-shod hoofs on cobbles.

Dick's voice called out, as the cart halted nearby, and a horse snorted its relief.

Another kind of footsteps sounded; hobnails, like Will wore.

It was Will – she heard him hail Dick!

Wildly Charlie renewed her efforts, but they didn't hear.

They were unloading something heavy, the coal-hole was opening. Oh God, if only she could get there in time.

As the trap-door was lifted, a shaft of daylight lit the whole area, blinding her with its brightness. She half-scrambled, half-fell to the bottom of the log pile, cursing both men for not hearing her.

An avalanche of coal drowned her cries, and caused a thick cloud of choking dust. She fumbled for her kerchief to cover her nose and mouth.

It seemed ages before the black dust settled enough for her to draw proper breath, but the trap-door was still open. She moved forward, prepared to shout for all she was worth, for Will and Dick stood nearby, yarning.

'Friday, I dunno,' she heard Dick say. 'It'd be more'n me job's worth if Squire got back and found out I'd lent his best horses.'

Charlie's yells died in her throat. Through a haze of shock, and disbelief she realized both men were involved in smuggling.

'Nobody's askin' fer the thoroughbreds,' Will went on peevishly. 'The old man says the kids' palfreys'll do. You'll be well paid, and if all goes accordin' to plan, you'll get a cut when *Esmerelda* brings in the big haul at th'end o' July.'

'That's two months away,' said Dick. 'The brats'll be home fer the summer, I can't let you have horses then. Besides, I got me own plans; me an' Maisie's gettin' married, an' I don't want no trouble—'

'Listen,' said Will, 'Maltravers just got back from London. I heard'n tellin' th'old man that 'parlyment's passing new laws to interfere wi' the racket. We got to make the most of it while us can.' He paused, then added more persuasively: 'We must have fast horses in case we need to outrun the ridin' officer.'

Charlie gasped, not wanting to believe her ears. Dick was risking dismissal at the very least, but Will was in with the ringleaders – and thriving on it!

Smuggling was a way of life for many, even if they only took payment for hiding contraband. But Ma would be horrified if she knew Will was so deeply involved.

Was Maltravers also involved, or had Will heard him making innocent conversation with the old man? Somehow she doubted it.

And who was 'th'old man' if not Henry Warren? Will had mentioned *Esmerelda*, their grandfather's ship. She remembered Warren calling for Will in the snow, because his ship was stuck in Holywell Bay. Her instincts had told her then he wasn't to be trusted; now she knew it was more than coal he was after.

Warren and Maltravers were ringleaders, and her brother was putty in the hands of those rogues. Neither would risk getting caught, and would betray him to save their own necks.

Will could hang, or be transported to the colonies – God, where would it all end?

Charlie felt helpless. If she shouted now they would know she'd over-heard.

She wavered, and as if to settle her dilemma, the trap-door slammed shut and dislodged another cloud of coal dust.

Once more she was trapped, and alone in the dark. There seemed nothing for it but to wait on the scullery steps until she heard someone in the kitchen.

She groped her way to the failing light of the candle at the scullery door, wishing Sir Alan were here. Everything seemed all wrong while he was away.

Using the velvet dress to cushion the cold stone, she sat at the top of the steps, drew up her knees, and leaned her head against the oak door.

God, how she hated men. Dick was a rogue; would he be good to Maisie if they married? Will would never listen to sense while he was earning easy money, and she couldn't tell Ma.

Poor Ma, reconciled at last to Grandfather Warren – the wicked old louse. Then there was Maltravers. They were all louses.

Excepts her dad, and . . . Sir Alan . . . .

She must have dozed off after all. A scraping noise jerked Charlie to her senses. She opened her eyes to darkness, and took a moment to real-ize someone had unbolted the cellar door.

'Maisie?'

There was only the sound of footsteps scurrying away. The kitchen-maid must have seen Mrs Biggins coming. It would be Maisie's word against hers.

Charlie pulled herself up stiffly on cramped legs. Her bottom felt numb, and she shivered with cold. She pushed open the door, and staggered through the scullery into the kitchen just as Mrs Biggins walked in.

The cook stared in amazement. She took off her hat, and removed the hatpin clamped between her lips.

'What on earth – what you bin doin' down that cellar? You look all in! Where's that Maisie?' Her voice rose to a shriek. 'Maisie – come quick, and get Miss Freer a tot of brandy!' She ushered Charlie into a chair, then draped her coat around Charlie's shaking shoulders.

'Now, what's bin goin' on?' It sounded as if she already suspected trouble between the two young women.

Charlie sipped the brandy which made her cough. She was cold, and hungry, and her nerves were shattered, but she didn't miss the hostile look Maisie gave her. The last thing she wanted was a shouting match with the jealous girl, Mrs Biggins would pass it off as another tedious quarrel, and she'd be no better off.

Charlie waited until the fiery liquid had warmed her and she'd stopped shivering before she tried to speak.

'I feel such a fool,' she admitted at last. 'I – er ran out of candles, and got lost down there.' She turned huge eyes on Cook.

'Oh, Mrs Biggins, thank God you came back when you did. I was afraid to move half the time, then when I heard you in the kitchen I got my bearings, and found the steps.'

'Well, I never thought the day'd come when you'd be glad to see me,' said Cook.

She ran off a pail of hot water from the boiler, muttering about a mere chit of a girl being too inexperienced to be a housekeeper.

'Here,' she said, turning back to Charlie, 'you'd better go an' clean yerself up, then get to bed. I hope you learned from your mistake.'

'Oh, yes,' said Charlie, taking the pail gratefully. 'I won't make that mistake again.'

She aimed a blazing look at Maisie, so that the maid flinched and stepped back to let her pass. Charlie snatched the chance to reassert herself.

'Be so good as to bring me up some bread and cheese, will you, Maisie?'

Maisie looked at Cook, but Mrs Biggins compressed her lips and nodded.

'Do as she says. I don't s'pose she's had anything to eat all day.'

By the time Maisie arrived with a tray of bread and cheese and a dish of Mrs Biggins's pickle, Charlie had washed, and changed into her night-dress.

'Mrs B sent some hot milk as well,' said Maisie docilely, and set the tray down on a chair beside the bed.

'Thanks very much,' said Charlie, her voice heavy with sarcasm. There seemed no point in recrimination, but she shut the door and stood in front of it, enjoying the expression of alarm that flitted across Maisie's pinched face.

'What you gonna do?' the maid asked, warily.

'I just want to talk to you. First, please understand there is nothing between Dick and me. I didn't choose to go to market with him, and he's the last man . . . oh, never mind.'

Clearly, Maisie's love for Dick made her want to believe in him.

'Where d'you go then, of an evenin' if not somewhere with 'im?' Maisie asked carefully. 'I notice you'm both gone sometimes.'

Charlie felt a spurt of sympathy, and gave the girl a small smile.

'Oh Maisie, if we seem to disappear together it really is coincidence. You know I spend as much time as I can studying.' She made a vague gesture that encompassed her room. 'I don't want to spend the rest of my life kowtowing in this place. I do go out now the evenings are lighter, to meet Tommy. Then I don't have to walk all the way home.

'As for Dick, well.' She shrugged, and tried to sound casual, for he probably met others involved in smuggling. 'If he doesn't go to the pub, I don't know what he gets up to.'

Maisie nodded miserably, then shook her fair curls out of her eyes. Charlie changed the subject abruptly.

'And, second – if you ever play a trick like that again, I'll see that Dick is relieved of his duties – without references.' She paused to let this sink in. 'All I have to do is tell Sir Alan that Isobel is in danger from Dick's advances.'

Maisie looked at her in mute appeal, all animosity gone.

'Don't do that, Charlie. He's all I got, an' he ain't so bad.'

'No, I know. He just needs to be anchored. What I can tell you about market day is, he mentioned that men complain about nagging wives.' She allowed herself a smile. 'No doubt they deserve it, but it sounds like your Dick's afraid of marriage. If it's any comfort, I think you'd make him a dam good wife.'

'You reckon?' Doubt and hope wrestled across Maisie's face.

'Yes,' said Charlie, as she opened the door. 'Now, will you take Mrs

B's coat back to her?'

Maisie snatched the coat, and Charlie called after her:

'Remember what I said. You can *trust* me!' She locked her bedroom door, and added softly: 'Take that any way you like.'

She devoured every bit of the food, and drained the mug of hot milk. Afer which, she got into bed.

It was only early evening, but she drifted into the dreamless sleep of exhaustion.

CHAPTER TEN

WHEN Charlie awoke the following morning, the sun was streaming through the curtains reminding her of the light beaming through the open coal-hole.

Painful thoughts assailed her while she dressed, as she recalled Dick and her elder brother's conversation.

Will was more deeply involved in contraband than men who merely carried tubs, and took no part in the dealings. The organizers were always of a higher standing in society. What if they were Maltravers, and old Warren? And Dick was about to hire out Sir Alan's horses behind his back!

Charlie's thoughts were interrupted when her gaze lit on the pile of filthy clothes she had discarded last night. They were covered in coal-dust, and needed a good soak in the scullery wash-tub.

She emptied the pockets. Among the candle-stumps and lucifers was the crumpled paper she'd found in Lady Lackford's dress.

Curiosity made her forget everything else. She sat on her bed, and smoothed the paper out on her lap. It was yellowed, the ink gone brown, for it was dated almost four years ago: 19 June, 1829.

Charlie noted the date was two days before the lady's death. She began to read, and her mind leapt from curiosity to wondering disbelief. The words were those of an educated person, but the handwriting was poor, and uneven, like her own when she first learned to write.

My dear Helen the faded words began, *How it grieves me to pen these words. I fear you read too much into our acquaintance, for I cannot run away with you to London. You may say you are now married in name only, but you are married with two children—'*

114

As the strange letter continued, it became plain to Charlie that someone went to great pains to hide his identity.

*As you know. I have no legitimate heir, and am about to marry the
lady whom fate decrees. She is not beautiful like you, but she adores
me, so your letters must cease. I feel sure you will not begrudge me
my chance.*

*About your "news". An illegitimate child cannot inherit, and
running away is not the answer. Believe me, I have your best interests at heart when I say the fairest thing for everyone is to do away
with this unwanted child.*

Here, Charlie paused, horrified. Dear God, what had been going on?
An affair, obviously, but what a false lover the man was, and Sir Alan
apparently had no idea.

Your husband, the letter continued, *will not learn of your indiscre-
tion from me, but – should you bring the matter to his notice, I
shall deny your allegations. You would heap disgrace upon yourself,
make a laughing-stock of him, and no one in London society will
open their doors to you*

*Do not try to see me again, or write. Go and see the witch, she
will rid you of your burden.*

I repeat, it will be the fairest thing for everyone.

I remain, your well-meaning friend.

The letter finished unsigned.
A well-meaning friend – little better than a murderer!
Charlie clasped the letter to her breast, and stared unseeingly ahead.
Who was it from? Clearly a man protecting his identity in case it fell into
the wrong hands.
He must be well known to go to such pains.
And who was 'the witch'? Biddy Cauldon? Getting rid of an unborn
child could well be one of her 'services'.
All that aside, what about Sir Alan? Charlie remembered his behaviour in the cellar that night, when he spoke of his dead wife. How guilty
he felt for having failed her, and all along Lady Helen had been unfaith-
ful to him! London society was important to her, and in her despair
she'd been past caring about anyone or anything.

Charlie remembered her ma saying how desperate she and her dad were, when they began life together with nothing. If the young Sir Alan hadn't gone over Maltravers' head to allow them to settle on his land, they and baby Will would have been in the workhouse, and separated. As it was they were in debt, but they coped because they had each other.

Lady Lackford had no one to turn to. She wouldn't dare approach her own relatives, her children were at boarding-school, and Sir Alan was away most of the time. She couldn't have *loved* him, surely?

Was this what Maisie meant, about Isobel taking after her mother?

How much did the maid know, and what made her keep quiet?

Charlie couldn't believe it was respect for Sir Alan. Perhaps Maisie knew the unknown lover, and he had some hold over her.

As questions raced through her inquisitive mind, Charlie's instinct told her that if the confusion was sorted out, it would somehow benefit Sir Alan. Which thought surprised her. None of it was her business; why should she care? It was then that she saw a potential danger to Isobel.

If Maisie knew of the affair, she must also know why Lady Lackford killed herself. She wouldn't want to be involved, so would have done nothing – not then.

But now, after four years, Isobel was almost a young woman, flirting with Dick, and Maisie was jealous. What mischief the maid could cause if she felt inclined. The sooner Dick married her, the better!

Thinking of Dick made Charlie sit up. She'd forgotten her immediate worry over him and Will.

'Oh, sugar,' she groaned, just as someone knocked at her door.

'You awake, Charlie? Be you all right?'

It was Maisie, and she sounded genuinely concerned. Charlie hastily pocketed the letter. 'Yes, Maisie,' she called, 'I'm coming.' She gathered up her soiled garments, and opened the door.

'You all right?' Maisie asked again. Her brow furrowed uncertainly.

'Yes, I awoke late. I was just fetching these clothes to soak.'

'Give 'em to me, I'll dunk 'em,' said Maisie. 'You better hurry if you want breakfast, Mrs B ain't too happy this mornin'. Ponsonby's told her the master's comin' back this weekend but he ain't sure which day. She's got to have everything ready for tomorrow, just in case.'

It was the longest speech Charlie had heard Maisie make. Clearly the maid regretted yesterday's incident. Charlie meant to stay on the right

116

side of her; there were questions to be asked, but it wouldn't do to be too soft.

'Thank you for the warning, Maisie.' She let Maisie follow her down with her dirty clothes.

She might have been glad the master was coming home, but with so much on her mind, she worried about the letter all morning. Instinct warned her to show it to him might do more harm than good. She had no desire to hurt him by raking up the past to inform him he'd been cuckolded.

She also worried about Will. Dick would be alerted by now, but would he warn her brother?

At present she had enough to do helping Maisie to pacify Cook. When her own chores were done, she went to ask if she was needed in the kitchen.

'Yep. Help Maisie get them vegetables ready fer soup,' said Mrs Biggins grumpily. Charlie went to the sink and began peeling and chopping carrots, onions and herbs, and washing leeks.

'I likes to know where I stand,' grumbled Mrs Biggins, wiping a plump hand across her brow. 'If I prepare table creams fer dessert this evenin' it might be too soon, an' they'll spoil. If I leave 'em an' he comes, it'll be too late. As fer main courses I reckon I'll do a beef-casserole that can be reheated, and roast a chicken he can have cold.'

Charlie tried to make conversation.

'I suppose he's been wining and dining, at some grand gentlemen's club, in London?'

'Hmph,' grunted Cook. 'I worked fer his father, so I've known him since he was a lad. Never did care fer city life, an' always glad to come home.'

'So, he's more likely to arrive sooner than later,' said Charlie. 'I'd best keep his bed aired.' She went to put a warming-pan in his bed, relieved that Cook seemed easier now she'd made up her mind about the menu.

When she came down Mrs B was up to her elbows in pastry, while Maisie had washed rhubarb, and chopped it into a pie dish.

'Sugar an' butter,' Cook said shortly to Charlie, nodding towards the larder. 'Weigh up eight ounces of each, please.'

Charlie fetched the items, and weighed them.

'How often does Squire go away?' She asked casually. 'His business interests must be growing; he seems prosperous, anyhow.'

She expected to be told not to be nosy, but it seemed Cook and Maisie had decided to show her due respect. While they would back one another if she reported yesterday's incident to Ponsonby, they knew the master wouldn't tolerate such a malicious prank.

'Oh aah.' Mrs B replied amicably to Charlie's question, as she began rolling pastry. 'Funny you should say that. He don't go away so often, nor so long since *she* passed on, an' he likes to be yer when them kiddies is home.'

Hearing Cook refer to the children as kiddies, rather than brats, meant her mood was improving.

'So, they began boarding-school at an early age,' said Charlie.

'Hmph.' Cook coated the rolling-pin with flour, and thumped it down again. 'Some time afore her Ladyship died, poor mites. Then when Miss Isobel was ten he sent her to the young ladies' seminary at Blandford, where she be now. Master Hugh's at Sherborne School. Squire'll want him to go to Oxford, I reckon, but the next thing for Miss Isobel will be a finishin'-school on the Continent, I shouldn't wonder . . .' Cook turned the pastry vigorously between rollings, '. . . as if she ain't got 'nuff airs an' graces already.'

As Maisie spooned sugar and ginger over the rhubarb, Charlie saw the frown on her face disappear. By the time Isobel finished school she wasn't likely to even look at a horse-groom.

Cook raised the circle of pastry on her rolling-pin, slapped it down over the rhubarb and trimmed the edges expertly with her sharp knife. It would go into the top of the oven while the chicken and the beef-casserole were 'doing' underneath.

Charlie tipped the butter and sugar into a mixing bowl.

'There was quite a scandal at the time of Lady Helen's death, I believe,' she observed. 'Ma said we weren't to pay heed to rumours, and I never knew much about it.'

'They was prob'ly scared you'd say the wrong thing at the wrong time, knowin' what little 'uns is like,' said Mrs Biggins scathingly.

Charlie grinned, 'I had no idea I'd be working for an ogre one day.'

'Where'd you hear that name?' Cook asked sharply.

'I overheard it in town once, when I wasn't supposed to be listening,' Charlie answered apologetically.

'Since coming here, though, I think the gossip was exaggerated and unfair.' She glanced at Maisie, who was delving in the potato-sack. 'Especially after he saved the town when we were snowed in,' she added.

'You'm right there,' said Cook, putting the rhubarb-pie in the oven. 'He got that reputation 'cause o' her. Like I said, she got bored. She never understood the locals like he did.'

Charlie marvelled at Cook being so chatty, nor was she as fond of the mistress as she'd thought. She guessed that in her gruff way Mrs B sympathized with the children.

Maisie, she noticed, was listening keenly while she peeled potatoes.

'What her ladyship didn't realize,' Mrs B went on, 'was that Sir Alan grew up among our local boys, and fought side by side wi' some of 'em.'

'Yet Squire was heart-broken when she died,' said Charlie, making hard work of creaming the butter and sugar with a big wooden spoon. 'Perhaps he felt he failed her somehow—'

'Yer, gimme that.' Mrs Biggins was more concerned about her cooking. 'You go an' weigh up eight ounces o' flour, an' sift it twice wi' half a teaspoon o' bicarb, an' half o' cream o' tarter, an' a pinch o' salt!'

She took the bowl from Charlie and soon had the mixture slapping around its sides.

'You young wimmen don't know how to make cakes,' she remarked scornfully. 'Maisie, leave them spuds, and fetch me three eggs.'

Charlie hid a grin at being relieved from the creaming.

'We don't often have cake,' she protested. 'We can't afford butter, but Ma makes lovely jam tarts with lard.'

'I can make pastry, and jam, too,' put in Maisie, as she cracked an egg into a chipped teacup. She began to beat it with a fork.

'You two thinkin' o' takin' over me job?' asked Mrs Biggins with a smirk.

'Oh no,' said Charlie quickly, and tried to steer the subject back to Sir Alan. 'I don't think Squire would like my cooking. I can fry fish of course, and make a fair rabbit stew . . .'

'Oh aah, bin poachin' on Master's land, 'ave you?'

'Wouldn't dare,' said Charlie non-committally, and inadvertently went off at a tangent. 'Anyhow, rabbiting's better on Maltravers' land, up cliff. When I was young we always knew when he was away because that's when we had rabbit stew.'

'You must-a had it pretty often, then,' sniffed Mrs Biggins. 'He was always gallivantin' off to London, or Dorchester. Soon as quarter days was past. Mind you, that's when he was stewardin' fer Squire. Then after Sir Alan come of age, he went away fer a couple o' years to squander the money he'd creamed off Squire's profits. Bin a rotten landlord ever since.'

Charlie listened, intrigued, as she weighed the dry ingredients.

'He settled down after Sir Alan got married. Took a great interest in his little great-niece and nephew; always visitin' 'e was.'

Mrs B stopped her mixing, and paused thoughtfully.

''S funny, y'know, despite her bad heads, how much happier her lady-ship was after Hugh's birth – and 'twas a difficult one.'

While Mrs B prattled on, Charlie saw Maisie go red, and wince as she cut a finger. She sucked it without even a swear word. How unlike her, not to make a fuss.

What Cook was saying must mean something, as if Maisie knew more about Lady Helen than Mrs B.

'Then Maltravers got married, too,' Charlie said softly.

'That's the strangest thing,' Mrs B went on, as she resumed her mixing. 'A real what-you-call-it, er – coincidence.'

'What?' Charlie persisted. 'What was a coincidence?'

'Well, 'twas only after *it* happened, you understand, that I thought 'twas queer how 'er ladyship did 'erself in the day after the Honourable Mr got married. On the twentieth, to that banker's daughter from Poole, an' Lady Helen died on the twenty-first. She was too poorly to attend the weddin' so Master went alone – with Miss Isobel, and Hugh, of course . . .'

Cook's voice faded into the background as Charlie's brain hammered the date at her. The twenty-first of June 1829, and that letter was dated the nineteenth – two days before the lady's death. Surely it was from Maltravers!

The lady must have made one last desperate attempt not to be cast aside, by telling him she was pregnant, and failed. He'd visited her often, Mrs B said, and with Sir Alan away . . .

'Yer – watch what you'm doin' wi' that flour – it's goin' all over the table!'

Cook's voice brought Charlie out of her reverie, and she saw the sprinkling of flour on the table where she'd missed the bowl.

'Oh, sugar. I – I'm sorry, Mrs B.'

'Give me the sieve,' snapped Cook. 'You'd best get back to yer house-keepin'. Go an' count sheets, or summat! Maisie, weigh out another ounce o' flour. If this cake don't sink in the middle, we'll see pigs fly tonight!'

Charlie gladly vacated the kitchen. She hurried to her room, locked the door, then pulled out the letter.

The date was definitely the nineteenth. Now she was convinced Maltravers was the false lover.

Charlie had learned from Widow Hyer to use her imagination. As she re-read the letter, she tried to put herself in Lady Lackford's place.

Even the first sentences belittling the affair must have been hurtful. Charlie murmured the callous words: *I have no legitimate heir*. Why, he virtually admits to other mistresses, and how cruelly he points out that an illegitimate child cannot inherit, meaning he wants nothing more to do with her.

He has the gall to say: *I have your best interests at heart*, then tells her to kill her unborn baby!

Charlie felt a lump in her throat. She'd learnt from Ma what it meant to lose a child – the little boy still-born between her and Tommy.

No wonder the poor, silly lady killed herself. She'd betrayed her husband and children with a man who deserted her, and the only option was to see the 'witch'.

The only 'witch' Charlie knew of was Biddy Cauldon. Could she be an accomplice to Maltravers?

There were two ways by which the old woman could have profited. One from the potion Lady Helen needed, and later the possibility of compromising her.

As for the covetous Maltravers, Charlie felt she would never understand what Lady Helen saw in him. Apart from Maisie, or Cook, whom could she consult? Her ma?

Charlie hid the letter in her drawer under the clothes she would wear next time she went home.

Had Lady Helen gone to Biddy? An overdose of laudanum, Cook said, obtained from her doctor for headaches. Yet, if she had got rid of the child she could have continued the pretence of a respectable marriage.

Why hadn't she? Because Maltravers had a hold over her?

He was often short of money, and might himself have compromised Lady Helen sooner or later. Perhaps she couldn't endure the prospect of further humiliation.

Whatever the reason, it seemed she had no wish to go on living under such duress.

'Dear God, what a louse,' Charlie muttered. She felt so angry at

Maltravers she stood up and yelled at the wall, 'The louse!'

Maltravers had probably intended Lady Lackford's downfall all along, to ruin Sir Alan. He'd nearly succeeded.

If Lady Helen had confessed to her husband, to avoid blackmail from either party, he would still be devastated to know his wife had been seduced by his own uncle.

Maybe she'd thwarted Maltravers and 'the witch' in the only way she could.

Charlie gave a mirthless laugh. Maltravers was no better off because he still had no heir. Something Widow Hyer would call poetic justice.

She thought of the haughty but miserable Jane Maltravers, who appeared to have long ago ceased to adore her husband.

Maltravers had been instrumental in leaving two children motherless, was responsible – with no thanks to Henry Warren – for her own family's poverty, and could still punish Ma for rejecting him long ago by ruining Will. The man was evil.

Charlie sat bowed on her bed, her fists pressed against her forehead. She too had put herself on the wrong side of Maltravers with her headstrong defence of her father.

'Oh God,' she gasped aloud, 'I must think it out!'

There was such confusion in her mind. A walk might help, perhaps she would meet Tommy from school.

Through him she could let Will know Sir Alan was due back, and stop him coming for the horses.

Sometimes, when Charlie had time for a walk, she went to the cliffs to gaze across the Channel. She would think of her French grandmother seeking refuge, some forty years ago, from the dreadful Terror that raged in Paris, and imagine the scene.

The billows smashing the ship to pieces on the rocks below, and a younger, more attractive Henry Warren rescuing a bedraggled female survivor.

Of course, she told herself sceptically, he was after salvage, and rescuing Charlotte Annereaux was a bit of luck – for him.

Today, however, her thoughts were far from the grandmother she'd never known as she headed into the wood below Lackford Hall.

Her path was almost obliterated by bluebells spreading in a huge carpet between budding oaks and beeches, their blueness punctuated by unfurling spears of young ferns. As the heady scent of flowers and

122

mosses pervaded her senses, she began to think more clearly.

Because Will was deeply involved in smuggling, Maltravers could ruin her family. It might not be his intent, but she feared the nature of the man.

If she was right, how could she stop him? Even if she could prove he was a ringleader to the preventive men, it would mean incriminating Will.

Sugar. What if Will was betrayed before she found a way?

Suppose she spoke to Sir Alan, showed him the letter? Could she risk hurting him, in order to protect her own family?

She shook her head, she had no positive proof it came from his uncle.

Charlie found herself in the ancient monastery ruins Sir Alan had mentioned. They were now so overgrown they were part of the wood. In her present mood she almost feared that an invisible presence was watching her. She hurried on until she came out of the wood and on to the track that led to Underhill Manor.

And there near the track, half-hidden by trees, was Biddy Cauldon's cottage.

Lackford Hall, built over the remains of a brewery, was in a direct line with the ruins, and Biddy's secluded cottage would have been easily accessible to both Lady Helen and Maltravers.

Another thought flitted through Charlie's mind. It was said that grown men went a mile out of their way to avoid passing Biddy's cottage, especially at dusk. It was one place where even the preventive men were reluctant to search for fear of her evil eye.

She could well believe Maltravers and Biddy worked together in the racket.

Charlie's thoughts ran on. Biddy might have seen Lady Lackford pass by, when she was supposedly in her room suffering headaches. Or she might have observed Maltravers, when he visited Lady Helen during Sir Alan's absences.

She thought of the chestnut-tree outside the lady's bedroom window. Any able-bodied person could climb up, unnoticed.

As Charlie passed the old woman's cottage she crossed her fingers behind her back, just in case.

The track wound on through high hedgerows bordered by horse-daisies, and thistles tall as herself. Tendrils of honeysuckle, yet to flower, wrestled with bindweed among the wild rose buds.

Charlie looked back, and saw that Lackford Hall was hidden from view in this downhill direction. Nor could she see Underhill Manor, which meant anyone standing here couldn't be seen either.

She gained the top of the rise. Down in a sheltering dip, surrounded by trees was Underhill Manor.

To one side a field lay fallow, and stinging-nettles lined the track. By contrast the garden was a riot of bright spring flowers, and Charlie warmed slightly towards Jane Maltravers, who was most likely responsible.

She walked on to a point where three narrow lanes met. One came over the hill from Holywell, while another from the sea in the east crossed her track to continue westwards to Corvesgate. Thus were all the farms hereabouts linked. With their high hedgerows, these lanes formed a natural tunnel which was useful to smugglers, and none was far from Biddy's cottage.

Charlie rested on the bridge over a stream, and shaded her eyes against the sinking sun. It was time to meet Tommy.

She recrossed the valley to the parish church, and saw children already straggling up the hill. Seeing no sign of Tommy she knocked at the schoolroom door and went in.

Martha Hyer's bright, boot-button eyes met Charlie's.

'Your brother's well ahead of the others, so rather than see him bored and tempted to make mischief, I sent him home early.' Her thin lips tugged into a smile. 'I'm hoping that such a reward may inspire the others to try harder. And how are you, Miss Freer?'

'I – I'm very well, thank you, ma'am,' said Charlie. She felt awkward with this unplanned interview. 'Squire seems satisfied; he's made me his official housekeeper. I get on well with his children, you see, which I believe takes a lot off his mind.'

'Yes, I'm sure,' replied the schoolmarm, 'but don't let it rest there, my dear. You have it in you to go far, if you put your mind to it.'

'Thank you, Ma'am.' Charlie took her leave. 'I must catch up with Tommy.'

To herself she added: or I won't be going anywhere. Her reason for seeing her little brother was to drop the hints he would pass on about Sir Alan returning sooner than expected.

Will mustn't know she was aware of his secret employment, or she too would become entangled.

Now that she'd missed Tommy, she would have to go all the way home, and that would make her late getting back.

It couldn't be helped; Will must be warned not to go after Squire's horses.

CHAPTER ELEVEN

CHARLIE reached home just as Will arrived. She watched him, covered in clay and like their dad, he sat wearily down for Ma to wash his face and neck, the traditional privilege accorded to the head of the house.

'Hello Charlie!' Amelia smiled up from her task, surprised to see her daughter.

'I can't stay,' said Charlie, quick to drop meaningful hints for Will. 'Sir Alan's expected, and if I'm late he'll think I've taken advantage of his absence.

'I was out walking, and thought I'd meet Tommy from school. But I missed him. Is he all right?' She could hardly say she knew Widow Hyer had sent him home early. 'Only with Squire back, I shan't be able to see him for a bit.'

She glanced at Will. His eyes were closed against the soapy lather, but a muscle flicked in his cheek. Her message was getting through. She smothered her relief.

'Where is the little scallywag, anyway?' she added casually.

'Gone with Sandy to look for fossils along the undercliff,' said Amelia. She handed Will a towel, and chuckled. 'They've got some get-rich-quick scheme. Martha Hyer's been telling them how Mary Anning of Lyme found remains of strange sea-creatures, with even stranger names – Will – where are you going? Supper's ready.'

Will had dried himself, and was heading for the door.

'I got to see someone first,' he grunted.

Amelia tut-tutted, and raised an eyebrow at Charlie.

'Sorry, Ma,' said Charlie, 'I have to go.'

She was none too soon. It was dusk when she arrived at the hall, and the sight of Dick rubbing down Sir Alan's big hunter alarmed her. The master was back already!

Thank goodness she'd got to Will in time!

Dick grimaced at her, no one had expected Squire before tomorrow.

Charlie looked down at her old mud-stained clothes in dismay. Her hair was a mess, too. Hastily she filled a pitcher with water and was about to climb the back stairs when Sir Alan appeared.

'Ah Miss Freer, there you are. You were not at your post. I expect to be greeted by my housekeeper – at least to take my things and hang them up. And what if I'd brought a visitor?'

Charlie quailed. She'd wanted to look her best, and greet him with a smile and a curtsy, not be all scruffy and guilt-ridden.

Previously if she was at fault, he'd seemed indifferent, but now he sounded distant. She was stung by his manner. Although nervous with guilt over Will and Dick, her own failings were unintentional.

'I'm very sorry, sir,' she began, distractedly pushing strands of hair back off her face with her free hand. 'I – I wasn't sure you were returning today, or your exact time of arrival.'

His mouth twitched, but his eyes were like steel.

'You should have been prepared like the others, you of all people. Do I have to remind you of your duties as housekeeper, or that your time belongs to me?'

Charlie remembered how much she'd missed him when she'd been locked in the cellar, now here he was, treating her as if she were in disgrace. She bridled.

'You bought my services, sir,' she corrected him obstinately, 'for one year.'

'That's enough, Miss Freer. Go and make yourself presentable, then come and see me in the library.'

He barely gave her time to say 'Yes sir', before he strode down the hall, and left her feeling small and frustrated.

She passed Maisie on the stairs.

'What's wrong with *him*? He's not usually so bad-tempered.'

'It's your fault,' hissed Maisie. 'When he galloped into the yard, he was cheerful 'nuff, 'til you didn't show. Then he got into a right huff, an' marched to his room – boots an' all!' The maid shrugged. 'I tried to cover for you. Said you was gone to see yer little brother – so I reckon we'm quits, don't you?'

'Thanks, Maisie.' Charlie was only too glad of the truce with Maisie and Mrs B. Life was getting more complicated by the minute.

She felt disappointed and angry, but washed and changed quickly. If the master took away her new position, she dam well would do whatever it took to protect her family from Maltravers, and if it upset the Lackfords, too bad.

Only when she looked presentable, and was half-way down the stairs, did she realize that she felt hurt by the master's attitude. After all she'd learnt and put up with during his absence, she'd so looked forward to his return.

Sir Alan sat by the library fire, having put a taper to it himself, for the evening was chilly. Deep in thought he crossed his long legs, put his elbows on the arms of his chair, and pressed his fingertips together.

He felt calmer now. Despite his irritation, he'd almost burst out laughing when the dishevelled Miss Freer tried to creep up the back stairs.

He felt perplexed by his own aggressive mood. Almost two months he'd been away, and had only felt happy on his way home. He could scarcely admit he'd anticipated a welcome from his new young housekeeper, for when she was nowhere to be seen, his buoyant spirits fell flat.

Well, he would make her pay. To put her in her place he'd left his room in disarray and lit the fire. She'd have her work cut out tomorrow.

He pursed his lips at the thought of her in his room, and remembered the day he'd forgotten the ledger. He'd returned, and had to pass Isobel's room to fetch it. He'd noticed the door was ajar, and had gone to close it, intending to tell Miss Freer to be more careful in case the cat got in. When he peeped in the sight of Miss Freer posing, and preening herself before his daughter's full-length mirror was completely unexpected.

Far from being angered, he was charmed. Then he'd been puzzled as her display of exuberance ended suddenly in tears. He had no desire to confront her with her misdemeanour, if misdemeanour it was, and quietly pulled the door to. Being a gentleman, he respected her need for privacy.

Recalling the scene had brightened his waking hours while he was away, yet puzzled by her sadness, he became increasingly aware that he liked her . . .

Devil take him, he was attracted to the girl!

Now he considered the good breeding in her blood, from her French grandmother, that her grandfather was a well-respected merchant, and that she had an educated mother who might have done better for herself.

Miss Freer was young, eager to learn, and affectionate towards his children.

His children – she was only a few years older than Isobel! *We had Aesops Fables at school . . .*

He recalled her words, so shyly spoken, and felt a stab of misery. What, in God's name possessed him? He was seventeen years her senior. She was far more likely to prefer a handsome young man – like Dick – someone her own class, and nearer her age.

Dash it, had the time come to take another wife? Four years ago the doctor and the parson had tried to console him, saying he would remarry one day. He'd refused to even think about it. Until now, thanks to Miss Freer of all people. What foolishness!

Yet no other woman had made such an impression on him.

Sir Alan coughed with embarrassment as Charlie's gentle tap sounded on the library door. Turning his head to the fire, he called:

'Come.'

He kept her standing, to exact his due portion of respect.

'Miss Freer,' he murmured menacingly, still staring into the fire. 'I found it most irritating that you were not at your post when I returned.'

Charlie forced firmness into her voice.

'Yes, I'm sorry, sir.'

There followed an awkward silence. She felt unsure of herself, and it seemed he didn't know what to say. How many apologies did he want?

At last he turned to her, with a slight frown.

'Am I to take it from your earlier remark that you'll be glad when your time here is up? You must tell me if you are dissatisfied with our arrangement.'

'Oh, no sir. It's not that.' She floundered. But her pride would not allow her to make excuses. 'I – I was rather rude, sir, and I apologize if I forgot myself.'

'Hmm. I understand you went to see your little brother. Do you have problems at home?'

Will's face flashed through Charlie's mind, but she assured her master all was well. Politely she pointed out that apart from her absence everything was ready for his return.

'Had I been at my post, sir, I wouldn't have lit the fires until you arrived.'

He'd galloped into the yard, eager to be home and was angry only when she didn't appear.

Charlie's legs felt weak, and she wished he would tell her to be seated. She put a hand on the mantlepiece to steady herself.

'You're not going to dismiss me, are you sir?' She half-whispered. 'I – I was looking forward to seeing Miss Isobel and Master Hugh again. They are coming home at Whitsuntide?'

Something like jealousy flickered in his breast. She was dashed fond of his children.

'No,' he replied shortly, and Charlie's heart sank as his melancholy expression deepened. 'I'm afraid they will remain at school until summer term ends.' He shook his head as if annoyed at her changing the subject. 'And no, I'll not dismiss you. I shall overlook your . . . ahem . . . misdemeanour this time. I accept you were not to know the time of my arrival; besides there's a deal to be done before your year is up.'

Before you've had your money's worth, she thought. Yet she felt relieved and peeved at the same time, and dared to look him in the eye.

'Thank you, sir.'

'You look disappointed,' he said, curiously.

'I am, sir.' Her grey eyes widened with genuine concern. 'I had hoped the children would be home for the Whit Tuesday Fair.' The fair on the first Tuesday after Whit Sunday was the biggest event of the year in Swanwick, and Charlie thought it would have been a good chance for Sir Alan to enjoy being with his children.

'I'm leaving them where they are for their own good,' he said, and motioned her at last to draw up a stool. Hiding his pleasure at watching her, he waited until she was settled.

'Do you know, Miss Freer, that influenza is rampant in the cities?'

Charlie gasped. 'I thought the cholera was more to be feared.' Perhaps he was moody because he had to keep the children at school.

'On the contrary, my dear,' he said absently, 'it is reported in the *Medical Gazette* that more people died from influenza in London during the last two weeks in April than from the cholera, which is now contained.' He sighed. 'Sadly, one of them was the husband of my favourite niece.'

'Oh sir, I am sorry,' said Charlie. No wonder he was worried about his children.

'Ye-es,' he went on slowly. 'She's too young for widowhood; they were only married a year ago, and hadn't even started a family.'

Charlie didn't know what to say, then he seemed to shake off his melancholy.

'Anyway, Miss Freer, I believe I can trust you not to spread gossip. The fact is, Her Royal Highness the Princess Victoria, who recently celebrated her fourteenth birthday, is to accompany her mother, the Duchess of Kent, on a tour of the south-west counties.

'I rather suspect her parents want her out of the capital until these epidemics are over. Be that as it may, she will end her tour on the Isle of Wight.' He gazed earnestly at Charlie. 'We shall keep this to ourselves for the time being.'

'Oh, yes we shall – I mean – yes, of course sir!' Charlie almost leaped off her seat. 'Will they come here, do you think? Shall we see them?'

'As to that, I've no idea,' said Sir Alan. He stood up, to indicate the interview was over.

Charlie wanted to stay and ask him more about the young princess, and life in the city. But he'd dismissed the subject of their royal highnesses.

'Do you see the package on my desk?' He crossed the room to fetch a large oblong parcel.

Charlie nodded. 'I did notice it when I came in.'

'It's yours, the material I promised. Take it, and decide how best to use it. The dark stuff is for your position as housekeeper.'

'Thank you, sir!' Having feared his wrath and her dismissal only minutes ago, she was overcome with relief and gratitude. As she held out her arms for the package, she unwittingly gave him the charming look he'd anticipated earlier. Her smile was wide, and her grey eyes shone up at him.

Seeing her so genuinely pleased made up for his earlier disappointment.

'I like to see my servants well-attired,' he said gruffly, and opened the door for her.

This year, after the Easter festivities were snowed off, Whit Tuesday holiday was particularly welcome. There would also be a half-holiday on the Wednesday.

Charlie was sorry the squire couldn't share it with his children, but she looked forward to spending the day with her own family. Will had finished the lean-to, so there was room for her to stay overnight, then return to Lackford Hall by lunchtime on Wednesday.

While she and Maisie finished the spring-cleaning the aroma of baking, and meat cooking wafted up the back stairs to tickle their nostrils. Mrs Biggins was stocking the larder with pies, boiled ham, and cold roast meats.

Early on the Tuesday morning Hart brought in salad vegetables from the glasshouse, and now everyone had the day free.

As soon as she'd cleared away Sir Alan's breakfast dishes Charlie got ready to go home. She'd opened the master's package some days earlier, to find not only navy-blue serge for her housekeeper's dress, but a bolt end of creamy linen for a best dress, and some fine white lawn for undergarments. In her excitement she forgot her worries. There'd been no time to make anything for Whitsun, so she'd let out the bodice darts in one of Lady Helen's summer gowns and removed the furbelows. It still looked smarter than anything she owned. She wanted to look her best because Ma was hiring a booth to display the straw-plait items she'd worked on all winter.

Below Lackford Hall the stalls lined the highway all the way down the street to Sam Roper's smithy. Men had strung rows of bunting from one side of the road to the other. Among the goods on display were woven and knitted goods, rush baskets and matting, ropes of varying thicknesses as well as twine for fishing nets, all smelling fresh and new. With dressmaking in mind, Charlie eagerly examined the buttons and fingered smooth satin ribbons on the haberdashery stall.

Besides traders, there were coconut shies and Aunt Sallies – great favourites with the quarry boys – and strategically placed near each inn was a skittle alley. There were all sorts of fairings to choose from, including minty humbugs, peppermint sticks and sticky brandy-balls.

A Russian sailor from Poole strolled along the street with a dancing bear, whose odour was rather less attractive than the cakes and pastries.

The day began officially with payouts made to members of the sick benefit club, and free pints of beer at the Dun Cow.

Wearing one of Amelia's spanking new bonnets, Charlie helped the boys to set up her ma's stall. They could see the men who had erected the bandstand on ten-foot-high scaffolding decorating it with flags and evergreens. As yet there was no sign of Will.

'He said he had some unfinished business to see to first,' Amelia told her.

Her mother assumed it was to do with the quarr, and Charlie tried to ignore her own misgivings. She didn't want to spoil Ma's day.

Across the road Biddy Cauldon set herself up as a fortune-teller, no doubt hoping to sell her remedies. She wore a white eye-patch, and a bright blue kerchief tied around her head. The young woman who stood out front to welcome customers into the curtained booth must be Hetty. She was plain, and rather simple-looking.

By nine o clock, there was an air of anticipation as people gathered along the roadsides to greet the gentry who would grace the club as honorary members. Charlie was relieved to see Henry Warren among the first officials to arrive. Whatever Will was up to wasn't important enough to keep their grandfather from the festivities. After the merchant came the Honourable Simon Maltravers with his wife in their gig. They made little impression, but when Sir Alan Lackford rode into view the crowd surged forward, knowing he liked to be seen to do the right thing.

The squire wore a dark-grey broadcloth suit, and a silk top-hat in keeping with the other dignitaries. Charlie's stomach tweaked, and a hot flush crept up her throat to her cheeks when she saw him look their way. He doffed his hat, and inclined his head. They returned his greeting with polite bobs. Amelia said what a nice gentleman he was, to notice them like that, and Charlie saw her ma blush, too.

Reining his horse to a walk, Sir Alan pulled a purse from his pocket, and opened it. He flourished it in a wide arc, and showered pennies among the onlookers. Tommy and Sandy joined the other youngsters who scrambled after the coins, then ran off to examine Mariner Joe's curiosity stall. The old sea-dog had seen service in Lord Nelson's time. While Amelia walked about displaying her bonnets decorated with feathers, or imitation flowers, Charlie watched the stall. Maisie strolled by with Cook, who for once had her sleeves rolled down and fastened at the wrists.

As soon as the payouts at the Dun Cow were finished the church bells began to peal, a signal for the procession to begin. The town crier, in his scarlet robe and black tricorne hat, strode ahead with his long red pole held horizontally before him to clear a path.

'Make way, make way!' he boomed.

As the crowd moved back two bearers advanced, taking turns to carry the club flag. Behind them came two lines of dignitaries headed by the mayor and Sir Alan, then the rector and his curate.

The other officials, led by the Honourable Simon Maltravers and Henry Warren JP, were an impressive sight. They wore rosettes in their lapels, and each carried a six-foot-high club stick. Then came the town band, with its brass instruments gleaming in the sunlight. Sam Roper caught Charlie's eye, winked, then made her jump with three fierce thumps on his bass drum, as the band struck up the club march. The remaining members brought up the rear, with smaller flags and garlands of greenery, and the public fell in behind. Charlie studied the marchers carefully but she couldn't see Will or Dick.

The Freers followed the procession with Hart's wife and children to the parish church. Inside, the marchers hung their flags and garlands over the galleries, and the club sticks stood beside each official where he sat.

The rector kept the service short, and based his sermon on a text from Hebrews 13:

'Never cease to love your fellow-Christians. Remember to show hospitality. There are some who, by so doing, have entertained angels without knowing it . . .'

Martha Hyer had organized an angelic-looking group of youngsters to lead the appropriate hymn. They drew several 'oohs' and 'aahs' from proud parents.

Immediately after the benediction the bells pealed again. The double crocodile re-formed, and the band led the way up the hill. A quick march brought them back to the inns at the town centre, and the procession dispersed in minutes.

Charlie still couldn't see her older brother, it was like looking for a needle in a haystack. People swarmed up and down the pavements, weaving across the road from one booth to another, or in and out of the inns.

The bandsmen drowned out the bells. They would play all day, apart from when they stopped for refreshments. Children joined in with toy trumpets, tin whistles and drums; dogs, startled from their search for dropped crumbs and sweets, began to bark and howl.

Stallholders shouted themselves hoarse, crying their wares above the rumpus, and at the skittle-alleys, where heavy wooden balls and hobnail boots thundered up and down the boards, the noise was even more deafening.

Never could Charlie remember the town being so busy and noisy. As the day progressed so did the children's shrieks, and the high spirits of the tipplers. When a fight broke out over a disagreement, it was seen as further entertainment.

The Freers did a brisk business and soon took orders. Even Jane Maltravers, who saw the mayor's wife buy a bonnet, thought the straw-plaits 'most fetching'. Once, a young lad came shyly to buy one for his sweetheart, and Sir Alan himself came to admire.

He chose one for Isobel, and two more for his sisters in London. Afterwards, Amelia remarked that, while he seemed interested in her work, he was watching Charlie.

'He's not used to seeing me look smart, that's all,' said Charlie, embarrassed. 'When he sees me at the hall, I'm nearly always doing a dirty job in old clothes.'

Amelia smiled wistfully.

Refreshments were laid out on trestle-tables in the Dun Cow and the White Horse, the two inns with the biggest upstairs rooms. Charlie and her mother went to a smaller inn, the Swan, which had a canvas-awning extension.

As the afternoon wore on, people lost interest in the stalls in favour of merrymaking, and the vendors dropped their prices. The crowd had thinned when Henry Warren, impressed by the Mayor's interest in Amelia's straw-plait work, paid his respects. It seemed his daughter's industry and skill appealed to his business nature.

'Come and have some refreshments with me, m'dears,' he offered, hoping Charlie would refuse the invitation. She'd been so fond of her father, he had little hope of winning her respect. He needn't have worried. Amelia looked pleased, and raised an eyebrow at her daughter.

'You go on, Ma, you deserve a spell,' said Charlie. 'I'll pack up and take the stuff home before the dancing.'

Henry Warren nodded at her as if she'd sought his approval.

'Bring one of your bonnets,' he said to Amelia. 'I'll wager you'll get more orders. I might even think about setting you up in a small shop.' He gave Amelia his arm, and she laughed as they drifted away.

'A boutique! Now, *that* will be the day . . .'

Charlie grimaced. If Ma but knew what she did! Angrily she stuffed the few remaining bonnets into a sack. Then, seeing that one sack would suffice to carry home the leftover stock, her anger cooled. Ma had done well.

Hetty chose the moment to come over.

'I'm packing up,' said Charlie shortly. Resentment towards her grandfather had put her in just the mood to keep a wary eye on the girl Sir Alan had dismissed for stealing.

'I be on'y just lookin', Miss Freer,' said Hetty softly, in a broad accent.

Charlie was surprised by the girl's timid manner, but Hetty seemed genuinely taken with the bonnets and baskets.

'D'you think yer ma'd teach I?' she asked.

'It's not up to me, you'll have to ask her,' Charlie replied, guardedly.

'I wouldn't want much pay, an' I be quick to lurn,' said Hetty earnestly. 'Me Gran says I got nimble fingers . . .'

'So I've heard,' said Charlie, with a note of sarcasm, which wasn't lost on Hetty.

'I know what you be thinkin',' she said. 'I spose you've heard about them logs, an' that I be a good-fer-nothin'. Well, 'tain't true. I never stole 'em.'

'Are you calling Squire a liar?' Charlie's eyebrows shot up in exaggerated scorn. 'You could get into trouble—'

'Naow, I ain't sayin' thaat,' said Hetty hastily. 'I was told I could 'ave them logs, then 'er what said I could 'ave 'em, went an' told on me!'

'Who was that, then Hetty?' asked Charlie, half-believing.

'Maisie, craafty bitch. She wanted to get rid of I 'cause 'er Dick fancied me!' Hetty's ample bosom heaved with indignation. 'I know I beain't pretty, but 'tweren't me face 'e was int'rested in!'

Charlie could see the girl was in earnest, and for a moment she didn't know what to say. In view of her recent experience she could well believe Hetty, but would Sir Alan have dismissed the girl unfairly?

'Didn't you tell Squire that Maisie said you could have the logs?'

'Aah, I tried, but she 'ad to say she never did, or *she* would've bin in trouble. Then 'e sez: "One o' you is lyin'", an' asked Cook what she knew.'

'And,' prompted Charlie, as Hetty paused to gulp back sobs of resentment.

'Cook sez she di'nt know about logs, but she 'ad noticed things missin' from the laarder.' Hetty's eyes bulged with pained frustration. 'I swear I never stole 'em—'

Charlie suddenly remembered a more valuable object, and interrupted.

'And you were never tempted by Lady Lackford's jewel casket? It went missing.'

She immediately regretted the accusation. Hetty became so passionate, she felt sure the girl was telling the truth.

'Miss, that ain't fair! Just 'cause I told you 'bout them logs you think I pinched everythin' thass gone missin' from the hall. Well, I never did. I weren't never tempted, an' I never pinched 'er rotten of jewel box!'

'I'm sorry, Hetty,' said Charlie. 'That was mean of me, and I believe you. It's just that I know you had to clean her ladyship's bedroom, and must have seen it.'

It wasn't often anyone apologized to Hetty.

'Oh aah, I knowed 'n, but I ony seen 'n once or twice,' she added, mollified. 'Anyway there weren't no jewels in 'n, on'y papers—'

'Papers! What papers?'

'I dunno, I cain't read, but they wuz precious to 'er, like jewels. Kept it locked away, an' hung the key round her neck, 'er did.' Hetty screwed up her nose and leaned towards Charlie. 'An' what's more, I never seen 'n fer ages afore 'er ladyship died.'

Charlie had to fight her rising excitement. She stared at Hetty, who pleaded again.

'Miss, I'll swear on the Holy Bible if you want, I never took nothin' except them logs.'

'All right Hetty, I believe you,' soothed Charlie. 'So Squire didn't even give you the benefit of the doubt?'

'Naow. He believed Maisie 'cause she'd bin there longer'n me, an' was recommended by his Uncle Maltravers.'

'Aah,' breathed Charlie. It seemed Maisie was Lady Helen's go-between. And she must have, unwittingly or not, aroused suspicion towards Hetty by smuggling things from the larder for Dick, to win his favour. Poor Hetty, and poor Maisie. Charlie shook her head.

'It's all past now,' she said guardedly, 'but Ma *might* be glad of some help after doing so well today. Unless – haven't you got enough to do helping your gran?'

'Huh, she do work I aard,' said Hetty frowning down at her boots, and stubbing a toe into the dust. ' 'Twould be nice to get away from 'er moanin'. Takes advantage 'er do, 'cause nobody else wants me.'

Mud sticks, thought Charlie. Out loud she said:

'I know. It's hard to get work without references. How long's Maisie been with Squire, then?' she asked carefully.

'Since maaster Hugh was born. The Honourable Mr said he could spare her 'cause he 'ad no kids of 'is own, so Maisie 'ad reference 'nuff . . .' Hetty pouted at the thought.

'Of course,' murmured Charlie. She changed the subject. 'Well, you and Biddy have done good business today, I think?'

'Oh aah. Me Gran's bin convincin' everybody what an 'armless ol' dear she be really. Even gie I tuppence to spend.' Hetty's voice was heavy with sarcasm. 'Mean ol' thing 'er is!'

137

'She's looked after you, though. At least you're not in the workhouse, but I do think you're brave not to be afraid of her . . .'

Hetty snorted, and looked so downcast that Charlie felt sorry for her. There was something appealing about the girl.

'Hetty, I can't promise anything, but if Ma can afford help I'll put in a good word for you.'

'Thank you, miss.' Hetty sounded so humbly grateful that on impulse, Charlie picked up the last bonnet.

'Here, have this one for twopence. If anyone asks where you got it, tell them to see me.'

Hetty's wide smile made up for her plainess. Delighted, she gave Charlie the coins and donned the bonnet. Her eyes sparkled, as she sought approval.

'It's very becoming, Hetty.'

'You'm a good'n,' said Hetty, 'so I'm gonna tell 'ee summat.'

Charlie's brow creased with amused curiosity.

'What's that, then?'

Mischievously, Hetty beckoned her close to whisper in her ear.

'Me Gran's o'ny got the evil eye at full moon.'

Charlie put a hand to her mouth to suppress a laugh. Hetty sounded so sincere.

'But Hetty, I know people who've seen her when she's taken off her patch, and been frightened silly.'

'Yer – watch this,' said Hetty. She held up her right index finger and stared fixedly at it. Slowly she drew it towards her nose until it touched. The terrible squint this produced made her really ugly, despite her wide, wicked grin.

Charlie doubled up with laughter.

'You mean,' she gasped, 'that she does it on purpose, and lets folk think she's affected by the moon?'

The wicked old witch, what power she wielded by fooling people! Charlie stopped laughing, and muttered, to herself: 'And when smugglers are busiest.'

But Hetty heard.

'Now, miss, I ain't sayin' thaat, but I trust you with me gran's secret, 'cause I like you. I got to go now. She's expectin' more customers when it gets dark.'

Hetty clamped her bonnet to her head and ran back to her gran's booth.

Charlie smiled wryly. The fortune-teller was the only one to stay open when the others had closed.

She bundled the empty sacks under one arm, hoisted the full sack over her other shoulder, and started for home, glad to get away from the noise and bustle, and for the chance to think.

She hadn't seen Will all day, and was worried about him. Where could he be, or, more important, what was he up to?

CHAPTER TWELVE

CHARLIE returned to the town as a cavalcade of wagons loaded with dismantled sideshows headed into the sunset.

She was hungry, and hastened to the Swan where Amelia found her. She was without Henry Warren, Charlie was glad to see. Instead, her ma had Tommy and Sandy in tow.

'There you are, Charlie, just in time.'

The musicians had finished playing, and preparations were being made for the dancing in the upper room of the Dun Cow. The windows were thrown up and furniture passed out to make space. Tommy and Sandy rushed upstairs with the other youngsters, to race about the dance floor until the grown-ups shooed them out. All the chairs were pushed back against the walls, except one which was lifted on to a table. As soon as the fiddler was hoisted up to take his position the dancing began. It was the moment all the young people were waiting for, and Sandy shyly asked Charlie to dance the first jig with him.

Maisie was alone too, which meant Dick was still missing. So was Will.

Sir Alan made it his business to give all the ladies a dance, and Charlie remembered Cook saying he enjoyed being with the locals. When he claimed Amelia for the polka she felt a stab of jealousy, yet it was good to see her ma enjoying the evening.

Then, at long last, Will and Dick staggered in, already tipsy. Maisie quickly pulled Dick into the dance, while Amelia spoke to Will over her shoulder as Sir Alan whirled her past.

The young quarryman swilled down the contents of his tankard, and swaggered over to Charlie. There was a smug, lopsided grin on his face, and he slurred his words.

'Ma says to give you a dance, sis.'

He reeked of liquor, but Charlie was relieved to see him. He and Dick had managed without Squire's horses, which was the reason for their being away so long. They'd clearly consumed their share of the contraband.

She tilted her nose.

'All right,' she said, 'but only to please Ma.'

She tried to act like a fond sister, but when he trod on her toes and overbalanced, she lost her temper.

'You've had more than your free ticket's worth of booze. Where'd you get the money?'

Will leered at her, and slyly tapped the side of his nose.

'Now that would be tellin'. Let's just say me ship came in.'

Charlie averted her head from his foul breath.

'What ship's that then, Will?' she asked, casually.

'Thash my little secret – whoops!' He tripped over his own feet, and she had to grab him to stop him falling. He sagged against her as she steered him towards the door.

'Let's go outside for some fresh air.' She felt herself grow red with embarrassment in case anyone, particularly Sir Alan, was watching.

But Will wasn't the only one in an inebriated state, and no one took any notice as he stumbled downstairs.

Among the less active folk in the company below were Simon Maltravers and Henry Warren. Charlie guessed they'd taken the opportunity to talk without being overheard.

The wooden ceiling-props shook as above them hobnails pranced to the fiddler's jigs. Jane Maltravers rubbed her brow. She looked if all hell had been let loose.

Charlie dragged her brother out into the moonlight, then prompted him.

'C'mon, Will. Did you get lucky in the boxing-ring, or have you been gambling? You know what Ma thinks—'

'Naow,' said Will, stupidly emphatic. 'I told you, me ship came home. I got me own little treshure-trove.'

'I don't believe you,' she snapped. 'You're drunk, and don't know what you're saying.'

Will prided himself on being able to hold his liquor, and took offence. His eyes grew wide as he concentrated on his speech.

'I'll tell 'ee summat,' he gulped. 'Remember the founder that killed our dad? The tunnel fell in 'cause it was too close to old workings. Them walls an' ceilin's was weak. I cleared a way through, see, and got meself a nice hidy-hole on t'other side.'

Charlie didn't want to be reminded of their dad's death.

'Why tell me all this? If you get caught it'll break Ma's heart—'

'I won't get caught,' Will snarled. 'What's down there is earnin' me money just sittin' there. I'm lookin' after it until 'tis safe to shift it.' He paused, then added mutinously: 'If our ma do find out she cain't blame me. She went an' married our dad when she could have done better. She chose to be poor.'

Charlie hit back.

'It was Maltravers who kept us poor. Our Dad flogged himself to death to put food in our mouths, and a roof over our heads.'

'You never think about the way I've lived,' said Will angrily. 'I was the one to suffer, bein' his bastard, dragged out o'school an' in to the quarr afore I was ten.'

He thumbed his chest, his face looked tortured.

' 'Twas me had to crawl inter them tiny spaces where 'tweren't safe fer him to go. Riskin' me neck while you soaked up learnin' thass useless fer a maid. An' now you'm at the hall, pickin' up airs an' graces.'

'I'm not exactly living a life of ease, Will—'

'You got nothin' to lose, then!' He shoved his jaw at her. 'I'm still down there, hackin' me guts out to keep Tommy at school. Our dad never cared fer me like he did you an' Tommy . . .'

Charlie drew back as tears pricked her eyes. 'Oh he did, Will. He just couldn't show it. He would've helped you get to London soon as he was out of debt. He was ill.'

'Well, if you think I'll sweat underground 'til I get bad like him, you're mistaken. I know a better way to earn money, an' I'll soon have 'nuff to git to London an' set up on me own.'

'Will,' she pleaded, 'can't you see? Thanks to you, Ma's got her own business going. I don't want to be a servant all my life, and I don't begrudge you wanting to make something of yourself. But not this way!' She stepped closer. 'Listen, if you've got money saved, why not set yourself up here? You'd have room in the lean-to for another apprentice to sleep, or a partner, then you'd have time for monumental work—'

'I ain't payin' no partner,' barked Will. 'I work bloody 'ard fer what I've got!'

Charlie felt exasperated.

'You talk about our ma keeping us poor, what about dear granddad? Wouldn't lift a finger to help his own daughter!'

142

'He's makin' up fer it now they'm friends again,' argued Will.

'And why's that, Will? Why is he suddenly so fond of her after all this time? Could it be because he needs you?'

Oh why couldn't Will see he was being used? She only succeeded in needling him.

'That'sh fer me to know, an' you better keep yer nose out o' my business if you don' want to upset Ma, or ruin Tommy's chances.'

Charlie struggled to control her temper.

'My God, Will,' she hissed, 'you don't half take after our granddad. Between you both you'll pull us all down in disgrace!'

Will's answer was to make an ugly cut-throat gesture.

'If you know what's good fer you,' he repeated, 'you'll keep out o' my business.'

He staggered away from her, and Charlie watched him sway down the road to the White Horse. At least he had more sense than to betray himself further, for if Maltravers suspected him of giving away their secrets . . . Charlie shuddered.

She returned to the dancing feeling defeated. But, flushed and panting at the end of a progressive reel, she found herself facing Sir Alan.

He imprisoned her hand until the next dance, and she gazed shyly up at him. He looked happy, and with his high-browed head thrown back, seemed even taller. She was sorry when the dance moved her on to another partner.

She sat the next one out with her laughing, breathless ma.

'Where were you?' Amelia asked. 'Squire asked for you during the waltz, he said 'twas his right as our landlord to claim a dance with my lovely daughter. What d'you think of that?' She studied her daughter quizzically. Was Squire interested in her Charlie – or was he just being gracious?

'He's merry with drink, same as everybody else,' said Charlie quickly, to hide her confusion and disappointment. To think she'd been rowing with Will when she could have been waltzing with Sir Alan! 'Anyway,' she added, 'I thought he was rather taken with you, our Ma.'

Amelia gazed at her daughter as if about to say something, then shook her head. What would Squire want with a middle-aged matron, other than as a chaperon? How little Charlie really understood, and how could she, without the advantages she herself once had?

Charlie explained, in blunt sisterly terms, how she'd taken Will outside before he made a complete fool of himself.

'Besides, I'd rather not dance with Squire because there's some as would make something of it, especially as I live in at the Hall.'

Amelia raised her eyebrows as Charlie jerked her head towards the door where Maltravers hovered on the threshold.

'Him?' Amelia frowned. 'Oh, I know he's no friend of ours, but he *is* Squire's uncle.'

'I'll tell you later,' muttered Charlie, seeing Maltravers take leave of Sir Alan.

Word soon went round that Mrs Maltravers was suffering one of her abominable headaches, and no one was sorry to see them go.

It was the early hours of Wednesday morning before everyone had gone home, including the Freers, and the town was quiet once more.

Amelia Freer counted her earnings, and smiled at her success, for there was more than enough to renew her supply of good-quality straw.

Perhaps she should invest some of the money in the quarr, yet she'd resent giving it to Will, who behaved too much as though he were the head of the house, and she his drudge. She'd worked hard, often going to bed with sore, aching fingers from the straw-plaiting. No, she would do as she wished with her money.

She put the coins into a small earthenware pot, then hid it behind a loose stone in the fireplace. How serious had her father been, she wondered, when he'd mentioned setting up a shop? Was it the drink talking, or did he mean it?

Another thought crossed her mind, and she gazed out through the open sunlit doorway. Yes, that was it, another use for the money, a wonder she hadn't thought of it sooner!

She carried a stool outside and sat in the sun with her mending.

Will and the boys were still asleep, but she could hear Charlie moving about. She'd been alarmed by her daughter's vehemence towards Maltravers last night, for he was no longer to be feared. Life was full of promise now that her father wished to let bygones be bygones.

Cowslips and pink soldiers' jackets were in full bloom, and Amelia closed her eyes to enjoy the sun's caress, and the heady scents of early summer.

Relaxing thus, long-buried memories began to surface.

How pleasant it was, at this time of year when she and *Maman*, as her mother had liked to be addressed, would gather cowslips to make wine.

She hadn't known then how happy she was.

Maman called her father Henri, and it seemed that Amelia was different from her playmates, whom she amused by speaking French, her mother's tongue. She taught her little friends to sing *Frère Jacques*, and *Sur le Pont d'Avignon*.

They were all quarrymen's children, and never thought of themselves as peasants, or realized how poor they were until the big boy, Simon Maltravers, spoiled their fun. He used to come and visit his relations when he was on holiday from his London school.

Amelia had despised him long before he wrecked her plans to elope with William. A younger son of one of the landed gentry, he delighted in ridiculing their ignorance. She retaliated by taunting him in French, and when the others laughed, he called her 'Frogspawn', which was worse, apparently, than being a peasant.

She couldn't understand, if it was such a poor thing to be a peasant, why the son of a rich man should bother about them. *Maman* told her he was jealous of their fun.

It was in school that she'd first begun to grow apart from her friends. 'Say "Mother", not "Maman",' the school-mistress would say. A frigid spinster, she lacked the malleable heart of Widow Hyer.

Amelia answered back. 'But *Maman* likes me to call her so,' she said, and was made to stand in the corner. *Maman* did her best to comfort her *chérie*, and explained that she was half-French.

But *Maman* was an 'alien', England was at war with France, and Simon Maltravers led the teasing.

The only person bold enough to stick up for her was William Freer, a strong, handsome little boy. One day, when she'd been trying to get her own back by singing 'Simple Simon' at the top of her voice, Maltravers chased her in fury. William grabbed his coat, swung him round, and shot his fist into Simon's face. The bigger boy ran off howling, then it was his turn to be teased because a smaller boy had given him a bloody nose.

Soon after, William was among the boys taken away from school to help the war effort against Napoleon. The government was frantically building fortifications around the coast in case of invasion, and a lot of cliff stone was needed.

Later, it was *Maman's* idea to send her to a young ladies' academy and because her father's circumstances were improved, he agreed.

Then *Maman's* death from the cholera acted like a wedge between Amelia and Henry. He buried himself in his business, and instead of the life *Maman* had planned for her, Amelia became little more than his secretary-cum-housekeeper.

She found consolation in her clandestine meetings with William – dear William, by which time Maltravers had changed his tune.

She was a well-off, educated young lady, and he paid court, using her mother's death to ingratiate himself with her father.

Henry Warren never gambled, or drank excessively, and was successful in his business dealings, yet he would have sacrificed her for the prestige of a title in the family. Now he was a lonely old man.

To Amelia, her love for William was all that mattered then, but now the thought of sacrifice brought her back to the present.

Hadn't she sacrificed Charlie, for the family's sake?

Amelia resumed her sewing with a sigh. After last night, dare she hope for a better future for her daughter? She resolved not to drink so much next holiday time.

'Morning, Ma.' Charlie came out chewing a crust of bread. She grinned ruefully. 'Ooh, my head.'

Dressed in an old skirt and blouse, her hair pulled back from her face in a clumsy attempt at a top-knot, she stood barefoot on the doorstep. Some of her heavy dark tresses broke free and hung untidily around her face. Amelia chuckled.

'Last night you were beautiful, just like your grandmother. This morning you look like a gypsy.'

Charlie shrugged good-naturedly.

'Come and sit by me,' said Amelia. 'I want to talk to you.'

Charlie fetched a stool and sat down. She stretched her legs, and wriggled her toes in the warm sun.

'What about, Ma?'

'What did you mean last night, about Maltravers?'

Charlie wished she'd never brought the subject up, but she'd been so worried about Will.

She tried to explain, saying no more than necessary, and it was a relief not to be keeping it all to herself.

'Since I've been at the hall I've heard that Maltravers envies his nephew because of his wealth.'

Amelia nodded. 'That seems quite possible. Go on.'

'Well, after that business with the snow at Easter, Squire's more popular – you saw that before the procession started yesterday.'

'Ye-es, that's true,' Amelia agreed. 'Anything else bothering you?'

Charlie bit her lip, deciding, then looked Amelia in the eyes.

'Maltravers hates us, too.' She related the incident in the dining room at Easter, and how she'd riled the Honourable Mr by saying he was the last person she'd want for a father.

Ma looked horrified.

'Oh Charlie, I wish you hadn't.'

'Well he was so horrid, he's trouble, Ma. I wouldn't put it past him to spread lies about Squire, or us.' She held back on her suspicions about his having an affair with Lady Helen.

'He tried to ruin you and Dad, and I can tell by the way he sneers that he still bears a grudge. I don't trust him.'

She longed to say that Will could be in danger from him, but wouldn't burden Ma with that. As it was, her ma thought she was exaggerating.

'It was so long ago,' Amelia objected, 'and he's your grandfather's friend. I can't see Maltravers upsetting him by hurting us.' She bent to her sewing again, the subject closed.

Charlie almost blurted her doubts. She felt angry that old Warren never understood Ma's need for love, and at the way he'd allowed Maltravers to ruin her parents.

'Anyway,' Amelia went on, 'what I really want to say is, after our success yesterday I hope to expand my business, especially if your grandfather meant what he said. In which case I'd be glad of help. Would you come in with me?'

'Me?' said Charlie, halting the last piece of bread before her open mouth. 'How?'

Amelia darted a look at her daughter. 'We did better yesterday than I dared hope. There's enough money to buy good straw *and* pay off Will's debt to Squire.'

Charlie gaped at her, and Amelia put down her sewing. She took Charlie's hands in her own, and gazed tenderly at her daughter to gauge her reaction.

'You would be free to come home, I did promise I'd make it up to you.'

It would be good to have Charlie back; life could be tiresome for one woman in a household of men. Yet, if there was a chance for Charlie to improve her prospects – even to marry well . . .

Deliberately she added: 'Of course, if staying where you are will help your prospects of better employment . . . Well, it's something to think about. Now, how about some tea? See if the kettle's boiling, will you?'

Charlie obeyed numbly. With so many things on her mind, Ma's proposal was unexpected. A few weeks ago she'd have jumped at the chance to buy back her freedom, now she felt dismayed at the idea of leaving Lackford Hall. Despite her fears about Maltravers, she enjoyed her new position. She was wearing nice clothes, and was looking forward to the children coming home. She was needed there – but how could she let her ma down?

Deep inside she knew it was her feeling for Sir Alan, too. Having penetrated his reserve she could almost say they were friends, but would they remain so if she was independent of him?

What was the matter with her? Why should she care whether they were friends or not?

She was afraid to even think of an answer.

She brought two steaming mugs outside, and seeing her mother intent on the mending, felt a great surge of love. What a hard life Ma had chosen, always scraping to make ends meet. Now, though eager to pursue her new business, she was offering her bit of money to end her daughter's bondage.

Well she wouldn't let her Ma make any more sacrifices; somehow she must help.

Then Charlie remembered her promise to Hetty. She swallowed.

'Ma, I need time to think,' she began. 'I like being housekeeper, and I – the children will be home next month. They're expecting me to be there, they miss their mother . . .'

'I understand,' Amelia said softly, agonizing. Charlie was growing up, yet was unaware that she was falling in love.

If only it were a possibility. She'd suffered this same helpless feeling over her first-born, when Will left school to work long hours in the quarr. Now it seemed she couldn't save Charlie from a love that was surely doomed. She sighed.

'Well maid, I expect I can find someone, we'll see. The offer will be there if you change your mind. I suppose even as a paid housekeeper you're cheaper than hired help.'

'Yes, well,' said Charlie defensively, 'the place only comes alive when the children are home. Anyway, I know someone who could help you.'

She explained about Hetty, and how the girl wasn't as bad as folk thought.

'Will you give her a chance, Ma? She's honest at heart, and I know it would be good for her.'

Amelia nodded.

'All right, Charlie. If that's what you want I'll give her a month's trial.'

Charlie felt relieved, and pleased for Hetty's sake.

'I'll let her know, soon as I can.'

On Amelia's insistence Charlie made more effort over her appearance before she returned to Lackford Hall. She was glad she did, for she was immediately summoned to the library.

Sir Alan regarded her politely, his hands clasped beneath his chin.

'How did you enjoy Whit Tuesday, Miss Freer?'

'Very much, thank you, sir.' Apart from Will, she added to herself as she curtsied. 'It was the best I can remember.'

'Oh?'

There was humour in his appraisal, and she blushed to think she'd danced, albeit briefly, in his arms.

'My mother's new venture was a success; she wants to expand her business.'

Charlie was pleased by his reaction.

'Really? That's excellent. We must secure more orders from Bridport, and Dorchester, perhaps London, too. Hmph—' He coughed politely, the signal to change the subject. 'The reason I wished to see you, is to inform you of my daughter's birthday.'

'Oh, yes,' said Charlie eagerly. 'She'll be thirteen, in July.'

'Indeed, the thirtieth.'

'She will be home from school in time?'

'Yes,' he became businesslike, 'so we must make preparation.'

Of course, thought Charlie wryly. His 'we' never failed to amuse her. Aloud, she said: 'I do hope Miss Isobel will like her room, and sir, shouldn't we allow her to choose her own birthday dress?' If he could say 'we' why shouldn't she?

'That will be your first duty as her chaperon, Miss Freer. You and she are to shop in Dorchester as soon as she's home. There won't be time to employ a seamstress.'

'Her chaperon!'

He seemed not to notice her surprise for he added; 'Which reminds me, how are you getting on with the material I gave you?'

'Oh, quite well, sir. I have my housekeeper's dress cut out and ready to sew.'

'Good, good. But I want you to have your best dress ready for Miss Isobel's return. She is of an age now to adopt more ladylike pursuits; I

149

cannot always accompany her.'

'No, of course not, sir.' Charlie smothered an urge to giggle, he was so pompous at times. Isobel would be just as happy paddling barefoot on the shore with Hugh, as dressed up for social calls and museum visits. He was still speaking.

'I'll get Ponsonby to collect details of excursions and concerts. Between us we'll draw up a schedule.'

'What about her birthday, sir? Will there be entertainments?'

His raised eyebrow caused Charlie to bite her lip, and lower her eyes. She was being too forward again.

'I was coming to that, Miss Freer. As a woman, you know the female mind, and I was hoping you could see to that.'

Whoops! Charlie sucked in her breath and met his eyes again. What did she know about young ladies' birthdays? Ma would know, she thought in relief.

'Yes sir, I believe I shall cope,' she said, pretending assurance. 'But you will be there, won't you, sir?'

He frowned slightly.

'What makes you think I might not?'

Charlie looked down at her feet.

'Nothing, sir. I just feel she misses you more than you might think. She needs you more than ever now she's growing up.'

She was thinking of Dick. The slightest encouragement from the precocious Isobel . . .

'Thank you for your advice, and concern, Miss Freer,' Sir Alan's voice was as soft as his tone was curt. 'I believe I know where my duty lies.'

'Yes, sir.' Fearing she'd offended him, she missed the glow in his eyes.

'Now, two of my sisters are coming from London with their families, including the widowed niece. I want you to be especially attentive to her.'

'I'll do my best sir.' There were limits to her capabilities!

As usual he seemed to guess her thoughts.

'We are a little tired, are we not, after last night? There is much to do, but you must make the dress your first concern. That is all.'

Charlie had looked forward to having more spare time with the light evenings; now she realized her mistake. With the master's relatives coming in six weeks, and Isobel's birthday to organize, she'd hardly find time to sew, let alone study. Two dresses still to make!

Puttin' on airs an' graces, Will had accused. Hardly that!

150

She forgot her worries. Leisure hours were scarce but she made time to go home, and while Amelia helped with the dressmaking they discussed ideas for Isobel's party.

The last two weeks in June were wet, so that haymaking was delayed. Concerned for the coming harvest, Sir Alan rode around his estate to visit his tenant farmers.

Charlie busied herself with the birthday arrangements. She wrote to Isobel, to suggest a beach-party and picnic, weather permitting, and asked Ponsonby about hiring a conjurer for the evening as a surprise. She was sealing the letter when she remembered she hadn't spoken to Hetty.

Early next morning Cook saw Charlie take off her apron.

'You ain't goin' out, are you, with so much to do yer?'

'I have to give Mr Crabb a letter before he takes the post to Frometown,' Charlie told her. 'It's for Miss Isobel, and must go today.' Mrs B couldn't argue with the master's business.

'Well, you better hurry back,' said Mrs Biggins grudgingly.

'I'll be as quick as I can.' Charlie didn't say she intended to visit Biddy Cauldon's on the way back. That would be an ordeal in itself, without having to endure Cook's grumbling as well.

CHAPTER THIRTEEN

WILL scrambled up the slide to help Sandy off-load the stone just hauled up. It was the sort that would split, for roof tiles, and while Sandy began to knock in the wedges, Will stretched, and rolled his shoulders to ease the strain in his back.

As he wiped his brow with his neckerchief he stared down into the valley, and recognized the tall lean figure of Simon Maltravers riding their way.

'Sandy, leave that, and take these chisels down to Sam Roper. While you're there, go an' see Henry Warren. Tell him I need to hire his team, there'll be a load ready this afternoon.'

'Right, Will.' Errands made a welcome break, so Sandy jumped at the chance.

Aping a man's grunt, he hoisted the toolbag on to his back, and set off with long strides.

Will watched him go, and saw Maltravers nod at the boy as they passed on the track.

'A good lad,' remarked Maltravers as he dismounted.

'He's strong an' willing,' said Will. 'He'll do. What've you got for me today?'

Maltravers told him a list of names, receivers of contraband. It was a good ruse to hide a few bales and barrels in the wagon beneath a layer of stone, to be left at certain back doors.

'You can trust the lad?' asked Maltravers, referring to Sandy again.

'Oh aah,' said Will. 'I treat'n fair, an' he says here's better than the orphanage. Does as he's bid.'

'Good, I'll leave you to it, then.'

Will nodded. He had no liking for his granddad's partner, nor any use for idle chit-chat.

*

The Swanwick district had so far escaped the unrest of other places; Sir Alan had little use for newfangled machinery that caused rioting, and firing of haystacks. As long as his farms had enough manual labour to cope with the harvest he was satisfied. But if the weather didn't improve as the summer progressed, he might have to think about it. Machines could do the work in half the time if a dry spell was unlikely to last.

This morning, as he inspected the crops, he was considering the idea of a threshing machine, when he caught sight of Miss Freer running down the hill. She had a letter clutched in her hand.

'Hmph,' he muttered. As housekeeper she had authority to send Dick, or even Hart on such an errand, particularly as it looked as though it could rain again at any minute.

Hearing a horse behind him, he turned. It was Maltravers; he too had seen Charlie.

'Your housekeeper is fleet of foot, Nephew.'

'Morning, Uncle. I believe she has a letter for Isobel concerning birth-day arrangements.' For some reason Sir Alan found himself on the defensive. She probably deserved a break from routine, he had rather burdened her. 'My sisters from London are joining us for the occasion, so there is much to do.'

Maltravers sniffed. 'A good test of her capabilities. I wonder how she'll handle herself with them, eh?'

Sir Alan gave his uncle a tight little smile, being curious himself to observe his sisters' reaction to Miss Freer. Would they condone her intimacy with his children?

'I hope she will receive their approval. She gets on with Isobel and Hugh better than I expected—'

He didn't see the shadow that flickered over his uncle's face, and was taken aback by Maltravers' interruption.

'Oho, not getting ideas, are you, Nephew? No doubt she'd be a delectable little dish to bed, but not to wed. A bit beneath you, I'd say.'

Sir Alan coughed in embarrassment, but tried to make light of his uncle's remark.

'Ha, it would be nice to have a mother for my children, but I fear I'm too old for such a tender young virgin.'

He was startled by the older man's snort of ridicule.

153

'You think she's a virgin? With a lusty, handsome groom like yours around? I've seen them a bit too close for comfort at times, like coming home from Dorchester market—'

'Really, Uncle, I don't think—'

'You'd be surprised what servants get up to while the master's away.'

Sir Alan knew his uncle's flair for making disturbing remarks, but his last words went too far. He had wondered about Miss Freer and his groom, for he'd seen them in conversation. Miss Freer seemed completely at ease with the young man, but he had never thought she would allow Dick Farmer to have his way with her.

He was about to object, but Maltravers was still trying to demolish the young woman's character.

'How old is she, almost eighteen?' Maltravers sneered. 'I hear she enjoyed herself at the Whitsun dance with the young orphan lad you found, to help her brother. Likes 'em young, I'll warrant.'

Riled though he was, Sir Alan recalled the way Miss Freer looked at him during the dance. Her eyes had glowed, and her gaze had never left his face.

He knew she had little respect for Maltravers; the incident in his dining-room at Easter proved that. His uncle was having a bout of sour grapes, and he had no wish to continue this conversation.

'I expect you're right, Uncle. She's like a mother to the children in her capacity as housekeeper. Perhaps I should expect no more than that.'

Abruptly he bid Maltravers 'Good-day', and rode on his way, aware that his usual calm had deserted him. His uncle had spoiled his morning, and he groaned with despair. Only four years off forty, and she not yet twenty.

Miss Freer seemed mature beyond her years, and was no loose woman, even if she did have an eye for Dick. Leaving him aside, just suppose he took it into his head . . . She was fond of the children, and he could give her security – but would his family approve?

She had a way with her, and just as she'd won over his children she might do the same with his sisters, if he decided that was what he wanted. *But would she have him?*

Oh, dammit it all to hell! He spurred his horse, and galloped the long way home.

Maltravers rode by Biddy Cauldon's cottage on his way home, never dreaming that the girl who reminded him so much of Amelia Warren at that age was inside, talking to the old crone.

'Why should my Hetty go an' work fer your Ma, when she got 'nuff to do yer?'

Charlie had expected an argument, but it took all her self-control not to lose patience. She no longer feared Biddy, and noted the flicker of respect in the old woman's one visible eye.

'It will do Hetty good to get out and meet people,' she said firmly, 'and it wouldn't do your reputation any harm.'

'Yer, what d'you mean? There's nothin' wrong with me reputation, I be respected—'

' 'Tain't respect, Graan,' put in Hetty. She felt brave in Charlie's presence. 'Folks is afeared o' you. They'd like you more if they saw me earnin' me livin'. I can do the housework an' the garden in th' evenings.' She hesitated, then added: 'You never let me help with your potions anyway. Don't you want folks to like you?'

'No, I don't. I'd rather they kept their distance.'

Charlie was all politeness, but it was hard work.

'Mrs Cauldon, surely you want Hetty to better herself? She can't even read and write—'

'Don't 'ee go givin' she any ideas above herself,' whined Biddy. 'You cain't make a silk purse from a sow's ear.' She turned her head sharply, so that her uncovered eye was fixed on Hetty's face. 'All right, she can go, but she better remember her place.' She wagged a finger and added; 'I know what I'm talkin' about!'

Charlie knew what Biddy meant. Education made peasants realize how poor they were, and that's when trouble started.

'I understand,' Charlie said. 'As long as Hetty can keep house and cook, and has skill with her hands, she'll be fine.'

Biddy gave her a grudging nod, then turned on Hetty.

'You mind you behave yerself, maid, and make sure you bring all yer earnings back 'ome!'

'Yes, Gran.' Hetty beamed. A proper job! 'Thanks Charlie.'

'Come and see Ma tomorrow, then.' Charlie turned to Biddy. 'Thank you, Mrs Cauldon, Ma will appreciate this.'

She grinned as she let herself out. The old woman was scowling at her, but she didn't care.

Half-way through July the skies cleared, promising a fine hot spell.

Charlie prayed it would last for Isobel's birthday. She'd been busy, but her new dress was ready for its final fitting, and she meant to take it home to her ma the next day.

But in the morning, Mrs Biggins was frantic.

'Maisie's took sick, and I got all me summer preservin' to do.'

Hart the gardener had brought in enough raspberries and strawberries to make jams and delicious desserts. Which meant beating lots of egg-whites to make meringues, the Master's favourite.

'You'll have to help me,' Cook demanded. 'Them kids'll be home soon, and everything's got to be ready for her *ladyship*'s birthday. There's still the cake to decorate.'

'How ill is Maisie?' Charlie doubted the girl was really ill, just lazy.

'Ill 'nuff,' sniffed Mrs Biggins. 'Silly bitch come in all wet through t'other night, after chasin' that Dick. I hope she ain't gettin' th' influenza – or worse. 'Twould be a fine to-do if we was all to get it!'

Charlie thought Cook was merely panicking, with so much to do, and went to see Maisie for herself. Yet she crossed her fingers as she ran up the back stairs. Squire had said the cholera and smallpox were contained, but influenza could be as serious.

The maid had a fit of vomiting as Charlie entered the attic dormitory, but said she felt better afterwards. Perhaps it was just something she'd eaten. She came down later and helped in the kitchen while Charlie hurriedly attended to her own duties.

Next morning, Maisie was again absent, and while Charlie did her best to fill in, she and Cook both knew they couldn't go on this way.

' 'Tis your job, as housekeeper,' said Cook, 'to inform the master.'

Reluctantly, Charlie went to see Maisie first, and was alarmed by her pallor.

'Maisie, I must tell Squire you're ill, I think he should send for the doctor.'

'Don'ee tell him, Charlie,' moaned Maisie. ' 'Twill be more'n me job's worth.' She was almost in tears with no sign of her usual antagonism. 'I ain't really sick – nothin' Biddy Cauldon cain't cure. Will you go an' see her for me, please Charlie? Tell her I need the same as before—'

'You've had this trouble before?' cried Charlie, perplexed. 'I've never seen you like it.'

' 'Twas afore you come here.'

Maisie looked down at the coverlet, and Charlie suddenly understood. Why else had the girl been so desperate to find Dick that she must go out in the pouring rain?

'Maisie, you're not ill, are you. Tell me the truth or I can't help you. Has Dick got you with child?'

Maisie nodded sullenly.

'We both got drunk at Whitsun, an' spent the night – everybody was tipsy, an' nobody would have known—'

'Except that you've fallen.'

'Nobody needs t' know,' pleaded Maisie, 'if you get me the stuff from Biddy.'

Charlie ignored this remark.

'Has Dick mentioned marriage to you?'

'No, an' I don't want him to think I done it on purpose to make him marry me.' Maisie began to cry.

'Doesn't he know about the child?'

Maisie shook her head.

'No. That's why I got so wet, 'cause I couldn't find him. I thought if I asked him to go to Biddy, he'd ask why, an' he might just say he'd marry me . . .' She broke off in another burst of weeping. 'I don't know what'll happen if I don't get rid of it, 'cause then the master will have to know.'

Charlie sighed. Poor, foolish Maisie, and she could strangle Dick. She had little to thank Maisie for, but she didn't want to see the girl put out with no references, and it would be tragic to get rid of the baby when they should so obviously be married. When Sir Alan knew, it could mean the sack for Dick, and the workhouse for Maisie. Unless . . .

She had spoken truly when she told Dick the master valued him. If the groom could be persuaded of his duty to marry Maisie, and with Sir Alan's blessing . . .

It would mean extra work during Maisie's confinement, for Sir Alan wasn't likely to employ anyone to fill in; but that was months away, and there were some big 'ifs' to deal with.

Charlie's imagination prompted her wishful thinking. Dick would no longer be living over the stables, and one must hope that he would be less keen to help the smugglers.

Then there was Isobel. She would have more respect for Dick as someone's husband, and a father to boot.

'I'll see what I can do,' she told Maisie, resting a hand on the girl's shoulder, 'but you must trust me.'

As Maisie dried her eyes, Charlie went out, and closed the door behind her.

She clenched her fists; she had no intention of seeking the kind of help Maisie meant. The master must be told, which meant taking risks on behalf of both Dick and the maid. Oh dear, there were so many ifs and buts running through her mind.

'Please God,' she breathed, 'let me get it right.'

She was steeling her nerves when she met Sir Alan at the bottom of the stairs.

'Miss Freer,' he began, sounding puzzled, 'last night you were late clearing the dinner dishes, and this morning I find my breakfast table somewhat haphazardly laid.'

Charlie smoothed her skirt with damp hands.

'I'm sorry, sir, it won't happen again.'

Her courage was failing just when she needed her wits about her. Before she had a chance to consult him about Dick and Maisie, he was finding fault with her over petty things. She forced herself to look at him, and saw he was more concerned than annoyed.

'You give me no excuse?' He studied her face, 'You look pale, you are well, I hope? Come . . .'

He motioned her to precede him into his study. It was much smaller than the library, and had a more masculine feel. Against one wall was a gun cabinet, and on the black oak desk were his smoking things, and an accounts ledger lying open.

Sir Alan sat down in the leather-upholstered easy-chair behind the desk, and dipped his quill in the crystal inkwell. He wrote a few figures, then without looking up he murmured:

'I am curious to hear your answer, Miss Freer.'

Charlie took a deep breath to summon her courage.

'Oh, me? I'm quite well thank you, sir. It's just that there's been so much to do, and Maisie has been – er unwell these two days past . . .'

She was unprepared for his almost violent reaction.

He looked up sharply, dropped his pen, and stood up.

'Maisie unwell – what do you mean? You've seen her vomiting? Has she a headache, or sore throat? Send for Doctor Simpson, immediately!' Pumping clasped hands behind his back he went to the window. 'If it's cholera, or smallpox we shall have to stop Isobel and Hugh coming home. How dashed inconvenient. Blast!'

He turned to see Charlie staring dumbly at him. She hadn't moved. He glowered at her.

'Well, don't stand there, send Dick for Doctor Simpson, then pack a bag so I can leave at once. I'm taking no risks if it's contagious. I'll go to the children and break the news myself!'

'Oh sir,' cried Charlie, plaintively. All her prepared explanations receded, yet, though he looked distraught, he seemed more disappointed than angry.

'Sir, I must speak to you first.' Her anxiety made her words sound like a command, and caused him to blink.

'There's no time to waste,' he snapped. 'It had better be important – is it?'

'Yes sir,' she stated, more firmly than she felt. 'It does have a bearing on what you will do next. You can depend upon it that Maisie's health poses no threat to anyone.' She nodded her head. 'But I do think the doctor should see her,' she added.

'Is she ill or not?'

'Sir, there's no need for alarm. I beg you, hear me out. I know what's wrong with Maisie, and I swear it is not contagious.'

He continued to glower at her, but sat down as she asked. He'd looked forward to bringing the children home, with her here, and for his sisters to meet her. Easter had been ruined by snow, and if he missed the summer with Isobel, who was no longer a child, he feared the estrangement that could grow between them.

'Well?'

Nervously Charlie laced her fingers before her breast in an effort to keep looking at him.

'Sir, there's something I've longed to suggest for some time, but until now, well, it's not my place to do so . . .'

'What the devil are you talking about? Get to the point, woman!'

Charlie was startled into boldness by his tone.

'Sir, I wish you might use your imagination.' He probably thought she was spouting nonsense, but at least she had his full attention. She licked her dry lips. Please God he would see things her way. She began again, stumbling over her words.

'Sir, I have been aware for some time that Maisie and Dick, that they are – Oh sir, they should be married. You mustn't blame them, they're both orphans, with no one to care for them.'

Charlie's hands fell to her sides, and she looked down at her feet.

'They . . . it seems they both had too much to drink at the Whit Tuesday fair,' she finished lamely.

For a full minute she endured his ominous silence while he absorbed her meaning, then, fearful of his reaction, she slowly raised her eyes.

To her surprise and relief, his expression softened, as though a great weight had been lifted from his shoulders.

'Miss Freer . . .' As he relaxed, his blue eyes regained their kindness. 'Am I to understand that my groom has got the kitchen-maid in the family way?'

She bit her lip, and gave him a tiny nod.

'Good lord!' His hand slapped the desk as he stood up. 'If they were ready for marriage, why didn't they come to me? And you,' his voice rose ever so slightly, 'my housekeeper, say you've known for some time. Only now you tell me, *you* think they should marry!'

The change in his attitude encouraged her.

'Please sir, I think they would have married long ago, except that Dick is . . . that is, he fears commitment.'

Oh dear, that wasn't right either. The master was frowning again.

'You seem to know him very well?'

'I've known him longer than Maisie,' she said, pursuing his better mood, 'and when I accompanied him to Dorchester market, he hinted that he was afraid to marry—'

'You mean the subject cropped up between you, just like that?'

'Y-yes sir.' Puzzled by his sarcastic tone, she continued doggedly with her explanation. The damage was done now, and all she wanted was his goodwill towards Maisie and Dick.

'I felt I had the right to tell him that I thought Maisie would make him a good wife. I – I knew she loved him, you see sir . . .'

She paused, praying he wasn't even further offended.

'Go on,' he prompted quietly.

'Dick said he didn't want to marry, he didn't want children in case they became orphans like him,' she floundered. 'He -er, lacks confidence, sir, and I think they should marry, because the responsibility, and having his own cottage would be good for him. I-I know you value him, sir. He is good at his work.'

Sir Alan remained silent, and she feared she'd gone too far. There seemed nothing left but to plead her cause.

'Oh, sir, Maisie is so worried. All she can think of is to get rid of the baby.' Charlie gulped the sob that rose in her throat at the thought. 'If

160

they married they would gain self-respect, and . . . Sir?'

His face remained expressionless.

'Yes?'

Her words came in a rush.

'If I might say so, sir, it seems to me that Maisie's . . . condition . . . is good news compared to our earlier fears.'

She dared to use 'our' in accordance with his 'we'.

At last she detected a glint of humour in his eyes.

'Ha! Looking at it that way. I admit it is a relief. It would please you then, Miss Freer, if this outrageous pair were to marry?'

Was he mocking her? Not in a cruel way, certainly. She smiled with relief, and pleasure.

'Oh, yes sir. And as I said, I'm sure they'd have married before if . . .'

He gave her one of his rare boyish grins.

'Quite the little match-maker, aren't you? I'll give Dick's confidence a boost right now, the rogue shall marry the girl whether he will, or no.'

He would have swept past Charlie, but she stepped in front of the door.

'Sir?' He stopped, eyebrows raised, his wide blue eyes entrancing her.

'Please sir, neither of them knows I have come to you. Maisie believes I am gone on – on a quite different errand.'

His expression flickered with quick understanding, and when he put his hands on her shoulders, their warm firm touch sent a thrill of pleasure and reassurance through her.

'Rest assured, Miss Freer, I shall respect your confidence.'

He went out, leaving her bewildered, and elated.

He'd taken the news far better than she dared hope, she'd never seen him look so pleased.

She would have been more surprised could she see him stride across the stable-yard in search of Dick. Sir Alan rubbed his hands together, threw back his head, and laughed aloud.

The day Sir Alan went to meet the children, Charlie wore her new housekeeper's dress. Its colour, midnight blue, suited her, with her grey eyes and dark, almost black hair. A neat white apron emphasized her narrow waist.

She handed the squire his hat and cape, and saw approval in his eyes.

'Very nice, Miss Freer. I'm glad you were able to put the material to such fitting use. What of the other dresses?'

'One is ready, sir, the other almost.' She curtsied to hide the smile she couldn't suppress.

Dick pulled up outside the open front door in the immaculately prepared carriage-and-pair. He gave Charlie a cheery nod, and winked.

She hadn't heard what had taken place between him and Squire the other day, but within an hour he'd delivered Sir Alan's message to Dr Simpson. As soon as the doctor had confirmed Maisie's condition Charlie escorted Dick to the attic on the master's orders, where she left him to propose to Maisie.

The maid and groom became different people. Charlie let Maisie think Dick had plucked up courage to speak to Squire at last, and a light, happy atmosphere settled between them.

When Maisie asked what had come over her beloved, Charlie shrugged.

'I never spoke to Dick,' she said truthfully, but she wasn't going to let on she'd taken the matter into her own hands and spoken to the squire. This was a chance for Dick to rise in Maisie's esteem.

Dick and Maisie visited the parson to set a date for the wedding at the end of August, which allowed time for the banns to be read. They then went to inspect the empty cottage Sir Alan allotted them.

Now Charlie's attention was absorbed with Isobel's birthday. Everything was ready, and so far the weather held. Isobel's latest letter was full of enthusiasm for Charlie's plans, and Sir Alan's two sisters from London were due to arrive the day before, on 29 July.

Charlie tried to dismiss her apprehension over their coming, and hoped the children would like their new rooms. She decided to go for a walk to settle her nerves in the little time she had left to herself.

She wandered down the lanes, listening to a hundred different bird-songs. The hedgerows were bursting with life; elderberry flowers dominated purple nightshade, and the sweet scent of dog roses and honeysuckle pervaded her senses.

In tranquil mood she recognized real happiness for the first time since her Dad had died. Until now she'd been motivated by obedience to her ma, and concern for her family. Now that so much had happened, she realized she was happy for herself.

Her latest confrontation with the master was still fresh in her mind; she could still feel the warm touch of his hands on her shoulders. She closed her eyes and imagined herself reaching her arms up around his neck, and could almost feel his lips on hers . . .

She opened her eyes, and chided herself. What a romantic fool she was. Squire was just relieved that it was safe for his children to come home, with no danger from any dread disease.

Even if he was fond of her how could she, a poor quarry maid with a brother up to his neck in smuggling, risk shaming him?

CHAPTER FOURTEEN

CHARLIE waited dutifully at the front door as soon as Hart reported the coach coming up the drive. Her fear of the children reverting to their previous attitude was soon dispelled.

Immediately Sir Alan handed Isobel down the young girl rushed to Charlie, barely able to restrain herself.

'Oh, Char- Miss Freer – I've been so looking forward to coming home. You have wonderful ideas for my birthday, I can't wait!'

Charlie laughed, and bobbed a curtsy.

'Thank you, Miss.' She shook hands with Hugh, who was pushing Isobel aside. 'My, how well you both look. I hope you will like your new rooms.'

She had to stop herself from hugging them, for it might be unseemly in front of their father, and when she'd taken their hats and capes, they rushed to inspect their rooms.

Charlie carried the afternoon tea-tray into the sitting-room as they bounded back, followed sedately by Sir Alan. She could see by their faces and his appraising glance that all was well.

She poured the tea and handed round slices of Cook's best fruit-cake, then withdrew, to leave them together.

Dick looked handsome as ever in his Lackford livery as the carriage-and-pair bowled along the highway to Dorchester. There was an element of self-respect in his manner, a noticeable new maturity.

Isobel sat quietly, hands in lap, her delicate little nose tilted, and a pout on her lips. Was she offended, Charlie wondered, because Dick paid her less attention than usual?

Wary of upsetting her, Charlie tried to break the ice.

'Has your father told you the news about Dick, Miss Isobel?'

Isobel stared stubbornly ahead.

'What news about Dick would I be interested in?'

'Well,' said Charlie carefully, 'perhaps he thought it unnecessary to mention that two of his servants are being married, after your birthday.'

'Dick married? Not to you?' As Isobel turned her face towards her, Charlie was surprised by the girl's shocked look. It hadn't occurred to her that anyone could think she was involved with Dick.

'Oh no, to Maisie,' Charlie added gently. 'They've been walking out for some time; your father has given them the old gatekeeper's cottage.'

Isobel appeared to bite back some comment, then feigned indifference.

'No, it was not necessary for Papa to mention the matter, I have more important things to think about. My aunts and uncles and cousins are coming for my birthday. You wait until you see Cousin Robert, he's tall and handsome and extremely wealthy – or will be, one day.'

'I'm sure,' murmured Charlie, not a bit fooled by Isobel's fickleness. She wished she could say something to ease the girl's bruised ego.

Any spite Isobel felt was taken out on the Dorchester shop-assistants. She made them take out every dress, including those on the models in the windows, and showed not the least embarrassment at their barely hidden exasperation.

At last she consented to a gown she and Charlie both liked. Pale blue, with a white sash and a frilled skirt that almost swept the floor, it complemented Isobel's gold-red hair perfectly.

Isobel stood back from the shop mirror, and held up her hair.

'It makes you look quite grown up,' said Charlie. 'I'm sure your father will like it.'

To complete the outfit Isobel chose a white lacy shawl to drape around her shoulders. She looked lovely, and was pleased to let Charlie tell her so.

She behaved impeccably all the way home, and asked Charlie to please hang up her birthday gown while she ran to find her papa.

When the relations arrived the following afternoon, it was Charlie's turn to suffer deflated self-esteem. She stood beside a glowing Maisie, with the other members of staff at the front entrance, while Sir Alan and his children stepped out to greet the two carriages.

Down spilled several youngsters, followed by two aristocratic-looking couples. The last to alight was a young woman dressed entirely in black: clearly the widowed niece.

The two sisters and their husbands were older than Sir Alan, and of the children four were the same age as Isobel and Hugh, and two a little older.

Charlie saw Isobel's eyes on a tall handsome youth about a year younger than herself, and guessed he must be Robert.

After a few minutes of rowdy welcome, the grown-ups made the youngsters stand still to be introduced to the staff, so the servants would know how to address them all.

The young woman in black lifted her veil to reveal flaxen hair beneath her bonnet, as she was introduced as Mistress Sylvia.

Despite the shadows under her blue eyes, Sylvia was extremely pretty, with a slightly turned-up nose giving her a pert expression. She couldn't be past nineteen, and Charlie's heart went out to her.

As they exchanged candid looks, Charlie sensed they would like each other, and smiled warmly.

Sir Alan's elder sister and her husband were Sir Mervyn and Lady Kingsly, Robert's parents, while the younger couple, Mr and Mrs Scott-Wilson, were Sylvia's parents. Sorting out who was who among the younger ones would come gradually.

'I say, all that paint and perfume, how lah-de-dah!' sniggered Maisie, as she and Charlie climbed the stairs laden with capes, hats and small baggage. Dick and Hart brought the heavier luggage.

'Never mind,' replied Charlie. 'You'll look a real lady on your wedding-day, when you become the distinguished Mrs Richard Farmer.'

They both giggled, but Charlie was aware of a sinking feeling in her stomach. Perhaps it was the way the ladies lifted their noses at her, as if they feared an infection. Or was it their use of each others' first names?

She felt a sharp pang when Lady Kingsly observed:

'Alan darling, she's a little young to be your housekeeper, isn't she?'

'I think it's high time Alan thought about marrying again,' said Mrs Scott-Wilson, 'you need a wife to take over the household. You should come to town more often. What do you think, dear?'

Her husband only coughed with embarrassment.

Charlie was glad not to hear any more. Until now she'd ignored the instinct that warned against familiarity with the master. She knew the situation would be different, had he a wife, nor would she have grown so close to the children.

Now it seemed a barrier had distanced her from the Lackfords, marring her happiness of the last few days. The master had no time for his servants other than to give orders, and those testily, if his sisters voiced dissatisfaction. They were aggrieved over his appalling lack of staff.

'There should be a personal maid for Isobel, if not for Hugh,' declared Lady Kingsly.

As it was, the younger children were commandeered to deliver messages, while Charlie and Maisie were run off their feet.

For all that, Isobel's birthday went well. The weather was warm and clear, and the picnic on the beach was a great success.

As well as the usual pork-pies, sausage-rolls and sandwiches, Charlie had Hart light a brazier on which Cook and Maisie grilled fresh fish and meats.

It was a fetching novelty, and Sylvia insisted on helping Charlie serve. She smiled at Charlie when her father nudged Sir Mervyn and muttered:

'We may have underestimated this young housekeeper's efficiency, what!'

Cook said later that she'd overheard Mrs Scott-Wilson praising 'Miss Freer' to her brother. Evidently the change and the sea air were doing her daughter good.

Squire's sisters however, both looked on disdainfully when the children took off their shoes and stockings to paddle in the sea, the girls lifting their skirts to avoid the waves. The boys rolled their trousers up to the knees.

'Really,' sniffed Lady Kingsly, 'they're behaving like common quarry-men when they load the stone boats, and the girls are showing far too much of their legs!'

But even she unbent to laugh at the ensuing mayhem, which involved the children in running-games along the sand, to dry out. Isobel's father and two uncles joined in a cricket match in which anyone was allowed to field the ball rather than let it roll into the sea.

Later, when Charlie helped Isobel to dress for dinner, she gave her a satin gardenia she'd made herself, as a birthday gift. Isobel was delighted, and asked Charlie to fix it in her hair.

'Are you enjoying your birthday, miss?' Charlie asked the obvious because she was pleased to see Isobel so happy. She was pleasantly surprised by the girl's response.

'Oh yes, Charlie, thanks to you,' she breathed.

Touched, Charlie gently admonished her.

'Don't let your aunts and uncles hear you call me Charlie, they might not like it.'

'Pooh,' said Isobel, but she promised for Charlie's sake.

It was good to see so many happy young faces at Lackford Hall, though it meant extra work. Charlie and Maisie were kept busy serving all evening, until they cleared up at long last.

The conjurer had finished, and they could hear Sylvia playing the piano in the drawing-room while the older women put the youngsters to bed. The men were smoking their pipes.

Charlie looked at Maisie.

'You must be tired, why don't you go to bed? I'll finish here.'

There was genuine sincerity in Maisie's voice as she thanked Charlie, and accepted the suggestion.

When Master Robert came into the scullery, scavenging for left-overs, Charlie shared a jest with him, then cautiously she said:

'Young mistress thinks very highly of you, Master Robert, I believe you're her favourite cousin.'

She could hardly explain Isobel's recent crush on Dick, so sought another way to protect the adolescent from any further hurt.

'Hah, for the moment at any rate,' said Robert. He grinned. 'No doubt she'll find plenty of beaux on the Continent when she goes to finishing-school next year.' He frowned slightly. 'You seem concerned about her, Miss Freer, almost like a mother.'

'Or an older sister,' said Charlie quickly, to keep the conversation light. 'Gracious, I hope I don't look old enough to be her mother!'

They both laughed until he stopped suddenly, and looked horrified.

'Good lord, you don't think she's in love with me, do you?'

'No, but she may think she is. Even little girls fall in love as soon as they're old enough to tell the difference. They don't consider age, or—'

'Is that so, Miss Freer?'

Charlie almost dropped the pile of dishes she was about to carry to the dining-room. The heady scent of lavender accompanied the scornful sound of Lady Kingsly's voice.

Robert's mother had apparently missed her son and come looking for him. She was clearly displeased to find him and the housekeeper behaving like old friends.

Already flustered, Charlie suffered more acute embarrassment when Sir Alan appeared behind his sister in the doorway.

'Y – yes, your ladyship, that is . . . what I believe,' she somehow managed to stammer.

Lady Kingsly jerked her head so high it was a wonder she could see below her nose.

'What about you, miss? Do you have any marriage plans – perhaps with an older, rich man in mind?'

The thinly veiled accusation annoyed Charlie.

'Oh no, Ma'am. The man I marry would have to be very special to replace my father in my affections.'

She glared defiantly at Lady Kingsly. The woman had insulted her first.

Sir Alan cleared his throat, and held out an arm to his nephew.

'Come Robert, let's join the others in the drawing-room. Shall you come and play bridge, Beulah?'

Lady Kingsly glanced at him over her shoulder, then pulled herself up to her full height.

'In a moment Alan,' she said haughtily, and turned back to Charlie. Her voice rose an octave.

'It has to be said, Miss Freer, your handling of Isobel's birthday was excellent. One cannot help but wonder how you came by your abilities.'

She raised an eyebrow, her remark being more in the nature of a question.

Charlie's pride came to the fore, the woman was saving face.

'I have my mother to thank, your ladyship,' she answered, in a low, calm voice. 'She had a lady's education.'

'Well then,' said Lady Kingsly, 'it's a pity your mother married beneath herself, I must say.'

Charlie caught her breath in anger, why should she bother to justify herself? Fortunately, her ladyship lifted her skirts and swept after Sir Alan and Robert.

Inwardly shaking, Charlie went to the dining-room with the pile of dishes.

Meanwhile, in the drawing-room Sylvia was examining some music with her mother. They exchanged knowing looks at Lady Kingsly's pained expression. Something had upset her.

Beulah tut-tutted as Sir Alan handed her a glass of port.

'Really, Alan, you should have more servants. You rely too much on that young miss. If you're not careful you'll be enamoured of her. She's an unsophisticated, fortune-hunting nobody.'

She meant ill-bred, but Miss Freer's lack of sophistication was what Sir Alan liked about her. It was how she'd won over his children, and it gave her that artless ability to stick up for herself.

'Yes,' he murmured, looking over his glass of port at his sister. 'You're half-right, Beulah . . .'

Beulah turned away impatiently.

'You tell him, Mervyn!'

Sir Mervyn, however, had reached the limit of his tolerance of his wife's belligerence. He gave her an aggrieved wag of his head, and looked Sir Alan in the eye.

'Beulah has your interest at heart,' he began, 'The girl's clearly fond of the children, and they of her.' He glanced at his wife. 'You must agree, m'dear, that's no small thing.'

'Hm,' said Lady Kingsly, grudgingly. 'She is also fond of my brother – too fond. Mark my words, Alan, I've seen her eyes following you, even her complexion changes colour when you—'

'Really?' Sir Alan interrupted her, his eyebrows raised humorously. 'How amusing.' He tapped out his pipe. 'I could do worse, Beulah, but you heard what she said about her father. I doubt she'd have me!'

'Really, Alan,' cried Beulah, shocked. 'It is no joking matter!'

'Oh Alan,' said Adèle Scott-Wilson, shaking her head with a smile. 'Stop baiting Beulah.'

'Listen, sisters,' he said, serious now. 'Miss Freer is honest, sincere, and unassuming, and Mervyn is quite right about her and the children. She was in tears when they returned to school last time, and actually reprimanded me when I refused to allow them home for Whitsun.'

He took a pack of bridge-cards from a drawer and began to deal. 'I understand your prejudice against such a one as you imagine, but I can assure you, she's not like that. Her father died last year, and she works hard to help support her family.'

Lady Kingsly sniffed, as she arranged her cards.

'Even so, she's a common peasant and can hardly replace the children's mother.'

Before Sir Alan could mention Miss Freer's aristocratic French connection, Sylvia joined them at the card-table.

'Oh, Aunt Beulah, Miss Freer's no peasant, and what's more she speaks French quite well.'

'French?' Disparagingly.

'Yes, Aunt,' said Sylvia, 'I've heard her practising with Isobel. I believe,' she glanced at Sir Alan, 'Isobel wants to take Miss Freer to the Continent for a chaperon.'

Ignoring her aunt's shocked expression she rushed on: 'Let me tell you what happened. One of the children asked Isobel how she could be friends with a peasant, and – you know how hot-tempered Isobel can be – even though it was her birthday they would have come to blows if Miss Freer hadn't intervened.

'She told them the word peasant comes from the French *paysan* meaning countryside, therefore peasants were just people who lived in the country. Hugh immediately made a joke, saying that you, Uncle Alan, are a wealthy peasant.'

Sylvia waited for the mixed reaction to this remark to die down.

'But Miss Freer forbade him to make such jests, and never at the expense of others. Do you know what she told us then?'

Sylvia's gaze swept the group of adults, her eyes wide with mischief.

'She said that while a peasant is one who works on the land, her folk are an élite. Quarrymen keep their trade within the family, with skills handed down through the generations. Which means they have long pedigrees . . .'

She looked deliberately at her aunt. 'Do you know, Aunt Beulah,' she said casually, 'Miss Freer's family goes right back to the time of William the Conqueror. That's way beyond any of us. Our family's knighthoods were only given after the Civil Wars—'

'How absurd,' said Lady Kingsly, not at all pleased with this unwelcome information. 'The wench is still poor!'

'Well,' said Sylvia airily, 'I wouldn't mind having her for a cousin if—'

'Sylvia!' cried Beulah incredulously. Robbed of speech, she looked distractedly at her younger sister, Mrs Scott-Wilson.

Sylvia's mother was trying to keep a straight face. She eyed her husband, then lightly shook her head at Sylvia, and bent over her cards.

'Let me tell you all something,' put in Sir Alan. 'Miss Freer's grandmother was a wealthy *aristo* who settled here after escaping the dreadful Terror, in Paris. So whatever you think, this quarry maid has breeding and,' he shrugged, 'I know my children are much happier since she's been in my employ.'

'And so are you,' said Mr Scott-Wilson. 'But come, Alan, let's be serious and concentrate on our game.'

So their conversation ran, unbeknown to Charlie who was eating her heart out. She couldn't know that Beulah's interference only made the squire more aware of his feelings towards her.

She'd finished in the dining-room and was passing the main staircase when she heard a 'Psst!'

She looked up and saw Isobel leaning over the banisters.

'I'm not going to bed until you come and say goodnight!'

The girl hissed so loudly that Charlie looked round, fearful the guests might hear. She pretended to make stern agreement, but felt extremely touched.

'Oh Charlie.' Isobel smiled as she settled back on her pillow. 'It's been the best birthday ever!' She reached out and kissed Charlie, who could no longer resist hugging her.

'I'm so glad, dear. Now you must go to sleep.'

She went to check on Hugh. 'Will you do a picnic for my birthday please, Charlie?' he murmured sleepily.

'We'll see, Master Hugh,' said Charlie non-committally. She kissed his forehead, but he was already asleep, a contented smile on his lips. She would point out to him later that his birthday was in the middle of winter.

The warmth of the children's affection eased the overwhelming ache she presently endured. She knew now she was in love with the master, and when at last she climbed into bed, she cried herself to sleep.

In the morning, Charlie tried to think, through a haze of misery. It was foolish to indulge in such romantic feelings towards the squire. She could understand Lady Kingsly's assumption that she was a fortune-hunter.

With a sigh, she resigned herself to Ma's suggestion that she should pay off the debt to Squire, and buy her out of his service.

As soon as his relations left, so would she.

CHAPTER FIFTEEN

IT wasn't difficult to avoid Sir Alan with such a lot to do, so Charlie was surprised when he cornered her two evenings later.

She'd seen him come in from his rounds and had tried to run up the back stairs, but he strode after her without bothering to remove his boots.

'Don't run away, Miss Freer, I'm not contagious!'

Charlie halted on the second stair, and felt herself go red. He knew she was avoiding him.

He placed a hand on the banister rail, and stood with one foot on the bottom stair so that their faces were level. There was a faint smile on his lips.

'Sir?' she said, wondering what could be wrong.

Before she lowered her gaze he saw his eyes darken a shade, just as Beulah had said.

He surveyed her lazily.

'I haven't had time to thank you properly for making such a good job of my daughter's birthday. It was an enviable success.'

'Thank you, sir,' she replied meekly, and hoped for dismissal, but he spoke again.

'The trouble is, I fear, you've started something. Both my children are asking when they might have their next picnic.'

She looked up and caught the glint in his eyes.

'It seems you've given yourself an extra duty, because they say they won't go without you.'

Oh dear, it was the last thing she wished to discuss.

'I – yes, sir,' she faltered. 'Master Hugh asked for a picnic on his birthday. I haven't the heart to remind him it falls in January.'

His smile pierced her like a dart.

'Then we had better pray for a fine winter.'

She only managed a quiver of a smile, for she ought to tell him she wouldn't be here then. She tried to sound casual.

'Perhaps you should plan a picnic after your relations leave. It would make up a little for the children missing their cousins. They are having so much fun.'

'Ye-es,' he agreed. 'You're right, we should leave it for a bit.' He would prefer to have her and the children to himself.

'Might I ask how long your sisters will stay?' she ventured.

'Until they become bored,' he replied. Suddenly he removed his hand from the banister, and stood up straight. 'I wish you goodnight, Miss Freer. Sleep well.'

Barely able to mouth 'goodnight' in return, she fled up the stairs, knowing he stood there watching her.

She slept, but not for a long time, so mixed were her feelings and desires. Never had she wanted so much to stay, yet never wanted more to go home, where life was uncomplicated.

Next morning, the men went riding with Sylvia and the children while the older ladies sat in the shady garden, reading the *Dorset County Chronical* which had just arrived.

Charlie would have to wait until they discarded the newspaper before she could study the advertisements for posts for young ladies. Now that Hetty was working for Ma, she would rather be independent.

As she approached the sisters with their tray of morning coffee she heard them discussing the royal progress in the West Counties.

'Do you see this, Beulah?' Mrs Scott-Wilson indicated a paragraph. 'Their Highnesses are due in Lyme at the end of this week.' She clasped her hands like a young girl. 'Wouldn't it be exciting to see them?'

She smiled at Charlie as she put down the tray, but Lady Kingsly could not resist a sneer.

'Well, their Royal Highnesses aren't likely to come here, to a quarry-stone port.'

'Oh,' said Mrs Scott-Wilson, 'you think they'll continue on around Poole Harbour?'

Lady Kingsly nodded.

'Tell you what, Adèle, would you like to spend some time at Lyme? I remember last summer, we walked out to sea on the Cobb. Most invigorating!'

I wish you would go to Lyme, thought Charlie as she returned to the house. Lady Kingsly was so overbearing, the others would agree to whatever she wished. No one would think she'd been born and bred in Swanwick.

The royal tour was discussed at dinner that night, and as the ladies so desired to see royalty, it was decided they would pack the very next day, and be ready to leave the day after.

A note was sent by special messenger to book rooms at a hotel in Lyme, and Charlie felt an immense wave of relief. Isobel, though, was upset about losing Robert's company. Thank goodness Sir Alan had agreed on a picnic.

The evening before they left, Sylvia came to look for Charlie as she was putting the crockery away. Charlie closed the cabinet door, and stood up, smoothing her dress.

Sylvia smiled shyly.

'Miss Freer, I'd like to say goodbye to you now, in case I don't get a chance in the morning. I enjoyed meeting you, it's lovely to see Isobel and Hugh so happy.'

'Thank you, mistress. They will be sorry to lose their cousins so soon.'

'They'll only miss us for a day or two, I'm sure,' said Sylvia. 'There's plenty to do; they've learned to enjoy themselves, thanks to you.'

'Me, mistress?'

'Oh, Charlie – may I call you Charlie? Miss Freer sounds so pompous. Isobel told me lots about you, now you've always got time to talk to them, and read to them at bed-time.'

There was a yearning in the young widow's eyes, Charlie thought, perhaps for the children she'd been denied.

She wanted to say something to comfort Sylvia, who was young enough to remarry, but knew it wasn't her place.

'As long as you don't let the master hear you call me Charlie, I don't mind.'

'Uncle Alan likes you very well. He says he's never seen his children so happy, and they're much more considerate. He's easier with them, too.'

'I like children, miss,' Charlie said, fighting the pain that Sylvia had unwittingly caused her. 'I hope to get a post as a governess, or a nanny when I leave here—'

'Leave? You mustn't leave, it would break their hearts!'

Charlie smiled wryly.

'I doubt your parents or your Aunt and Uncle Kingsly would agree. I'm afraid they suspect me of having ideas above myself.'

Sylvia put a hand on Charlie's shoulder, and looked at her searchingly.

'Let me tell you something. They think success means money and possessions, but when I see the effect you've had on Uncle Alan and my cousins, I know there is more to it.' She smiled and added: 'I admire you, Charlie, and I know my uncle . . . likes . . . you. It doesn't matter what anyone else thinks . . .'

She broke off awkwardly. 'Charlie, I must go now, but please promise not to make any hasty decisions. I for one should like to see you again.'

She took both Charlie's hands in hers, and Charlie thought how like Sir Alan she was around the eyes. The same clear, blue, candid look.

Sylvia tightened her grip in earnest.

'Don't worry about Aunt Beulah, my parents like you, so don't fret about any of them. They would change their tunes if – Oh, I cannot say . . .' She loosed Charlie's hands and turned to go. 'Just think about Uncle Alan, and my cousins. They need you.'

Charlie swallowed.

'Oh, goodbye, Mistress Sylvia. I hope I see you again, too.'

Later, she tried to soothe Isobel, who was more put out than Hugh by their cousins' departure.

'Why couldn't they have taken me with them to see the Princess,' she pouted. 'When I asked Papa, he said it was best for me to stay here – and I thought he loved me!'

'Your father would be very lonely, Miss Isobel,' said Charlie. 'Whatever you may think, he misses you both while you're away at school, but he wants you to have the best life you can.'

She tilted Isobel's chin, and smiled into her eyes. 'Soon he'll no longer have a little girl, he wants to make the most of your company.'

She told Isobel how disappointed her papa was, not having them home at Whitsun for fear of the illnesses that prevailed.

'He's always so busy,' complained Isobel, with an angry sob.

Charlie hugged her close.

'Try not to mind,' she whispered. 'Your childhood is very precious, and it's such a tiny part of your whole life. Don't blame him, you'll understand one day, I promise.'

'All right, Charlie. I'll believe you, but I shan't be happy tomorrow!'

'No one expects you to be, dear. I hate goodbyes too. Goodnight.'

Early next morning Charlie saw the Lackfords wave farewell to their relations. She felt relieved. and thought she detected something similar in Sir Alan.

They re-entered the house, and the children went to their rooms, leaving her and Sir Alan alone. He seemed quite relaxed, and she thought this might be a good a time to broach the subject of her future.

'Please sir, in a few months my time here will be up . . .'

'You want to leave us?' He regarded her as if puzzled by such an unnatural desire. 'I thought you liked it here. You must realize by now that the position is permanent, if you so wish. Isobel will need a chaperon; wouldn't you like to travel?'

His words tore at Charlie's heart. She gulped, and plunged on.

'Ma – er my mother, says she can pay you off, so I needn't stay until my time is up. Oh . . .' Her eyes widened, imploring him. 'Your sisters are right. The children should not be told what to do by a common quarry maid.'

She stopped, and bit her lip as he murmured:

'Oh, so that's it.'

Next moment he startled her by his sudden sharp tone, and bleak expression. His eyes grew pale.

'Miss Freer, I should be obliged if you would leave my sisters out of it. I cannot accept your mother's offer because I am not willing to release you. The bargain I struck with your brother was that you should work for me for one year. When your time is up – we shall cross that bridge when we come to it.'

'Oh, sir—'

'Don't argue. You're forgetting Dick and Maisie. They're to wed soon, and Maisie's confinement is due in February. No, no. We couldn't possibly manage without you.' He paused, then frowned. 'What has upset you?'

Mercifully, she was saved from having to answer by a shriek from Hugh. He tore along the hall, chased by Isobel.

The squire's expression changed swiftly from irritation to anger.

'What is the meaning of this rumpus?'

'Izzy's after me,' panted Hugh. He threw himself on Charlie as Isobel raced up, scarlet with fury, her fists clenched.

'He keeps teasing me – I'm *not* sweet on Rob!'

They both stopped as they became aware of their father's stern expression.

'Hugh, desist at once, and apologize to your sister!'

The boy feared his father's wrath more than Isobel's, and obeyed immediately.

'I'm sorry, Izzie, I won't do it again.' At least now she couldn't punish him.

As the glare on Sir Alan's face faded, his mouth twisted humorously.

'I have problems of my own,' he told them. 'Miss Freer is tired. Do you agree, children, that she has been working very hard lately, and ought to rest?'

He looked at Charlie, and spoke in that quiet, but persuasive tone she'd first heard when she was hiding in his stable loft. How long ago that day seemed!

'I shall cope with breakfast in the morning,' he said, 'and Isobel shall bring yours upstairs, shan't you, Isobel?'

Both children approved loudly, amused by the idea that they should wait on Charlie.

'I shall like that,' said Isobel, while Hugh immediately intervened.

'Stay in bed all day,' he suggested, 'and I shall bring you luncheon.'

Isobel hooted with laughter.

'You're all so kind,' said Charlie, smothering a sob. Though her nerves were jangling she saw a way of escape and clutched at it. 'Very well, sir, if you say so. In which case I had better make sure everything is ready for tomorrow.'

She bobbed a curtsy, and left them in the hall.

'Why was she so upset?' asked Isobel, who missed nothing. In her most grown-up voice she added: 'Miss Freer does look a bit tired,' and mischievously mimicked her aunts:

'Brother dear, I think it's high time she had a husband to look after her.'

She glanced at her father, knowing she risked rebuke, but he turned to Hugh.

'And what do you think, my son?'

In all innocence the boy replied; 'I think we should marry her, Papa.'

While Isobel shrieked with mirth, Sir Alan smiled indulgently, and patted his son on the head.

The following weekend found the squire supervising the bands of reapers in his cornfields. The sky had clouded, and the sultry air threatened thunderstorms. Because of the bad weather early in the season the harvest was late, and he was anxious it should be brought home before the weather broke. He plied the reapers with ale, and bread and cheese, and promised an extra shilling for working through the weekend.

Aware this would meet with the parson's disapproval, Sir Alan nevertheless attended Sunday morning service with Isobel and Hugh.

Hetty came to church with the Freers. She sat between Amelia and Will, so with Tommy and Sandy there was no room for Charlie. Sir Alan insisted that she should sit in his family pew.

After the first hymn Hugh joined the other youngsters who went out for Sunday school, leaving Charlie with Sir Alan and Isobel.

Charlie saw the heads nodding together, and eyes turned in her direction. Nor did she miss the Maltravers' stares.

Anxiously she glanced at Sir Alan. While an ambiguous smile lifted the corners of his mouth, his eyes gleamed provocatively, as if to say: Let them think what they will.

She found it hard to concentrate on the rest of the service, folk were bound to talk. At least it was out of Maltravers' hands to start rumours.

Charlie felt embarrassed and confused, but gained a measure of comfort when she caught her ma's eye, and saw her proud smile.

When the service was over, Sir Alan said to Isobel:

'I must do the rounds, but I haven't forgotten my promise. We shall picnic next weekend.' He glanced at Charlie. 'Miss Freer will take you for a walk, and I'll be home for luncheon.'

Hugh gave an impatient grunt. 'It's too hot for walking.' Isobel grumbled. She stared moodily after her father.

'I know,' suggested Charlie. 'It's cooler on the river bank. Let's follow it to the wood, then play hide-and-seek in the shade. It's only a short walk home from there.'

'Yes!' shouted Hugh.

'Bags I get to hide first,' Isobel cried, and danced ahead.

'Oh, you always want to go first,' protested Hugh running after her.

Apart from calling out to them not to climb trees in their Sunday clothes, Charlie let them argue it out; it was better than having them miss their cousins.

The river path skirted Biddy Cauldon's garden, then rounded a bend to be swallowed up in the trees. When they reached the abbey ruins the children explored and played their game while Charlie tried to make sense of the overgrown mounds.

Ancient stone steps led up to what once must have been the doorway to a refectory, or a chapel. Half an archway stood sentinel, smothered in ivy. A chapel, she decided, for in the remains of one wall was a piscina niche. Further on, a long hollowed-out stone at shoulder-level was probably a squint, where lepers could watch the sacraments being administered.

The thought of leprosy, and the disfigurements she'd heard it caused, made her shudder. She had a creepy sensation that someone was watching, then she heard a twig crack. She jumped, and whirled around. All she could see was a low branch stirring. It couldn't have been the breeze, for on such a hot day there was hardly a breath of wind.

'Boo!' Suddenly, Hugh popped his head up from behind the stone altar which still remained.

'Oh, you rascal, you startled me!' Charlie's heart thumped against her ribs, and she laughed shakily as Isobel appeared.

'It's a jolly good hiding-place, it's hollow,' Hugh told her. 'Charlie – er – Miss Freer, come and play with us?' He begged with a warmth she couldn't resist.

'Very well, go and hide both of you; I'll count to fifty.'

As she shut her eyes and counted, the feeling of being watched persisted. She made her voice louder as she neared fifty, then yelled: 'I'm coming!'

Hugh's sniggering gave him away. He helped her find Isobel.

'It's not fair, you looked together,' she promptly declared.

'I think it's time we went back for luncheon,' said Charlie.

'Just one more go,' pleaded Hugh. 'You hide this time, and we'll look together. Then it won't take long, and that'll make it fair for you, won't it, Izzy?'

'We'll only count to thirty,' shrilled Isobel, 'and save time!'

They turned their backs on Charlie to chant in loud unison.

Charlie ran into the chapel, and squeezed into the hollow part behind the altar.

She'd deliberately chosen the place Hugh recommended so they would find her easily, but hearing their voices get louder then fade, she knew they would search everywhere else first.

'Come on, you artful brats,' she muttered: her limbs were getting cramped.

She stretched her legs to ease them, and one foot came in contact with something square and solid. It moved too easily to be a stone. Curious, she manoeuvered the object with her feet, and brought it out to see what it was.

Caked in black mould, it looked heavy, but felt surprisingly light. At first it was difficult to see that it was a casket, until she realized it might be tarnished silver.

A silver casket! She suddenly remembered the one Sir Alan had mentioned. For the first time for days, her thoughts turned to the children's mother, Maltravers, and the strange letter.

The ruins were in a direct line between Lackford Hall and Underhill Manor, with the path hidden by trees. Could this spot have been the lovers' trysting place?

The casket was locked, and when she shook it something rustled inside. Did it still contain Lady Helen's love-letters?

The children chose that moment to find her.

'We know you're in here, Charlie Freer,' Isobel sang out cheekily.

'You're trapped!' shouted Hugh, gleefully triumphant.

Swiftly Charlie wrapped her shawl round the box, and in the ensuing horseplay of being dragged from hiding, managed to tuck the bundle beneath her arm.

The path was narrow, so Hugh marched ahead, being a famous explorer leading the way, while Isobel fell in behind Charlie. Presently, as the path widened, she put her arm through Charlie's.

'You're the next best person to be with when Papa can't come,' she said affectionately.

Charlie was touched; it was true, the children needed her.

'Thank you, Miss Isobel.'

And that was how Sir Alan saw them, as he returned from his rounds. They emerged from the wood, arm in arm.

Isobel loosed herself, and ran with Hugh to greet their father.

Sir Alan slipped down off his horse, to lead it, and walk the rest of the way with them, while they told him breathlessly what fun they'd had.

'I'm glad you enjoyed yourselves,' he said, 'but go and tidy up quickly for luncheon.'

Charlie hurried to her room and put the casket beneath her bed to examine later.

Sunday afternoon, a time of rest for everyone, was very hot. Even the toilers in the fields would be dozing in the shade of the nearest tree or hedgerow.

Charlie was thankful to be alone in her room with her disturbing thoughts.

She had fallen in love with the master. It wasn't the first time a fool-ish maid had done so.

She'd heard of country squires who dallied with their maids, only to tire of the sport, which it was to them. She could imagine Simon Maltravers as such, but not Sir Alan.

It was impossible to rest, so she took a cloth and some silver-cleaning powder from the pantry, and began to clean the casket. It *was* tarnished silver.

She polished hard until it gleamed, thinking how every step she took was fraught with problems.

She'd promised to return the casket to the master, but it would be difficult to explain how she'd found it in the monastery ruins. He would think someone had stolen it, and was bound to suspect Maisie or Hetty. And she couldn't let him find the letters, if they were inside.

She looked through all the keys on her housekeeper's chain. None was small enough, so she tried the one from a locking drawer in her dressing-table. It wasn't a perfect fit, but after some jiggling it turned reluctantly. Holding her breath, she slowly opened the lid.

Inside were several musty-smelling sheets of paper. Her fingers trembled as she examined them, for she was interfering in something that was none of her business.

She flung a hand across her mouth to stifle a cry.

The letters all began: *Darling Helen*, . . . he missed her . . . he looked forward to their meetings, and each was signed *Your loving Simon*. Another, and another . . .

Immersed in the letters, Charlie vaguely heard the insistent ringing of the front door bell. Maisie would answer it.

A short while later she became aware of footsteps running upstairs, and hurrying along the landing to her room. Hastily she shoved the letters back into the casket and relocked it. She barely had time to push it under her bed before Isobel burst in without knocking.

'Charlie – Miss Freer, I've a message from Papa . . .'

The girl was so excited that Charlie overlooked her lack of manners.

'Sit down, Isobel, and tell me calmly—' she began, but Isobel didn't calm down.

'A messenger just called,' she gasped breathlessly, 'all the way from Bridport, where the Princess Victoria is expected tomorrow—'

Witheringly, Charlie interrupted the overwrought girl.

'Isobel, it's marvellous news for Bridport, but how does the royal progress affect us, that you should be in this state? And what am I supposed to do about it?'

Isobel burst into peals of hysterical laughter. Charlie feared she would have to slap her, and gripped the girl's shoulders.

'Isobel, pull yourself together, or I shall have to call your papa!'

'Dear Charlie,' gasped Isobel, and took a deep breath. 'Their Royal Highnesses will come through Frometown, not Poole. Then they are coming here – to *Swanwick*! They intend to spend the night at the Manor Hotel and take ship on the morning tide for the Isle of Wight. The royal yacht will pick them up – Charlie – we are the first to know!'

Now Charlie was excited. She clapped her hands over her mouth, twirled around, and fixed her eyes on Isobel.

'And you, miss? Shall you meet her? She is but one year older than you. Oh, perhaps the rest of us will see her pass by. What a wonderful occasion for our town!'

They gazed rapturously at each other, until Charlie came to her senses.

'Your papa asked you to come and tell me? What does he . . . ?'

Isobel grinned wickedly. 'Papa says it's my duty to be part of the Princess' welcome, as a flower-girl. All our presentable young ladies will be flower-girls, and I said I wouldn't, unless you can be one too!'

'Isobel! How could you! And he . . . ?'

Isobel nodded, her face full of happy mischief.

'He thinks it's a good idea, and asked me to tell you, while he goes to see your mother—'

'My mother? Sir Alan has gone to see Ma?' Charlie opened and shut her mouth. 'Isobel, if this is a practical joke—'

'Oh no, Miss Freer, indeed it is not.' Isobel spoke soberly now. 'Papa says we must present the Princess with a gift. Something of local interest, and useful, for a souvenir. He will ask Mrs Freer to make a special straw bonnet, fit for a queen – well, a princess anyway. You, dear Miss, Charlie, must make sure we are properly attired. Papa said something about not having seen you in your new dress.'

'Oh, dear God,' said Charlie, at a loss for words. 'Let's hope the weather's fine.'

The silver casket lay forgotten under Charlie's bed. In the hustle and bustle of the next forty-eight hours, she suffered many vague misgivings; her life had become complicated. It seemed the more she struggled to be free of Sir Alan, the more involved she became.

One grim thought penetrated her excitement and confusion. Life had a horrid habit of dealing a blow to knock you down, just when you thought you were doing well.

CHAPTER SIXTEEN

THE following afternoon Henry Warren climbed the hill to Amelia's cottage. The deeply rutted track would not permit a horse and carriage, and the merchant was no horseman.

The heat of early August made the slope seem steeper than ever. He removed his stovepipe hat to mop his brow, and fingered his stiff white shirt collar.

'I hope she's home,' he muttered.

As the track evened out he walked more easily. He straightened his hat, and stuffed away his handkerchief, and his thoughts made him forget the heat.

Timing safe landings was tricky. It was easier in the old days when the customs service was short of good men; what with the wars against America and France, then the Turks, the navy needed them all. But since the great war with Boney, the Royal Navy had gradually taken over the coastguard service. It was as difficult to avoid the authorities' cutters at sea these days, as it was to hide the goods on land.

The preventive men had lately found so many of the best hiding-places that Warren guessed there must be an informant at work.

He checked, and double-checked all his arrangements with Maltravers and Captain Ford, and laid second plans in case something went wrong. This meant extending their code of signals, another aggravation.

Peace had ruined the trade. The government was always reducing taxes on something, and had blockaded the Channel. There was a price on the heads of the most wanted smugglers, and many a boat had to cut and run, to escape the fast navy cutters.

Illicit cargo was tossed overboard, and the only way to make any profit was to deliberately sink the goods, tied to marker buoys. Captain Ford would then boldly 'discover' the tubs, under a watching coastguard's spyglass, and hand them in at whichever port he was delivering stone. At least he and his crew shared the £30 salvage reward, and a portion of the auction money. And Warren kept sweet with the authorities.

No, smuggling wasn't what it used to be. He remembered the trade in its heyday, when Amelia was tiny. Customers actually came to the caves along the coast to buy the cheap goods. Now it all had to be kept under wraps.

So far he was above suspicion, as was his coal store which was handy to the landing-slips. It faced the bay, so was in full view of any man on the look-out for contraband.

At the back of the coal store, the empty premises he had done up for Amelia fronted the street near the Manor House Hotel. Beneath this shop, a cellar connected with the coal store. It was known only to himself and a few trusted employees.

The shop was ready, and the sooner Amelia opened up, the better. Who would suspect a shop full of women's bonnets?

Henry Warren stroked his beard as he thought of his daughter. A fine-looking woman still, Amelia would add to the respectability of the place. She wouldn't know, of course, that a cellar full of contraband lay beneath.

He wasn't troubled by conscience, for his purpose today was twofold. He was genuinely glad the rift with his daughter was healed, and he had a growing fondness for Will. He wanted to see his grandson better himself.

As he approached Amelia's cottage, he saw her busy with her plait-work in the open doorway. Young Hetty Cauldon was there, splitting and soaking the lengths of straw.

Henry frowned at how hard Amelia was working. Even between chores, when she sat down to rest, her fingers kept busy. He must find her more help when she was established.

Amelia looked up and greeted him with a smile.

'Hello, Father.'

She must be doing well, he thought, how else had she come by such fine quality white straw? The plait her nimble fingers produced looked light and sparkly. But that wasn't important.

He expected her to put down her work, but she kept rapidly plaiting, and setting in more lengths of straw. Every so often she would measure the plait between her chin and finger tips then, as she coiled it around her arm, Hetty slid more damp straws under her armpit.

He observed the obvious.

'You'm busy, something special?'

'Haven't you heard the news, Father?' Amelia nodded at Hetty who went inside to fetch a chair for the old man.

He flicked out his coat-tails, and sat down. He'd spent the morning sorting the remainder of the last haul, marking kegs and bales, and making room for the assignment due next evening. It was the reason he was anxious to get Amelia set up.

'What news?'

'Why, the royal visit,' said Amelia, surprised at his ignorance. 'The Duchess of Kent and Princess Victoria are coming through Frometown tomorrow, and will spend the night at our new Manor House Hotel!' Her eyes shone as she looked at him, but her fingers kept going. 'Squire has asked me to make a bonnet specially for the Princess,' she added, breathlessly. 'He only heard himself, yesterday, and brought me some best straw that he'd purchased in Dorchester.'

' 'Twill be a gurt procession,' put in Hetty, too excited to keep quiet. 'There'll be her own royal guard, an' all the sojers, an' the town band. I reckon everybody'll stop work tomorrer.'

'Yes.' Amelia smiled. 'The officer who brought the news to Sir Alan has passed on orders for the Yeomanry to assemble as a guard of honour to escort the royal party all the way from Frometown to Swanwick.'

'Well, I'll be . . .' For a moment Henry Warren was overcome. 'I never knew, I've been busy. I just came to tell you the shop's ready.' He paused, as if seeking an extra incentive. 'I've ordered some splitting-machines to make your work easier—'

'Oh, I can't *think* of moving stock until after the royal visit,' said Amelia, her eyes bright with enthusiasm. 'Hetty and I shall be up all night as it is. I need at least three-score yards of plait, then there's the lining, and ribbons – oh, I do hope it will be suitable for Her Royal Highness!'

Amelia paused in her work to focus round eyes on him.

'Father, if she is gracious enough to accept it, think what an advertisement it will be for the shop. The timing couldn't be better!'

'Er, yes, you're right.' He could hardly disagree. His mind worked at top speed. 'Tell you what, m'dear, I'll ask Squire to let Charlie help you shift, when their Highnesses have left.'

'That would be splendid. Thank you, Father!'

'I'd best get on then, leave you to it. Got some people to see; I'm sure to be on the welcoming committee. Good luck, m'dear.'

Amelia smiled after him as he hurried away. She could forgive his pomposity now that things were looking up. Tonight she could afford to light extra candles.

The merchant could hardly believe his luck. Tomorrow night's haul, including tea, and spices, was the largest yet – and probably the last. He'd already had word that *Esmerelda* had met the Chinaman off the Isles of Scilly. She would even now be sailing up Channel, her progress necessarily slow, for she must be ready to shelter in any one of the innumerable coves along the coast should a warning signal be given.

The royal visit suited his plans admirably. The Princess would be guarded by all the trained men available, and with complete attention on the royal progress, it would be safe for his ship to move with all speed.

Henry Warren walked towards the White Horse, where he hoped to find Will and send him to Maltravers with a message. He was almost there when the Honourable Mr himself appeared. He'd heard the news, so the two men sat on a bench outside the public house to discuss the situation over a pint of ale.

'It'll be easier to get the stuff ashore,' said Maltravers, a satisfied gleam in his black eyes. 'Trouble is, as official dignitaries we'll both have to attend the welcome.'

'No matter,' said the merchant. 'Captain Ford's crew are reliable enough, and I can trust my grandson to guide them. We'll have to stow the cargo in the old ruins for the time being. I suggest we use the underground storeroom Will knows about; it'll be safer than Biddy's cellar.'

Will had discovered a well-preserved cellar under a densely overgrown part of the ruins, after Charlie repeated what Squire had said about the hall being built over an ancient brewery.

Henry Warren looked enquiringly at Maltravers, and jerked a thumb towards the bay.

'We can move it to my store when the hullabaloo dies down, an' folks go back to the harvest.'

'Hm, I suppose so,' Maltravers muttered. He rubbed his chin. 'We'd better tell Biddy Cauldon to watch out for anyone nosing around.'

They finished their drinks, then went to see the old woman.

'I expect you'm right.' Biddy nodded her scraggy head, her one visible eye fixed bright and sharp on Maltravers. 'No one ever comes there now, 'cepts them kids.'

'What kids?' asked the merchant, exasperated. Children were the worst for snooping and prying, what they called 'exploring'. It wouldn't do for them to find the barrels and bales, and go bleating to their parents.

'Squire's kids!' exclaimed Biddy. 'They bin playin' hide an' seek after church. I seen 'em when I was out pickin' me herbs.'

'They was with your granddaughter, Miss hoighty-toighty Freer,' she added accusingly. She resented Hetty's high-falutin' ideas of bettering herself. The silly girl wanted to go to school and learn reading and writing 'like Miss Freer'.

Maltravers scowled. He'd seen Isobel and Hugh on the river bank with the Freer bitch, but it hadn't occurred to him they might mess about in the woods.

'Everyone will be at the big event,' he growled. 'It's the bit between the royal visit, and getting the stuff shifted that'll cause problems.' He swore. 'Damn and blast!'

'Leave it with me,' said Henry Warren. 'The Lackford kids won't go into the woods on their own.' He explained about the shop he'd prepared for Amelia's straw-plait business. 'When the royal party leaves I'll ask Squire to allow my granddaughter to help her ma move stock.'

Grudgingly Maltravers agreed it was the best plan.

'I'll be on, then. I'll alert my runner to signal *Esmerelda* to make full sail – and I'll call on my nephew, drop the hint that you want to borrow young Charlotte.' He almost spat the name, for he despised her more than his wife.

While the merchant went to give Will his instructions for the morrow, the Honourable Mr rode to Lackford Hall to see what his nephew's arrangements were.

He was received by Maisie, who seemed somehow different. She glowed with confidence. He blinked.

'Where's the new housekeeper, then?' he asked sarcastically.

Although she'd gained her present position through him, Maisie had no liking for the man. Soon to marry Dick, with Sir Alan's blessing, she knew which side her bread was buttered. She owed Simon Maltravers nothing, but was wise enough to be on her guard.

'Miss Freer's gone on an errand for the master,' she said, warily. 'Did you want to see her?'

Glad not to see the Freer girl, he overlooked Maisie's bluntness.

'Not necessary m'dear, it's Sir Alan I want to see.'

'Squire's in the stables; everything's got to be spick an' span for tomorrow.'

The words were barely out of her mouth before Maltravers strode off, and led his horse around the back.

He noticed, smugly, that his nephew was all of a dither.

Sir Alan had both Dick and Hart grooming the horses, polishing bits and brasses, and cleaning everything in sight. He was even helping them.

'All this is interfering with the harvest,' he explained snappily. 'The whole town's gone mad. It's been such a poor year weatherwise, we really can't afford to stop.'

About his plans, he said; 'I have the perfect gift for Her Royal Highness, but it's a secret until tomorrow, and Miss Freer will be out early with the children, picking flowers.'

'Hmph, I'm glad everything's under control,' grunted Maltravers. He forced a smile. 'Well, if there's nothing I can do here I'll go home, and see to my own arrangements.'

As he remounted his horse he spoke again, for at the moment it suited him to keep Miss Freer in the conversation.

'So, your little housekeeper is to be a flower-girl tomorrow?'

'Isobel's idea,' chuckled Sir Alan. 'Says she won't do her duty unless Miss Freer accompanies her.'

Maltravers averted his eyes from his nephew's gaze.

'That reminds me,' he said, flicking a stray hair from his jacket. 'You'll be pleased to hear Merchant Warren is opening a spare premises, near the hotel, for Mrs Freer to expand her business. He may ask you to lend him his granddaughter as soon as this royal affair is over, to help her mother move in. I trust you will accommodate our merchant friend.'

'I'd heard their feud is ended,' said Sir Alan, 'and if it will help the family I shall certainly permit her.' He pursed his lips, 'I believe Miss Freer, though, doesn't get on with the merchant. I don't know why.'

'Warren tells me she can be stubborn,' said Maltravers. 'She's very like Amelia at that age, except she's prettier . . . eh, Nephew?'

'I had noticed,' said Sir Alan evenly.

'All the same,' added Maltravers abruptly, 'she does get strange ideas . . .'

'Such as?'

'Oh . . .' Maltravers shrugged, as if unwilling to smear the young woman's character. 'Such as not allowing anyone to call her Charlotte.

I wonder what she'd say if the Princess were to ask her name?'

'An interesting point, Uncle,' murmured Sir Alan thoughtfully.

Maltravers changed the subject.

'What about Isobel and Hugh? What shall they do while Miss Freer is away?'

'I shall take them riding.' His nephew smiled. 'As they have no mother I feel I ought to spend more time with them. What do you think?'

Maltravers swiftly agreed, and seized his chance to ensure that the children would go nowhere near the woods.

'Strange you should say that I was thinking along similar lines. Jane has no children, she'd be pleased for them to visit. Why don't you finish your ride at Underhill – join Jane and me for luncheon?'

He lowered his voice confidingly: 'She doesn't really have enough to do, you know . . .'

Immediately he'd persuaded his nephew to accept the invitation, Maltravers lifted a hand in salute and rode off.

The sun was setting as a lone rider cantered along the upper coast path. On he rode, past the cliff quarrs, skirting coves and inlets until he reached the last outcrop of rock where the seam of stone that men quarried ended in the sea. From the top of this rock he made his signal.

Way out to sea he saw an answering light. Invisible in the dusk, *Esmerelda* would make all speed, and drop anchor off the Swanwick cliffs to wait for the signal to unload.

A preventive man on cliff-top duty had seen the lone horseman. His eyes narrowed as the rider grew tiny in the distance. Guessing the messenger's destination, and putting two and two together, Horace Skinner, informant turned auxiliary coastguard, made his plans for the morrow.

His reward this time would be more than a mere pittance.

CHAPTER SEVENTEEN

S WANWICK was in holiday mood. The street was hung with flags and bunting, houses were decorated with flowers and laurel-branches, and folk left their daily toil to come out in their Sunday best.

The day had dawned fine and warm, and time passed quickly with last minute preparations. By midday all the trained men in the district had ridden off to assemble at Frometown to form the guard of honour.

The Princess was due at five in the afternoon, and after luncheon Charlie helped Isobel and Hugh to dress. Isobel wore her birthday gown, and Charlie combed her copper hair into ringlets which bounced fetchingly beneath a *broderie anglaise* bonnet.

'Now I shall help you,' Isobel insisted, when Charlie laughingly protested. 'I shall put up your hair like a lady's.'

Dick was to drive Maisie, the Harts, and Mrs Biggins, and Sir Alan would bring Charlie with his children, and Ponsonby. Ponsonby ushered them into the carriages, and tethered Hugh's pony to trot behind.

Sir Alan motioned Charlie to precede him through the front door, and laid a hand on her shoulder as she did so.

'Turn around, Miss Freer. Let me look at you.'

Her expression was unintentionally coy as she glanced at him and blushed, as she meekly obeyed.

She looked down at herself as she turned. The creamy satin hung in smooth layers from the waist to finish in a double hem-frill; the bodice was a snug fit. Puffed sleeves were visible beneath the matching wrap she'd draped around her shoulders for modesty.

'I see you are a skilled needlewoman,' he said softly. He saw the way Isobel had left enough of Charlie's dark hair showing beneath the bonnet to enhance her glowing complexion. 'The dress suits you admirably.'

Shyly she murmured her thanks.

'You look every inch a lady,' he added. 'and any gentleman would be proud to escort you. Won't you take my arm?'

'Oh, but sir . . .' Startled, she hesitated. What would the others think? But she had no choice.

'Do not argue, Miss Freer.' He took her hand and tucked it firmly beneath his arm as they walked to the carriage.

Not daring to look at Maisie and the others, Charlie saw that Isobel and Hugh were smiling.

She should have been happy, but once again that inward voice persisted, warning how life had a horrid habit of knocking a person down.

By late afternoon all was ready, and the crowd had followed the band to the crossroads on the outskirts of town. Stalls were set up to provide refreshment, and the band practised their tunes.

Being so hot, time began to drag and Charlie gazed idly around. She smiled at Isobel, who looked demure, mindful that she was to present the gift to Her Royal Highness. Hugh's chest swelled with importance, for his was the task to ride to the parish church and alert the bell-ringers as soon as the first rider appeared.

Not far from where they stood were the Maltravers and Henry Warren, who seemed in an extremely good mood. He smiled and joked with those around him.

At five o'clock there was no sign of the royal party, and seeing her ma with Tommy and Sandy, Charlie went across to them. Once again at a public gathering she couldn't see Will.

She tried not to think what he was up to, yet she realized there would never be a better time for smugglers to land their contraband. Was that why Warren looked so pleased with himself?

Amelia was too excited and apprehensive about the bonnet she had been up all night making, to notice Will's absence. She smiled broadly at her daughter, and said how lovely she looked. Proudly she held out the hat-box that Charlie had taken her the day before.

'We managed it, didn't we, Hetty?'

The fact that Hetty was with Ma drew attention to another absence – that of Biddy Cauldon. Now Charlie was sure something was going on, most likely in those woods a mile away.

She suppressed her anxiety, and lifted the box-lid. The new bonnet was immaculate, made of the best shiny white straw, with satin lining and ribbons to match, and decorated around the crown with flowers.

'Oh Ma, it's gorgeous', she breathed. 'Sir Alan will be pleased.'

'Thank you, Charlie,' said Amelia. 'You'd better take it and show him, then.'

Before Charlie could do so Henry Warren came over; he'd been talking to Sir Alan.

'Squire's given permission for Charlie to help you move your . . .' he began to tell Amelia, then stood and stared at his granddaughter.

For once Charlie liked the look he gave her, despite her misgivings about him and the trade. She'd rarely spared him more than a passing glance, but now she watched his open-mouthed expression until he spoke in a wondering whisper.

'Charlotte Annereaux, you've come back to haunt me.' He removed his top-hat, and swept her a bow. When he straightened again, Charlie saw tears in his eyes.

He blinked furiously. 'You look grand, maid. Where did you get those clothes?'

He clearly had no idea of her suspicions, and for the first time she found herself smiling at him. This appreciation in his manner was so new, she felt extremely self-conscious, and spoke awkwardly.

'I made it, er . . . granddad . . . Thank you for the compliment.' She wouldn't tell him how she'd come by the material, but added hastily: 'Ma helped me with the fitting. I finished it just in time. I – I'm glad you think I look like my grandma.'

'Aah, she were a real beauty,' he said, 'and so be you, maid.'

He coughed against the back of his hand, and looked at Amelia. 'Don't reckon I noticed the resemblance afore, her bein' such a tomboy.'

Amelia laughed.

'Yes, until now it's been difficult to tell. Here, Charlie, take the bonnet to Squire, do. I must know he approves.'

Charlie pulled herself erect, and walked as gracefully as she knew how. She wished Sir Alan's haughty sisters could see her now – and her town. The quarry port wasn't good enough for them, but it was good enough for a princess to end her tour of the West Country!

Her elation was dampened when she saw Maltravers and his wife talking to Sir Alan. Conscious of Maltravers' eyes flicking over her, she gave Jane a glimmer of a smile, unsure of what else to do, then averted her eyes.

Unable to look at the master, Charlie fixed her eyes on the box as if she were afraid of dropping it, and held it out to him. 'Ma – my mother has made the most beautiful bonnet, sir, that I have ever seen . . .'

Isobel leapt down from her seat in the carriage.

'Let me see,' she cried, and elbowed her way to Charlie's side.

Sir Alan spoke in the mocking tone he used when amused. 'Please, do open it, Miss Freer.'

She obeyed nervously, but thought it best to display the bonnet without taking it out. She was gratified when Jane Maltravers leaned over her shoulder, and gasped:

'Your mother has truly surpassed herself.'

'Yes,' said Charlie, 'but she wants it known that it is done with Hetty Cauldon's help.'

'They both have skilled fingers,' said Sir Alan, closing the lid.

Charlie looked up then, and smouldered beneath the look in his eyes. He gazed down at her as if there were only the two of them present.

She knew she was blushing, and fumbled with the wrap that slipped revealingly while she held the hat-box. Mercifully he changed the subject.

'Let us hope, Isobel, you will not have to wait much longer to present this delightful gift to Her Royal Highness.'

Isobel gave a nervous shriek, and turned to her great-aunt Jane.

'You'll look after it, won't you, until I've performed my duty as a flower-girl?'

Jane nodded, and smiled, and Charlie thought how much nicer everyone seemed today.

No trouble was expected at midday when *Esmerelda* hove to, off the rocky ledges of Maltravers' disused cliff quarr, but a man was still posted on the heights above.

He had a panoramic view encompassing three miles, but apart from cattle, a few sheep, and sea-birds, the area looked deserted.

Will had given Captain Ford his grandfather's message that an informant was at work, so they would take no chances with the usual tub men. With the captain's promise of more bounty for the extra labour involved, the crew rowed the long boats back and forth until all the cargo was landed.

Will shouldered a keg, and led the file of laden men up the hill, and through the shady yard of Grange Farm. The occupants had long since gone to join the celebrations in town.

The farm stood by an ancient roadway sheltered by high hedgerows.

The road ran from an equally ancient cliff-top chapel, down into Swanwick, winding across the valley, dipping and rising onward over the ridge to Holywell, a distance of seven miles in all.

But Will knew all the short cuts, and within an hour he'd led the crew into the woods between Lackford Hall and Underhill Manor. Instead of going directly to the ruins, he took an overgrown path that crossed a disused open-cast quarr. It dipped steeply amid a covering of ferns and brambles, to disappear underground. After about a hundred yards it ended in what was once a storeroom under the refectory.

Meanwhile Horace Skinner settled down in a barn at Grange Farm to wait. At intervals he lit his clay pipe, careful not to tap it out on his bed of hay, and congratulated himself on being right about the haul being bigger than usual.

He'd watched Will and the smugglers go by, and knew it would be some time before they returned. There were about a hundred of them, some armed with clubs.

Oh yes, old Skinner had guessed the gang would move while the town awaited the arrival of the royal party. All he had to do was sit tight for an hour or two. He knew the Princess was due at five o'clock, then the time taken up with welcome speeches would be just long enough for the goods to be hidden – probably in Biddy Cauldon's cellar. If so, it could only be temporary as the authorities were already suspicious of Biddy. Where the contraband was to go after that he had yet to discover, but if his plan worked it wouldn't matter. It should be enough for him to alert the yeomanry before the gang could regain their ship. He'd wait until six, make his way to the edge of the wood, and run hell for leather into town. He'd soon find some horsemen relieved of duty, send them after the gang, then claim his reward.

'What time is it now, Papa?'

Hugh looked up at his father, his face crumpled with boredom. Five o'clock had come and gone an hour ago, and he was tired of endless games of 'I spy with my little eye'. He and Tommy had been stopped from playing tag because the grown-ups moaned about them getting messed up.

For the third time Sir Alan took out his fob-watch.

'Thirty minutes past six o'clock,' he said.

Isobel gave out a long heavy sigh.

'How much longer will they be?'

The squire looked up the road, his mouth tight.

'As long as it takes; something must have delayed them.'

'It wouldn't be so bad if it wasn't so hot,' complained Jane Maltravers, fanning herself vigorously. She was sitting next to her great-niece in Sir Alan's carriage with Amelia and Cook.

'I don't think they're coming,' pouted Isobel.

'Now, my dear,' soothed her Aunt Jane, 'I'm sure word would have been sent if their plans were changed. We must be patient a little longer.'

'I wish I was an orphan,' lamented Tommy. He watched enviously as Sandy, who had elected himself look-out, shinned up an elm-tree.

'I don't belong to anybody,' he'd said, 'and I ain't got no best clothes to spoil.'

'We're half-orphans,' offered Hugh sympathetically. 'I only have a father, and you a mother—'

'Stop bleating, you two,' laughed Charlie, who had been to fetch a jug of water for the ladies in the carriage. 'Look, Hetty's coming with some of Widow Hyer's lemon cordial for you.'

Suddenly Sandy gave a shout.

'There's a rider coming!'

He nearly fell in his haste to scramble down the tree.

Amelia climbed down from the carriage to dust him off and straighten his collar.

'Only one?' she asked. She gave him the cap she'd been minding, and he tugged it on, almost too excited to reply.

'Oh, I didn't wait to see no more.'

Minutes later a rider galloped into view, and reined his horse to a halt in a cloud of dust.

Worried-looking officials stepped quickly forward, and the mayor barely acknowledged the soldier's salute.

'What's happening?'

The young officer rapidly explained how the royal party had been held up by great crowds in Frometown.

'But they were through Corvesgate without even stopping, when I came on,' he said encouragingly.

Mayor Phillips turned to the people, and raised his arms.

'They're on their way!'

To Charlie it seemed a miracle the way everyone instantly revived. The band struck up, and Hugh mounted his pony and cantered to the parish church. Soon the bells rang out in frenzied peals that would be kept up for the rest of the evening. All petty differences were forgotten when the drumming of many hoofs was heard, and the procession came into view.

Three preceding officers acknowledged the huzzas that rent the air, then everyone stood solemnly to attention. As the royal carriage pulled up, men and boys doffed their hats while the band played *God Save the King*, then the crowd gave three hearty cheers.

Amid the ensuing mayhem, Sir John Conroy, Irish equerry to the Duchess of Kent, went into a huddle with the local dignitaries. The whole gathering simmered down while the mayor, Sir Alan and others listened, then spoke in their turn. Reverend Barton made a gesture that encompassed the crowd, and Sir Alan and Maltravers nodded in agreement.

They turned back to the waiting onlookers. 'Their Royal Highnesses, are very tired, they have travelled over one hundred miles today,' the mayor announced. 'They are much obliged for your splendid welcome, but crave your indulgence. They wish to continue immediately to their accommodation.'

Sir John Conroy promised that the Duchess of Kent would receive presentations and give her address next morning, when she and the Princess Victoria were refreshed.

With that the crowd had to be content, and Charlie sympathized with those who grumbled. For most folk like herself, it was their first and probably only glimpse of royalty. They'd all gone to so much trouble, and waited for hours in the heat of the day.

The occasion, however, was too exciting for any resentment to last.

The three officers led the procession into town, with the band and everyone else marching behind the guard of honour.

At the Manor Hotel a white banner hung across the street bore the words: Welcome, thrice welcome, Victoria, and when their Royal Highnesses alighted the acclamations broke out again.

Hearts a-flutter, Charlie and Isobel led two columns of flower-girls up the double flight of steps to the hotel entrance, strewing blooms from their baskets all the way to the royal apartments.

No sooner had the royal party gone inside than someone yelled: 'We want the Princess!'

The cry was taken up until the whole populace was chanting, over and over: 'We want the Princess.'

Charlie shared in the mass elation. It was intoxicating, a moment of a lifetime, and the humble folk of Swanwick were making the most of it.

Eventually the fourteen-year-old Victoria came to the casement window on the pedimented top floor, and looked down at them.

The crowd hushed as Charlie gazed up at her.

'She looks like a china doll!' she heard one onlooker say.

Next moment, the Princess lifted a tiny hand, waved to them, and shyly bid them all a good night.

Unaware of the long delay in the proceedings of the royal visit, Horace Skinner climbed down from the loft and made his way warily across the fields. He was armed with a cutlass and pistols, but wouldn't risk using the narrow route of the old monks because there'd be no escape if he met the gang returning. He had to go the long way round.

He'd barely gained the woodland path when he heard the tramping of feet. Fearful now, he hid in a leafy oak and held his breath until the last man was gone.

Will wasn't with them; he must have gone back into town. Sure that the royal welcome must be over by now, and that he was bound to find some off-duty soldiers at the nearest inn, Skinner hurried through the wood.

Will wasn't gone; he'd stayed to check that there were no broken branches or fern-fronds to betray the entrance to the underground store.

Once satisfied, he ran to catch up with the others and see them safely away before he reported to his grandfather.

He ran straight into Horace Skinner.

The coastguard shoved Will back, and for a moment both men glared at each other. Then with a leer, Skinner drew his cutlass.

'Out of my way boy, I got some important business to attend to.'

The look on his ugly face told Will everything, and his heart sank. He saw his dream of making his fortune in London crumble around him, for his arrest would mean prison – or worse!

'Not if I can help it,' he muttered.

He bent quickly to snatch a piece of fallen branch. As Skinner rushed him, cutlass raised, Will ducked and caught the older man a blow behind the knees. Skinner staggered, and Will smashed the branch across the man's sword arm, forcing him to drop his cutlass with a howl of pain and rage.

In that moment Will appreciated his own strength, built up from years of handling heavy tools and stone. He closed in confidently, meaning to use brute force to intimidate the man into keeping his mouth shut.

The idea was naïve, and even as he moved, Skinner had loosed a pistol from his belt with his good hand.

Will paused, there was so much hatred on Skinner's face that the quarryman knew he would be shot even if he kept still. He fixed his eyes on the man's pistol hand, and tried to judge his moment.

Suddenly he ducked his head and charged his enemy in the belly. He heard a shot, and a groan of agony in the same instant. A searing pain tore at his left arm, and in the mist before his eyes he didn't know whether the cry was Skinner's or his own.

He looked up as he sank to his knees, and saw *Esmerelda*'s mate standing over the crumpled Skinner, his tight-held cosh still raised at the end of its deadly swing.

The mate rolled Skinner over with his booted foot. Satisfied that the coastguard was unconscious, he came to Will and looked at his arm.

'He only winged ye,' he growled.

'I'm glad to see you,' said Will struggling to his feet. 'I thought you'd be back on board.'

'Aah, I like to make sure we ain't follered, and I had a feelin' all weren't well.' The mate jerked his thumb at Skinner's inert form. 'That bugger knows ye, don't he. We'll all be done for if we leave 'im here.'

He seemed unconcerned that Will was bleeding. 'Yer, give us a hand with 'im.'

With his good arm Will held Skinner's head down while the mate bound his wrists. Then they dragged their hapless prisoner up to the cliff where the rest of the crew were swilling rum from a keg they'd saved for the purpose.

Skinner regained consciousness, and began swearing. He demanded in the name of the King that they release him.

'Aah, we'll release ye all right,' snarled the mate. 'Cut him loose, lads, and let's show him how much we respect a dootiful King's man!'

They unbound him, then jeered and laughed as they pushed him around before beating him up.

'Just bruise him up, lads,' growled the mate, 'we don't want no knife or bullet wounds.'

Will looked on in horror, oblivious to the blood that trickled down his arm to drip from his fingertips. The drunken rabble knocked Skinner senseless again before the mate called a halt.

'That's 'nuff! We want h_m to live long enough to drown, don't we, lads?'

The last thing Will saw before he fainted was Skinner being thrown over the cliff.

When Will came to, he found himself propped against a dry-stone wall. His wound had been bound with his own neckerchief, and in his lap was a small leather flask of brandy. He took a sip, choked, then sipped again. Memory flooded back, and he pulled himself up.

Weak from shock and loss of blood, he stepped forward groggily until he could see there was no vessel in sight, nor any sign of a scuffle. There was nothing to tell the tale of Skinner's end, except the turmoil inside himself.

Faced with the enormity of what had happened, Will realized the disgrace he was bringing on himself, and on his ma's good name. Nor was he comforted to remember that Charlie had warned him he would bring them all down.

In the twilight he managed to stagger as far as his quarry. Too ashamed for his ma to see him in this state, he bedded down for the night beside Trixie the pony.

CHAPTER EIGHTEEN

Between its finger-and-thumb downs, with gleaming cliffs mirrored in the calm blue sea, Swanwick Bay seemed to smile in the sunshine. In mid-bay, flags a-flutter among myriad small craft, was the royal yacht, waiting to take the Princess Victoria to the Isle of Wight.

For Charlie it was a second chance to see the Princess! At 10.30 Sir Alan brought her and the children to the Manor Hotel where Henry Warren and Amelia met them.

They both looked so proud and pleased, and Charlie was aware of watching eyes as Squire escorted them into the ballroom for the reception.

The rector was there preparing to address the assembly, and all the ladies and gentlemen were greeted by Sir John Conroy who conducted them into the royal presence.

When Charlie was introduced as Miss Charlotte Freer, chief flower-girl of the previous evening, the sound of her own name was so alien she coloured, and glanced at Sir Alan in embarrassment. She could swear there was a triumphant gleam in his eyes, and she felt an absurd dart of anger. What else should he use but her correct name?

There was no time for absurdity, she was face to face with their Royal Highnesses.

She gasped. How beautiful the Princess looked after her night's rest. Her shiny chestnut hair was parted in the middle, swept back from one side of her small round face to cascade loosely over the opposite shoulder. She had a small, straight nose, large, brilliant blue eyes, and a pink rosebud-like mouth.

It took all Charlie's concentration to curtsy low and not stumble, and when Sir Alan handed her up, his firm grasp calmed her. Now she felt thankful he stood beside her.

The Duchess of Kent addressed the assembly, conveying the message that the purpose of the tour was for the Princess to meet the people as future Queen, and be conscious of her duty towards them.

As return speeches of loyalty were made, Charlie couldn't help thinking that while the dignitaries promised fealty under divine providence on behalf of the whole town, Warren and Maltravers' gang were robbing the King of his revenue.

The moment came for the presentation, and Charlie thought the Princess seemed shy, and more nervous than Isobel. She accepted the bonnet with a small sweet smile.

'Say thank you, Victoria,' said her mother.

When the Duchess thanked the ladies who made the bonnet, Amelia blushed deeply and curtsied, while Charlie relished the pride on her grandfather's face.

The royal party was escorted the short distance to the quay where the guard of honour stood to attention. Victoria and her mother walked between their ranks to the barge that would carry them out to the royal yacht. As it pulled away, the cheering of the crowd drowned the band playing *God Save the King*.

Not until the royal yacht was a mere speck on the horizon did the crowd disperse, many of the men in the direction of the pubs.

After a few words with his Uncle Maltravers, Sir Alan joined the small group of women.

'What shall you do now, Mrs Freer?'

'Go home and sleep, sir.' smiled Amelia. 'I must gather strength to see to the shop tomorrow.'

'Ah, yes.' Sir Alan nodded, 'I've given your daughter permission to help you.' As Amelia thanked him, he added: 'Won't you allow us to escort you home?'

Only one thing marred Charlie's happiness – the feeling that Will was involved in something more than the accepted dabbling in the trade. Thank goodness Ma had been too excited to notice his absence during the whole royal occasion.

Now Amelia hesitated before climbing into the carriage.

'What about Sandy and Tommy?'

Charlie feared she would think of Will next.

'They ought to go to the quarr and check the pony's all right,' she said quickly.

'Deary me,' said Amelia, 'I'd forgotten all about the poor pony.'

She called to the two youngsters, who seemed full of energy still. 'Will you boys go and feed Trixie – but get changed first – oh, I wonder where Will is?'

'Ma, don't worry about him,' said Charlie, fighting exasperation. 'I'm sure he's with drinking–companions.' Of one sort or another, she added to herself. 'You must get home and rest. Please stop fussing!'

She felt embarrassed that Sir Alan was waiting to help her ma into the carriage, but he came to the rescue.

'Your daughter is quite right, Mrs Freer. We all need to gather strength for the work ahead. The harvest's been waiting long enough, and you have your work cut out now. I'll warrant you'll be flooded with orders for bonnets just like Princess Victoria's.'

Amelia laughed and accepted his assistance.

'Thank you sir, for thinking of the idea in the first place.'

To Charlie's relief, her ma seemed content to sit back and be driven to the track that led to their home. Sir Alan helped her down, and thanked her again for her part in the success of the royal visit.

Amelia waved as the carriage drove on up the highway, but stared anxiously after Charlie. Then her mouth softened, and she felt tears prick her eyes. She clasped her hands in front of her, prayer fashion.

Will was woken by Tommy's shrill voice calling to Sandy as the two boys climbed the slope to the quarr. He staggered dizzily to his feet, for he'd lost a lot of blood, and hadn't eaten for nearly two days. His wounded arm felt stiff and sore, and he cursed, thinking it would be some time before he could work properly again. Meanwhile, no one must know why he wasn't hewing stone.

Hastily he rolled down his sleeves to cover the bandage, and stepped outside as the boys arrived with their arms full of green stuff.

'I got to see Merchant Warren,' he said gruffly. He still found it awkward to refer to the old man as 'grandfather' to other people. 'I want you boys to put the pony out to graze, while you go and help with the harvest. I'll come an' join you soon as I can.'

Noting by their incredulous looks that they needed an explanation, he added: ' 'Tis our duty by the community.'

'Gosh,' said Tommy, wide-eyed. 'It'll be like a holiday for you, Sandy.'

Sandy was glad to escape from underground toil, and the struggle with cartloads of stone. He grinned.

'I think 'tis only right an' proper to do our duty by the community.'

They tethered Trixie to a tree where she could graze, then hared off to find the nearest team of reapers.

Will knelt by a stream and cupped his hands to drink some water, then steeled himself to walk the half-mile to his grandfather's shire stables.

As he approached, Hercules poked his head out of his stall, and whinnied softly. Will stopped to stroke him and nuzzle his cheek against the horse's neck.

'He needs shoein',' said Henry Warren. He eyed Will curiously. Hercules was the only one to whom the lad displayed any emotion. He didn't even seem interested in young maids.

The merchant had expected a visit before this. So far he'd only got the thumbs-up sign from Biddy as she walked past his stables. Now, seeing the unkempt state of his grandson, he led Will into the house.

He called his cook and general help.

'Mrs Harris! Warm up that stew, and make us some tea, will you?' To Will he said: 'You look all in, lad. Nothing wrong, I hope?'

Will shook his head as he collapsed on a chair at the kitchen table.

Warren waited until Mrs Harris put the stew and a hunk of bread in front of Will.

'Here, get this lot down, then let's have it,' he said then, curtly.

While Will ate ravenously, the merchant took the tea-tray from his cook and dismissed her.

Will couldn't keep the panic out of his voice as he described the previous evening's events.

'When I agreed to join the trade I never thought 'twould come to murder! I had nothin' to do with killin' Skinner, all I done was defend meself from his cutlass.' He shook his head vigorously. 'I ain't havin' no more to do with it!'

Henry Warren put his head to one side and looked shrewdly at Will.

'You didn't want him to arrest you, so what did you think would happen afore Matey came along?'

Bewildered, Will shrugged.

'I would have broke his arm, unless he promised not to tell.'

'Haa – you'm a greenhorn, boy, you cain't trust a man like him. Only a dead man don't tell tales!'

Will sat with his head in his hands. He couldn't remember ever feeling so afraid.

' 'Twas your crew who beat him up and chucked him over the cliff. How long d'you think they'll let me live? You're right, I don't trust 'em, an' they ain't like to trust me!'

'So, why d'you think they bandaged yer arm, an' left you propped up comfy-like, wi' a flask o' brandy?'

Will admitted this puzzled him.

'Because they know I'm your kin?' he wondered.

'Aah.' Warren nodded. 'I'm the one who pays 'em. I could shop the lot if I was minded. But look, lad, it ain't goin' to help nobody to go shoutin' off your mouth, nor would it bring Skinner back. They owed you one – think on it. 'Twas you stopped him first. The way they see it, they was helpin' you an' me, not just savin' their own skins.'

Will frowned, and shook his head.

'I ain't blabbin'. I just want out.'

'So you will, m'boy, so you will. Listen, you got the makings of a good stonemason, and I'm gonna get you established in London.'

Will looked at him sharply, unable to take the old man seriously.

'How? How can I go to London wi' this lot hangin' over me. And what about me ma, an' the quarr—'

'One thing at a time, Will. First you got to sit tight, an' don't say nothin' to nobody. When they find Skinner – 'cause his body's sure to get washed up, let 'em think he lost his footing in the dark an' fell over th'edge. I'll put it in their heads he got drunk celebratin' the royal visit, like everyone else.'

Warren bent closer to Will, to emphasize his next words. 'When the rocks didn't finish him, he drowned. An' that's the truth – he died by drowning, now don't 'ee forget it. Anyway, he won't be much missed.' He paused.

'Why should you bother helpin' me when you hated my Dad so?' Will muttered doubtfully.

The question was unexpected, and the old man drew a deep breath.

'I never hated your dad, just thought he weren't good 'nuff fer your ma. I certainly didn't want him to die the way he did, an' I want you out, afore the dust gets you.

'Besides, your ma deserves a better life. I let her down, an' I want to make up fer it. I'm getting on, and you'm the nearest I got to a son. Anyway,' he added gruffly, 'look what it'll do fer my reputation when you're famous, an' tell 'em you're Henry Warren's grandson!'

A sarcastic grunt accompanied by a casual shrug was the nearest Will managed, to show humour.

'Carry on as if nothin's happened,' coaxed his grandfather. 'Then by the time 'tis all died down, your ma will be in her shop – I'll help her out if need be – an' she can sell the quarr.'

He was businesslike once more. 'You can work your passage to London on a stone-boat, and I'll give you a letter of introduction, and references. But for now, keep in with Maltravers an' help move the goods tonight while folks is still getting over their excitement. You do feel up to it, I hope?'

Will nodded. What else could he do but go along with his granddad?

'Good,' said Henry Warren briskly. 'Perhaps you'd take Hercules along to Sam Roper, then bide yer 'til dusk.'

Back at Lackford Hall the squire left Dick to put away the horses and carriages, and rode his own hunter back into town. There he found his uncle and joined him in rousting men out of the pubs.

'Unless we save the harvest before this good spell breaks, we'll have another hard winter,' he told them. It was the only apology they could expect for the interruption to their holiday.

Loath to leave their celebrating, some of the men made half-hearted attempts to resist.

'Just one more, Squire,' and. 'Soon as I've finished this'un, zir.'

Sir Alan's eyes glinted dangerously.

'You'd best get to it now, and put your backs into it, or I shall make it my business to invest in mechanical reapers. It'll be quicker, and I shan't need so much help next year. It's up to you!'

They scowled; he meant what he said. Banging down their mugs, they began to move out.

'Bloody ogre,' muttered one. ' 'E's a slave driver,' agreed another, but they knew they should be grateful that their squire was opposed to change.

By the time Sir Alan returned to his fields, he found Charlie with Isobel and Hugh. They'd changed into old clothes, and were helping the village women to bind and stack sheaves of wheat. He picked up a scythe and joined the line of men.

That evening, all through dinner, Isobel and Hugh talked of nothing but the future Queen of England. When Sir Alan grew weary of their arguing about which one of them the Princess liked best, he sent them to bed. But they wouldn't settle down until Charlie had read to them. She and Hugh sat on Isobel's bed while she read the tale of Snow White.

It was a long story, and at last Isobel yawned and began to close her eyes, while Hugh's head drooped. Charlie carried him to his own bed, and he was asleep as soon as his head touched the pillow.

She turned his lamp down low and, intending to return to Isobel, she almost bumped into the squire who stood quietly in the doorway. He nodded at her with an expression of such warmth, she couldn't tell whether it was for Hugh or herself.

'Excuse me, sir,' she whispered. 'I'll just say goodnight to Isobel.'

He followed her. Isobel roused herself.

'When are we going for a picnic?' she asked drowsily.

Surprised that with all the recent excitement Isobel was still thinking about picnics, Charlie hesitated.

'Soon,' she promised guardedly. Squire was unlikely to commit himself. 'Not tomorrow, I must be away early, for your father has said I may go home to help my mother set up her shop in town.' She turned to Sir Alan. 'Perhaps we could discuss it later?'

'Yes, why not'?' said Sir Alan, bending over his daughter to kiss her goodnight. 'In fact I shall discuss the matter with Miss Freer now, but only if you go to sleep.'

'Very well, Papa.' Isobel yawned and turned over. 'It had better be soon,' she murmured, 'or we'll be back at school.' She was asleep almost before she'd finished speaking, and Charlie couldn't help smiling at the irony in the sleepy girl's voice.

Charlie longed for her own bed, and didn't relish the prospect of an interview with the master right now. Couldn't it wait until after tomorrow?

In her tired state, with him beside her, she felt she was gliding downstairs in a dream.

He put a hand under her elbow, and gently guided her into the library. The low-burning oil-lamps bathed the room in a soft glow.

'I shall not keep you long, Miss Freer,' he said, as if guessing her thoughts.

When he motioned her to sit in the fireside chair opposite him, she sank down gratefully, but with a sudden urge to giggle. What would his sisters think if they could see her now? They hadn't been introduced to royalty!

'About this picnic,' began Sir Alan. 'As I've promised the children, I think we'd best have it next weekend. Will that give you and your mother time to sort things out?'

Hardly giving her time to nod, he added: 'I'll get Mrs Biggins to arrange the food, so all you have to do is come along.'

'That will be lovely, sir, I look forward to it.'

She wasn't prepared for further conversation, but he went on:

'The other thing, of course, is that we mustn't forget my groom and Maisie's wedding.'

'Oh no,' gasped Charlie, 'we mustn't, sir.' She *had* forgotten, with so much else going on.

'Precisely,' he said, with that familiar humorous twist at the corner of his mouth. Why was he so often amused by her?

'Er – do you wish to discuss arrangements for the wedding now?' she asked, desperately hoping he didn't.

'Yes, briefly.'

She barely managed to suppress a sigh at his reply.

'I think you know best what is suitable for the occasion.' He made a vague motion with one hand. 'I'll provide the breakfast of course, but I have no idea what they would like, so I want you to supervise, give Cook a hand.'

'I should like that, sir,' she replied wearily. 'Er – shall we all attend the ceremony?'

'Indeed. Ask Maisie whom she would like to come. Perhaps your mother and Dick might like to invite Sam Roper, and what about your brother? Will shall be best man if Dick wishes.'

Charlie started. He was going too fast, her usually clear mind was befuddled with tiredness. She had a sudden vision of Will and Dick sneaking away with Squire's horses to help the smugglers.

Sir Alan wouldn't be so kindly disposed towards any of them, if he knew!

'Do you agree, Miss Freer?' he asked again.

She nodded feebly, and blinked as she swallowed a yawn.

'Mm, yes, thank you, sir. You are most kind, they should all be very grateful—'

'Not at all. As master of this estate I believe that harmony among my servants – and the community – makes for a happier, more successful life for us all.'

He stood up as he spoke; she was being dismissed at last.

She should have been glad, but she never could get used to the way they seemed like friends one minute, the next he was the master, putting her in her place.

Slowly she rose, her gaze fixed on the floor. To look him in the eyes and say goodnight was for an equal, not for her. She bobbed a quick curtsy.

'Thank you for everything, sir. Goodnight.'

As she turned towards the door he halted her sharply.

'Miss Freer.'

Charlie's eyes smarted with tears of exhaustion. Couldn't he see how tired she was?

'Sir?' Fatigue gave way to exasperation, and she refused to turn to him. She took another step, and put a hand on the doorknob.

His next words stopped her completely.

'*You* have no plans to marry, I hope?'

Now she did turn around to look him straight in the eyes. What right did he have to ask such a thing, even if he was the master?

'Not before my year is up,' she flashed at him, almost hysterical with frustration.

She immediately regretted her hasty reply. The numbed look in his eyes surprised and pained her, for his expression was that of an apprehensive schoolboy.

Puzzled by his capricious mood she asked: 'Did you think I had?'

Suddenly he was all meekness again. Relief flooded his face, and he gave a helpless shrug, his hands outspread.

'I don't know what I – or my children – would do without you, Miss Freer. We are very fond of you. Goodnight, sleep well.'

The royal yacht had sailed on the noon tide. Twelve hours later, two yeomen, returning in the early hours from their off-duty session at the pubs, paused to see what the incoming tide had brought in. Wedged between the rocks at the base of the fort was the battered body of Horace Skinner.

CHAPTER NINETEEN

As soon as she'd cleared away the Lackford family's breakfast dishes, Charlie went home. She would be gone all day, while Sir Alan was to take Isobel and Hugh riding along the coast, then have luncheon at Underhill Manor.

Her suspicions that contraband was hidden in the ruins were confirmed when Maisie told her Maltravers had come in person to invite the children.

Anything to keep them clear of the woods today, thought Charlie, while the goods were distributed, or hidden elsewhere. There was nothing she could do without implicating Will and bringing ruin on her family.

She remembered that Whit Tuesday night, when Will had let slip about the hiding-place in his quarr. Why must trouble always spoil the good things?

She was angry with Granddad Warren too, certain he'd involved Will in the first place. Oh, if only she could make her brother see sense before he spoiled all their lives!

At home her fears were magnified. Tommy and Sandy ran in and out, loading bundles on to a cart by the door.

'Mornin', Ma,' she began brightly enough. 'Where did you get that handcart?'

Amelia smiled. 'Sam Roper. He sent it up with the boys last night when they finished work in the fields.'

'In the fields,' echoed Charlie. 'You mean Sandy was away from the quarr?'

'Yeah,' said Tommy, 'we bin helpin' with the harvest. Will said—'

'Where is Will?' asked Amelia sharply. 'It was only when I noticed his bed hadn't been slept in that I realized I haven't seen him for two days.'

211

'He was at the quarr yes'day,' said Sandy, 'when we went to feed the pony. That's when he told us to go help the reapers.'

Charlie's fear grew, it wasn't like Will to let Sandy off work. He must have wanted Sandy out of the way, and she knew why.

'What else did he say? Didn't he want you to tell Ma if he wasn't coming home?'

Tommy shrugged. 'He said he'd come and help with the reapin' soon as he could. He was going to see Merchant Warren first.'

'Huh!' Charlie smothered her anxiety with contempt. 'Fancy our Will being so public-spirited!'

'We ain't seen him since,' put in Sandy unhelpfully.

'Perhaps he's been working in the quarr all night,' said Amelia defensively. 'I hope he's not overdoing it, he must sleep sometime.' She looked worried when she should have been in high spirits with the opening of her shop.

Oh, he's been in the quarr all night, Charlie thought malevolently. She felt furious with Will, and disgusted that Ma couldn't see any wrong in him.

Even so she was concerned, not only that he took a chance by having smuggled goods in his quarr; she also feared that the old workings might collapse.

Oh dear God, such risks! Life was so uncertain, and when things changed for the worse they never seemed to get quite right again.

Her family had been poor when Dad was alive, but at least they had each other, and knew where they stood.

It did no good to brood.

'Where's Hetty? Isn't she supposed to be helping?'

'I told her to meet us at the shop,' said Amelia. 'There's no point her coming all the way up here to go down again.'

They started down the valley; the boys pushed the handcart, while the women carried the lighter bundles. The town was waking up, but the shops weren't busy as most able-bodied folk were gone to help in the fields.

Which made the presence of the yeomanry even more conspicuous. They were seeking something, entering every shop, pub, and dwelling.

'All right, boys,' said Amelia, as they stood and gaped at the soldiers. 'It's none of our business, and we can manage. You'd best get on to the fields.'

Tommy and Sandy went off to join the reapers who, having worked

212

the drink out of their systems, now looked forward to the promised harvest home celebrations. Charlie and Amelia began to off-load the cart.

The workmen whom Henry Warren employed had done a good job on the premises. The little shop looked quite new.

One corner was equipped with a trough and water-pump, for soaking the straw to make it pliable, and chairs were provided for Ma and Hetty to sit on while they plaited. There were shelves for the finished bonnets and other items, and drawers for cottons and ribbons, and sewing-equipment.

Rush matting covered the floor, in the centre of which was a counter with a cash-drawer, where Ma could do her accounts. They would display the best items on the wide window-ledge.

Charlie stowed bundles of straw beneath the counter, and was outside fetching the last one when Hetty ran up.

'You're late,' snapped Charlie.

'I know, I'm sorry,' gasped Hetty, her plump bosom heaving. 'I couldn't help it, miss, 'tis me Gran . . .' She paused to catch her breath.

'Your Gran, is she ill?'

'Naow, not she.' Hetty shook her head, 'The sojers come, see, an' asked if she knew anythin' about ol' Skinner . . .'

'Horace Skinner, why would they ask her about him?'

'They bin askin' everyone, to find out who saw him laast,' Hetty panted, still excited. 'He bin drowned, the sojers found'n this mornin', washed up on shore.'

'Horace Skinner – drowned!' Charlie repeated stupidly, as an icy hand gripped her heart. The man was unpopular before he joined the coastguard as an auxiliary, but he and Will in particular didn't get on.

'He was all bruised an' battered,' she heard Hetty saying. 'They think he might'a bin murdered. They searched the ruins, then had the cheek to turn me Gran's place upside down. They dint find nothin'.'

'So, there was a landing on the night of the Princess' visit?' said Charlie, gravely.

'I ain't sayin' thaat, miss. They was only lookin' because ol' Skinner got drowned. They don't *know* there was a landing, and me gran got so mad she sent me to fetch Merchant Warren, 'cause e's a JP, an' a friend o' hers. Thass why I be late.'

'Well, what did he do?'

'He told 'em good an' proper, oh aah. Jus' 'cause ol' Skinner's a coastguard, he told 'em, don't mean there was foul play. If theer was, he asked 'em, then where's the goods? "You ain't found nothin' 'ave you," he says—'

'What about Maltravers?' interrupted Charlie snappily. 'Did they search Underhill Manor?' Hetty must know her gran, Warren, and Maltravers were all in it together.

'Ooh, they wouldn't do thaat, he's more feared than yer granddad. Naow, ol' Warren got ever so hoighty-toighty with 'em. Said Skinner got drunk celebratin' the royal visit same as everybody else, an' when he went to the look-out, he must o' wandered off the path, an' fell over th'edge. He got all bruised fallin' on the rocks. Oh aah, 'e sent 'em off wi' their tails 'tween their legs.'

It was evident from her expression that Hetty admired Charlie's granddad. She gave a big grin. 'I reckon they was glad to stop lookin'. They all got hangovers.'

'Hm, I see.' Charlie sighed inwardly. Perplexed, and not at all satisfied, she dumped the last bundle of straw on Hetty. 'You take this in to Ma, tell her I'm returning Sam's handcart.'

'All right, miss.' Disappointed that Charlie hadn't shown more interest in her news, Hetty entered the shop gearing herself up to repeat her tale to Mrs Freer.

There wasn't much the blacksmith didn't know. Sure there was a landing yesterday with Will mixed up in it, Charlie hoped Sam Roper could make sense of what was going on.

Dick at least was in the clear. He'd been at the royal reception, and had been working hard in his free time to do up his and Maisie's cottage.

In the smithy yard she was surprised to see Will with Henry Warren, who was settling a bill. She couldn't speak to Sam, apart from thanking him for the loan of the handcart, but she fairly leapt on Will.

'I want to talk to you,' she said and dragged him out of the two older men's hearing. 'Where the hell have you been all this time? Ma's worried stiff about you. She thinks you're working too hard, but I know what you're up to!'

Will stared at her, his face white and passive, most unlike his usual aggressive self. Still he tried to bluff her.

'I don't know what you'm on about.'

'Don't lie to me, Will. It's not like you to leave the quarr for harvesting.' Unknowingly, she punched him on his wounded arm and made him wince.

'You're hurt,' she gasped. 'How did it happen? Tell me, or I'll tell Ma what you're up to, and that you've got contraband hidden at the quarr.'

To her dismay, Will folded on to a bench and hid his face in his hands. His shoulders shook, and he moaned through his fingers.

There was something badly wrong. She'd never seen him cry, not even when their dad was killed. Even so, she insisted she knew his trouble was to do with smuggling.

'Was it you beat up Skinner and pushed him off the cliff?'

He blurted out the whole story, and finished by explaining that he'd sent the boys harvesting because he couldn't work until his wound healed. He wouldn't tell her where the stuff was hidden.

'Only some of it's in our quarr, an' I'll get rid of it.' His dark eyes were full of pain, and pleading. 'You got to believe me, Sis, I had nothin' to do with killin' Skinner, and the crew's loyal to our grand-dad.

'He's goin' to help me get to London, and I'll be out of it all, leaving you and Ma in peace.'

'That's if nobody discovers the truth, if they do you'll be arrested as an accomplice!' Charlie felt frightened and angry, but for Ma's sake she promised to keep quiet on condition he kept his word to get rid of all he was hiding, and leave the trade. She saw Warren and Sam looking their way.

'Pull yourself together, Will, before they guess what you've told me. Let 'em think I've been telling you off, and Ma's after you for not coming home for two nights.'

She took Will's good arm, and offered him a crumb of comfort. 'Now you know how our dad must have felt; he saw worse things on the battlefield.'

'Ye-es,' said Will. Unaccustomed respect crept into his voice. 'Our dad must 'a killed a few. No wonder he was glad to get back to quar-ryin'.'

Charlie walked slowly back to her ma's shop, trying to gather her scattered thoughts. Everything was spoilt. She would *have* to leave Sir Alan's employ for his and the children's sake. If Will was found out after she'd left Lackford Hall, at least that family would be spared any disgrace.

She wouldn't confide in Ma – how could she, without hurting her.

215

If only things would settle down, and allow Will to get to London. It seemed the best she could hope for. No doubt Sir Alan would go away when the children returned to school, and then, she hoped, it would all blow over.

Impatiently she wiped away a tear. She'd made one sacrifice for her family; now, because of Will she had to make another. She must leave the man she'd grown to love, just when it seemed he might love her, too. Hadn't he said he couldn't do without her?

Ah well, it served her right. She'd always wanted to better herself, but she'd aimed too high. Huh! She grimaced through her tears; wouldn't it have been one in the eye for Granddad Warren!

It was all she could manage to put on a brave face in front of Ma and Hetty. By the afternoon the shop was straight, and she made her excuses to get back to the hall. Now she must think of a convincing reason to give Sir Alan as to why she had to leave.

As she dragged her steps back to the hall, she remembered how once, during a quarrel with Will, she'd told him that one day he would come to her, cap in hand.

Well, he had, and it brought her no joy or satisfaction. Only misery.

After their exhilarating ride along the cliff-top, Isobel felt rather flat as she, Papa and Hugh crossed the valley and walked their horses up the winding lane to Underhill Manor. She could think of nothing worse than dining with the Maltravers. Great-aunt Jane always complained of headaches, and Uncle Simon had shifty eyes. She'd seen the sly way they'd narrowed in church when the banns were read for Dick and Maisie, and the contemptuous look he gave Charlie during the royal visit.

Come to think of it, she'd enjoyed seeing Charlie, looking like a real lady on Papa's arm . . . She made faces at Hugh behind their father's back.

'It's a pity Miss Freer couldn't come,' said Hugh, pointedly, and poked out his tongue.

'Yes, it is,' replied Isobel. She wrinkled her nose at him. 'If she hadn't had to help her mother, she could have looked after us, and we wouldn't have to go to Uncle Simon's.'

'Don't you enjoy my company then?' asked their papa. He gave them a look of mock hurt. 'You made enough fuss the other day when I couldn't come walking with you.'

'Oh, Papa, we love every minute with you,' purred Isobel endearingly, 'but Aunt and Uncle Maltravers are so, well, boring, to be quite frank!'

Sir Alan chuckled. 'And Miss Freer isn't?'

'No,' said Hugh, 'she's fun.'

'Well, my son, I'm sorry, but it's as well to learn there are times when duty must come before pleasure. We owe your aunt and uncle a visit. It would be rude not to accept their invitation. Besides, it gives Cook a rest.'

'When duty calls,' sighed Isobel theatrically.

'Tell you what,' began Sir Alan, suddenly remembering what it was he'd forgotten. He'd had a vague feeling all morning of something missing. Dammit, if Miss Freer had been with them he would have remembered sooner.

'If you behave yourselves today Miss Freer and I will take you for a picnic on Sunday.'

'Oh, yes!' cried Isobel. 'You said you would discuss it with her.'

'That's right. We also discussed young Master Dick and Maisie's wedding. Would you both like to attend? They'll be wed before you go back to school.'

'I suppose so.' Isobel was still a bit put out that Dick had been courting Maisie, whom she had never got on with. He could at least have sought her approval. 'Is Char – er – Miss Freer going?'

'Of course.' Her papa nodded. 'We're going to make it an occasion that everyone on the estate will celebrate. Give them a half-holiday.'

'Another duty to perform,' conceded Hugh as if it were a matter of life and death. 'Well, I don't mind going if Charlie's going.'

'Who?'

'Sorry, Papa. Miss Freer.' Hugh grimaced at Isobel who was glaring at him.

Neither child realized how they amused their papa. He was enjoying this time alone with them, thanks to Miss Freer's hints and gentle admonitions. Also, the harvest was almost done.

Now Underhill Manor was in sight.

'Look, we're nearly there, so settle down, and behave yourselves.'

The garden was in full bloom; eye-catching colours and the scent of roses attracted bees and butterflies. Inwardly, Sir Alan sighed. It would be nice if Miss Freer was with them.

'Perhaps, if you're very good,' he said, 'Aunt Jane will allow you to cut some roses for Miss Freer.'

Both children agreed.

'I promise we'll be on our best behaviour, Papa,' said Isobel. To show how well they meant, they greeted their great-aunt and uncle with radiant smiles.

They behaved impeccably throughout luncheon, and listened intently to the news about Horace Skinner, and the conversation surmising as to how he had met his end.

But when that topic was exhausted, and Maltravers asked their papa: 'How goes the harvest?' they began to fidget.

'It's starting to cloud, so there'll be storms building up, but I believe we'll make it,' said Sir Alan. 'I'm glad I insisted on having the teams work on Sundays. Actually, I was thinking of combining the harvest supper with Dick and Maisie's wedding at the end of the month.'

'It will be our duty to attend,' put in Hugh, trying to sound grown-up.

Isobel could no longer contain her boredom. Aunt Jane looked weary too; perhaps she didn't want to hear about Dick and Maisie either. However, the mention of marriage made her forget her promise.

'Papa is thinking of marrying our Miss Freer,' she declared impulsively, her face full of wicked pleasure. She knew she was being outrageous, but the thrill of making mischief was greater than her sense of caution.

'Isobel!' gasped her papa, but she was engrossed in studying Aunt Jane's face for her reaction. She was not disappointed.

Aunt Jane's mouth dropped open; then, as words failed her it pinched up, and nearly disappeared. She stared blankly at her husband.

Uncle Simon was first to regain his senses.

'Nephew,' he blustered, 'your young scallywag is jesting?'

When Sir Alan made no reply, he added; 'You can't be serious!'

Seeing the black look on her papa s face, Isobel's excitement waned. She'd livened things up, but now would come the reckoning.

She was saved by her little brother.

Hugh resented the venomous look Uncle Simon directed at his papa.

'Yes, he is, we all want her to marry us. Can we go and pick some flowers now, please Aunt Jane?'

Jane Maltravers blinked.

'Er – yes, why not?' She was too startled to refuse. 'But – you won't trample on them, will you?'

'No, Aunt. Thank you, Aunt,' they chirruped, and gleefully made their escape.

Sir Alan recovered himself, and decided to make a clean breast of the matter. If the idea caused a scandal, it would pass, and that would be preferable to exaggerated rumours.

'Would it be so shocking?' he asked. 'After all, you would have married her mother once. Besides, nothing's been said to her, and she may well refuse. I do know she's fond of Isobel and Hugh, that's why they want to pick flowers – for her.'

'My boy, you don't know what you're doing,' said Maltravers, trying to sound reasonable. 'It would be most unwise.' He reminded his nephew of his sisters' visit. 'Beulah's right, she's a fortune-hunter, and you know my opinion of the wench.'

'Well, you were wrong about her and my groom,' said Sir Alan, petulantly. 'He and Maisie are made for each other. Miss Freer is young, and willing to learn. As you know, there is French aristocracy in her blood. She has enough breeding to make a darn good hostess—'

'But she is *not* her grandmother,' said Maltravers, slapping the table. 'She has peasant ways – teaching your children rough games – and the way she dresses when you're away! Do you really expect to turn her into a lady?'

'She was every inch a lady at Princess Victoria's reception,' said Sir Alan doggedly. 'A tomboy, perhaps, but she has great charm and knows how to behave. She's tactful, and most reliable, I should hate to lose her.'

'I still say you should be guided by your sisters,' persisted Maltravers.

'My sisters are a little above themselves, since they've lived in Town. Anyway the subject was broached with them and when they heard of Miss Freer's background their attitude softened. I believe they'll get used to the idea.'

He glanced at Jane. Her pale face was devoid of expression.

'They'll accept her once she is my wife,' he added persuasively. 'They do have my happiness in mind.' A whimsical smile teased his lips. 'Miss Freer is good for the children, and for me . . .'

He paused, then looked fully at Maltravers. 'She's brought a lot of meaning back into our lives. In short, Uncle, I love her, and I intend to marry her – if she'll have me.'

'*If* she'll have you!' thundered Maltravers, his black-browed eyes fierce. 'Don't you realize she's as two-faced as the rest of her kind? Half her folk are engaged in smuggling, but you wouldn't think butter would melt in their mouths.

Jane gave a resigned sigh, but neither man took any notice. They were too busy glaring at each other.

'She's dishonest, m'boy,' cried Maltravers, furiously. 'She's after wealth and position. A man of your status should never trust a chit of a woman like her!'

He wagged a finger vigorously under his nephew's nose, 'Don't forget, you're years older, and in my opinion she's playing you for a fool, worming her way into your affections. She'll marry you for what she can get, then take a lover when your back's turned. Love, be damned!'

'I didn't ask for your opiniom.' Sir Alan retorted.

Suddenly Jane Maltravers stood up.

'If you'll excuse me, gentlemen, I'll go and cut the children some roses.'

She went to find the straw bonnet she'd bought from Amelia at the Whit Tuesday fair, and a pair of secateurs. The truth was she could no longer bear to listen to her despicable spouse.

She'd been disillusioned long ago. He'd married her for money, and she'd been fool enough to think it would buy his affection. He soon tired of her when no babies came, and what money he didn't waste over-planting his wheatfields, he'd lost gambling.

The conversation had begun to irritate her when they mentioned the forthcoming marriage of Dick and Maisie. She had no idea what her husband did when he was in London, and on those occasions when she went home to visit her father, she wouldn't be surprised if Simon made hay while the sun shone with that sly Maisie who once worked for them.

Not that it bothered her now, but lately she'd become aware that her husband had some bugbear, other than their dismal marriage. And why should he care if Alan wanted to marry beneath himself?

Jane felt sure that for some reason Simon was using Miss Freer to vent his spite. She herself hardly knew the girl, but quite liked her mother.

'Ohh!' She breathed a long, vexed sigh; her head throbbed from the men's quarrel. Her garden was her only consolation in this miserable life of perpetually putting on side to impress or to save face.

What fools we women are, she thought. Someone ought to warn Miss Freer, not Sir Alan. Look what happened to his first wife!

She dismissed the men from her mind, and helped Isobel and Hugh make up a bouquet for Miss Freer. How lovely, to be so appreciated.

*

Rather than endure further unpleasantness, Sir Alan left immediately. The children were happy to go home and put their flowers in water before they wilted.

'I'm sorry I spoke out of turn, Papa,' said Isobel penitently, seeing her father's sober expression. 'I only meant to liven things up, not cause trouble. I didn't know they disliked Miss Freer so much. Does it mean, if you marry her, she can never go to our uncle's house?'

Sir Alan reached across from his horse and squeezed his daughter's hand.

'She doesn't care for them either,' he said, with a tight-lipped smile. 'I'm sure our Miss Freer would find something else to occupy her.'

'You can't call her Miss Freer when you're married, Papa.' Isobel's brow creased at the thought.

'She doesn't like being called Charlotte,' Hugh stated flatly from behind.

'What'll you do?' asked Isobel, and both children gazed wide-eyed at their papa.

'We shall cross that bridge when we come to it.' He smiled, his good humour restored. 'And you two should remember we haven't yet come to it. Never take things for granted, and don't go bleating about it to Miss Freer. We don't want to frighten her off, do we?'

'All right, Papa,' said Isobel sweetly, 'but we can put the flowers in her room to surprise her, can't we?'

'I don't see why not.' He nodded absently, he was thinking pleasurably of ways he might cross certain bridges.

As his two excited children searched the pantry for a suitable vase, Sir Alan felt a tug at his heart. He'd forgotten what it was like, to be a child planning a surprise.

They made their selection, and he was about to retire to his study when he saw Fudge the ginger tom follow them upstairs.

'Mind that cat,' he called after them. 'Make sure he comes down again, won't you?'

'Yes, Papa,' they replied dutifully. They put the vase on Charlie's dressing-table, and stood back to admire their handiwork.

'It looks like two lots of flowers,' said Hugh, waggling his head from side to side at the reflection in the mirror.

'Quick, she's coming,' squealed Isobel, looking out the window.

'She's just crossing Farmer Brown's field.' They rushed to the top of the stairs.

'Oh-oh, where's Fudge?' said Hugh, 'I can't see him.'

'Go and find him,' urged Isobel. 'I'll keep watch at the landing window.'

Hugh saw the tip of Fudge's tail poking out beneath the coverlet on Charlie's bed. 'Come out, you pesky cat,' he cried. He ducked down on all fours to crawl after the animal.

'Hurry, Hugh,' called Isobel from the landing window. 'She's at the garden gate!'

'Coming,' she heard Hugh's muffled reply. Next moment she was startled by his sudden shriek: 'Hey, Izzie – what's this?'

Groaning with impatience, Isobel hurried back to Charlie's room.

Hugh scrambled out from under the bed, his hair and clothes awry. In his hands he clutched the shiny silver casket.

'You shouldn't touch other people's things,' shouted Isobel bossily.

'Well, why would she hide it under the bed?' piped Hugh, genuinely puzzled.

Isobel frowned. 'I've seen it before,' she said, 'I'm sure it belonged to our mama.'

She had been nine when their mother died, and she vaguely remembered such an object on Mama's dressing-table.

She grabbed the casket from Hugh and rushed on to the landing.

'Papa, Papa! Do come and see what Hugh's found!'

Sir Alan was already on his way, having heard their shouts. He couldn't bear them being noisy in the house.

Isobel held the casket out to him as he reached the top of the stairs.

'Oh, Papa, did you give it to Char – to Miss Freer? I haven't seen it for years and years. What's the matter, Papa?'

Sir Alan stared as if he couldn't believe his eyes. Nor did he want to.

'Neither have I,' he said slowly, his face ashen.

'Is it real silver, Papa?' asked Hugh, unable to understand what the fuss was about.

'Yes,' said Sir Alan, 'and no, I didn't give it her. I asked her to keep her eye open for it, and bring it to me if she found it.'

He'd mentioned the missing casket to Miss Freer months ago, when he promoted her to housekeeper, and asked her to sort out the things in the cellars.

She'd obviously found it, and kept it.

'Finders keepers?' suggested Hugh hopefully. Even he realized the serious implications.

'She'd never steal it, would she, Papa?' Isobel shook his sleeve. 'Surely not. Oh, not Miss Freer?'

A muscle flickered in his cheek as he looked miserably at the casket. She must have had it in her possession since April. What other explanation was there?

CHAPTER TWENTY

C HARLIE knew something was wrong as soon as she arrived at the hall and bumped into Cook.

Mrs Biggins surveyed her with a mixture of triumph and contempt.

'I was tidyin' the attic,' she said shortly, 'when I heard Master's kids run upstairs to your room.'

'They're back already?'

'Aah, they was all excited, shriekin' like, then the master comes up, an' it all went quiet.' Cook put her head to one side, and looked quizzically at Charlie. 'I dunno what you bin up to, but I don't think they'm very happy. I come on down the back stairs . . .'

Charlie was already running up the stairs to the first landing. Her heart pounded ominously. What were they doing in her room? As if she didn't have enough on her plate!

She slowed to a halt as she reached the open door. The three Lackfords stood rigid as the statues in their niches, their faces almost as white. At the open window, the flapping curtains emphasized their shocked stillness, and three pairs of eyes stared accusingly at her.

Her gaze slid to the silver casket Sir Alan held in his hands. She'd forgotten all about it with the hectic events of the past week.

She guessed what they were thinking, and how guilty she must look.

Sir Alan's expression was the worst, there was such a haunted look in his eyes she felt too stunned to speak. Isobel broke the silence.

'How *could* you, Miss Freer? We thought you were our friend!' Choking on a sob she pushed past Charlie and ran from the room.

Hugh eyed her dumbly, his eyes sad like Shepherd Tom's dog.

'We brought you some flowers,' he said petulantly, 'then Fudge hid under your bed, so I went after him.' He nodded at the casket, 'And I found . . . it.'

Charlie barely noticed the beautiful roses on her dressing-table. How stupid of her to have forgotten the casket.

'Leave us, Hugh,' said Sir Alan. 'Go and keep your sister company. I'll join you both directly.' There was such disillusion in the look he levelled at her, Charlie couldn't bear to think what the misunderstanding was doing to him and the children. She must explain.

She dared to meet his eyes with indignant denial, but shocked by the sudden change in his manner, her words came clumsily.

'Sir, I can explain if you give me time . . . I have my reasons—'

'I'm sure you do,' he snapped. 'It seems my uncle was right.' He paused, then added more in sadness than anger: 'Do you really take me for such an old fool?'

'What? No! Oh, no, of course not . . .' So, Maltravers had got at him before they found the casket. They'd returned so early – if only she'd been back before them!

'Please sir, please give me time to—'

'I'll give you time, Miss Freer. I shall go and settle the children down, they are very unhappy. Perhaps I shall be calm enough to listen to you by the time I return.'

He took the casket, and shut her door behind him.

Only an hour ago he'd defended her to his Uncle Maltravers, confessed he loved her, and declared his intention to marry her!

Now, seeing her look so guilty and caught on the hop, Maltravers' words rang in his ears: *She's a fortune hunter, out for what she can get. She is not her grandmother . . . has peasant ways, unruly, her folk engaged in smuggling – dishonest . . .*

For the second time in his life he felt rejected by a woman he'd been fool enough to fall in love with. Only this time he wouldn't give way to weakness or despair. For his children's sake he would be strong.

Charlie collapsed on her bed and wept. This was too much. Why, oh why had she so stupidly left the casket under her bed?

She shuddered in despair, and tried to pull herself together, to think.

Should she simply tell the truth? That she'd found it only a few days ago, and kept it to clean? Which meant whoever stole the thing must have hidden it and forgotten all about it.

Even if Sir Alan believed her he was bound to think someone from the hall had stolen it. He'd blame Hetty, or Maisie, which would spoil everything for her and Dick. And what about those letters? She'd shoved them back quickly when she'd been interrupted by Isobel, the day they heard of the royal visit. It hadn't occurred to her to hide them separately, because she forgot them in the excitement.

They would prove her words, and he would learn of his wife's affair with his uncle.

God, how she hated Maltravers! She had all the proof she needed against that evil man, yet something held her back. What would the discovery of such a dreadful secret do to Sir Alan, and his children?

In the back of her mind lay the intention to keep the matter from him until Isobel and Hugh returned to school for the autumn term, to spare them any needless torment.

But she'd hardly had time to turn round, let alone consider such puzzling things. First the sisters' visit, then the Princess, and her worries over Will – and what with the harvest, and helping Ma in the shop . . . Not only had she had no time to think, she was always too tired by bedtime to even remember.

She was tired now, and her thoughts ran in circles.

Even if she had remembered, and returned the casket to Squire without the letters, how could she have explained finding it? He would still think Maisie or Hetty had stolen it.

Well, he had it now, love-letters and all.

Before she could decide which course to take, Sir Alan threw open the door and stood looking at her.

As he watched her jump up, and stand before him wide-eyed and childlike, groping for words to proclaim her innocence, he could well believe Maltravers. *You're years older than she is, she's playing you for a fool!*

She was crying, a feminine ploy to weaken him. Yes, he really had been stupid enough to be taken in by her youth and beauty.

He shook his head. It was so hard to believe that her patience and tact with his children was a front. She had brightened their lives, and brought the three of them closer. Yet how cruelly she'd let them down. The promised picnic was off, and they would miss the harvest supper. Their hurt was as great to them as his own was to him; it made him angry, and in no mood for excuses. He thrust out a hand.

'The key to the casket, if you please, Miss Freer.'

She winced at the sarcastic way he spoke her name.

'I don't have it, sir. There wasn't one when I found it.'

His hand dropped as he scrutinized her with eyes pale as cold steel.

'Very well, that is the least of our problems.'

226

Oh, dear God, she thought, he believes I've stolen jewellery from it!

'Sir,' she pleaded, 'I promise you the casket has only been in my possession for a week! I kept it to clean it, before handing it back to you – then . . . then I forgot about it.' She took a step towards him, her hands outstretched. 'You know how busy it's been since your sisters came . . .'

A plausible attempt . . . His sisters, yes. Besotted with her, he'd paid no regard to their warnings either.

'Miss Freer, if you had merely forgotten the casket, why hide it under your bed?'

She had no answer. She bit her lips, and blinked away tears.

'No, I don't accept your explanation,' he went on coldly. 'Must you add lies to your deceit?'

She had been using a deception of sorts, but she was no liar. She swallowed a protest as anger began to rise. It cleared her brain. Being called a liar on top of being accused of stealing, roused her stubborn pride, and lent her strength.

She'd always tried to please to the best of her ability, and this was all the thanks she got. Let him think what he liked, and to hell with his sisters and Maltravers. He would get the casket open soon enough, then he would know the truth. In the meantime she was in disgrace, and nothing she could say was going to make any difference. She stood erect, and glared at him defiantly.

'Do you have nothing to say?'

Behind his icy gaze there was disappointment. She could at least have the decency to make some apology, promise to make amends. He could almost forgive her, even now, if only she showed some remorse. He understood temptation.

'Yes sir.' She threw back her head and returned his gaze unwavering. 'You will never know how sorry I am, to cause your children unnecessary distress. I would not hurt them – nor you – for the world. As it is, I have no choice but to leave your employ.'

She had to leave anyway, because of Will, but she hadn't reckoned on leaving because of her own disgrace. 'Shall you have me up before the magistrate?'

There would be a few sorry faces if he did, she thought, darkly.

He flinched, taken aback by her vehemence. Except for the hurt to his children he could still admire her, despite his anguish.

'Miss Freer, I *am* a magistrate. You are right, you're dismissed, but no, I shall not press charges. I wish to avoid a scandal, and I respect your mother. Therefore I shall not make an issue of this matter. You may tell her what you will.'

As far as gossip-mongers were concerned it would be nothing new for him to get rid of a servant without good reason.

'Also,' his expression wavered briefly, 'because, whatever you are, you have taught my children and myself to appreciate each other. For that at least, I thank you.'

Anger spent, she lowered her eyes, and tried in vain to stem her tears. When she looked up he was standing at the window, his back to her, his hands clasped behind him.

'In the morning I shall take the children to Lyme, and spend the rest of the summer with the family. It may raise their spirits.'

He turned abruptly, and walked to the door. 'Leave as soon as you're ready,' he said, without looking at her. 'I will tell the other servants that I'm letting you go as there will be little for you to do here. I shall be gone for some time, and no longer need a housekeeper. Ponsonby and Mrs Biggins can see to arrangements for Dick and Maisie.'

And that was all. Nothing about the time she still owed him, nor a chance to say her ma would pay him off.

She trembled with resentment at the injustice as she packed her few belongings, and left her best dresses hanging beside those of Lady Lackford's that she'd altered for second-best.

She would take nothing that wasn't hers alone.

Gathering her last shreds of pride, she took her bundle, and went to say a tentative goodbye to Cook and Maisie. To her surprise they were sympathetic.

'I always knew 'e was tight,' said Cook, 'but I'm blowed if this don't beat all. Sackin' you to save wages while he's away!'

Maisie was genuinely sorry to see her go.

'You will come to me weddin', won't you?'

Well, *he* wasn't likely to be there.

'Yes, I'd love to, Maisie. Ma, and Hetty, too?'

'Oh, everybody,' said Maisie, her eyes shining. 'I want whoever to come who wants to, excepts ol' Maltravers and his wife. "They ain't invited," I says to Dick, and he says, "Fine by me"!'

Has she guessed he had something to do with my going, Charlie wondered.

'All right, and I'll come and visit you when you've moved into your cottage,' she promised.

Amelia was surprised to see her, 'You've come home – with your things! What's happened?'

Charlie had never felt so miserable. She'd been falsely accused of theft and deception by Sir Alan, and now she must deceive her ma. What would it do to Ma, if she told the truth, that she'd been dismissed in disgrace, and Will was up to his neck in smuggling and murder?

'Squire's decided he doesn't need me any more,' said Charlie. She repeated what he said about going to Lyme. 'The children will go back to school from there.'

She was thankful that her ma seemed satisfied.

Charlie wondered how long it would be before Sir Alan opened the casket and found the letters. Perhaps he wouldn't bother, then he'd never learn the truth. . . .

Late into the night, in his study, Sir Alan sat with furrowed brow surveying the casket he'd once valued so much. Somehow it didn't seem important any more, and he wished fervently he'd never mentioned the damned thing.

He had no key to fit the lock, which was loose as if someone had tampered with it. It felt light, and whatever rustled inside wasn't jewellery. Well, there was no hurry, he'd take it to Lyme and find a locksmith who could furnish the right key.

'Don't you want your breakfast?'

Amelia watched Charlie stirring her porridge lethargically. Will had been strangely quiet, too, but had gone to the quarr with Sandy.

Charlie took a mouthful, then lay down her spoon.

'I'm not really hungry.'

Amelia saw the sorrow in her daughter's eyes. Charlie was mooning over Sir Alan, and his children. He was out of her life, so she'd just have to get over it, and perhaps it was just as well. She must realize that a match with Squire wasn't to be, because last night she said she'd been thinking of leaving the hall anyway.

'What will you do today?' Amelia asked. 'Come and help in the shop?'

Charlie grimaced inwardly. In her present state she couldn't stand Hetty's chatter.

'Not today, Ma, would you mind? But if Tommy brings me a bundle of straw, I'll do some plaiting at home.'

'All right, Charlie. Perhaps you'll be better on your own for a bit.' Amelia held back a sigh of exasperation. 'Come on, Tommy, I've got a lot to do.'

She had no time to worry about her daughter's love-sickness, or Will's moods. Maybe it was to do with the royal visit. Too much excitement wasn't good for anyone.

Thank heavens things were getting back to normal. She just wished Charlie wasn't so pale.

It was noon when Amelia left Hetty in charge of the shop, and came out for a break. She strolled along the river bank, and met Jane Maltravers wearing a wide-brimmed sun-hat.

Surprisingly, Jane wanted to stop and chat. It wasn't like her, but then she seemed easier without Simon around. They discussed Amelia's business, and how Hetty was doing, then Jane asked after Charlie.

Amelia was about to reply when they saw the Lackford coach pull up at the crossroads. It turned left and took the highway to Corvesgate. There were trunks on the back, and Dick Farmer was driving.

'Oh?' Jane Maltravers craned her neck. 'Sir Alan and his children. They came to luncheon yesterday, but they didn't say they were going away.' She turned to Amelia, her eyes curious. 'Your daughter isn't going with them, then?'

'Why, no,' said Amelia, startled. 'She came home last evening. I'm surprised your nephew didn't tell you they were going to Lyme for the rest of the summer. My daughter said something about the children missing their cous . . .'

She broke off, seeing Jane's sudden strange expression. 'What made you think she might be going with them? She was told she's not needed any more because the children will go on to school from there. Squire plans to be away a long time.'

'Oh, nothing really.' Jane Maltravers shook her head, 'One sort of assumes these things, knowing how well she got on with them.'

There was no point saying Alan wanted to marry the girl; Simon had obviously caused their nephew to change his mind. Now he was putting distance between them.

Jane untethered her pony.

'I'd better be going, Mrs Freer,' she said guardedly, 'or I shall be late for luncheon. Good day to you.'

'Goodbye, Mrs Maltravers, it was nice talking to . . .' Amelia found herself addressing thin air. The Honourable Mrs Maltravers was already trotting towards Underhill Manor.

Charlie's ma shrugged, and returned to her shop. She had better things to do than concern herself with the goings-on of the quality.

Simon Maltravers stood in the garden, his hands tucked beneath his coat-tails, and scowled at the sunflowers. Thanks to his nephew's meddling the harvest was well in hand, therefore flour and bread prices in this area would remain stable this winter.

Alan was too soft. He even disapproved of pressing leases on the quarrymen to make more money from the land they quarried. Why, he would have no money at all if he followed Alan's ideas of sharing his land for nothing more than royalties on the stone. And what with the recent news in the *Chronicle* of Parliament's endless reforms session . . .

Even spending up to twelve hours a day in the House, members weren't expected to finish before the end of the month. Not that he was bothered about the state of Ireland, or the renewal of the charters of the Bank of England and East India Company. Nor did he care that old Wilberforce had worked himself to death trying to get slavery abolished.

His one concern was the House's intention to repeal certain taxes. The smuggling trade was dying. Soon he'd have no use for Henry Warren, or his precious grandson.

Another thing: if they amended the dower and inheritance laws, Jane would have the right to own her own property! It was to be hoped that her elderly father would die soon, before – talk of the devil, here she was, back from her jaunt to the village.

For once her cheeks were rosy, and her eyes alight, but her passion was not to his liking.

'I hope you're satisfied, *Mr Maltravers*!' she cried, deliberately snubbing him, for he was less than honourable in her eyes.

His scowl deepened. What vexed her now?

'I met that nice Mrs Freer in the village. Honestly, Simon, I don't know why you dislike that family so much. Anyway, it seems you've persuaded Alan not to marry Miss Freer. He's gone to spend the remainder of the holidays in Lyme, and Miss Freer is dismissed.'

She dismounted, and handed the reins to the stable-boy who

appeared. 'Mrs Freer and I saw them driving off with all their trunks on board the coach.'

'My dear.' He smiled the sarcastic smile he knew she hated. 'For once you've told me something I'm glad to hear.' His face became sober. 'Who was driving?'

'Why, Dick Farmer of course,' she answered, and walked past him into the house.

She ate luncheon in silence, her brow puckered, while her husband smiled to himself.

He'd finished Amelia's young whelp, now it was time for that brother of hers.

By the time he'd finished, it would be the ruin of the whole family of Freers.

CHAPTER TWENTY-ONE

THE smell of limewash greeted Maisie as she climbed the stairs to the upper room of the cottage that was to be hers and Dick's. Her work done for the day, she was within her rights to look around. Dick had spent last night at Lyme, and should be back by suppertime.

Now that he'd mended the doors and windows and the decorating was finished she'd soon have it looking cheerful and cosy. She'd picked some lavender from the garden, and opened the windows and let in the scent of climbing roses.

Maisie felt free and easy, knowing at last where she stood with Dick, and she hummed a tune as she chose a corner for the baby's cradle.

She heard footsteps come in below, and thought it was Dick already.

'I'm up here,' she called, and loosened her bodice to show off her breasts, plump with pregnancy. There'd been no chance for love-making lately, with so much going on, and them kids racing about. Now everyone was away, and the morning sickness had passed.

But it was Simon Maltravers who came upstairs. He paused in the doorway to ogle her.

'My, what a pretty sight,' he said, leering at her. He strode towards her.

Maisie shook her head, and stepped back.

'Don't you dare!'

'Oh, I forgot, we're respectable now,' he mocked.

'What do you want,' she snapped, hastily retying her bodice-ribbons. 'If you're looking for Dick, he'll be here any minute.'

'Then I'll wait, and maybe teach you more respect for your old master, to pass the time—'

'And p'raps I could tell Squire I was go-between for you and his wife,' she retorted. 'He'd love to know he was cuckolded by his own uncle!'

As Maltravers' expression changed, she added: 'I don't know what the mistress saw in an old man like you!' Insults were the best way to cool a man's ardour.

'You bitch!'

He lifted a hand to strike her, then to Maisie's relief she heard a horse canter up to the front door, and a sharp whinny.

Dick threw himself down, and ran inside and up the stairs.

'You here, Maisie? Cook said I'd . . .'

He stopped as Maltravers turned to face him.

Dick looked from one to the other, and Maisie made an appropriate face behind Maltravers' back. She didn't want her future husband getting the wrong idea.

'He wants to see you,' she said emphatically. 'I just happened to be yer lookin' round.'

'Yes, Master Farmer,' said Maltravers, sarcastically polite. 'Could we go outside and talk?'

'Don't mind me.' Maisie was annoyed by his interruption to her planned welcome for Dick. 'I'll stay here. The less I know about your smuggling, the better!'

Dick frowned, and led the way downstairs. Maisie peeped out of the dormer window, and saw them standing below. She listened intently as their voices floated up.

'I won't do it!' she heard Dick exclaim.

'You have no choice, m'lad,' said Maltravers evenly.

'It's bad enough betraying a mate,' groaned Dick, 'but telling lies makes me a false witness. Something you don't make no bones about!'

Maltravers shrugged. 'You can either tell the authorities you saw Will Freer push Horace Skinner off the cliff, or I will inform Squire that Skinner had told me you lent out your master's horses behind his back. Which would point to *you* wanting him silenced.'

'That was nothing to do with me, and you know it,' Dick cried, aghast. 'I drove Squire to the royal reception, I was nowhere near the cliff!'

'All the same,' retorted Maltravers menacingly, 'I can see to it that there is sufficient reason to have you and your bride dismissed. Without references or a roof over your heads, what would happen to you both then, eh?'

Dick's shoulders sagged.

'All right, you win. I'll go to the fort.'

'Wait until morning,' said Maltravers, falsely soothing, 'and we'll go together. Don't worry, you needn't be present when the soldiers arrest Master Freer at his quarr. They'll find his contraband, and that will clinch it. He need never know who betrayed him.'

His tone became icy as he mounted, and turned in the saddle. 'Don't forget, if you're not at Underhill by nine, I ride to Lyme!'

Groggily, Maisie came downstairs. Only half an hour ago she'd been so happy. What a way to begin a new life, with the betrayal of a friend on their consciences. She and Dick were no angels, but neither would have stooped that low from choice. Maltravers knew how to drag a person down.

'That man needs shooting,' she said vehemently when she saw Dick's worried face. There would be no love-making tonight.

'You heard?' Alarm showed in his eyes.

'No,' she lied. For his sake she pretended ignorance. 'I can see by the look on yer face he brought bad news – and I'll tell you this . . .' Maisie put her arms around him. 'I dunno what he wanted, but there'll never be anyone fer me but you, Dick Farmer. Don't 'ee fret, now. Me and the young un'll make up to you for all your troubles – and one o' these days, that Honourable Mr will get his come-uppance!'

Sir Alan strolled arm in arm with Sylvia along the Cobb. Isobel and Hugh had perked up, being with their cousins again, and he smiled a little when Isobel put her arm through Robert's to drag him ahead of the others.

But he still thought of Miss Freer. He'd dismissed her from his service, but he could not dismiss her from his mind. How could he have been so taken in? Could she have explained away the damning circumstances, had he allowed her to?

He bowed his head; wishful thinking was no use. Better that he found out now than make another disastrous marriage.

'Is anything wrong, Uncle?' Sylvia sensed that he would hardly desire to be with his sisters for Isobel and Hugh's sakes alone.

They had turned back, and he was saved from answering his niece as a messenger-boy dashed up. He recognized him as the locksmith's son.

'Here y'are, sir. Father says the new key works a treat.'

Sir Alan nodded at the boy as he took the package and put a coin in his hand. The boy doffed his cap, and grinned with pleasure.

'Thank you kindly, sir.'

Sir Alan left the package in his room while he ate luncheon with the family; later, tormented still by his emotions he went to lie down. He'd always thought Aunt Jane made too much of her headaches, but actually having one wasn't agreeable.

First, he sat on the bed, and unwrapped the package. He sighed heavily at the sight of the silver casket, and reluctantly decided to open it.

The new key turned easily in the lock, and he stared curiously at the folded sheets of paper inside. When he began to examine them, his blue eyes bulged as he saw that some were written a year or more before Helen died.

'*Dear Helen*,' said the first, '*I want to thank you for a most enjoyable day at the races . . . such pleasure in watching your excitement . . .*' It was signed, '*Simon*'.

There was only one Simon he knew who took his wife to the races at Dorchester: his uncle.

Well, nothing wrong in that . . . but then the letters became more intimate. It seemed the races were a front for what followed after. '*Such bliss . . .*' he adored her too, longing for the next time . . .

'Oh, God!' He dropped the letters, and bowed his head in his hands. No wonder Helen had been so cold. She clearly preferred the excitement of an illicit affair with an older man.

He remembered then how often Maltravers had visited after Hugh was born, and made them a 'present' of Maisie. Had she been their go-between?

Unable to believe it all, Sir Alan forced himself to read the letters again. They made him think.

As tiny tots, his children were often with Maisie while Helen busied herself arranging balls. She never organized local functions, or shared his fondness for the locals. And why should she?

She'd never experienced things like going to war, and mingling with ordinary men who were just as brave and patriotic as their superiors.

She must have found his devotion flattering, he realized now, but the affection she showed, which for him filled the gap left by his parents' deaths, bordered on pity.

How bored she must really have been.

Sir Alan lay down and closed his eyes. He could see now that she had withdrawn from him after Maltravers came into their lives, lavishing attention on her after his return from five years in London.

And he, fool that he was, had allowed the intrusion. Unable to bear her increasing coolness, he'd made himself scarce by going away frequently on business.

Yielding to the truth of his wife's infidelity with his own uncle, his sense of outrage was profound. All this time he'd blamed himself for her death, and the humiliating rejections he'd suffered at her hands. She didn't feel well, or she was too weak since Hugh's birth, and couldn't bear to be touched.

He remembered those times, when he was home, she'd locked herself in her room for two or three days on end with terrible headaches, worse apparently, than Jane Maltravers'.

Jane! Had Helen killed herself because Maltravers had married? Jane had a wealthy banker father, and Maltravers' relationship with Helen would always have to be clandestine . . .

At last he recognized his uncle for what he truly was, and rocked to and fro, groaning. Was Simon's rejection so bad that she had to kill herself – and abandon their children?

Ah yes, the children. When Isobel was old enough, Helen had insisted on sending her away to school. Because children noticed things, and told tales?

Hell, to think his children had been in their mother's way. How little she'd cared for them! What selfishness – and what a contrast to Miss Freer, who irritated him with her concern for them!

In an agony of disgust and anger he crushed the letters in his fists, and threw them to one side. As he did so, another piece of paper, jammed in the bottom of the casket, caught his eye.

It was another note, anonymous this time, the writing disguised. He studied it with shaking hands, and was astounded further by what he read.

His wife had been with child by her lover – his own uncle – who had casually abandoned her!

So that was it! The note was dated two days before Maltravers married Jane, and Helen had dosed herself the following day.

Sir Alan was devastated. He stayed in his room for two days, tormenting himself with old self-doubts, and guilt. At midday on the second day there was a knock at the door.

'Who is it?' he snapped. He was ready to tell either of his sisters to go away.

'It's Sylvia, Uncle. I've brought you some refreshment.'

He unlocked the door, and she stared at him in dismay as she stood there with a loaded tray. She wasn't used to seeing him look so haggard, and unshaven.

'You've had no breakfast, and you ate nothing yesterday,' she said pointedly, but there was gentleness, and genuine compassion in her eyes.

'I told your mother and your aunt, I am not well—'

'I know,' said Sylvia firmly, as she pushed past him. 'But I don't believe it's the sort of unwell that won't benefit from a good feed!'

How practical she was, like Char- Miss Freer . . .

'So, please eat,' she ordered, 'and you can listen while I speak. You must do as I ask, please, for my cousins' sakes. They are very unhappy.'

He sat down and took a bite from a piece of bread to please her.

'I thought they enjoyed being here.'

'They've tried, for your sake. They were unhappy when they arrived, but now you've locked yourself away it's unbearable for them, and they're being naughty.' She watched him eat some cheese, and cold meat. 'Have some wine, Uncle. It will put new life into you.'

She poured as she spoke, and pushed the glass towards him. 'Isobel told me what happened with the casket. I was very sorry to hear it. That's how I know they were unhappy when they came. They're upset about Miss Freer, and missing her.' She paused, then boldly added: 'I think they would forgive her, if you did.'

He was impressed by her forcefulness, and her attitude which was so different from his sisters'.

'Could you forgive her then, Sylvia?' he asked.

'No, Uncle. I could not, because I don't believe she had any intention of stealing the casket. I fear 'tis you who needs her forgiveness for misjudging her. I believe she *did* forget about it.'

'You are that sure of her?'

'Yes, and I know you miss her, too. But that's not why you're up here fretting, is it? I'm sure there's more to your melancholy, and I think you'd feel better if you talk to someone. Shall I fetch Mama, or Aunt Beulah?'

'No, no!' He pushed the tray aside, and sank wearily back on his pillows. He gave her a slight smile.

'How discerning you are, my dear.'

He gazed into the glass of wine he still held in his hand, and made up his mind. Sylvia, young as she was, had been married.

'Perhaps I can tell you, my dear, but not my sisters. I prefer your common sense to their vindictive attitude.'

Particularly Beulah's. If he confided in Adèle, who was more sympathetic, it would cause friction, for Beulah would have to know.

'It's not what happened before we left, it's far worse . . .'

He spent an hour unburdening himself, and showing his niece the letters.

'Can you follow it all, Sylvia?' he said at last.

'Ye-es,' she said thoughtfully. 'I appreciate how you must feel. It's a terrible shock. But I also understand that it happened five years ago, so is not fair on the children.'

'They're not to know about this,' he cried. How could I possibly tell them!'

Sylvia was thinking ahead. Maltravers was badly at fault, and Uncle Alan couldn't let the matter rest. The children must be told something.

'Perhaps not now, Uncle, but they may have to know sometime. For the moment I think you owe it to them, and to Char- er- Miss Freer, to explain that you were mistaken about her motives regarding the casket.'

'Ye-es, Miss Freer . . .'

Sylvia caught the tenderness in his tone as he mentioned the name.

'I never could believe il of that young woman, Uncle. I don't care what anyone says. I came to know her rather well that week, and I think it far more likely that she was trying to protect you from the truth.'

It would have been comical the way his eyebrows shot up, if things hadn't been so serious.

'You do? You think she opened the casket somehow, and read the letters?'

'How else could that anonymous note be in there, with those that Aunt Helen treasured? No. I'm certain Miss Freer spoke the truth when she said she'd forgotten it. In fact, I think she was waiting for the children to go back to school, to spare them any upset. She knew what a shock it would be for you. As indeed it is.'

Sylvia stood up. 'The past is past, Uncle, and none of us can change it.' She swallowed. 'I should know that.'

She laid a hand on his arm, and looked appealingly into his eyes. 'I hope you'll pardon me, but Miss Freer, and your children are your *present*. Please, Uncle, don't let this chance of happiness slip away.'

'What a wise head for such young shoulders,' said Sir Alan fondly. 'All right, tell the children I'll join them soon, after I clean up – and Sylvia . . .'

'Yes, Uncle?'

'Thank you, my dear.'

She smiled, and left him absently finishing the food.

He was thinking of Charlie again. Charlie – Miss Freer! She'd been telling the truth when she'd reminded him how busy they'd been, and really had meant to give it to him.

The only lie she'd ever told him was about the key, and that had been for his sake.

She must have known, and as Sylvia suggested, had been waiting for the right moment to tell him.

Another thought struck him. What about the anonymous note? And where had she found the casket? Only she could tell him.

He must go home at once. But first he would have to give Isobel and Hugh some sort of explanation.

CHAPTER TWENTY-TWO

CHARLIE sat in the doorway of the Freer cottage listlessly plaiting straw. Every so often she let her hands fall idle in her lap, then she sighed and carried on.

Will and Sandy had long gone to the quarr, and her ma to the shop. Tommy had gone with her to run errands, and Charlie was glad to be left alone.

Glad! One of these days she'd have to tell Ma the whole truth. Will hadn't yet got rid of all the contraband he'd hidden in his quarr, otherwise things did seem to be settling down, apart from her own troubles.

It was unbearable to know that the Lackfords thought ill of her.

She looked wistfully in the direction of the hall, but it was two miles away, with quarries and hills between. She must stop visualizing how things might have been.

A movement in the distance caught her eye. Someone was running, then slowing to a walk, then running again. It was a woman coming this way. Maisie?

Charlie stood up. It *was* Maisie. Why was she in such a hurry? It couldn't be more trouble from Sir Alan, he was at Lyme.

She went to meet the maid who was stumbling, and steadied her.

'Maisie, whatever is it? Come, sit down and catch your breath.'

Maisie sat down, and looked sorrowfully at Charlie.

'I come as quick as I could, but I had to wait 'til Dick was gone, he had 'nuff to worry about. I couldn't stop him or Maltravers . . .' She paused, still panting. 'Charlie, I had to come and tell you—'

'What are you talking about?' Charlie knew it was bad as soon as Maisie mentioned Maltravers. 'Is it to do with your wedding? Is that awful man meddling while Squire's away? The child's all right?'

'Me an' the babe's fine, and the weddin's spoilt anyway wi' the master gone. Oh, thanks.' Maisie took the cup of water Charlie brought her.

'He was goin' to give me away,' she whimpered between gulps, 'and Will was goin' to be best man—'

'I know Will . . .' Charlie felt a sickening fear grow inside her. 'What do you mean, he *was* to be best man? For God's sake Maisie, get to the point!'

A sudden rush of anger overcame Maisie's distress.

'It's that rotten Maltravers,' she burst out. 'He come lookin' fer Dick last night—'

'Dick? I thought you said Will—'

'Oh aah, 'tis Will he's after. He wants my Dick to tell the law he saw Will push Skinner off the cliff . . . that he was too scared to come forward afore.'

Ignoring Charlie's horrified gasp, Maisie rushed on: 'Then he – Maltravers – is goin' to take the soldiers an' arrest Will at his quarr—'

'Surely Dick wouldn't . . . But why?'

'Oh, my Dick told'n he weren't tellin' no lies. I heard'n say: "No, I won't do it!" But *he* made'n. Otherwise, he said, he'll tell Squire about Dick lendin' his horses fer smugglin' runs.' Maisie let out a loud wail. 'You know what that means. Squire'll dismiss us wi' no references. No roof – oh, Charlie, I don't know what to do!'

The maid dissolved in a fit of weeping.

'Yes,' said Charlie bitterly. 'Squire believes everything that man says.'

Maisie gulped. 'He likes you, Charlie, you could put in a good word for Will, and Dick—'

Charlie gave a mirthless laugh.

'Nothing I could say to him would help now. Do you know why I was really dismissed? Because Squire listened to his uncle blackening my name. He believed all his lies. You remember when I sorted out those things in the cellar?'

Maisie nodded, and listened tearfully.

'Well, Squire asked me to look out for a silver casket – which you know about, don't you? Don't fib, Maisie, I can tell by your face. You knew about Lady Helen's affair with Maltravers . . .'

Charlie stopped, her fear made her angry. She stood over Maisie, hands on hips.

'I found the casket when I was in the woods with the children. It was full of love-letters.'

'But how?' gasped Maisie. 'I threw away the key – I panicked when her ladyship died. If the master found out about the affair, and me passin' notes, 'twould be more'n me job was worth . . .'

'So it was you hid the casket in the ruins,' cried Charlie. 'Well I'll tell you something else! The day you locked me in the cellar I found a note in the pocket of that black dress. It was from Maltravers to Lady Helen. He rejected her because he was getting married.'

Charlie exhaled heavily, she saw no need to tell Maisie her mistress was carrying Maltravers' child.

'I'm only telling you all this because *Sir Alan thinks I stole his darn casket!* That's why I was dismissed, so you see, Maisie, he'd never listen to me now.'

Maisie's face was a pale mask of terror.

'Anyway,' Charlie went on, 'none of this can help Will.' She stamped her foot, and swore. 'Damn Maltravers!'

Maisie stopped crying and looked at Charlie with a mixture of respect mingled with despair.

'That man has the luck o'the devil. He's gettin' away wi' everything!'

'Not if I can help it,' said Charlie. 'I'm going to the quarr to warn Will. He'll have to hide until we can sort something out. I want you to go to my granddad, and tell him what you've told me. He is a JP and might have some influence, after all he convinced the military that Skinner was drunk, and fell off the cliff.'

It was a dismal hope, but what else was there to do?

Maisie didn't move. She was afraid of what she was getting into, and what she'd already done.

'Maltravers'll get me for tellin' you,' she whined.

Fighting tears herself, Charlie persisted.

'Maisie, I'm grateful to you for coming to me like this, but you've got to help me some more. Maltravers has had it in for my family for years. Now he's finished me with Squire, he's after Will. Merchant Warren will be next. It'll slay Ma, and ruin her business.'

She drew breath, and became threateningly firm. 'It's what Maltravers wants, then he'll claim the reward for helping to smash the smuggling-ring as if he had nothing to do with it!'

Impatiently she pulled the dazed Maisie up from the chair. 'Can't you see? He'll never leave you and Dick alone after this, because you both know too much. Every time he wants some dirty work done he'll be on your doorstep.'

Maisie sniffed, and swallowed a sob.

'Aah, all right, I'll go fetch yer granddad, but you better hurry – and Charlie . . .'

243

'Yes?'

'Do 'ee take care.' With that, Maisie scurried off. Fortunately it was all downhill to Warren's stables.

Charlie didn't waste another minute. She couldn't see her way clear, but with Maisie to back her up there must be a way to settle Maltravers once and for all.

First, she must find Will.

'Sandy, where's Will?'

'Right down under, Miss Freer. Said he didn't want my help yet, and I was to carry on cleavin' these yer old slabs into roofin' tiles.'

'Sandy, listen to me. Will's in trouble. He's done nothing wrong, but there's been a terrible misunderstanding, and I came to warn him. I need your help.'

Sandy put down his tools and gave her his full attention.

'Would you go down the track, and if you see soldiers coming, waylay them? Say Will's not here, anything you can think of. Can you do that?'

The lad looked worried.

'I'll try, miss. I'd do anything to help you and Will, but you bain't goin' down *there*, be you? Wouldn't 'ee rather I went?'

Down in the valley Charlie glimpsed scarlet jackets.

'No, I must go to him myself.' There was no time to lose. 'It's all right,' she assured Sandy, 'I've done it before. Hurry now, they're coming!'

She scrambled down the slide, heedless of knocks and grazes, and hurried inside the mine-entrance to find the tinder-box. Almost immediately the darkness enveloped her, and for a brief moment she shuddered with the memory of finding her father beneath the founder.

A candle lit, she began the journey underground. She guessed Will had gone through to the old workings he'd told her about.

They would catch him red-handed, shifting out contraband.

Stumbling along as quickly as she dared, she came to the corner into the lane where her Dad had been killed. Part of the fall remained, but there was a gap where Will had cleared a way through.

'Will, Will,' she hissed loudly, fearing what a vibration could do. 'Are you there? For God's sake answer me!'

Seeing greyness rather than blackness beyond the opening, she clambered through into a roomy cave. The rock walls and the legs supporting the ceiling were dangerously slanted.

Daylight filtered through a passage which sloped gently upwards to the outside; at the bottom were three brandy-barrels.

Charlie met Will coming down the passage, and briefly sensed relief. She'd found him!

'Sis! What . . . ?'

'You've been betrayed, Will,' she told him breathlessly. 'There's no time to explain, the soldiers are coming. Granddad's on his way to help, but right now you've got to hide!'

Will's knowledge of the quarries was second nature, he'd soon find a place, and she would bring him food.

Sir Alan was their best hope – once he'd read those letters. But what would they do to him? Charlie remembered his emotional collapse in the cellar when he showed her his wife's things.

Even if he coped with the shock, *would* he help? He might rather save face, he'd covered up the reason for her dismissal to avoid scandal.

In her frustration she felt angry with everyone concerned, except Ma. She who'd done nothing to deserve any of this would be the one to suffer most.

There was no time to think; Charlie insisted on going ahead up the passage to see the way was clear, but when she came to the entrance she found a worse nightmare beginning.

She was in a hollow. Hercules stood nearby, harnessed to the contraband-laden cart. Even as she realized the soldiers would see the horse and find the hiding-place, a detachment of uniformed men swarmed into the hollow.

Charlie fled back down the passage.

'We can't get out that way,' she cried, 'they've found Hercules!' Already they could hear booted footsteps.

They tried to hide near the founder, but soldiers bearing torches had found their way in from the main entrance. Charlie and her brother were trapped.

Will was grabbed, and hustled back into the hollow.

Charlie followed in a state of shock, it had all happened too quickly. Her sudden dismissal, and a day later, Will's betrayal. All her efforts had proved useless; nothing seemed real any more.

From somewhere in the confusion Sandy ran to her side.

'I'm sorry, miss, I tried to stop 'em, like you said, but *he* was with 'em. Wouldn't even let 'em stop an' listen to me.'

As though in a trance, Charlie turned her head to see where the lad pointed.

Above the hollow stood the triumphant figure of Simon Maltravers.

An ugly sneer distorted his features as he watched the men examine the cart, and question Will. When her brother protested that he was obeying Maltravers' orders, he was laughed to scorn.

Will fought to reach Maltravers then, but they held him fast.

'Your smuggling is a minor charge,' announced the sergeant. 'We're arresting you for the murder of Horace Skinner!'

'You what – I never did it!' cried Will. His head went back, and pulling one arm free, he shook his fist at Maltravers.

They tied his hands then, and even from where she stood Charlie could see the evil look on Maltravers' face, the twist of his cruel mouth.

His word was accepted so easily against Will's. She leaned on Sandy, feeling faint.

Suddenly Henry Warren appeared behind Maltravers, his chest heaving from the climb, and Charlie straightened. She saw the broken-hearted look on her grandfather's face as he levelled the pistol in his hand at Maltravers' head.

She stopped breathing. As in a nightmare she was unable to move, or speak.

A shot rang out, but it was Henry Warren who tottered forward, and rolled into the hollow, arms and legs flailing like a rag-doll's.

Near Maltravers stood a yeoman with a smoking rifle.

'No-o!' With a terrible cry, Charlie ran to her grandfather's side. Despite all the years of estrangement, and her mistrust of him, tears gushed down her cheeks as she knelt by the dying man. For he was not quite dead. His eyes fluttered open and he tried to speak.

She leaned closer, but caught only part of what he said.

'Mistake – tell Amelia – letter . . .' as he breathed his last.

He knew Will's arrest was a mistake, thought Charlie frantically, but why tell Amelia, and not the sergeant? Oh, how could anyone think in the throes of death? Clasping his hand, she held it against her cheek. Was he apologizing to Ma for all that had gone wrong?

A soldier's strong arms dragged her, kicking, away from the body.

'He spoke,' she cried. 'He said Will's arrest was a mistake!'

She tore herself free and ran to the sergeant, to repeat her plea.

He looked at her with gruff compassion, he had his duty to do.

'Take her home, boy,' he told Sandy.

While the soldiers bore her grandfather to the Freer's cottage, Charlie felt more distraught than ever. In a peculiar way her dad's death had fused her family together, but now they were being torn apart.

Sandy put his arm around her in a boyish gesture of comfort.

'I am sorry, miss. Yer ma'll be upset so, about Will – and yer grand-dad.'

Charlie was touched by his concern, but felt completely defeated.

'Sandy,' she sobbed, 'that was the first time I ever asked Granddad Warren for anything in my whole life.'

The sergeant said her ma would be told what had happened, and Dr Simpson would come to issue Warren's death certificate.

Charlie sat silently beside the body until Amelia arrived home from her shop, with Dr Simpson and Sam Roper supporting her. She tried to be rational, and explain to her ma how she had known of Will's doings, but hadn't wanted to worry her.

'Will meant to finish with smuggling, and Granddad was going to establish him in London.'

But Amelia could only see that she'd lost her father, and was about to lose her son.

'I'm so sorry,' Charlie kept saying. She blamed herself, yet knew there was nothing either she or Ma could have done, had Ma known sooner. Nothing would have stopped Will once he'd set his course.

While the two women wept, and tried to console each other, Sam Roper kept Tommy and Sandy busy, fetching wood for the fire, and water to make pots of tea.

Charlie was grateful for the tea, and Sam coaxed Amelia into swallowing some.

'I think Mr Warren should be conveyed to his own home,' said Sam when Dr Simpson had finished the death certificate.

The doctor agreed.

'I'll send the undertaker, but meanwhile I'll give Mrs Freer some laudanum. What she needs most is a good sleep – you, too, Miss Freer.'

'Laudanum?' Charlie couldn't say why the suggestion bothered her, but it forced a stray thought into her foggy mind. ' 'Twas laudanum killed Lady Lackford . . .'

Dr Simpson cleared his throat. Shock could cause patients to ramble; best to indulge them.

'Not if the proper dose had been followed,' he said. 'What I've prescribed for your mother will just help her to sleep. Of course, if she took it on top of – she's not taking any other medicine, is she?'

Numbly Charlie shook her head, while Sam laid a hand on her shoulder. His presence comforted her.

'No, no laudanum for me, thank you I need to think how I can help my brother.' She looked anxiously at Sam, then at the doctor. 'What will happen to him?'

When they shook their heads, she whispered in terror:

'They won't . . . hang him – not without a proper trial?'

'They'll keep him at the Fort until his turn comes up at Dorchester, won't they, Doctor?' Sam said tentatively.

'I should think so,' sighed Dr Simpson. 'What with rick-burning, and machine-smashing, Dorchester jail's overcrowded with hunger-driven criminals.'

'How long before . . . ? Charlie gulped, unable to finish the question.

The doctor shrugged.

'It will depend on what influence Maltravers has on the case. No doubt he will press for an early hearing.'

'No doubt,' Charlie echoed bitterly. Even Dr Simpson hadn't used the 'Honourable Mr' title.

He repeated his offer of laudanum, but she declined.

'Are you sure you'll be all right?' he asked.

'I want to look after Ma,' she told him.

'I'll stay until the undertaker's been,' offered Sam. The doctor nodded, and as soon as Amelia was asleep he left.

Charlie sat at the kitchen table with Sam, too wrapped in her own misery to notice Tommy's and Sandy's drooping faces.

'Go and pick some blackberries,' Sam said to them. 'When Mrs Freer wakes up she'll need to keep busy. Get her to make a pie. Tell her she can take one to Will at the fort.'

'Sam's right,' Sandy told Tommy manfully. He found a basket. 'C'mon, Tommy.'

'Penny for your thoughts, maid?' said Sam when they'd gone.

Charlie answered him numbly.

'I can't stop worrying about Will, and I'm sorry about Granddad Warren, I was just beginning to know him. But 'tis me ma who's worst hit.'

Amid the turmoil in her mind, she thought of Sir Alan. Despite all her doubts and fears, she felt everything would come right if he were here.

But he wasn't. Henry Warren was dead, and Ma would never know happiness again. Unless – If only Will could go free, it would make up to Ma for Granddad's untimely death.

'What d'you say, maid?'

Charlie didn't realize she'd muttered aloud. She gave Sam a tremulous smile.

'It's what history would call a tragedy, eh, Sam?'

A tragedy because Maltravers had succeeded in ruining everything. She couldn't begin to count how many lives he'd spoiled.

CHAPTER TWENTY-THREE

'MY girl, Charlotte.'
Charlie started, as if she'd heard her Dad's words spoken aloud. If he were here now, what would he do?

He wouldn't sit here moping. *Attack is the best form of defence*, he'd told her once, and right now he'd be out looking for Maltravers.

Charlie's mind began to clear. She did have a weapon to fight that man with. If he could be persuaded to tell the law that Dick was mistaken after all, they'd have to let Will go.

At least he wouldn't hang.

She looked across at Sam Roper. He would stop her do anything 'foolish', so she'd wait until he left.

'Squire's a magistrate,' she said. 'Do you think if he was on the bench . . . ?'

Sam looked gloomy.

'There's no tellin', maid, but he'd be as fair as anyone. A darn sight fairer than that Frampton who tries most poor buggers in Dorchester. Regular Judge Jeffreys he be. Enjoys makin' an example of his victims.'

Charlie was horrified.

'Oh, Sam, is there nothing we can do?'

He was spared trying to answer her, because Mr Grey the undertaker arrived with his assistant. Charlie was surprised to see Martha Hyer with them.

They expressed their condolences, then the school-mistress gave Charlie her 'no nonsense' boot-button stare.

'When your poor mother is more herself, tell her that Tommy must come to school. I shall waive the fourpence a week until times are better.'

Charlie almost wept with gratitude for her kindness. It seemed not everyone thought badly of her family. They could do worse than have the school-mistress on their side.

'It's little enough,' said the widow kindly. 'You must tell me if there is anything else I can do.' She turned to Sam. 'Mr Roper, I believe it is high time the squire was sent for; his community needs him. I don't fancy leaving Will to the tender mercies of the military.'

'Aye, ma'am. I quite agree. I'll go to Lyme myself and return with him the morrow.'

As soon as the undertaker and his assistant had taken charge of her grandfather's body, and Sam had left, Charlie said:

'Thank you for coming, Mrs Hyer. There . . . is something else.'

Martha gave Charlie an encouraging nod.

'I – I'd be much obliged if you could stay a while. I – I'd like to go for a walk . . .' She hardly knew how to ask, but she needn't have worried.

'Excellent idea,' said the widow briskly. 'The fresh air will do you good. Moping won't help Will at all. The best thing you can do is go to the church, and ask the Almighty for a miracle. Why not take the pony? A ride will be something different, help you get to grips.'

Charlie went. I'll pray for help all right, she thought. If not for a miracle, then for the strength to kill that man.

She untethered Trixie and shuddered at the sight of the silent quarr. Compared to the others, with their sounds of metal ringing on stone, and the stone wagons constantly rumbling down to the shore, it seemed dead.

There was no saddle or stirrups, so she threw a sack across Trixie's back and stood on a stone to hoist herself up.

She rode down the hill, and across the valley to follow the lane to Underhill.

Widow Hyer was right. Trixie became frisky with the unaccustomed exercise, and in concentrating on handling the pony Charlie's spirits lifted.

Her thoughts turned to what Dr Simpson had said about laudanum. Being ignorant of Lady Helen's pregnancy, he'd assumed she deliberately swallowed an overdose of the sleeping draught.

What if she *had* gone to Biddy for something to rid her of the child, then taken the laudanum to help her sleep? She would have been unaware of the terrible consequences, and accidentally poisoned herself!

Charlie decided to go to Biddy's first. If she could get the old crone

251

to admit she'd administered that potion . . .

She had Maisie to back her up over the affair, but she needed more amunition to confront Maltravers, and a witness to what occurred between her and that devil would not be amiss.

It wasn't fair to ask Maisie, and Dick was out of the question. He would hardly welcome any proceedings that might put him at risk. It would have to be Hetty.

Now she'd made her decision she felt stronger, strong enough to deal with Biddy at least.

If she ever got the chance to tell Sir Alan that Lady Helen's death was an accident, he would surely think better of her, for the stigma of suicide in his family would be lifted.

As for herself, Charlie felt she'd already lost whatever she might have had with the squire. All she wanted now was to free Will, and see her ma happy once more.

It occurred to her then that she was gambling everything on one thing. The casket, and those fatal love-letters. But they were no longer in her possession!

Sir Alan Lackford slowed his horse to a trot as he recognized the mounted figure of Sam Roper approaching him from the far side of Frometown bridge. The blacksmith waved his hat frantically.

'I was on me way to Lyme to find you, sir,' he panted in his gravelly voice. He wheeled his horse. ' 'Tis mighty glad I be to find 'ee so near to home.'

'What's wrong, Sam? What's happened?' Until now, the squire's thoughts had been not unpleasantly engaged in how to approach Miss Freer . . .

They walked their horses while Sam explained the tragic events during Sir Alan's absence.

' 'Tis plain 'nuff the lad's bin handlin' contraband, but there's some doubt about him killin' Skinner,' said Sam, looking earnestly at the squire. 'The other bad thing is,' he added hesitantly, 'Merchant Warren went gunning for Maltravers at the quarr when Will was arrested.'

'Aha,' murmured Sir Alan, frowning.

'Thass how he got shot, y'see, sir. One o' the yeomanry saw him take aim, and fired first.'

Sir Alan swore. 'So Henry Warren never had a chance to defend his grandson, and now Will's a prisoner at the fort?'

'Yes, sir. We'm all hopin' fer his fam'ly's sake he don't go afore
Frampton at Dorchester. The lad would have no chance. He swears he
never done it, sir, an' I believe him. Warren's dyin' words were of a
mistake. I reckon he must've known something . . . something that made
him want to kill your uncle.'

The feeling's mutual, thought Sir Alan.

'What were his exact words?'

Sam Roper shook his head.

'I dunno, sir. You'd have to ask Miss Charlie—'

'Miss Freer was there?'

'Yes, sir, and near demented with worry she be. I don' like leavin' her
alone, but the schoolmarm was with her when I left.'

'Hm,' said Sir Alan worriedly. 'I think we'd best go to the fort first,
and see about Will.' Half to himself he muttered: 'I'm sorry for Warren's
death, but I'd rather deal with my dear uncle—'

'You . . . what, sir?'

'It's a long story, Sam. You'll find out.' Once Maltravers was brought
to trial the whole story would be made public, love-letters and all. 'The
whole damned community will know soon enough. Let's save our
breath, friend, and ride!'

Hetty opened the door to Charlie's knock and stared uncertainly. Her
mouth sagged open.

'Hetty, I need your help . . .' Charlie began.

'Who be it?' called Biddy from within.

Hetty looked too scared to answer, and Charlie pushed past her, in
no mood for politeness.

'It's Charlie – er Miss Freer, Gran,' stammered Hetty belatedly, for
Charlie was already in their kitchen facing the old woman who hastily
fixed her eyepatch in place.

'What you come fer?' she growled. 'We don' want none o' your
murderin' brood yer.'

'That's unfair, and you know it,' snapped Charlie. 'If anyone does
murder in my family it'll be me – unless you co-operate!'

'Don't 'ee threaten me,' shrieked Biddy. She threw up her hands, her
fingers curled, clawlike. 'I'll curse you, then your family will be in worse
trouble!'

'You don't scare me!' Charlie reached out and snatched off the old
woman's eye patch.

Biddy clawed the air and screamed in fury.

'I'll get the law on you. Hetty – run an' fetch the sojurs!'

'Yes, do!' Charlie shouted, while Hetty dithered between the two. 'Then I can tell them how your Gran cheats people. She trades on their fear, and superstitions – when she's not helping Maltravers!'

The old woman groaned, and sank into a chair.

'Sit down,' Charlie told Hetty. 'When I've finished with her, I shall need your help.'

Hetty shut her mouth with a gulp, and obeyed.

'O-oh, don't 'ee go ruinin' a pore ol' woman's reputation,' whined Biddy. 'I got to live, ain't I?'

'Listen then,' said Charlie. 'All I want is information, and if I don't get it, you'll find yourself accused of being an accomplice to murder.'

'Murder – me?' cried the old crone. 'I never murdered nobody in me life!'

'It amounts to the same thing,' said Charlie crisply. 'I have it from Dr Simpson that your bayleaf potion to kill an unborn child would kill the mother too, taken with laudanum.'

Biddy clenched her hands against her wrinkled cheeks as Charlie told about the letter proving Lady Lackford's affair and pregnancy.

'I know the letter was from Maltravers. All I want from you is an admission that Lady Lackford came to you to buy that potion.' Relentlessly she added: 'If Will hangs, so will you!'

Biddy shrank back as Charlie leaned closer.

'What sort of people are you and Maltravers, to allow an innocent man – no – two innocent men to suffer so? Even if you escape the law, who will do business with you when they hear what really happened?'

'Aah, don't 'ee go tellin' nobody,' wailed Biddy. 'All right, I admit she come yer, but I dint know she took laudanum. An' I'll tell Squire how Maltravers made me help with the smuggling.'

'He didn't make you,' said Charlie grimly, 'you did it for the money. And if Lady Helen had lived, you would have extorted more money in return for your silence, you crafty old witch.'

Charlie tossed her head in disgust. 'But she died, unexpectedly, and you and Maltravers were happy to let everyone think Squire drove her to suicide. That was most despicable!'

Biddy waved her hands in agitation.

'Stop, stop! I'll do what you want, an' Hetty can go with you. But 'tis no good relyin' on she.'

Charlie glanced at Hetty, her gran had a point.

'It's all right, Hetty. I only want you to listen to what's said. You won't have to do anything, just be a witness.'

The girl looked terrified, and shook her head.

'You must,' Charlie insisted, 'so we can sort out this dreadful muddle! It will be all right, I promise. No one will learn your gran's secret from me, and you can go back to work in Ma's shop. You want to, don't you?'

Hetty nodded doubtfully.

'All right, I'll come, if I don't have to say nothin'.'

'You won't. There's nothing to fear, I promise.'

The Honourable Simon Maltravers relaxed in his easy-chair, his feet crossed on a footstool, while he smoked a cigar. Languidly he blew a perfect smoke-ring, and sighed with satisfaction.

Revenge at last. All that remained was to dispose of the contraband.

He debated with himself whether to disclose the secret cellar beneath Amelia's shop to the authorities, and heap even more disgrace on the family. On the other hand, he was due for the reward money, why not keep quiet and peddle the rest of the goods for more profit?

He heard the front door-bell ring, and a minute later, Jane herself going to answer it. A housekeeper is all she's good for, he thought contemptuously.

She'd been gone for some minutes before he heard women murmuring. His curiosity was aroused: had Amelia come to plead with him?

He smiled, and removed his feet from the footstool. What a welcome thought. He stubbed out his cigar as Jane appeared in the open doorway. She looked more frosty than ever.

'It's Charlotte Freer. I told her you won't see her, but she refuses to leave.'

He stood up, gloating. Not Amelia, but her daughter. He'd enjoy watching her grovel.

'Let her come in, she won't take long to deal with.' With a bored look for his wife's benefit, he waved her away as he would a servant.

He had a less pleasant surprise when Charlie marched in, her head held high, with Hetty Cauldon creeping after her. What did she think she was doing, bringing Biddy's shabby brood here?

'What can I do for you, Miss Freer? Miss Cauldon?' He was damned if he would invite them to sit

Hetty hung her head, and cringed behind Charlie.

'If you've come to discuss your wretched family's plight,' he sneered at Charlie, 'what business does *she* have, coming here?'

'It is her business,' said Charlie belligerently. 'Hetty works for my mother, and your actions are interfering with their business.'

'What do you expect me to do about it?' he asked callously.

'Tell the military there's been a mistake, and they must let my brother go.'

What bravado! He could admire the young whelp if it wasn't so satisfying to put her down.

'I'm very sorry about your grandfather,' he began placatingly, 'but he acted foolishly. As for your brother, I'm afraid he's beyond my help.'

He expected her to shed tears and beg for his help, but she remained undaunted.

'Beyond your willing help,' she replied, 'but there is no reason why you can't go to the duty sergeant and tell him Dick Farmer was drunk, and now admits he was mistaken about Will. My brother wasn't responsible for Skinner's death, it was *Esmerelda*'s crew—'

'If you know it,' he said coolly, 'the reason you haven't helped him yourself is because you can't prove it.' He could deny all her accusations now that Warren was dead.

He was not prepared for her next onslaught.

'That's why I'm here,' she stated bluntly. 'The military needn't know the truth, but unless you withdraw your charges against Will, I shall tell of your affair with Lady Lackford, and your involvement in her death – which was less suicide than murder.'

He froze, thunderstruck. That event, five years before, had been wiped from his mind, what with running the smuggling-ring, and his malice towards the Freers.

While he remained speechless, Charlie felt strong enough to go on. She told him how she'd found a casket containing letters which proved her story.

'Casket! What letters?'

'Those you sent to Lady Helen,' cried Charlie. Sarcastically she added: 'She kept them in her silver casket because she valued your so-called love! Unless you have my brother freed, I shall tell Sir Alan everything!'

He shook with rage, his face white as cliff stone. How dare this chit of a girl challenge him. But Charlie wasn't finished.

'Lady Helen took laudanum to help her sleep, after drinking the bayleaf potion that you persuaded her to use to rid her of the child she was carrying. Your child! Her death was an accident, not suicide.

Her voice rose, shrill with anger. 'But it was you who caused it, and you let people think ill of your nephew whilst pretending friendship with him – you hypocrite!'

Suddenly Maltravers understood why Hetty was there, nervously taking it all in. He let out a bellow of rage, and leaped at her.

It was too much for Hetty. With a yelp of fear, she dashed from the room and collided with Jane Maltravers who was listening, lips clamped, outside the door.

Maltravers paid his wife no heed, but rounded on Charlie.

'So much for your clever scheme. Your witness has fled.'

'No matter,' retorted Charlie. She feigned indifference with a shrug. 'She's heard enough. Now – Will's freedom for my silence – or shall you allow a scandal that will rock the county, and your social life?'

'And who will take notice of two lowly, hysterical women?' snarled Maltravers. He pounced on Charlie, gripping her arms, and shook her.

'Where is this casket?' he demanded hoarsely.

Charlie gasped for breath. She realized that the sudden confrontation with his past made Maltravers unsure of himself, but she'd gambled on her knowledge of his affairs being enough to secure Will's freedom. She couldn't produce the letters because Sir Alan had them!

The fear she'd been at pains to control rose like a dam-burst. She struggled frantically, but he was too strong, he would kill her to silence her.

Through her panic she remembered that Sam had gone to fetch Squire. Oh, would he come? How long would he be? She must play for time.

She summoned her last shreds of courage.

'I don't have the casket with me,' she cried. 'You shall have it when Will is free, and not before!'

'Let her go, Simon!' Jane Maltravers stepped into the room. 'I have heard enough.'

Maltravers relaxed his grip, and looked at his wife as if seeing her for the first time.

'I think you should do as she says,' she went on harshly, 'or my father shall hear what manner of man I was tricked into marrying.'

Maltravers was beside himself. He lashed out at his wife, and caught her a savage blow across the face that sent her reeling.

She crashed against the wall, and crumpled to the floor, moaning in pain.

Next moment he had Charlie by the throat. Despite her kicks and struggles, he pulled her up until her toes left the floor as he throttled her.

Her eyes bulged with fear and choking, her fingers clawing helplessly at his big cruel hands.

Suddenly a dreadful shout penetrated her swimming senses.

'I have the letters, Uncle. Come and face me like a man!'

The strident voice cracked like a whiplash, almost unrecognizable as that of Sir Alan.

Surprise was the last thing Charlie's mind registered as she slid into blackness.

She came to on a bed in a strange room. Gingerly she touched her burning throat which felt twice its size. Her dress had been unbuttoned down to her breasts.

Her eyes flickered with fear, drawn by the movement of the door as it slowly opened.

But it was only Jane, who came in with a bowl, and a piece of clean linen over one arm. When Charlie saw the woman's blackened cheek, she remembered.

'Where am I?' she croaked.

Jane dunked the cloth in the bowl of cold water.

'In Sam Roper's house,' she said calmly.

'Sam?' Charlie clutched feebly at her open bodice. 'He did . . . ?'

'No, it was my nephew.' Jane gave her a gentle smile, 'He saved your life, and carried you here while the doctor was sent for.'

'Sir Alan? Ohh . . .' Charlie gave a painful gasp. 'I thought I heard . . . How long have I been here?'

'Not long, Dr Simpson has just left.'

'And your . . . husband . . . is arrested?' said Charlie, barely comprehending anything.

'Oh, there was quite a struggle,' said Jane, 'but everything's under control now.' She wrung out the cloth, 'Let me apply this compress, then I'll give you a drink to help you sleep.'

She wrapped the wet linen around Charlie's throat, then put an arm behind her shoulders to support her while she sipped painfully from the cup.

'It's got laudanum in, hasn't it,' Charlie asked weakly.

'Don't worry,' said Jane, with a tight little smile. 'I'll not poison you. Dr Simpson said you should have taken some when he offered it earlier. He says you must rest here, until morning.'

'Oh, but Ma—'

'She'll be told when she wakes up. It will give her something else to think about.'

'More to worry about,' muttered Charlie, blinking. It hurt her throat too much to cry. 'What about my brother?'

'You mustn't worry about anything,' said Jane, 'Alan's at the fort now, he'll sort things out.'

'I – I don't understand,' croaked Charlie, 'How did he . . . ?'

'Hush, child. Stop trying to talk,' said Jane. 'Sam met him at Frometown bridge. My nephew had left Lyme hours before, for his own reasons – and now I know why. They were going to the fort until they almost ran down your friend, Hetty. She was in such a state, but she told them what was going on at Underhill so they sent her to fetch the soldiers.'

Jane Maltravers set down the cup, and gently pushed Charlie back on to the pillow. 'We all need time to take in what's happened, to see the truth.' She chewed her bottom lip. 'It's not easy to admit to being taken for a fool all this time,' she added. 'Apparently those letters, of which I knew nothing, throw an entirely different light on Lady Lackford's death. Sam Roper's been telling me all about it. It seems my husband was dreadfully at fault. He is charged with your attempted murder, and complicity in Helen's death as well as serious smuggling involvements . . .'

Her voice droned on, devoid of emotion, and Charlie couldn't tell whether she was concerned for her husband or not.

She felt sorry for Jane, but more so for Sir Alan, who would have the worst part of his private life made public. At least the children would be at school when the trial took place . . . Oh, thank God Will . . .

The sleeping draught was doing its work. Before Charlie could take it all in, her eyelids grew heavy, and she was asleep.

Jane Maltravers drew the covers up to Charlie's chin, then donned her cloak and went outside. Her pony was tethered alongside Trixie. She mounted, and leading Charlie's pony, she headed for the Freer cottage at a trot.

Someone must see Amelia and Martha Hyer, and put their minds at rest.

CHAPTER TWENTY-FOUR

A T the fort, Sir Alan Lackford began his examination of Will's case. First he summoned Maisie, and spoke to her alone.

On pain of dismissal without reference, she confessed her erstwhile dealings with Maltravers, and all she knew of his affair with Lady Helen.

He interviewed Biddy Cauldon and Hetty briefly, then let them go.

Will and Dick were marched in, and Dick told how Maltravers forced him to act as a false witness against Will.

He attempted to justify himself: 'I ain't a smuggler,' then was compelled to explain the hold Maltravers had over him. When he admitted lending out his master's horses to carry contraband, the young lieutenant in charge of the garrison looked worried.

'I'm relieved the charge of murder against Master Freer is dropped,' he said, 'but the other offences are still serious. Both these men could be sentenced to months of hard labour.'

'Master Farmer is here as a witness for the defence against the charge of murder,' said Sir Alan. 'It's up to me whether or not I charge him with an offence.'

'As for Master Freer,' he continued, 'he is charged with one crime only, which charge is now withdrawn. However . . .' He looked sternly at them both. 'It would be better for you to tell us all you know, and help the lieutenant stamp out the illicit trade in this area.'

Will twisted his cap in his hands, and stepped forward.

'Dick's told all he knows,' he began tentatively. 'Apart from your horses, sir, he had no hand in any of it. I can only add, the most valuable goods are stored in a secret cellar under my ma's bonnet-shop.'

He stared at Sir Alan with stricken eyes, then dropped his gaze, shamefaced. 'Please, sir, she don't know nothin' about any of it.'

'Hm, I see,' murmured Sir Alan. 'And what about your sister? Does she . . . ?'

'No!' Will cried. 'She only knew what I told her. 'Twas she tried to stop me. If I'd listened to her I wouldn't be yer now!'

Sir Alan nodded, and bent to scribble on the paper before him. After some moments he looked up and spoke to the officer.

'My uncle and Merchant Warren were the ringleaders, and somewhere out in the Channel is their shipful of pirates. Contact the swiftest naval cutters, then organize a detail to take Maltravers to Dorchester.'

His uncle would be hard put talking his way out of this lot to Judge Frampton.

The lieutenant clicked his heels and saluted, then turned and barked an order. The soldiers filed out.

Sir Alan gazed searchingly at Will and Dick standing before him. 'You're both free to go, but you, Will, pending further possible charges. Go home and look after your mother, and wait until I or my representative comes to see you.'

Both young men touched their forelocks, and mumbled their thanks, while Maisie fixed her eyes on the floor and attempted a curtsy. They were all relieved when the squire waved them away.

Early next morning, Sir Alan rode to the fort to watch his uncle's departure.

When Maltravers was brought into the drill yard, and saw his nephew, his lip curled with a venomous sneer. But docilely he mounted the horse they brought him and sat upright.

The sergeant in charge shouted an order, and the yeoman detailed to lead Maltravers' horse came alongside to take up his position.

Suddenly, as the gate was opened, Maltravers grabbed the yeoman's pistol from its holster, and whipped his horse with it. As the soldier tried to calm the startled animal, Maltravers fired a hasty shot at the squire, dug his heels into the horse's flanks and galloped away. For several moments there was pandemonium.

'After him!' yelled the sergeant as he ran to where Sir Alan writhed in a pool of blood.

The squire had taken a bullet in the shoulder.

'Don't let that devil get away,' he groaned, before he slid into unconsciousness.

Keeping his head low, Maltravers whipped his mount to greater effort as he rode uphill towards the cliffs. If he could outdistance his pursuers, he would lie low until nightfall, and escape in a fishing-boat.

He didn't see the loaded stone wagon until he heard the frantic blasts of a cowhorn.

Too late he saw the wagon almost upon him.

Despite using the brake, the driver could only run helplessly alongside, while the three shires struggled to contain their heavy load on the downhill slope.

Maltravers' horse sensed the danger. With a terrified whinny, she reared and threw her rider, and bolted.

Before Maltravers could scramble to his feet he was trampled by the snorting shires, then crushed by the wheels as they came to a stop.

The pursuing soldiers found the mangled remains; there was no point in riding to Dorchester.

When Charlie awoke, her throat felt tender, but she managed to pull herself up, and get out of bed. She remembered she was in Sam's house, then sat down suddenly. She was weaker than she thought, for she'd eaten nothing since breakfast the day before.

Expecting to see Jane Maltravers when the door opened, she was surprised to see her own mother, cheerfully carrying a tea-tray.

'Ma! What are you doing here?'

'Jane Maltravers came to see me last evening, and told me what happened. Aah, Charlie, I wish you wouldn't take such risks. Anyway, while she was there our Will came home.'

Charlie gasped, and clasped her hands in delight. Amelia poured tea and handed a cup to her daughter.

'I've just stirred up the fire to toast muffins. I'll fetch them, then I'll tell you all about it. Try and drink some tea.'

Charlie took a sip, which pained her throat, then suddenly experienced a great surge of emotion. It was true, things did come right when Sir Alan was around.

'Oh Ma,' she breathed at the open door, 'I do love that man.'

'Did you say something?' asked Amelia, carrying in the plate of buttered muffins.

Charlie blushed, and shook her head. She tore hungrily into a muffin despite her difficulty in swallowing. The memory of yesterday's events hit her suddenly.

'Where's Sam?'

Amelia hesitated. 'Gone to lend a hand,' she began carefully. 'Maltravers was killed, trying to escape from the military.'

Charlie was frightened by the solemn look on her ma's face, and the reticent way she spoke.

'There's something else, Ma? Please tell me.'

Amelia held her daughter's hands.

'Before Maltravers bolted, he shot the squire—'

Charlie would have screamed, had her throat permitted, but she could only manage a gasp. 'Ohh! Oh God, Ma, is he . . . ?'

'No, Charlie, but he's wounded – in the shoulder . . .'

Charlie looked frantically about her; she must go to him.

'Where are my clothes?'

Amelia gripped her hands now.

'Charlie, calm down!'

'Oh Ma, he saved my life, he's freed Will – he knows everything . . .' Charlie finished on a wail. 'I haven't even thanked him. I love him, Ma!'

'Charlie!' Touched by her daughter's announcement, torn from her in a way lesser events could never have done, Amelia almost choked on her own sobs.

'You must wait until he's had time to recuperate. The doctor is still removing the bullet.'

Charlie saw sense and calmed down, then Amelia helped her to dress, and took her home.

News of Maltravers' death burst on the community like a thunderclap, and as Sir Alan told Sam Roper, the whole town was talking.

While Squire recuperated from his shoulder wound, the scandal of Lady Lackford's death was augmented by that of her seduction.

The Honourable Mr had got his come-uppance, and now the 'ogre' was a jolly good fellow.

It was plain to Amelia that after her initial shock over the shooting, Charlie became increasingly subdued, rather than anxious to see Sir Alan.

She eventually coaxed out of her daughter the truth of her unfair dismissal.

'You'd think he would at least send word, or a note of apology,' said Charlie, vexed, 'now everybody knows the rest of it.'

'I'm sure he will, when he's better,' soothed Amelia. 'He's had a shock, too.' Optimistically she added: 'Sam told me when they bumped into Hetty that day and heard you were in trouble, Squire couldn't get there fast enough – and he insisted on staying with you until the doctor came. I thought you wanted to thank him – and for saving Will?'

'I do,' Charlie conceded, but somehow she felt unable to face him.

She was glad he wouldn't have to produce those letters as evidence in a court of law, yet she felt excluded. Squire had rushed back from Lyme on account of his wife, and Maltravers. The fact that he'd saved her life must seem irrelevant to him.

'I-I'll go and see him soon,' she told her ma, 'when I'm more my old self.'

Amelia sighed for the way events had stolen her daughter's precious innocence. Charlie doesn't realize how life changes a person, she thought. Once touched by evil, a person must grow up – or give up.

She didn't feel like trying to explain, with Charlie in her present mood.

A week passed, during which time the two funerals were held. Henry Warren's was well attended; he had the community's respect, if not its affection.

Afterwards his will was read to the Freers in the parlour of his house.

'He only recently altered it, Mrs Freer,' said Mr Harper, the white-haired solicitor, 'and did mean to tell you in writing.' He peered soulfully at Amelia over his half-moon spectacles. 'As you know, we were lifelong acquaintances, and I know he felt great remorse for having cut you off.'

He turned to Will. 'Your grandfather grew very fond of you, and wanted to make amends. He tore up the former document in front of me, saying how mistaken he'd been.'

'Oh,' murmured Charlie, 'so that's what Granddad meant when he died. He was thinking about his will!'

Mistake . . . tell Amelia . . . letter . . .

For the first time in her life she felt sorry for the old man. He'd died seeing Will arrested for murder, and the family in disgrace.

How awful to die beaten, feeling a failure.

'He has left everything to you,' Mr Harper told Will. 'House, business and stables – on condition that you look after your mother.' He went into numerous details.

Charlie watched the wondering look on her ma's face. Now she could have the life of ease she deserved.

She felt happy for her family, despite a certain heaviness inside herself.

Only the squire and his Aunt Jane attended Maltravers' funeral.

Sir Alan wore his left arm in a sling to ease his wounded shoulder. Jane's demeanour belied her widow's weeds, he thought, her face was far less pinched and careworn, she looked younger, and fully at ease.

When it was over, Jane thanked her nephew for coming.

'It was right I should attend,' he said. 'We've both been taken for fools, but he was my mother's brother. What will you do now, Aunt Jane?'

'My father will come and live with me,' Jane replied. 'Also I've spoken to Mrs Freer, who is most fair-minded, and capable.' She grimaced. 'As I've been landed with Simon's debts and shaky investments, methinks I could do worse than form a business partnership with her. She has the skill, and I have the business know-how, and connections.

'We shall employ more workers, and she will move into her old home. Her son will have plenty to fall back on.'

Jane paused, and regarded her nephew curiously. 'It could make an opening for her daughter, and young Tommy eventually.'

Sir Alan nodded, while a secretive smile hovered on his lips as he murmured: 'I see.'

'And what about you, Nephew?' Jane asked pertly.

'Me? Oh, I still have things to see to,' he said lightly. 'One being my maid's marriage.'

'So, you're keeping her and Dick on, then?'

Sir Alan shrugged. 'A good head-groom's not easy to replace, and would take time.' He chuckled. 'They don't know it yet, and it won't hurt them to stew for a bit.'

His aunt gave him a tiny smile.

'What of Will,' she asked delicately, 'and Miss Freer?'

She didn't miss the hastiness of his reply.

'I've arranged for Will to go to London, I know a building firm that has need of good masons. Once the military has smashed the smuggling ring, it'll be safe for him to come home.'

He neglected to mention Miss Freer, and Jane resisted the temptation to press the matter. It was her nephew's shyness she found endearing. For all his forcefulness when it suited, he was unsure of himself when it came to women.

'If Will is to go away, what of the Freer quarry?'

'I'm just going to see Mrs Freer to inform her of my arrangements,' said Sir Alan. 'I might suggest she keeps the quarry on to provide youngsters like Sandy with employment.'

'She will be a wealthy woman,' said Jane shrewdly. 'The family will be able to hold their heads up in any company.'

'That's true,' he agreed, and she saw the flush as he averted his gaze.

'I hope you will bring your father to visit me,' he said. He gave her a farewell kiss, and made his way to the bonnet-shop.

He hummed as he walked. Thank God he'd been wrong.

Disappointingly there was no sign of Miss Freer at the shop. He discussed his plans for Will with Amelia, then enquired cautiously about her daughter.

'She's at home,' said Amelia, and decided not to say she knew the true reason for her daughter's dismissal because of Charlie's plaintive cry that she loved this man. Now her hopes soared. 'I fear she has been a little dull since she came home. I believe she misses you – er – your children.'

'Ahem, that's partly why I want to see her. I've an idea for my groom and maidservant's wedding, and need her help after all. I thought to be away much longer, you understand?'

Amelia nodded, and hid a smile.

Sir Alan had left his horse at home, as riding would aggravate his shoulder wound, so he walked up the hill with a stick for support. He felt nervous as a love-sick schoolboy, for he'd wronged Miss Freer so much over the casket. All she'd done was try to protect him and his children from the truth.

Would she forgive him, and could she love him still? What if she refused to speak to him, or accept his apologies?

Charlie was tying the ribbons of her sun-bonnet when a shadow fell across the open doorway. She gasped, seeing Sir Alan so unexpectedly, for she'd just plucked up the courage to visit him. It seemed ages since her dismissal, and she felt embarrassed at the thought that he had carried her, unconscious, to Sam Roper's house . . . seeing her like that.

'I'm sorry to startle you, Miss Freer.' He removed his hat, and placed it over the top of his stick which he leaned against the wall. 'You're going out?'

'I was coming to see you, sir, to thank you for what you've done for my family, and for saving my life.'

'It seems we are in each other's debt,' he began, relieved that they were

266

on speaking terms. His gaze devoured her. Lord, how he'd missed her!

Neither could think what to say for a moment, and Charlie's pulse raced. He was so handsome. He seemed younger, somehow, and those blue eyes . . .

'How are the children?' she asked at last.

He smothered a smile. Not. 'How is your shoulder?' but, 'How are the children?'

'Missing you,' he replied simply. 'Miss Freer, I must beg you to accept my deepest apologies for that dreadful misunderstanding. Can you ever forgive us – er, me?'

She held her hands in front of her.

'Sir, there is nothing to forgive. It was only natural that you thought as you did . . . But do the children know?'

He gave a quick shake of his head.

'I've explained only as much as they need to know; they're more concerned about you.' He hesitated slightly, 'I have orders to bring you back to us.'

She laughed, then became serious again. She couldn't bear to be back in that house, close to him, and wanting him.

'I have no hard feelings, sir, but my mother needs me now she's beginning new ventures, and moving house – you know . . .'

Her voice trailed away, and he looked down at her tight-clasped hands. She wasn't teasing.

'There is much to think about,' he agreed, 'and I would not ask you to make a firm decision immediately.' He lifted his eyebrows hopefully. 'Would you at least consider lending a hand with Dick and Maisie's wedding? I shall bring my children back from Lyme, and we shall celebrate with a gala picnic.'

She couldn't trust herself to answer, she felt so torn.

'You still owe me a few months' work, you know,' he said, somewhat perplexed.

It was meant as a jocular remark, but she took it seriously.

'Sir,' she replied in desperation, 'your wife, and your honour are avenged, what can you possibly want from me?'

So, that was it; she thought he didn't care for her.

He stepped close, and laid a hand on her shoulder.

'Don't you realize how much I've come to rely on you?'

Her lips parted as she drew in her breath.

'Only because you have no wife—'

'Exactly. I need a wife, my children need a mother, and you have come so close to them – they want us to marry.'

She pulled away.

'I cannot marry you because your children want me to!'

Charlie had dreamed of such an intimate moment, but she had no intention of marrying him for his convenience. He'd made no mention of loving her!

She feared she was going to cry, and pushed past him. The last time she'd shed tears in front of him he'd mocked her.

'Please don't think me ungrateful,' she choked, and began to run, heedless of direction. The quarry – anywhere away from him.

Stunned, Sir Alan picked up his hat and stick to follow her. He could hear Sylvia's sweet voice saying: *Please Uncle, don't throw away this chance of happiness*, and cursed himself for his clumsiness.

In his frustration he lashed out: 'Charlotte!'

The sound of her proper name halted Charlie's flight, and her heart punched her ribs.

She remembered her vow when her dad died.

'Oh, sugar,' she whispered to herself in confusion.

Sir Alan came up behind her.

'I don't want your gratitude,' he said, his voice low and driven. 'I know you love me, I see it in your face each time I come upon you. Don't you know what that does to a man?'

No one confused her the way this man did.

'I don't know what to say,' she whispered helplessly, without turning round, 'or what to do.'

With his good arm, he took her by the shoulder and swung her round.

'Look at me!'

But she couldn't, not like this. She turned away again, to fumble for her handkerchief.

He misunderstood her reluctance to face him.

'You don't know how much I love you,' he cried, his voice choked with emotion, 'but I can understand your not wishing to marry an old man!'

She wanted to cry out that he wasn't old, but when she'd wiped her eyes and turned, he'd begun to walk back down the hill.

'Very well, Miss Freer, if that's the way you want it.'

In despair she called after him: 'I hadn't even considered such a thing, sir!'

'Well consider this,' he flung back over his shoulder. 'What *do* you want, Miss Freer? What do you want most in all the world?'

He heard her footsteps pounding after him, and swung round. His heart lifted. She was flying to him, her bonnet blown back from her face, and her cheeks smudged with tears.

As he dropped his stick and flung out his arm to catch her, she closed her eyes in earnest.

'What I want most in the world is to be with you,' she parted. 'Oh, you know I do!'

She heard his sharp intake of breath as he pulled her close.

'Charlotte, my Charlotte,' he whispered.

Her senses swam as he bent and kissed her lips for the first time. She responded by reaching her arms around his neck.

He caressed her face all over, then lifted his head to look at her.

She opened her eyes, about to protest that only her father called her that.

'I know what you're thinking,' he murmured, 'but Charlotte is what I intend to call you as my wife.'

More firmly he added: 'I shall be your provider, protector, friend and lover, all rolled into one. In short, my dear, your husband!'

She melted. 'Yes sir,' she said humbly.

'You'll get used to it,' he said, 'and now you must get used to calling me Alan.'

He laughed for joy at her expression.